Wilfr [illegible] umentary writer [illegible] s the Baltic and t [illegible] in 1959 to work [illegible] behind severa [illegible] *Plane Makers* and *T* [illegible] ters' Guild of Great [illegible] author of the feature film *Battle of Britain*. He has also written non-fiction books, including *Arnhem* (with Maj. Gen. R. E. Urquhart) and three novels – *The Freelancers*, *Crossover* and *Quicksand*. Apart from five years in the RAF Wilfred Greatorex has been a writer and journalist since leaving school. He now lives in Buckinghamshire with his wife, Beryl.

...ted Greekses, ...ex-journalist and now ... who has steered stories as far apart as ... the Snowy Mountains, left Fleet Street ... in television and films. He wrote ... major British TV series such as The ... The Power Game (of which he won Writers' ... ...nitain) awards. He [illegible]

Wilfred Greatorex

Airline: Take Off

based on the TV series by
Wilfred Greatorex

Futura
Macdonald & Co
London & Sydney

A Futura Book

First published in Great Britain in 1982
by Futura Publications, a division of
Macdonald & Co (Publishers) Ltd
London & Sydney

ISBN 0 7088 2141 3

Filmset, printed and bound in Great Britain by
Hazell Watson & Viney Ltd, Aylesbury, Bucks

Futura Publications
A Division of Macdonald & Co (Publishers) Ltd
London & Sydney
Holywell House
Worship Street
London EC2N 2EN

Author's Note

In the course of my research into the background for this fictional story I met and interviewed more than eighty pilots and others, who were in the thick of it when the independent fliers ('the bandits') moved into civil aviation in those early post World War II years, I am indebted to all of them, but my special thanks go to Mike Keegan, chairman of British Air Ferries, for his memories of those years, and to Dick Millward, AFC, a pilot from a later generation, who tried to keep me on course in the flying scenes.

Wilfred Greatorex

CHAPTER 1

He felt a surge of exhilaration as he looked at the bleak landscape below. It was Ruskin's first glimpse of Germany. Under its white cloak of January hoar frost it could have been Northern Ireland but for the ruins of Hanover, like broken teeth, and the Army trucks, which littered the roads like toys. Germany seemed drained of life.

But there was more going on down there than met the eye. Some of Ruskin's oppos in Transport Command had boasted of neat black market coups, and claimed that some aircrews were growing rich. With this in mind Ruskin had tried to fix a posting to the British Air Forces of Occupation. He had failed.

However he had got this one-off run with Spit and Mozzie spares, and he aimed to make good use of it.

'Pre-landing check, Skip?' It was his co-pilot, Flight Sergeant Gray, a good oppo even if he did come from the wrong side of the Pennines. He was also in a demob group well ahead of Ruskin's thirty-eight group, and that rankled a bit. Ruskin could not get out of the RAF fast enough.

'OK.' Ruskin's eyes fixed by habit on the hydraulic pressure gauge.

'Hydraulic pressure,' Gray said.

'Checked. Six six zero.'

'Brakes.'

'Off.'

'Fuel.'

Ruskin by reflex checked the gauges and selector pumps. 'Contents OK,' he said. 'Main tanks selected. Booster pumps on.'

'Undercart.'

'Undercart down.' He paused while the locks engaged. 'Locked. Green light on.'

They went through the rest of the checks like automatons. At the end Ruskin threw Gray a wink and concentrated on his approach. The airfield had that early morning look. Even during the war the RAF, contrary to general belief, seemed never to get up early.

'Looks like hangover time,' Ruskin murmured.

'As long as the cooks are good on bacon and eggs.'

Typical, Ruskin thought. He's thinking of breakfast when he could be thinking of making a bit of brass before demob. The Controller's voice came over the R/T giving him a clear to land. To Ruskin, it was like an invitation to join the gold rush. He teased the Dakota into a perfect touch-down, just in case any officers with lesser flying talents should be watching. There was the slightest of bumps as the tyres screeched against the tarmac of the runway once used by the Luftwaffe.

'Now where's that grub-hall?' It was, of course, Pip Gray.

Half an hour later they were in the sergeants' mess where news-hungry senior NCOs were reaching for that day's Fleet Street papers. The *Mirrors* and *Expresses* were most in demand. Ruskin recognized the plump little flight sergeant who was handing out the papers as Phil Barnes. They had served on the same squadron once at Driffield. Ruskin joined the scrum. 'You sucking up for a job with W. H. Smith on demob?' he asked, picking up an *Express*. Barnes whirled. His surprise turned to pleasure. 'Christ,' he said. 'Not Jack Ruskin? Another bad penny rolls up. What the hell are you doing here?'

Ruskin grinned. 'Thought we'd take a quick shuftie at the boom sector of Transport Command while the bonanza lasts.'

'We don't make a bean on the papers,' Barnes smirked. He was an alert Cockney with a wife and two kids, though he hardly looked old enough to be out of school. It would have come as a surprise to Ruskin if Barnes had not been in Germany: he would have seen the main chance long before the rest. 'You wangled a posting here or what?' Barnes asked.

'We'd be so lucky. It's a one-off trip. Spit and Mozzie spares.'

'And that's all?' Barnes whispered knowingly.

Ruskin stared back innocently. 'We're novices, mate. Mugs from the Aldergrove run with nothing in it bar Irish rain and legit loads. So come and have your cornflakes and fill me in on the Klondyke.'

For a moment Barnes eyed him warily. Ruskin was not celebrated for his peaceable nature or for being discreet. He had a chip on his shoulder about the officers, which made him a permanent threat to order and discipline, and marked him for special attention. And the last thing Barnes needed at this stage was attention.

'Well, come on,' Ruskin urged. 'You've not had breakfast yet, I take it?'

'Not yet, no,' Barnes said, with a glance at the reduced pile of papers.

'I've not been out east,' Ruskin said sharply. 'I've not got a dose or anything.'

Barnes reluctantly joined him over breakfast. He had little to say about the rackets. 'I thought you'd have been a WO by now,' he said evasively. 'How come?'

'Up and downer with a two ringer,' Ruskin said dismissively. 'I never actually hit him.' He paused. 'You used to be a good talker. What's made you clam up?'

Barnes' small bright eyes took in the mess hall. 'It's not only aircrew who use this mess, Jack,' he said. 'Provost sergeants linger.'

'Any about now?'

'Not that I can see.'

'So let's have it. We're still oppos, aren't we?'

'Sure.'

'So, gen me up on the game.'

Barnes eyed him warily.

'Listen, mate,' Ruskin urged. 'This is the age of socialism. We never put in Attlee's Government so that part of the RAF could help itself while the rest are left like Bisto kids getting less than a sniff of the good life.'

Barnes laughed. 'You know as well as anybody, Jack, this country's one bloody great black market. Part of the Jerries' penance, I suppose.'

'Now we're talking,' Ruskin said. 'I hear of one bloke on Daks who's bought a string of cafés right across Belgium and Holland. Out of his profits.'

'You get blokes shooting lines.'

'You shoot a few.'

'Anybody who's not helping himself a bit these days must be short of grey matter.'

'Right. The bloody war's over. So it's all change and fend for number one. I've got the message loud and clear, mate. I'm not criticizing. I'm not disapproving. I'm in demob group thirty-eight and when it comes up I'll be out faster than what the cooks put in the tea. But that's a few months off and I don't aim to spend 'em pissing about over the peatbogs.'

Barnes toyed with his tea. 'I'd have thought it wasn't beyond you to fix a posting here.'

'Listen. I've a CO who'd like nothing better than to ditch me in the drink with a punctured Mae West, and an Air Commodore who's virtually made sure I'll never make Warrant Officer.'

Barnes grinned. 'Still taking the bastards on, I see, Jack.' There was a hint of amused respect in the voice and he studied Ruskin for a long moment. 'Tell you what, Jack. You have a chunner with my skipper. You were once on the same squadron.'

'Squadron Leader Marlowe? He's around here?'

'Should be in the Mess right now.'

Ruskin's memories of Dickie Marlowe were all good ones. He was one of the few officers Ruskin had ever got on with – five, in fact, and three of those had bought it. He was also as good a pilot as Ruskin, and a lot of officers weren't. What was even more to the point, he was a born fixer who knew how to work the Raff system.

It took Ruskin less than ten minutes to get him on the line at the officers' mess. And Marlowe was friendly. 'Flight,' he enthused when Ruskin announced himself. 'You old rascal. What have you been up to, still not a WO?' The upper-class nasal accent was still clear, yet because it was Dickie Marlowe's it didn't grate on Ruskin.

'I dropped a clanger or two,' Ruskin said. He felt at ease. 'And had my own private war with a two-ringer.'

'What, another?' Marlowe laughed. 'How many's that, Flight?'

'Lost count, sir.'

'And now you're posted here?'

'That's just it, sir,' Ruskin said, lowering his voice as a cluster of sergeants went by. 'That's what I'd like a word with you about.'

'Not here,' Marlowe said confidentially. 'Let's see, Flight. I've my own billet in the town. Seventeen Hallestrasse. Apartment 2. Come and share some iron rations around lunchtime.'

Ruskin came out of the phone booth and went back to the mess hall, his elation reflected in the confident strides he took across the foyer. There was one thing he was sure about: there would be no genuflecting to rank once he was demobbed, and no return to that two-up, two-down terrace house where his father still lived. Never again would he live in that place, with its damp and its outside privy. He would not wait for authority to improve his lot: the RAF bureaucracy had destroyed any faith he could have ever had in authority.

Jack Ruskin knew that if he was to scale the bloody citadels, he could do it. But he would do it alone.

Number 17, Hallestrasse, was a nineteenth-century town house of some style and elegance spoilt only by a large eagle carved in the stone parapet over the front entrance. Ruskin pressed the button marked 'Apartment 2' and a stocky German in his forties wearing a neat Wehrmacht uniform came to the door.

He bowed and held the door open. Pale and solemn he pointed to the wide curving staircase leading to a pillared gallery. The war had clearly passed it by. No sign of troops' boots on the marble floors, the stonework and the teak rail on the staircase intact, the drapes at the head of the stairs looking almost new.

Ruskin started up the stairs.

'Flight! Jack! You old rebel!'

Ruskin looked up to see Marlowe leaning over the gallery rail, his blue battledress blouse unbuttoned and hanging free, a glass of lager in each hand.

'Hello, sir . . . Dickie.' His correction was quick to catch the mood of the encounter. Off the station Dickie Marlowe had always played down rank and now with the war over Ruskin could forget Marlowe's two-and-a-half rings. All the same he looked a bit of a prince standing between those stone pillars with their background of Renaissance-style paintings.

'I might have known,' Ruskin quipped. 'Who was here before you? Hermann Goering?'

The easy smile was still there, the intense blue eyes, the charm. And beneath it that same disdain – for hypocrisy and all things routine and expected. Marlowe wasn't very fond of the human race. Perhaps that was why they got on.

Marlowe laughed – without spilling a drop of lager from either glass. 'Old Hermann never had the taste, Jack. And I never did like bunks on the station, even back home. This, I would say, is a sort of halfway house to civvy street.'

'Halfway bloody palace.'

Marlowe handed Ruskin a glass as he reached the top stair. 'Get cracking on that and tell me as a light ale specialist if that lager doesn't beat anything you've put mouth to.'

Ruskin sampled it as they shook hands, then allowed himself to be ushered through the wide reception doors into Marlowe's apartment. The drapes covering the tall windows were in gold, and the rich furnishings and antique furniture could have come from some looted schloss. Most of the parquet floor was covered by a silk Persian carpet, and much of one wall by nineteenth-century French oil paintings.

'Jesus,' Ruskin said. 'You rent this place furnished? Must cost a bomb.'

'The contents are mine, Jack.'

Ruskin stood in the middle of the Persian carpet slowly circling and trying to take in the Aladdin's Cave.

'Picked up a piece here, a piece there,' Marlowe smiled. 'Rich old man and a few National Savings Certificates.'

'Bollocks . . . sir.'

'I'm more a magpie than a shitehawk.'

Ruskin gulped down the rest of the lager. 'I thought blokes got shot for looting?'

'Looting? Good Lord, Jack, I never even looted a souvenir swastika. I trade. Makes a change from just trundling spares between here and the UK.'

'I bet you're not pushing for demob,' Ruskin grinned.

Marlowe grimaced. 'All that rationing. All those controls. Attlee and his chaps. I'm not cut out for austerity. I take one look at Stafford Cripps and wonder where all the fun went.' He paused, his amused eyes on Ruskin. 'No, I'd rather stay here among the ruins we knocked about a bit. Another?'

He took Ruskin's glass. 'Same or Scotch?'

'Same please. It's a bit of all right.'

Marlowe opened a cabinet in rosewood to disclose a lager barrel. He ran Ruskin another glass. Ruskin said, 'I was going to ask if you could fix me a posting here but don't get the wrong impression. It seems you've cornered the market here anyway.'

'What's your demob group?' Marlowe asked, handing Ruskin his glass.

'Thirty-eight.'

'Gives you till May or June. Unless the Russkies turn

really nasty and it's all stopped. The buggers won't even look at us in the streets now.'

Ruskin sat on the four-decker sofa. 'If anybody wants another war they can fight it without me.' His tone was measured and bitter. 'I'd not mind trundling a few cameras and things back over the next few months, better than miscellaneous spare parts to Northern Ireland.'

'Count your blessings, Jack,' Marlowe said smoothly, dropping onto a matching sofa and stretching his legs. 'You could be on the trooping run to India, flying down the Gulf and catching prickly heat or malaria or some other pox. The erks out there are getting bolshie and who can blame 'em. I don't. At least you only get wet in Northern Ireland.'

'I'd rather get rich here,' Ruskin shot back.

There was a knock at the door and the stocky German entered.

'Ah! Time to eat is it, Gerhard?'

Ruskin took in the easy control Marlowe had over people. He was a natural. Some were born to give orders. Ruskin had always had to take them. Yet he and Marlowe were the same age, give or take a few days – twenty-seven – and had once shared a pub birthday party. Ruskin reckoned he had started his post-war recovery a bit late.

Gerhard said the meal was ready and left the room.

'Gerhard was an infantry corporal,' Marlowe explained. 'He went on that loony hike into Russia, wound up with frostbite and lost a foot.'

They moved through to the dining room.

'When I first came here,' Marlowe went on, 'nearly every other German adult male and some juveniles were without a foot or a leg and there were more crutches than matchsticks. And then somewhere back there, our politicians or top brass brought in the no-fraternization rule. Don't frat with the enemy. And the enemy were all on bloody crutches and in rags and they'd part with grandad's gold watch for a couple of bars of Naafi chocolate for their kids. The enemy? Don't fraternize? Well sod that for a lark.'

Ruskin wasn't swallowing the entire message but he was impressed by Marlowe's fluency with words. He could sit at Marlowe's feet and learn.

Gerhard held Ruskin's chair back from the twelve-foot long rosewood table as Marlowe took his place at the other end.

'Gerhard,' Marlowe nodded after the departing German, 'lost his wife in the bombing of Hanover, his two kids in Goch, his father had a heart attack when we cindered Lubeck, his sister was raped by the Russians and his mother committed suicide. His only remaining relative is a half cousin. He's been here ever since. Come on, let's dig into the hard tack.'

'Belsen's not far from here, is it?' Ruskin queried.

'Not all that far, no.'

'And I've got ambitions beyond my station. I should settle for what I've got and where I am?'

'Chip showing again, Jack. I never said that.' He sampled the paté and made a gesture with his thumb and forefinger to show he found it superb. 'I wasn't born yesterday any more than you were. When we first got here you'd have thought the Nazis were a figment of somebody's imagination, nobody had been a Nazi, and as for Belsen . . . Belsen? . . . it might have been a camp on the moon as far as they were concerned.' He paused savouring the paté. 'But you can't blame frostbitten infantry privates, old ladies and kids for the bloody horrors, can you?'

'Gerhard's no kid,' Ruskin said.

'No. But I tell you this, Jack. If Britain ever got itself a government that needed concentration camps there'd be no shortage of volunteers to join the camp guards.'

Ruskin thought he could be right.

'Come on,' Marlowe said. 'Soup's next. And you can't compare it to the dishwash in the sergeants' mess.' As he spoke a plump hausfrau of about forty with short blonde hair and competent, manicured hands came in with a bottle of Rhine wine and served them soup from a silver tureen. She looked formidably able to Ruskin. Just like Marlowe to set himself up with someone like her.

As if reading Ruskin's mind, Marlowe said, 'Elly's husband was in the Panzer division that copped it in the Falaise Gap when our Tiffies poured rockets into 'em. She has three kids under ten and nobody else. Her parents were killed in the Rhine crossing, she's not sure how. She has no English but she knows what I'm telling you.'

Elly nodded her understanding.

'She's just young enough to pick up the pieces,' Marlowe went on, raising his glass to Ruskin. 'To you, Jack.'

'To my posting here,' said Ruskin, raising his own glass.

'I can't walk on water, Jack.'

'I wouldn't be sure of that either,' Ruskin gazed around the opulent suite.

'Anyway,' Marlowe said as Ruskin checked on the departing Elly's strong well-shaped legs, 'don't threaten to clobber any more officers while I'm trying for you, eh?'

Ruskin shrugged. 'I was never charged. Think it went on my docs?'

'Probably. Docs are full of petty libels.'

'If postings can be fixed – and we know they can – it should be possible to fix docs.'

It was getting too solemn for Marlowe. 'You've not said how you like the soup.'

'I bet Attlee's doing no better in Downing Street,' Ruskin grinned.

It was another quarter hour before Ruskin really began to probe. Squadron Leader Dickie Marlowe was up to his eyes in the racket: it was part of the nature of the bloke, Ruskin thought, and his class, to get off to a head start in post-war survival. They were just digging into the roast pork, roast potatoes and fresh vegetables when Ruskin asked, 'So what's the game in sterling?'

'You must try those Brussels sprouts, Jack, they're sensational,' Marlowe said evasively.

Ruskin helped himself to some sprouts. 'You're flying currency over here.'

'Who is?' The eyes were bright, and the handsome face bland.

Ruskin swallowed his first mouthful of pork. 'Our blokes – erks and officers – are flogging coffee, fags, chocolate and maybe cookhouse supplies on the black market. For cameras – Leicas, Rolleis – and binoculars and things. Then they flog the gear for confetti reichsmarks and the reichsmarks for hard sterling brought in by troops back from UK leave. And by you and your oppos. Profit at every turn.'

Marlowe sipped the wine like a connoisseur. He eyed Ruskin over the gleaming cut glass. 'You should have made warrant officer, Jack. It's such a waste.'

Ruskin saw it as the usual neat and stylish brush-off that Marlowe was so good at. But if Marlowe had style Ruskin had stamina. He'd come again.

They were interrupted by Gerhard who limped round the table refillling their glasses. As long as he wore that Wehrmacht uniform Ruskin could not help but think of him as the enemy.

Marlowe had read his mind yet again. 'Good Germans do exist, you know. Though the first Jerry soldier I adopted and the first fraulein I took to were both hauled off by our Provost mob as Nazi SS. And the fraulein was a doctor's daughter you'd expect to be with the Red Cross. We're a bit better organized now, we've sorted 'em out.'

It was all part of Marlowe's evasion and Ruskin hadn't come to talk about the rehabilitation of the Germans. 'In Northern Ireland today,' he said with a mouthful of pork, 'I'd have been lucky to get bloody rissoles.'

'Glad you're enjoying it,' Marlowe smiled.

'And,' Ruskin said pointedly, 'there's no racket up there.'

'Jack,' said Marlowe, lowering his voice. 'Give me just one reason why I should try to get you posted here.'

'We're old oppos,' Ruskin said matter-of-factly. 'And

neither of us swear on King's Regs in preference to the Bible.'

'I swear on neither,' Marlowe said. 'Though I did pray rather intensely over Arnhem.'

'I nearly crossed myself on the Rhine drop.' For a moment they were united in their mutual fears and memories. Then Marlowe leaned back in the high-backed nineteenth-century French mahogany chair and held Ruskin's eyes. His mouth was set and he twirled the glass by its stem in his right hand. His pale face had lost its humour and he had the look of an examining magistrate.

Ruskin was being assessed – and he knew it.

Marlowe gave Ruskin a lift back to camp. They were near the station gate when he turned at the wheel of the jeep and said, 'Could work out quite nicely, Jack. Phil Barnes is due out soon. C Release. He has two kids and an ailing missus. And he's jumpy as a cricket.' He took the jeep round two potholes in the road and past a group of desolate German ex-soldiers hanging around a burned-out barracks, presumably on the look out for either work or erks with coffee and fags to sell.

The jeep stopped near the guardroom. 'OK to drop you here, Jack? Only I've a date back at the flat.'

'Fine,' Ruskin said. 'And thanks for the banquet.' He got down from the jeep. 'What are the chances?'

'I've warned you, I can't walk on water.'

'All the same you seem pretty good with the loaves and fishes.' Ruskin saw an SP corporal watching them from the guardroom window, and it was for his benefit that he threw Dickie Marlowe a salute. It surprised Marlowe until he caught Ruskin's wink. He saluted back, put the jeep into a U-turn around the pot holes, and called, 'I'll do what I can, Jack.'

As Ruskin went in past the guardroom window the button-nosed corporal pulled the window aside and said, 'You Flight Sergeant Ruskin?'

Ruskin nodded.

'The adj was looking for you, Flight. He left a message with one of your oppos in the sergeants' mess.'

'Thanks,' Ruskin said and hitched a lift in a 15-cwt cookhouse van to save time.

He found Pip Gray, and his other crewmen, Tiny Andrews and Jimmy Dawson, at the bar. Flight Sergeant Barnes was buying them a round and he was the only one with a smile on his face.

'Looks like a wake,' said Ruskin joining them. 'Who's bought it?'

'We have,' Gray said mournfully. 'It's back to UK day after tomorrow and then – give you one guess.'

Ruskin weighed them up. It could only be one thing. 'Not the bloody curry run,' he said. 'Oh no!'

'Signal came this afternoon,' Gray said tartly.

Barnes turned at the bar, his dark button eyes alight. He looked anything but jumpy, Ruskin thought. It was all right for him, he'd soon be out. 'Silver lining,' chuckled Barnes. 'It'll broaden your minds. All you've ever seen is Europe.'

'Wrap up,' Ruskin snapped, his mind churning with ideas for getting the posting stopped.

Gray collected his beer from Barnes and said, 'It's hell all the way from Bahrein down those pisshouse staging posts in the Gulf. You step out in nice starchy tropical gear and before you reach dispersal it's black with sweat.'

'Blood, toil and tears,' Barnes said in a lousy imitation of Churchill. 'Now the sweat.'

Nobody found it funny.

'Some shit has it in for us,' Ruskin murmured.

Barnes was not to be fobbed off. 'Still,' he said in mock consolation, 'you'll be well jabbed against the anopholene mosquito.'

'The *what*?' It was Gray.

'It's the little bugger that gives you malaria,' Barnes explained with the authority of an unqualified MO.

'The bugger who has it in for us,' Ruskin snapped, 'isn't

the bloody mosquito. It's some shit at Group with two legs and no wings.'

He took one sip of lager and went out to the phone to call Marlowe.

Ruskin lounged in the four-decker divan as Gerhard poured him a lager. The previous day's shaker of a posting was still troubling him. He had been on the phone to Marlowe almost immediately only to have Gerhard tell him that he was 'away'. And Gerhard had been guarded to the point of implying that Marlowe's whereabouts were top secret. It was not until just after breakfast that Marlowe had phoned Ruskin from an unspecified place some fifty miles from the camp – 'somewhere between Hanover and Hamburg' – inviting Ruskin to join him for a drink.

He still hadn't shown up.

'So how did you land this cushy number, Gerhard?' Ruskin said, hoping to prise some useful background out of the solemn, cagey German.

'I'm sorry, flight sergeant.' Gerhard was awfully correct.

'How did you meet sir?'

'On the Hanover road. I was walking.'

'And you hitched a lift?'

'I would never do that.' He was as proud as he was cagey.

Ruskin persisted. 'Sir stopped, did he?'

Gerhard nodded.

'Just like sir, that.'

Gerhard handed Ruskin the lager.

'Thank you,' Ruskin said, sprawling, his right arm dangling over the side of the divan. 'Have one yourself.' He had reservations about Gerhard. He wasn't used to Germans and the war hadn't been over long enough for him to feel easy in their company.

Gerhard declined the offer and began to leave.

'So what happened when sir stopped?' Ruskin asked.

Gerhard folded his hands over his belly, twirling his

thumbs, resenting Ruskin's noseyness. 'The squadron leader asked me if I had any children.'

'What? Just like that?'

'No,' Gerhard said. 'Just before we got to Hanover. I told him I had no children left and he asked if any of my comrades had children. I said I knew some. He gave me bars of chocolate to give them. *Give* to them. On the black market then some of your soldiers and airmen could get a Leica or a gold watch for three bars of chocolate.' He hesitated. 'I told him I would like to work for him at the RAF camp.'

'I bet you did.'

'He said he had a better idea. I was very lucky.'

From downstairs came the sound of the front door being closed. Ruskin got up and followed Gerhard to the gallery. He expected to see Marlowe, but climbing the stairs was a fresh-faced German girl with blonde hair tumbling around her shoulders from under a red wool bobble cap. Ruskin figured she was about twenty-two. She was unzipping a lined leather flying jacket that could have been RAF issue tailored for her. And her boots were wool-lined suede.

'Hello, Gerhard,' she called warmly in German, and then saw Ruskin. She frowned in surprise. 'Oh I'm sorry,' she said in good English. 'I was told Squadron Leader Marlowe would be at home.'

'You're not the only one,' Ruskin said, trying to guess what she looked like under all the cold weather gear.

She paused on the stairs as if she were about to turn back.

'Don't leave on my account, love,' Ruskin said, warming to Germans. 'Nothing in the rules about not having a drink with me, is there?'

He thought she blushed.

'I have many things to see to,' she said hastily. 'I am sorry.'

Ruskin leaned over the gallery rail. He put on a hurt look. 'Gerhard won't sup with me, now you, what if I'd been an officer?'

She looked unsure.

'I'm a friend of his,' Ruskin said, indicating his stripes. 'This is just a disguise.'

'Very well,' she said, and came on past Gerhard.

'Take your coat?' Ruskin offered. She let him take the heavy flying jacket and Ruskin was now sure it was RAF issue, and very well tailored. He took in the neat bosom under the white roll collar sweater, the pretty hands, her Alpine complexion and the total lack of make up. He was putting her coat on a teak chest when the front door opened and Marlowe rushed in, taking the stairs two at a time.

'Sorry I'm late, old son,' he called to Ruskin. He glanced at Gerhard and said, 'Hope you looked after him, Gerhard.'

'Very well,' Ruskin said. 'But you could have stayed away a bit longer. You spoilt a beautiful moment.'

Marlowe embraced the girl formally, and then introduced Ruskin. 'Helga . . . Flight Sergeant Ruskin . . . Jack in these parts.' He looked straight at Ruskin. 'Helga's sorting out my life for me.' He kissed Helga once more, indicated he would like to talk to Ruskin privately and gave her a parting pat on the backside. Ruskin could make out its shapely outline against the elasticized ski-ing slacks.

Marlowe closed the double doors and lit a cigarette.

'Noggin?' Ruskin asked, indicating the drinks cabinet.

'Not just now. Listen Jack, I've not even been back to London yet. Give me a chance. Patience, chum, patience.'

'It's a bit more urgent than it was yesterday,' Ruskin explained. 'Some sod's dropped me right in it. The bloody curry run.'

Marlowe was unsurprised. 'Trooping from India's got a high priority now. Like Welfare. The erks are getting restive over demob and the brass are shitting themselves.'

'Let 'em,' Ruskin said grimly. 'I've not come through four-and-a-half years of war to get bloody malaria after it.'

'Listen, Jack. Promise. I'll pull every string there is, but it's tougher now. Getting you on the German run's one thing, getting you off the India job's something else.' He looked as if he meant it. Ruskin drank up quickly. 'No hurry, Jack. Have another.'

'I'm in your way,' Ruskin said, indicating the doors.

'Oh Helga won't mind. She's very tolerant and even.'

'Even what?' Ruskin smiled. And for the first time, Marlowe laughed.

'I see what the bods were on about last year when they had the no-frat rule,' Ruskin said. 'With bints like her out of bounds it's no wonder some were qualifying for the hatch and the rest bending the Regs.'

'Crappy rule it was,' Marlowe said. 'I first met her when the ban was on. Her old man had lost both legs in the Falaise trap.'

Ruskin took in the pale and knowing face. 'Why is it nobody meets good Germans except you?'

'I don't know about good. But I'm buggered if I was going to freeze out a girl like her. Besides, the no-frat rule was to keep the ORs from running wild.'

Ruskin threw him a sharp look. 'Keep off. Except officers. And especially squadron leaders.'

Marlowe's face creased into that matinee idol's smile. 'I thought you'd rise to that. You don't change, Jack. I'll do what I can and that's a promise.'

They shook hands on it.

On the way downstairs Ruskin thought he might be lucky and see Helga. There was no trace of her. And he suddenly realized that it was more than a month since he had been with Jennie back in the north of England.

Ruskin and Gray threw anxious looks at the instruments as they came in low over the shimmering Indian Ocean. The oil temperature gauge for the port engine was way above normal while the pressure gauge showed a drop. Ruskin could see nothing visually amiss with the engine: no oil streaks. But he knew he would very likely have to shut it down.

The cabin behind had a full load of young sprogs posted

to India to replace veterans due for demob. And although he'd been back to cheer them up as best he could, their morale was low. Some had been airsick, others on their first flight were jittery, and many nursed painful arms from vaccinations and inoculations. A few hardly dared look out of the windows and buried themselves in out-of-date copies of the *Daily Mirror* and *Men Only*. One was deep into *Lady Chatterley's Lover* and another read through slim books of poetry all the way from the UK.

Ruskin pitied the poor sods.

He could feel the clammy heat and pitiless humidity of those Gulf staging posts already. The Dak was like some flying oven. Once back in the UK he aimed to get himself removed from curry runs for good. One was too many. He had never considered desertion before, but it had gone through his mind over the past two days. He felt bitter about Dickie Marlowe's failure to fix his posting to Germany.

They had met briefly in a pub in the Strand close to the Air Ministry. Marlowe had laid stress on the odds against his being able to oblige Ruskin. In fact he'd been so taken with his own problems that Ruskin had almost given up hope that Marlowe would look after anyone but himself. He'd said as much, and Marlowe replied, 'Sorry about the curry run, mate. But you can be sure you're not going to miss out in Germany. They're on our bloody tails with a vengeance now – Service police, the Provost crowd, Customs, even – they reckon – the bloody Bank of England. Trade's not what it was.'

All the same, the buzz around the messes in the UK was that the German run was still highly profitable for some, and that one or two elite operators were smuggling valuable antiques, including furniture, from the Zone to the UK. Was it true, Ruskin had asked Marlowe.

'Could be.'

In the end Marlowe had given a promise to try again to fix Ruskin's posting.

Ruskin ran the back of his hand across his face to clear the sweat. Gray's khaki shirt was soaked black.

'It's getting rougher, skip,' Gray said.

Ruskin peered out at the rough engine. 'Hello Tower,' he called into his R/T. 'Trader C Charlie. Our port engine's running very rough now.'

'Hello Trader C Charlie. You're clear to land.'

'Thank you, Tower.'

Another glance at those gauges. The temperature was still rising, the pressure falling.

Gray studied them a moment, wiping sweat from his eyes. 'She'll blow if we don't shut her down.' His voice was urgent.

'No, not just yet,' Ruskin said. 'We're heavy. We'd never hold the height on one. It's bloody hot out there. Plus twenty-five ISA.'

The engine began to bang and fart as if it were about to blow up.

Ruskin aimed the Dakota for the hot landing ground. His face was set, his pale blue eyes unblinking, his knuckles white on the column. He could feel the sweat running down his chest and from under his arms. The noises from the port engine grew in frequency and volume. The two flight sergeant pilots were almost mesmerized by the gauges, especially Gray, who watched the temperature thrust up to 120 and the pressure down through 30. 'For Christ's sake, she'll blow!' he suddenly blurted.

Ruskin threw a quick glance towards the port engine. Oil was flying and probably spraying the port side cabin windows. Ahead the airfield had all the look of a camp of the dead. Nothing moved except the heat shimmer. The runway looked hot enough to burst the tyres. The Dakota skimmed towards the start of the runway in a nigh-perfect attitude, the gauges signalling doom.

'Now!' Ruskin called. 'Chop it!'

Gray's reaction was instant but not quick enough. The bangs and farts gave way to a loud bang. The Dakota wobbled and dipped. But Ruskin held her, the tyres screeched on the hot runway, she slewed slightly, Ruskin righted her, and then she stopped.

'Jesus!' Gray murmured.

'Amen!' Ruskin said.

Over the R/T came the cultured voice of a ground control officer. 'Proceed to dispersal, C Charlie.'

'Piss off!' Ruskin murmured to himself.

The Dakota began to turn on the strength of its starboard engine with Ruskin compensating on the rudder.

The silence was suddenly invaded by the swelling sound of men's voices, singing:

'Sod 'em all
Sod 'em all
The long and the short and the tall
Sod all the sergeants and W.O. Ones
Sod all the corporals and their bleedin' sons' . . .

Grim relief showed on Ruskin's face. He saw Gray's left hand trembling across his neck. Sergeant Andrews and Flight Sergeant Dawson were already out of their seats and on their way into the cabin to reassure the sprogs.

Ruskin steered the Dakota towards dispersal. It was almost deserted. Apart from the men getting down from crash tenders and ambulances only distant birds moved. Ruskin's eyes narrowed. 'What the bloody hell's going on?'

Gray followed his glance.

The men leaving the crash tenders and ambulances were all senior NCOs.

Ruskin made his way down the cabin to the cargo door, running the gauntlet of the shaken, relieved sprogs. 'Did we lose an engine, Flight?' . . . 'Did an engine fall off?' . . . 'No favour bringing us here, Chiefie?' . . . 'Did somebody fire at us, Flight?' . . . 'The big bang? What was it?' . . . Ruskin made reassuring gestures, feeling pity for the poor sods. The cabin smelt of vomit and dope. And as the door swung open a blast of hot humid air enveloped them. Ruskin felt he couldn't breathe. Sweat rolled down his face.

He jumped down to the hot ground where a desperate-looking flight sergeant with a brown, thin, pock-marked face met him. 'What *is* this?' Ruskin said, indicating the bleak lifeless airfield. 'Everybody dead of the plague?'

'You're dead lucky there was no fire, mate,' said the flight sergeant, sizing up the port engine.

'You're telling me,' Ruskin said impatiently. 'So where is everybody? Why this sergeants' mess reception?'

'The ORs are on strike.' The sergeant's tired eyes were impassive.

Ruskin, whose eyes had been examining the damaged engine, turned back to the sergeant in disbelief. 'You what? Say again?'

'The buggers had a strike meeting last night. In the pitch dark so's nobody could make out the ringleaders.'

Ruskin felt his blood rising. 'This is the Raff. The Raff can't go on bloody strike. It's mutiny.'

The sergeant managed a resigned smirk. 'That's what the brown jobs would call it, and it's what our wet brass should be calling it.' He wasn't sweating all that much, Ruskin noticed. Maybe he was so bloody dehydrated he had no more to shed.

'What *are* they calling it?' Ruskin snapped.

'A stoppage of work.'

The sprogs began to spill out of the cargo door. Absurdly young-looking, their khaki drill spanking new, wide-eyed as they jumped down into a strange and alien world.

The sight of them made Ruskin even more angry. He fixed the flight sergeant with a glare.

'It's been brewing for months,' the flight sergeant said. 'The erks are brassed off something rotten about demob, and now they're out. Except the cooks. The erks don't intend to go hungry.'

The enormity of the problem was dawning on Ruskin. 'We got a signal saying we couldn't expect any servicing here but this—!' His voice trailed off as his passengers were formed up and began to march off.

'I can't see us putting out signals telling the world the Raff has mutinied, can you?'

Ruskin's crew were looking at that duff port engine. The engine cowling was smeared with oil, and so were the cabin windows on the port side. Oil dripped down and was forming a congealed puddle on the concrete. Other senior NCOs joined them. 'We only just made it on that duff engine,' Ruskin growled. 'A full load of young sprogs. Suppose we'd bloody pranged?'

The flight sergeant gazed at Ruskin with empty eyes. If he felt sympathy he was too drained to express it. The other NCOs, sensing Ruskin's temper, concentrated on that duff engine. One of them shot a worried glance at the hangar some two hundred yards away. Ruskin noticed. 'Buggers in there, are they?' he demanded.

The flight sergeant shook his head. 'I shouldn't, mate.'

'What do you mean? Shouldn't?' His face was set in fury.

'Look, Flight,' the flight sergeant pleaded. 'Don't accuse us, we're only the mugs who try to keep the place open.'

'And I've a duff engine that but for bloody prayer could have landed the lot of us in the 'oggin,' Ruskin shouted as he made for the hangar. 'And I need a new one, fast.'

The flight sergeant was at his limits. 'You'll have to take your turn for servicing, Flight. There aren't that many of us handy.'

'Order some erks to do it,' Ruskin shouted over his shoulder.

'It's been tried.'

'Where are the bloody officers then?'

The flight sergeant shrugged. 'We've got more top brass around here than mosquitoes. Somewhere.'

Ruskin continued towards the hangar. He heard the flight sergeant shout after him. 'No use, Flight. Those erks won't even man the bowsers.'

Gray broke into a trot and, sweating profusely, caught up with Ruskin. 'Jack,' he said, 'one of those NCOs said the Inspector General of the Raff spoke to 'em this morning. An Air Chief Marshal. Only the King comes higher. And the ACM got nowhere.'

'You keep those NCOs on our side,' Ruskin muttered. 'I'll see the mutineers.' He could make out vague shadowy movements inside the vast hangar. Somewhere a radio was playing high-pitched Indian music. He could hardly breathe in the heat and beads of sweat slid over his eyes. It was high noon. He went inside the hangar and had to adjust his eyes to the lower light level. He made out a group of erks in a shady corner. Four in a brag school, with others watching, two playing chess, and the rest reading copies of the *Daily Mirror* and *News of the World*. Faded, oil-greased pinups with lewd captions graced the wall and the spares' racks.

The erks hardly glanced at Ruskin. It was as if he were not even there. Ruskin tested the mood for a moment, curbing his rage, sensing some danger. 'Which of you's the spokesman?' he asked presently.

Nobody spoke.

Ruskin took one step nearer the brag school. 'I just brought in a load of sprogs,' he said quietly. 'On one engine. Suppose we'd pranged . . . ?'

They kept quiet but their glances were on a lean and pimply LAC with very short black hair and strong brown eyes.

'Suppose we'd pranged?' His voice was insistent.

'You didn't, did you, Flight?' the LAC said, weighing up his brag cards.

'We came in with a duff port engine.' Ruskin fixed the LAC with an accusing stare.

'Now you tell us,' the LAC said, folding his fan of cards then opening it.

'I'll do more than bloody tell you,' Ruskin spat. And he grabbed the LAC by his shirt collar drawing him upright. The LAC made no move to fight back. He said icily, 'Watch it, Flight. You're busting King's Regulations.'

There was a growl of support from the rest.

'I want you on your feet,' Ruskin snapped. 'Haven't you got feet to stand on?'

The grave LAC was impassive, his eyes challenging Ruskin to let go. 'We don't have bull, Flight.' His oppos were all on their feet now, their mood ugly. 'All right, lads,' the LAC said easily. 'Chiefie's seen the light, haven't you, Chiefie?'

Ruskin let go, not out of fear of the rest, but because of the LAC's calm authority.

'A bit of temper, that's all, that we can forget.' The LAC put his shirt straight. 'In case you never received the message loud and clear, Flight, we're on strike.'

Ruskin studied the LAC and the rest of the rebels, their war-worn tired faces, their thin brown bodies whittled down by dehydration, their boils and bites and pock marks, and their disillusioned eyes so full of bitterness. Bloody-minded to a man, their anger was greater than his. Ruskin knew it and he warmed to them. 'Suppose we'd come down in the drink?' his tone was softer now.

The LAC folded his arms, head-on to Ruskin. 'The air sea rescue lads are working, we've seen to that. Anyway you should never have been allowed to set off.'

Ruskin flared again. 'I was half way across the bloody Gulf with a load of sprogs when you mutinied.'

'Struck, Chiefie,' the LAC said quietly. 'Stoppage of work.'

'Mutiny,' Ruskin insisted.

There was a long silence broken only by the sound of a senior NCO distantly shouting orders to the sprogs Ruskin had brought in.

Ruskin gazed over the group, one face at a time. 'So who's going to get me off?'

Silence.

'Well?' The combined odour of aircraft dope, dried sweat and curry was getting to Ruskin. The place reeked.

'We don't have any blacklegs, Flight.' It was the LAC. 'We're solid.'

'Solid?' Ruskin snapped. 'Thick, more like. You're only

harming yourselves and your oppos. I'll be taking some of you home for demob.'

'Not us, Flight. We're the Army's bloody taxi service.'

'You lost all reason, have you?'

The LAC stared at him in disdain. 'Wouldn't you in a shithole like this?'

The silence was endless. Ruskin felt he needed to retch.

'Nothing personal, Flight,' the LAC continued, 'but we're on strike till our legitimate grievances have been seen to. We've blokes in demob Group twenty-three still here and they're up to twenty-eight back home. They've pissed us about enough, we've had it up to here, mate. Well past browned off.'

'You'll all be winding up in the glasshouse.' Ruskin felt for them: they'd had the rawest deal from a British Government supposedly grateful to its servicemen for having won the bloody war.

They waited for the LAC to speak up. 'Let 'em try putting us *all* under close arrest,' he said. 'And if they pick off a few as an example they'll need a regiment of commandos to guard the jail. There are thousands of us.'

Ruskin eyed each in turn, hoping for a hint of compromise. But the chess players sat down and took up their game. The brag school made a new foursome, excluding the LAC. A languid erk with bloodshot eyes and scarred hands played the first cards and threw a sharp look at Ruskin. 'As my oppos said, Chiefie, nothing personal. Some of us have been rotting up shit creek here for years. And nobody bloody cares. Well, they'd better.'

Ruskin knew one thing. If they could mutiny he could bend the Regs to counter them. He would get out of this humid, reeking curry hole even if it meant buying his way out. He caught the lean LAC trying to read his mind.

'Flight,' said the LAC. 'Dysentery, malaria, prickly heat, you name it we've had it between us, not to mention some of us in tents through the monsoons. And they're not just rain like in Kent. It's all flies, mozzies, and rats. We've even got a rat prevention officer. Hardly see the sod, mind.'

He paused to watch the game of brag. 'The war's over and we never put this government in to keep us in this black hole.'

'Oh yes,' Ruskin agreed. 'You mean "Vote Labour And Bring The Boys Back Home" . . . their bloody election slogan . . . Surely the quicker you turn blokes like me around the sooner you'll all be home?'

'Nothing personal, Flight,' the LAC said. 'And nothing doing.' He joined the brag school. 'Shuffle and deal me in, Len.' The languid erk cast his baleful pop eyes at Ruskin. 'And my oppo never said a word to you, Flight. Not one word.' Again, it was as if Ruskin were no longer there. He was cut off. He came near to kicking the cards out of their gnarled brown hands but thought better of it. He went out, his tropical gear already black with sweat, his head throbbing, his heart racing. And the smell made him want to vomit.

Ruskin stood on the starboard wing directing the hose into the fuel tank. Nearby the flight sergeant kept a hand on the flow control from the bowser.

Gray was in the cockpit doing a pre-flight check.

Ruskin felt shagged. They had worked with brief breaks for meals all through the night and now most of the morning, and with the help of four senior NCOs as well as the flight sergeant who first met them on landing they were nearly ready for off. They had found a replacement engine and Ruskin had taken charge of its installation, much to the surprise of the NCOs who helped and the erks watching from a distance. Ruskin told those working with him he'd once been a flight engineer. 'I knew it would be useful when I get demobbed, but I never thought I'd be working on an engine again in the Raff.'

It had been heavy work with the hoist, placing the engine. The Karachi night had been mercifully cool, but it had been a sweatshop operation just the same. At three in the morning they had paused for a break with tea and curry brought from the sergeants' mess.

'Bloody erks,' the flight sergeant had complained. 'If heads don't roll after this!' He came from Abergavenny and he found release for his tongue in the deep of the night, with a flood of dirty stories meant to prove that Welsh women were all nymphomaniacs. 'I'd give those erks bloody strikes!'

'They've a case, Chiefie,' Ruskin said, finding the curry hot but not unpleasant. The taste was superior to the smell.

'Not for mutiny, never for that,' said the flight sergeant. They were sitting in the hold of the Dakota, where someone had sprayed disinfectant. 'I mean what's it coming to? First they give the old heave-ho to the Inspector General, an Air Chief Marshal, then yesterday afternoon the AOC goes and meets the buggers in the station cinema and promises to send a signal stating their demands!' His voice was appalled. 'Their demands! Their bloody demands!' He nearly choked on his curry. 'And asking that they should be brought to the highest parliamentary authority. And even then the buggers say nothing doing. This isn't the Raff I knew.'

At that moment Sergeant Andrews had come in with a bottle of Scotch and some badly chipped enamel mugs. He poured and handed out drinks to Ruskin and the rest of his crew and their NCO saviours.

Ruskin had held up his mug in a toast. 'To getting off today.' They raised their mugs. But they weren't too hopeful.

Now the Dakota was all set. Ruskin came down from the wing and walked round, starting his checks at the main cargo door and working clockwise round the machine. He checked the port side fuselage and the port mainplane and flap, the aileron and the static earths. The port side was clean now. The oil smears had been washed off the fuselage and windows and the new engine was a near-virgin. He checked the security of the cowlings, the propeller and spinner, the position of the oil cooler shutter and the undercart. Gray joined him for the rest of the external checks. They had run the new port engine three times and she seemed good.

It was still not midday when their passengers for the flight back to the UK showed up. In total contrast to the young erks who'd come out, these were Army veterans, lean and tanned and tough, many wearing the ribbon of the Burma Star. Mountbatten's lot with leather skins and eyes that had seen hell. Dehydrated, edgy, expectant, a touch inclined not to believe they were at last on their way. 'I'll believe it,' one said to Ruskin as he went aboard the Dakota, 'when I'm on Euston Station.'

They all, to a man, ran the rule over Ruskin. He could read their thoughts. Can he get us back home? It was probably those moments that convinced Ruskin he would become a civil airline pilot when his number came up. He felt important. He felt he could do anything, not just fly a bunch of khaki jobs a quarter of the way round the world. He could deliver.

A little later, inside the cabin, he moved along checking the loading, the weight distribution, their safety harnesses. They weren't home yet by a long way. He'd heard talk in the sergeants' mess, and from the duty officer during the night, that the 'strike' was spreading not only through major RAF bases in India but also at those Godforsaken staging posts up the Gulf. What they'd managed here at Karachi would have to be repeated, if need be. The old soldiers were mostly silent, awed by the fact that they were finally on their way back to the civilized UK, dreaming of reunions and corner pubs and the Arsenal and Rangers and Welsh rugby on Saturday afternoons. They were highly-disciplined men, many with memories of the proximity of death from disease or predatory Japs. They had, however, little regard for rank. They were going to a new Britain where all would be equal. Officers would have to find their real place. Yet they were shy of Ruskin. They saw his three stripes topped by a crown not as the badge of a NCO, in their language a staff sergeant, but someone a bit nearer God's right hand. The miracle man who'd get them home.

Ruskin sensed it and felt twice as tall as his six foot two. He laid it on with his firm Northern accent just to make clear that he was one of them and not some toffee-nosed Brylcreem boy. He came upon a faded erk, lean like so many, and short, but with strong hands. Ruskin paused for a word. 'How come you fiddled it among all the brown jobs?' he grinned.

'C Release, Flight,' the erk said. 'My kid's in hospital.'

'Well you're on your way, lad.'

The boy raised a tight little smile, his eyes full of tears. Ruskin moved on to the cargo door where Dawson was set to close the aircraft. The lithe Welsh flight sergeant stood outside in the shimmering heat.

'You'll likely be on your own all the way up the Gulf, Jack,' the flight sergeant said. 'The staging posts are coming out.'

'I got the latest gen at the briefing,' Ruskin said, remembering that the briefing officer was as dim as a Tilly lamp.

'All the same,' the flight sergeant said, 'I'd not mind coming.'

'Right,' Ruskin said, feeling for him. 'One night here's one too many for me.' He bent down and leaned out and shook the flight sergeant's hand. 'And thanks for everything, Taff.'

The door banged to.

They were on their way.

It took Ruskin and his crew five days to get the boys back home. And it would have been twice as long if Ruskin hadn't pulled strings and bent the Regs all the way up the Gulf. Only after they'd landed at the Sharjah staging post, an oven in the middle of a hot desert, did they learn that scrawled in vivid dope along the Dakota's fuselage was the rebels' message: 'Strike! 0800 Hours!'

'Ernie Bevin the Second,' Ruskin said, gazing at the words.

'Young buggers,' said the sun-blackened ground staff sergeant who drove up in a 15-cwt crew truck. 'Which of you's going to drive the bowser? I'll take you across.'

It was Ruskin who climbed aboard and brought the bowser over the hot sand with a load of fuel. He could hardly breathe. The humidity was murderous.

And when he lifted the Dakota from Sharjah he vowed, 'One thing's for bloody sure. This is my first and last trip down these parts.' He indicated their load of veterans. 'I feel for the poor sods but compassion has its limits.'

Gray was a bit more cheerful now they were on their way back. 'Senior NCOs don't mutiny,' he said.

'Who said anything about mutiny?'

'You can hardly plead fallen arches or defective vision.'

'Eh?'

Gray smirked. 'Only I thought you wanted to join BOAC?'

Ruskin took the point. It reminded him he'd best be doing something about his future.

And that was why he now sat facing the careers officer back at his station in the UK. Careers officer! The fresh-faced flying officer with the navigator's half brevet could have been no more than twenty, Ruskin thought, laying odds to himself that the boy was a virgin. Here was the Raff snailing demob and making jobs for inadequate young officers who had joined too late to have a war to fight.

'BOAC, Ruskin?' The young man ran a hand through his shampooed blond mane. His accent was the standard public school one that so grated on Ruskin.

'It's the best way to stay in flying,' Ruskin countered.

The young man sniffed. 'They do have the cream of the Raff to go for, you know, Flight Sergeant.'

'Officers, you mean?' Ruskin felt the blood rising.

'I didn't say that, Flight, did I?'

'You implied it.'

The young officer glanced at his new gold wrist watch as

if to suggest it was time he was in the officers' mess. 'I doubt very much if BOAC would be interested in pilots with chips on their shoulders.'

Ruskin declined to take the hook.

The young man went on, loftily, 'I doubt very much if BOAC would be interested in pilots with chips on their shoulders.'

Ruskin outgazed him. The little prick, he thought, he thinks he's the boss of UK Ltd instead of being what he is, a prick with a commission at a trestle table in a bloody ante-room of the admin block of an unimportant RAF station. The officer made a point of consulting Ruskin's docs.

'I see from here you're a qualified flight engineer and that before you joined you were in the aircraft industry. You could, I suppose, return to that industry. Or to ground crew with BOAC, one supposes. I mean qualified artisans are in demand in civvy street.'

'Qualified artisans?' The tone was biting.

The careers officer nodded and met Ruskin's gaze.

'I don't want to be a qualified artisan,' Ruskin snapped. 'I want to stay flying.'

The young officer began to look irritated. He seemed out of place to Ruskin. In fact the whole room looked out of place. Even the bloody posters were irrelevant wartime propaganda, and the roneoed bumph in the wire trays on the desk reminded Ruskin of the bureaucratic adjutants he'd known. DROs, Group circulars, Command orders, drafted by penguins with not a single flying hour to their credit. The young officer tapped the edge of his desk with a pipe cleaner. His pipe lay unsmoked in one of the trays. 'It's possible,' he said, after deep thought, or what passed for it, 'it's possible the Raff will presently ask certain pilots, especially those in Transport Command, to consider staying on a bit.'

'I'm not staying in this lot,' Ruskin said firmly.

'This lot?' The young officer looked hurt.

'This lot.'

'I thought you were keen to stay flying.'

'Not as a flight sergeant.'

'Ah,' said the young officer, who thought that explained a lot about Ruskin's boorish behaviour. 'If you stayed on you might, I say might, get your Warrant Officer promotion, which could possibly help in any application you make to join BOAC. And by all the rules you should have made WO by now. Any reason?'

'A couple of two ringers I couldn't get on with.'

'I see. I'll not press the point.'

'Nothing to press,' Ruskin insisted. 'They were shits.'

The young officer coughed and ran his hand over that mane. 'All the same, it's peacetime now and . . .'

'Right,' Ruskin said. 'And when my number comes up I'll be on my way faster than Jesse Owens.'

The young officer's face went taut like that of a public schoolboy who'd run out of charm. 'You sound a touch bitter.'

'Not a touch bitter. Bloody bitter.'

'Airline pilots have to be very balanced, Ruskin, very stable.'

The superior tone was too much for Ruskin. He weighed up the boy, his head slightly to one side as he leaned with critical nonchalance on the chair arm. 'And what do *you* want to be when you grow up?'

Trapped between wishing to discipline Ruskin and his own sense of failure, the boy was lost for words.

'No, I'm interested,' Ruskin said.

The young officer made a point of shutting the file on Ruskin's docs and seeking some lost bumph in the in-tray. 'That will be all, Flight.'

Ruskin rose slowly. His eyes never left the young officer until he turned to make his way out.

'Has discipline gone out of fashion, flight sergeant? Haven't you forgotten something?'

Ruskin stopped, turned, fixed the young officer with a look of utter contempt. 'The war's over,' he said. 'Sir.' And he threw up the most limp-handed salute in the history of the Royal Air Force. If the bastards thought peace meant a return to the *status quo*, and its pre-war class privileges, they were in for a shaking. It didn't matter a sod what the Labour Government was doing about it: to Ruskin it was a personal affair. Not only would there be no outside privies in Ruskin's future, there'd be no toffee-nosed bastards pushing him around either. He had seven days leave after the India trip. He could either go back home and see Jennie and his father, or else he could use the time to begin setting himself up. But his first task was to see what the hell Dickie Marlowe was doing about his posting off the curry run.

He decided to hitch a Dakota ride to Germany.

Marlowe was jumpy.

It was so unlike him that Ruskin remarked on it. They were in Marlowe's apartment drinking lagers. At the base sergeants' mess earlier Ruskin had picked up a buzz that Marlowe's Dakota had been stopped just before take-off to the UK the previous Sunday and searched. A section of the RAF police led by Squadron Leader Colville had gone over every inch of the Dakota and every item in its load. The crew had been body-searched, Marlowe by Colville personally. All that Colville and his service cops had found for their pains was one Leica camera, one Rollei, and sterling, the secret property of some crafty erk with an accomplice back at the UK base. Colville had had a strip torn off him by the CO. But the feeling among the sergeants was that Dickie Marlowe had been lucky: he was considered to be up to his ears in the black market. And not only in deals in cameras and sterling but, so it was said, antique furniture looted and/or bought from the Germans.

Ruskin put it to Marlowe. 'Any truth in all this, Dickie?'

'Sergeants are gossips, Jack,' Marlowe said blandly. The voice was sure. The eyes were nervous. 'But it'll be a long time before Squadron Leader Sherlock Colville tries to duff us up again.' He paused. 'I made him see that the SPs put the load straight before I would take off. The CO backed me up.' He got up and poured Ruskin another lager. 'Anyway you're not here to discuss me.' He paused. 'Jack, it's easier these days to loop the loop in a Lanc than to get a posting to the trooping run cancelled.'

'You got yours cancelled,' Ruskin said, accepting the lager. 'You got yourself organized. You looked after number one like you've been trained to do, your class, the officers.'

'Bolshie rubbish,' Marlowe laughed.

Ruskin put his feet up on the nineteenth century footstool. 'Unless you're bolshie these days you're down the pan. Those lads in India and down the Gulf. Piss off, they said. Get stuffed. And look at the air marshals crawling to 'em and the Air Minister refusing to admit it's mutiny. And the Prime Minister, no less, saying their complaints are being dealt with. They even sent out Ensa to perform *Laburnum Grove*.'

Marlowe eased himself into the divan, glass in hand, and Ruskin thought he was a bit like Noel Coward. 'I can't challenge what you're saying, Jack. Not one word.'

'No,' Ruskin said. 'You're doing all right. And I'm volunteering to join the game before the final whistle.' He held out his glass like an accusing finger. 'You only fixed it for yourself in London. Esprit de corps? Bollocks. Sir.'

Marlowe crossed one elegantly trousered leg over the other. And tugged his silk scarf loose. 'Very well, Jack. I'll see if I can get any joy over your posting next trip. Even though the game's not what it was.'

'Raff Police?'

'And the market. It's being rumbled, Jack. In the biggest possible way.' He put his glass down and played with the gold ring on the little finger of his left hand. 'Anyway, I never could stand to see our blokes flogging chocolate for cameras and things to bombed out Jerries who only wanted to give their kids a treat.'

Ruskin eyed him sternly. 'You've been up to your hat in it.'

'Never chocolate,' Marlowe said. 'I drew the line at chocolate.'

Ruskin drew himself up in the divan. 'So would I. Given the chance.'

Marlowe went over to the radio and brought in British Forces Network, Hamburg. 'I'll have another go, Jack. Promise.'

'You promised last time.'

'I'll do what I can. Like a ride back tomorrow?'

Ruskin shook his head. 'I'm on seven days leave. And I can tell you, you need seven days between trooping trips to those dumps. No thanks. I thought I'd see what's going round here. I've a lot to learn.'

The phone rang.

Marlowe took the call. He was edgy. And cold January day or not, there were beads of sweat on his forehead. He looked at Ruskin and said, 'Jack, would you mind? This is a bit personal.' Ruskin suspected it was to do with the racket, but he took his leave instantly.

He went out, closed the double doors and leaned against the gallery rail looking down into the lavish hall below. Gerhard walked across it and Ruskin threw him an idle salute. It crossed his mind that Helga might show up. Or maybe it was her on the phone now? He didn't think so, somehow. He reckoned it was more likely a businessman, perhaps it was even one of those British Control Commission blokes who had the best of all worlds. Some of them were known to be operating on the black market, and they'd not even been in the fighting. Help yourself, Jack, Ruskin thought. It's the only way.

Presently Marlowe came out and said, 'Sorry, Jack. Urgent.' Ruskin followed him back into the living room. Marlowe said, 'One for the road, and I'll drive you back to camp.' He was more jumpy than ever.

They had one more lager apiece.

Less than twenty-four hours later Marlowe was dead.

Ruskin was packing his holdall in the sergeants' quarters when he got the message that Marlowe and his crew had all been killed in an abortive take-off from the airfield. He grabbed a jeep and drove himself to the scene of the crash.

The Dakota had failed to clear a German farmhouse on the fringe of the field. Both were still in flames when Ruskin got there. The Dak's back had been broken on the farmhouse roof and the front section lay face down in the frozen dung and mud. Scattered around the farmyard were the spewed-out contents of the Dak: Spit and Mozzie parts due for restoration in the UK and Leicas and Rollei cameras and binoculars, and Louis XV furniture and other German and French antiques. Some were still smouldering. Others were just smashed. It was like Aladdin's cave in hell, Ruskin thought.

He approached one of the rescue sergeants. 'Any survivors?'

'What do you think, Chiefie?' said the shaken sergeant. 'If they weren't dead when she pranged, they're incinerated now.' He indicated the farmhouse. 'And there were two kids in there. We all knew 'em. We used to give 'em chocolate.'

The flames began to die down.

Ruskin had a lump in his throat.

It was up to him – and him alone – now.

CHAPTER 2

Ruskin flipped through the pages of a year-old copy of *Picture Post*, but his eyes were on the three officers waiting with him, a squadron leader, a flight lieutenant, and a flying officer. The squadron leader read *The Times* and radiated a quiet confidence, the other two were self effacing, and Ruskin had it in his bones that the whole bloody show was cut and dried. They were about to face a selection board for civil pilots.

The room had the characteristics of a doctor's waiting room: silence and lots of out-of-date publications, including pre-war copies of *Punch*. The walls, however, set it apart: they carried photos of mainly Transport Command aircraft. The inevitable DC3, a Liberator, a Handley Page Heracles, a Junkers 52, and in pride of place, a repro of an oil painting of a Short S-23 flying boat in the livery of the old Imperial Airways.

It was June 1946, and Ruskin was still in his flight sergeant's uniform, though he had been demobbed three days earlier. Instead of going north right away, he had stayed on in London for this board and spent some time in the Wings Club, where ex-RAF aircrews tended to gather with crews still serving. The place was full of echoes of wartime associations they hated to lose, and all the talk was of flying. Demob was a wrench for many of them, and most wanted to stay with aircraft. There were times when Ruskin had thought the club was more than anything a labour exchange for pilots who could not bring themselves to return to the tame jobs they'd been in before they joined the Raff.

And the going wasn't good.

Like the vast majority of the returning Forces, Ruskin had voted Labour in 1945 to give Attlee a landslide. Any other vote would have been unthinkable. But Labour had chosen among its priorities to bring in a Civil Aviation Act which put air transport under complete State control through three public corporations. British European Airways was taking over British Overseas Airways Corporation's routes into Europe together with *all* UK airlines.

It was already looking too bloody regimented by far. Even in this waiting room there was a whiff of those very RAF values that irked him, the old social divide between officers and ORs, the class game. Certainly there were jokes in the Wings Club to the effect that Britain's socialist airlines were only looking for Group Captains from Eton, Harrow and Cranwell. Jokes? Ruskin wasn't so sure.

He glanced over the old mahogany table which had probably once graced some officers' mess. Apart from a bundle of copies of *Flight* magazine there were copies of *The Times*, the *Daily Telegraph*, and the bloody *Tatler* of all things. Not a *Mirror* or *Herald* in sight. They were probably seen as subversive. The door to the interview room opened and a squadron leader came out. He left, looking confident.

'Flight Sergeant Ruskin.' It was a veteran RAF corporal holding a brown file.

Ruskin stood up, donning his forage cap.

'No need for that, Chiefie,' the corporal said stonily. 'It's informal.'

Ruskin tucked the cap into his tunic belt and went through. The sun was strong through the windows facing him. He blinked and saw the board members sitting at a long table to his left. All were civvies apart from a white haired group captain with a leathery complexion. The chairman, a beaky middle-aged man in rimless glasses, peered at Ruskin as if he were a specimen, checked the file before him, and smiled. Ruskin knew what the voice would be like before the man spoke. Upper crust. Magisterial. Condescending.

'Ah. Flight Sergeant Ruskin. Do sit down.'

Ruskin weighed up the quintet in turn and knew where the flak would come from: the hard-faced dandy on the right flank with a Fred Astaire parting in his glossy hair. He had a mean, set mouth and ran the back of his hand across his jowl as he stared into Ruskin.

'Quite a service record, Flight,' said the chairman amiably, apparently to some extent impressed by Ruskin's docs.

'Yes,' Ruskin gulped.

The quintet swopped glances. He hadn't said 'sir'.

'So what makes you want to join a State airline?'

'I want to stay flying,' Ruskin said.

'It's not the same as dicing around in Spitfires, Flight.' The hard-faced dandy's voice was lofty.

'I was never on Spits,' Ruskin said, outgazing him. 'I was on Daks mostly.'

'All the same,' said Hard-face. 'Civil flying is different. You would have the safety of a lot of people in your hands.'

'I've just done a dozen trips to India and back ferrying blokes home for demob,' Ruskin snapped. Those ops had been hell even when the mutiny was over. 'And I flew paratroops on the Rhine crossing.'

His manner had been noted. The chairman made a play of perusing his docs very closely. 'Nobody is challenging your Service record, Flight. It's all here. Why do you think you were never commissioned?'

'That's yesterday,' Ruskin said dourly.

'Why?' he was insistent.

'Well I never ate sausage off my spoon,' Ruskin said. 'Even where I come from they don't do that.' There were looks all round. 'All that matters is I've had flight lieutenants second to me up there.'

The chairman adjusted his glasses, holding them by the frame join. 'Does it surprise you to know that your documents contain a recommendation that you were never to be commissioned?'

'Office boys will be office boys,' Ruskin said, and the group captain winced.

'Is that all you have to say?' the chairman asked. 'I mean you've no idea why that recommendation was made?'

'I have ideas who made it and when, but it doesn't matter. I didn't like bullshit.'

Hard-face said, 'Perhaps, Flight, you're not quite the pilot you think you are?'

Ruskin's hard blue eyes fixed him. 'I'm as good as any. Better than most.'

Hard-face rapped the table with his fingers. 'Possibly you didn't have the technical knowledge of your superiors?'

Ruskin pointed to Hard-face's copy of his docs. 'Have you read those?'

'I have seen them, yes.'

'Read them?' The voice was steely.

The group captain, a man of perception with a face that had gone through a lot of war, turned to Hard-face and coughed. 'I must say – er – Colin . . . Page Three . . . Ruskin was a trained flight engineer before he remustered as pilot.'

Hard-face began to look for it.

The chairman broke in. 'You got high marks on your engineer's course, Ruskin. Eighty-six per cent. Strange you weren't commissioned after that. Seventy per cent plus meant you were eligible.'

Ruskin shrugged. 'That was the Raff.'

Hard-face came back, stuffily. 'Any organization must have a certain amount of what you call bull, Flight. Even this one.'

'Don't you?' Ruskin said.

'Don't I what?'

'Call it bull?'

The other four stifled their laughs.

'It's a question of standards,' Hard-face went on. 'And ours in civil aviation are high.' He gazed at Ruskin as if he were dung. 'Not all wartime pilots would prove anything like good enough for us. Not by a long chalk.'

Ruskin curbed his anger. 'I got my civil pilot's licence on my last leave. I've also taken engineer's "A" and "C" licences.'

The chairman defused the cross fire. 'You seem to be in

a hurry, Flight. I see you were demobbed only three days ago. Have you been home yet?'

'I live up north,' Ruskin replied, wondering what in hell it had to do with civil flying whether he'd been home yet.

'You do have a family?'

'That's important?'

'I'm talking about your responsibilities, Ruskin.'

'I thought this board would be about flying.' He hesitated. 'My father's still alive. And I do have a girl friend.'

Hard-face and two of the others perused the docs looking for something with which to puncture Ruskin's cockiness. The chairman looked uneasy. There was a chance the group captain was actually on Ruskin's side. There were more questions meant to establish Ruskin's social status and he led them on by describing the two-up, two-down terrace house under a mill chimney from which he had joined the RAF. 'But I'll not be going back there,' he said tartly. He knew Hard-face would take the bait.

'Why not?'

'Would you?'

Hard-face had had enough, but a hitherto silent board member with a Royal Air Force tie and a moustache remarkably like Hitler's joined in. 'What's your handicap at golf, Ruskin?'

Ruskin thought it was a joke, but the quintet awaited his reply. He knew a lot about soccer, a bit about boxing, hardly anything about cricket, and absolutely nothing about golf.

'A hundred,' he offered.

The quintet consulted with their eyes.

'Come now,' said Hitler. 'You've never played golf in your life, have you?'

'Nor ever caddied,' Ruskin said. He sat up now, hands on hips, blatantly eyeing them in turn like some hanging judge.

'Now,' said the friendly chairman. 'Have you a question you'd like to ask us, Flight?'

'I've got two,' Ruskin said. 'First off – what are the wages?' He knew they wouldn't like that.

'If – I say if – you were to be accepted I have no doubt you would consider yourself well compensated,' the chairman said. 'And the second question?'

'How soon would I be flying?'

It was Hard-face again. 'As soon as we were satisfied as to your competence.'

'I only ask,' Ruskin went on, 'in case I decide to join you.' He was sure they'd gone against him from the moment he opened his mouth. He wished now he'd gone in with his top pocket full of cigars and offered one to each of them. Their prissy faces would have fallen a mile. Organization men. Part of the system. Parcelling up their corners of the peacetime world.

'Just one thing, Flight,' the chairman said. 'You can't get away from the Service fast enough. You *have* been demobbed. Yet you still wear the uniform.'

'It's allowed,' Ruskin said, nodding towards the group captain. 'For all and sundry.'

'But why do *you* wear it?'

'You should see my demob suit,' Ruskin flashed.

The quintet may have had the peace sewn up, but they were beginning to look trapped in it.

'Thank you for coming, Flight,' the chairman said easily. He stood up and offered his hand. Ruskin took it. He had little against the old buffer. But it took all his self-control not to bang Hard-face's nose against the table top.

As he went out he heard Hard-face's voice. 'The war hardly over and he's stopped saying "sir".'

Ruskin picked up his zip holdall and threw a look at those waiting for interview. The three officers had been joined by a warrant officer with an observer's half brevet. 'If it's any help get yourself some golf handicaps,' he told them. 'Well under a hundred, I think.'

And he left the building, hailed a taxi and made straight for King's Cross, where he'd left his kitbag and demob gear. He felt no disappointment. He'd half expected the board to get on his wick. If this was a Labour Government's idea of how State civil aviation should be run he wanted no part of it. In the Wings Club there'd been talk of a fight back, of privateers moving in on jobs the State airlines couldn't or wouldn't touch.

He'd have to look into it.

But first, it was home. He wanted to see Jennie and his Dad.

Jennie ran along the platform, level with Ruskin as he pulled down the carriage window. She had discarded her Women's Land Army gear in favour of a light summer print dress in shades of pale blue. She was what his Dad had called 'petite and pretty' with sparkling bright eyes, dark as her hair, with a dancer's legs and a smile that could light up a room. Ruskin had been unable to get off the curry run for her twenty-first birthday some weeks before, but she wore the gold necklace he had bought her. He jumped down to the platform and they embraced, a touch shyly. They kissed and held each other, one pair among many platform reunions. He caught the smell of her hair and it made him feel good.

There were tears in her dark eyes. 'I thought today would never come,' she said finally, taking his greatcoat and indicating the cardboard box under his arm. 'Demob suit, love?' Her face lit up. 'What's it like?'

'Fit for a gangster,' Ruskin said. 'Stretch James Cagney, it would be dead right for him.'

She laughed. 'Can't wait to see you in it.'

It was a hot June day and the dirty station shimmered in the soot and steam. The town looked like the back of nowhere to Ruskin. But for Jennie he might well have just looked his father up and gone straight back to London the same day.

'James Cagney,' she laughed as they approached the ticket collector.

'True,' Ruskin grinned. 'I'll never wear it. Flog the lot, trilby and all. Fifteen quidsworth in there.'

'And sixty-three clothing coupons. What colour is it?'

'Blue chalk stripe,' Ruskin said sheepishly.

She laughed.

'You've not asked how I did at the Board.'

'How, love?'

'There's enthusiasm for you,' Ruskin said, mock serious.

'You know what I think,' Jennie said. 'But we'll not talk about it now. For now we'll enjoy ourselves.'

Ruskin grinned. 'I turned 'em down.'

Her eyes flashed with joy.

'But I'll keep on flying.'

She handed in their tickets and they emerged in the drab concourse with its peeling rail schedules and propaganda posters. An ageing 'Careless Talk Costs Lives' poster was still there covered in graffiti.

Jennie was exhilarated. 'Promise you'll wear your demob suit tonight,' she pleaded.

'I'd not be found dead in it,' Ruskin said.

'Just the once, love.'

He shook his head. She laughed at his bloody-mindedness. Then tugging at his arm, said, 'Look who's over there!'

Ahead of them, pushing through the demobbed soldiers, sailors and airmen, was Ruskin's father, a compact figure in a trilby and his best suit. He had Ruskin's pale blue eyes and Ruskin's manner, but he was shorter and had a far more equable nature. He was probably the most completely unselfish man Ruskin had ever known. They embraced a touch self consciously. Bob Ruskin's eyes were moist. His wife, Ruskin's mother, had been alive when Ruskin went to join the RAF. She had died unexpectedly young in 1944, not in a bombing raid, but due to a neglectful GP and an anaesthetist who was clearly not up to the job.

'I was leaving it to Jen, but I saw you off to join five years back, it's only right I should see you back now.' He was hard up for words and was finding it hard to conceal the slight tremble in his voice. 'It's all over now, any road,' he said inadequately.

'No, Dad,' Ruskin said surprisingly. 'It's just starting.'

Jen thought she knew what he meant. Bob insisted on carrying Ruskin's oil-stained kitbag. And the three of them moved out to the station approach to find a taxi. Bob was not joining them in the ride to Jennie's parents' home. He was due back right away at his foreman's job in the paper mill. He knew of the plan for Ruskin to stay with her family for a time. And Ruskin thought he looked a lonely figure as he waved them off in their old pre-war Humber taxi.

Frank Shaw, Jennie's father, poured light ales for Ruskin, his father, and his own son, Alan. The evening was warm and the small living room's windows were opened out onto the backyard, where Mrs Shaw had miraculously created a rock garden. Curled newspapers lay in the grate ready for the next fire. The table was laid for supper with the Shaws' best china and some hardly-used cutlery.

Ruskin, still wearing his blue battledress trousers, lay sprawled on the chintz-covered sofa under the window. He'd only been back about seven hours and he was already wondering how long he could stay under the same roof with Jen's Dad. Frank Shaw, a wiry little northerner with a hawk's features, was shrewd, worldly wise, opinionated, and a fully paid-up member of the Labour Party.

'This town,' he pronounced, pouring the last of the pale ales for himself, 'has got to stop tying itself up in wool. They've got to get other industries in. Else I can see the place becoming a ghost town.' He ran a hand across his balding dome. 'With a team in the Third Division. We never won the war to end up in the Third Division. Least we know what we want. And what we don't want. We . . .'

'Like what?' Ruskin punctured Shaw's eloquence.

'Like what?' The tone was indignant. 'I'll tell you like what.'

Mrs Shaw came in from the kitchen, having overheard. Hands on hips, she nodded at Ruskin. 'Don't encourage him, Jack. It only makes him think he's Ernie Bevin.'

Ruskin threw her a wink.

Shaw chose to press on. 'They codded us it was going to be a land for heroes to live in after the last lot. We got one fit for heroes to starve in. Not this time though. Not this bloody time round. Eh, Jack?'

'We'll see,' Ruskin said, and he took a sip of pale ale.

Shaw frowned. 'We'll see? We will an' all. There's the Beveridge Plan for a start.'

'Cradle to grave security?' Ruskin said. 'Not for me.' It had irked him for some time to see his oppos in the RAF looking to civvy street as if it were to be a feather bed for the rest of their lives.

'Now don't you start.' Mrs Shaw's reproof was directed at her husband. 'And Jack just back. You know what he thinks.'

They watched Shaw packing his pipe. Alan looked out of it. He was still on farm work as a conscientious objector and felt like an intruder at what was in effect a supper to celebrate Ruskin's demob. Bob Ruskin, an intensely private man himself who had never visited anyone's house in the past fifteen years until through Jack he met the Shaws, sat in a straight-backed chair as if he were ready to leave.

'Anyhow, cheers,' said Shaw, raising his glass.

Jennie came in from the kitchen, smiled at Ruskin and said, 'Where's the demob suit then?'

'Upstairs.'

'You said you'd wear it.'

Ruskin shrugged. 'Only when you kept asking. I changed my mind.'

'You can always change it back.' Jennie hugged him.

'Perhaps Alan would like to buy it?' Ruskin taunted.

For a long moment nobody spoke, then Alan said, 'No thank you.'

Ruskin couldn't leave it there. 'Not only the suit,' he said. 'Shoes, men's, one pair. Socks, grey, two pairs. Shirt, blue, one. Collars, two. Cuff links, one set.' He was mimicking the RAF store bashers.

'No thanks,' Alan said stiffly.

'Twelve quid the lot.'

Jennie wished to God Ruskin would lay off.

Alan said, 'I'm not on air crew rates of pay. I'm still on the farm on pauper's wages.'

Mrs Shaw broke the ice. A neat and efficient woman in her fifties she considered a family was a family was a family, and should on no account be torn apart by petty feuds. She gave Ruskin a warming smile. 'Show us what your demob suit's like on, Jack. We'd like to see you in it.'

Ruskin drank up. 'OK,' he said. And to the surprise of all he went off upstairs.

Alan ran a nervous hand over his chin, a hand that was hardly work-ravaged. His farm work was mainly the supervision of German prisoners of war, not digging himself. 'He was getting at me,' he said. 'Sneering.'

'He doesn't sneer, Alan.' It was Jennie.

'He was getting at me! Selling me his demob suit!'

'If only you knew how he hates it,' she replied.

Mrs Shaw turned to Alan. 'That'll do, Alan. You're seeing a slight where there wasn't one.'

'It's the same every time he comes here,' Alan said.

Jennie snapped. 'He's as much right to be here as you have.' She had always supported Alan in his years as a conchie, and this was a switch of loyalty in his eyes. Alan put down his glass and got up to leave.

'Oh yes,' Jennie called. 'Turn your back. Run away. That's just like you.'

Alan made for the door. But Bob Ruskin's quiet words held him back. 'Nobody holds it against you, son, what you chose to do in the war.' And then he took the sting out of the moment by diverting the attention from Alan and turning to Mrs Shaw. 'You've got more sway over our Jack than ever his mother and me had. He'd not have put his demob suit on for us. Or anybody. Once he sets his mind there's no changing him. I remember when he made up his mind to join the Air Force. His mother hated the idea. And we thought he couldn't – being in that reserved occupation in the aircraft factory. So he made up his mind to hit the foreman, and get himself sacked so he could join up.'

In the small back bedroom that had been Jennie's for some years, Ruskin changed into the demob suit. He studied the effect in the tall mirror lining the Victorian wardrobe door.

Jennie came in, took in Ruskin and his chalk stripe, and began to giggle, holding her hand over her mouth.

'That's it then,' Ruskin snapped. 'Your conchie brother can have it for nothing.'

'Jack,' she pleaded, trying to smother her laughter.

'Like he wants everything for nothing. Like he's going to university for nothing. He had a great war, he did, genning up to get to university.'

'Unfair, Jack,' she said. 'He studied hard in his spare time.'

'He had plenty.'

'Very little actually. He's put in long hours at the farm.' She stood behind him so that he lost her in the mirror. Her arms came round his waist.

'Anyway,' Ruskin said. 'He can have this lot compliments of the Raff.'

'Don't say that to him, love.'

'Why not?'

'Because it's cruel.' He turned and she saw he was miles away, in his own world. 'It's not going to work out staying here, is it?'

'No,' he said, taking her face in his hands.

She lifted herself on her toes to reach him with a kiss. 'Did you know *Brief Encounter*'s on at the Royal this week?'

He raised his eyes as if praying for release from such romantic trash, and she laughed for a moment. Then she said, 'Oh, Jack, don't spoil it. You're back and we've waited a long time.'

He kissed her and held her to him.

Downstairs Frank Shaw was on another hobby horse. 'I know one thing for sure,' he said, dragging at his reluctant pipe. 'We'll never see Parliament full of hard-faced businessmen again. We'll never stand for it. We'll . . .' He cut himself short as he caught sight of Ruskin like some tailor's dummy from a Burtons shop window come to life. 'God. The man from Chicago.'

Jennie, coming in behind Ruskin, put a finger to her mouth to urge them not to laugh.

Mrs Shaw stepped forward to feel the material, running the jacket lapel between her thumb and forefinger. 'Oh it suits you, Jack,' she said warmly. 'Nice piece of worsted. I couldn't do better on the market.'

Ruskin suddenly saw the daft side of it. He burst out laughing. And everyone, except Alan, joined in.

'You'll be going away in it, will you?' asked Mrs Shaw.

Ruskin's face clouded. 'Going away?'

Mrs Shaw put a hand to her mouth. 'I've said the wrong thing. I thought you two were going away for a week to Devon?'

'We *were*,' Jennie said between clenched teeth.

Shaw knocked out his pipe against the back of the grate. 'Ah,' he said. 'You've seen the light? You're going to get wed first?'

'No, Dad,' Jennie said stubbornly.

Shaw fixed Jennie, then Ruskin, with firm looks, and raked out his pipe bowl. 'I'll say no more.'

'No you won't,' Mrs Shaw said. 'You can sit down and we'll start supper.'

The men took their places at the table. Mrs Shaw pulled out a chair at the head. 'You're here, Jack.'

Ruskin indicated Shaw. 'I thought that was his?'

'Yours tonight, lad,' Shaw said, waving a hand. 'It's all been agreed. Make yourself at home. Stay as long as you like till you're on your feet. You can have the boxroom and Alan can sleep downstairs meanwhile.'

Bob Ruskin listened intently. His gaze kept moving to his son, now set to become a lodger in his future in-laws' house rather than his own small one on the wrong side of Preston Road. He knew now that things could never be as they were.

Jennie was on her way to the kitchen when she said abruptly, 'Jack's sharing my room, Dad.'

It was like the end of the world. Nobody moved. Nobody said a word for a minute, and then a stunned 'You what?' came from her father.

'My room,' Jennie said firmly.

Shaw closed his eyes and held his hands palm down against the table edge like a mystic praying for guidance. 'I never thought to see the day when that would go on under my roof.' He picked on Mrs Shaw. 'What do you think about this?'

'Jen knows what I think,' she said primly.

Jennie shot looks at each of them. 'We can always go somewhere else.'

Ruskin clasped his strong hands behind his head and leaned back in the dining chair. 'Always go to our house.' And his pale blue eyes fixed his father. Bob Ruskin's face told them nothing: he was used to a close relationship with one woman and a son who'd gone away years ago. He just didn't know how to cope with family disputes. He sensed Mrs Shaw watching him.

'I don't think that would be fair on your father, Jack, especially if Jen's going out to work.' She looked at Shaw. 'Besides, this is supposed to be a welcome not a wake.' The reproof went unheeded.

Shaw ran a hand over his bald patch and said, 'I'd never have believed it, never.'

They had tinned salmon for starters, and Jennie served them. Shaw gave her a sideways look. 'I'd never have thought it!'

'Oh, stop it, Frank, and eat your salmon.'

'I don't want it,' Shaw fumed. 'I'd not have it if it was Royal sturgeon!' And he began to propel himself out of his chair.

Ruskin put out an arm to deter him. 'Don't be daft, Jen's Dad,' he said.

Mrs Shaw found it all too much. She went out into the kitchen fumbling for her handkerchief.

They came down to breakfast, Ruskin and Jennie, to a disapproving silence. Their first night together after demob had not been all they had looked forward to. Ruskin thought the wall between their room and Alan's was too thin. She had laughed at his fears. And then they'd made love. And Ruskin had slept heavily. His dreams were terrifying. He remembered sections of them. Looking from a Dakota cockpit at two children in a German farmyard as Dickie Marlowe leaned out of a jeep handing them bars of chocolate. It was weird, the way the Dakota *hovered* over the farm. The children's delight was clear on their faces. Marlowe was laughing his film actor's laugh. It seemed the Dakota took ages to pass over the farm. And then, suddenly, it all changed. The Dakota was taking off, its wheels leaving the ground just before the runway ran out. The farmhouse loomed. They were too close. Ruskin fought the controls, knowing they weren't going to make it. He began to scream in terror. And then the dream seemed to go into flashback. He and Marlowe desperately trying to get away from the German airfield with their load of cameras and antique furniture before the SPs searched the aircraft. Marlowe telling him to remove all the external locking pins except the undercart one, which could come out when the loading was complete. And then the refusal of the undercart to budge and the terrifying realization that the reason was those locking pins. His screaming, 'Shit! You said leave the bloody pins!' And fighting the undercart lever.

'Flaps?' His last shouted attempt to save them. Marlowe's reply drowned in the noise.

And then the crash. Flames and smoke and blood and Marlowe's burning skull. And the little girl from the farm running out like a human torch, roasted alive by aviation spirit.

Ruskin came awake to find Jennie running a cold sponge across his forehead. 'You were dreaming, love,' she said.

'Was I?'

'Tell me about it.'

'Don't remember,' he lied. He couldn't burden her with it.

And yet Ruskin couldn't shake the nightmare from his mind. Marlowe's Dakota *had* crashed, the inquiry proved, because the undercart locking pins had been left in place. It was the undercart that hit the farm. The foolishness of it all. He heard Shaw's voice from across the breakfast table, though it sounded as if it were coming from Australia.

'I know what I'd do if I were just coming out now,' Shaw was saying. 'I'd grab a job in the civil service or the town hall. Then a mortgage and a house. Any house. Even with an outside privy. And get wed.'

'You *are* wed!' Mrs Shaw said tartly.

He wasn't to be put off. 'If we get those hard arsed businessmen back . . .'

'Frank!' Mrs Shaw hated swear words, and he usually made a point of only using them at work. She said, 'I see Billy Melody's back in the rates office at the town hall. And him a Commando.'

'Sensible,' Shaw agreed. 'That job's safe as houses.'

Ruskin carried his empty cornflakes plate to the kitchen sink. 'He must be going nuts.'

'Why?' Shaw persisted. 'Jimmy Chambers is back in the public library sifting kids' books. He's happy as a pig in . . .'

'Frank!'

'And him in submarines.' Shaw waited till Ruskin had sat down to his eggs and bacon. 'Pity you hit that gaffer. You'd have had a legal right to your old job back now. I know the chairman of the Transport Committee. If you'd like me to have a word? He's in my Buffaloes Lodge.'

Ruskin grinned. 'As long as you don't stampede me onto the buses.'

'I was only thinking out loud,' Shaw said. 'I'd have thought you'd had enough of flying.'

After that dream, Ruskin thought, he had to be right. 'No,' Ruskin said.

Shaw was after him. 'Risking your neck in a just war while you're single, that's one thing—'

'He is single.' It was Jennie, eating a boiled egg. She never ate ham or bacon and trotters were unthinkable since she had worked with pigs with the Women's Land Army. She was near to being a vegetarian.

'Only on a technicality,' Shaw said.

'Oh, Dad, you're impossible!'

'Stands to reason,' Shaw said. 'Law of averages. You've licked it so far. Now you want to join BOAC or BEA.'

'I tried 'em on for size, yes.'

'Eh?'

'And they don't fit.' Ruskin's confidence had returned now the dream was fading. 'Too big. And I've had it up to here with Gentlemen and Players. Two and a half ringers and sergeants. It's daft. Labour nationalizes the airlines and says no independents. And then recruits these twits who talk like Tories and fly the planes.'

'It's only the bourgeois doing what it's always done,' Shaw said, picking his teeth with a match. 'Looking after itself.'

'They can have the State airlines.'

'It's no shame if they turned you down, Jack.'

'I turned *them* down.'

'So how'll you make a living?'

Ruskin looked at Shaw as if he were simple. 'Flying,' he said.

Shaw was baffled.

'I'll start my own airline.'

Mrs Shaw put a hand to her mouth in shock, Jennie shook her head in disbelief, and Shaw said, 'You what?'

'My own airline,' Ruskin said with a mouthful of bacon and egg.

'His own airline,' Shaw mocked.

'Right,' Ruskin said. 'Fried bread's super, Mum.'

'It's all that flying that's done it,' Shaw said. 'You don't look loco. I mean you just said, "no independents". And dead right. I don't want propellers dropping on my roof, and bodies all over the backyard.'

Marlowe's bloodied head loomed into Ruskin's vision. 'The law says . . . Civil Aviation Act . . . it says all air services will be under State control. But it allows non-scheduled private services.'

Shaw screwed up his face. 'What are they when they're at home?'

'The crumbs,' Ruskin said. 'The routes the State airlines aren't interested in. I'm not taking orders any more. Not from anybody.'

Shaw was far from convinced. 'Just one thing. Where are the aeroplanes coming from? You need money.'

'I'm working on it,' Ruskin nodded.

'How much have you got then?'

'My gratuity.'

'How much is that?'

'Seventy-one pounds nineteen.'

'And we've another hundred and fifty in savings certificates,' Jennie joined in.

'And there's dough sloshing around if you know where to go,' Ruskin said.

Shaw pushed open the kitchen window. He desperately felt he needed fresh air. 'Not London? Not that lot of thieves? You can't be in with that lot?'

Ruskin ignored him and forked a piece of fried bread around his plate, soaking up the egg and fat.

'How much is an aeroplane?'

'Varies,' Ruskin shrugged.

'Like how much?'

'What sort do you want?' Ruskin grinned. 'Dakota? Lancaster? Halifax bomber?'

'A bomber?' Mrs Shaw was horrified.

'They can carry a lot, Mum,' Ruskin said easily. 'Freight, I mean, not bombs. Freight. And people.'

'Never me,' Mrs Shaw said.

'Nor me either,' Shaw said. 'It's all Mother Riley anyway. He's not got the money to take a trip from here to Ilkley Moor, never mind buy an aeroplane.'

Ruskin buttered a slice of bread to soak up the remaining egg and fat. 'I know a corporal who's now got a string of garages all the way from Normandy to Nijmegen out of flogging coffee and fags on the black market in Germany.'

Shaw said coldly, 'What are you on about, Jack?'

'I'm saying there's money sloshing about.' He washed down the soaked bread with a gulp of tea.

'Dirty money!' Shaw rapped.

Ruskin put on his naïve young flight sergeant's look which could make him look a lot younger than twenty-seven. 'All I'm saying is there's money around. If you know where to look.'

'And you do?'

Ruskin nodded and threw Jennie a quick glance. He'd just made up his mind to do something which wouldn't please her. He was going back to London that very day.

Ruskin paid off the taxi in Mayfair and made his way to the Wings Club, a town house on such a scale it must once have been owned by an aristocratic millionaire. Now it was a haven for serving and demobbed airmen, with its vast bar and elegant dining and games rooms.

The bar was busy as Ruskin came in. But there was no sign of Peter Witney and he knew no one. He ordered a pale ale and studied the clientele, three with burned faces and hands and two walking on crutches. The whole place could have been a Royal Air Force museum, with its Spitfire propeller over the bar surrounded by squadron crests mounted on shields, and its gallery of photographs of fighters and bombers. Under a blown-up photograph of a Thirties airliner stood a group of fliers, most of them still in uniform. Their attention absorbed by a heavily-built civilian wearing the sort of bold chalk stripe suit Ruskin had been given on demob, only this one was cut with Savile Row quality. He wore an RAF tie which somehow looked out of place, and a carnation in his buttonhole.

Ruskin checked the time. It was unlike Pete Witney to be late. In the Raff he'd been so meticulous about everything. Maybe civvy street had changed him, maybe he had got married. The thought reminded him of Jennie, he must be sure to take her a present when he went back. She had seemed in good spirits when she saw him off but she had a way of hiding her feelings. 'One night back and you're off already,' she'd said in humorous reproof as she stood at the train door. 'It's worse than those forty-eight hour passes. I hate this railway station.'

'You liked it yesterday.'

'Mmmmm.' She had raised herself on the step to kiss him.

'And you'll like it when I get back.'

'When's that?' she had smiled.

'Soon as I get organized.'

'If you're not back the day after tomorrow, I'll come down and fetch you,' she had threatened with a laugh.

And he had chided her. 'Your old man let you go to the wicked city, would he? Not even with a Land Army pitchfork.' She had taken a light-hearted swing at him before kissing him as the train began to move off. There were tears in her eyes as she waved.

Ruskin felt a touch on his shoulder now. It was Witney. 'Jack, sorry I'm late,' he said, shaking Ruskin's hand. 'Got lost on the underground. Getting lost's a habit with me in civvy street.'

'You should have taken a taxi,' Ruskin said.

'I was an officer, mate,' Witney laughed. 'Only ex-corporals can afford taxis in Mr Attlee's paradise.' There was a touch of bitterness in the voice but the boyish smile was still there, and the officer-class charm. He was a lot like Dickie Marlowe, Ruskin thought. His accent, his style, his neatness, his touch of arrogance. Of the five officers Ruskin had got on with, he was the only one who hadn't bought it. And Ruskin knew him well enough to remember what he drank. Ruskin ordered Witney a large scotch.

'So what's it about? You didn't say on the phone.'

'I know you've got contacts here,' Ruskin said.

Witney laughed, showing those even white teeth. He could have been Marlowe. Twin squadron leaders. 'Right load of bandits. Anyway, what are you doing now you're out?'

'Nothing yet,' Ruskin said.

'Makes two of us.'

'I thought you were a lawyer in Lincoln's Inn?'

Witney sampled the scotch. 'Cheers. I was what's laughingly known as a pupil in chambers. Dogsbody to a bunch of barristers. Went back for two days. Couldn't stand the paper work or the dust that fell out of their wigs. Got my sinuses. Did you know barristers get a plague called scalp rash? Like nappy rash, only at the top end.'

Ruskin indicated Witney's squadron leader's uniform. 'So you've gone back?'

Witney shook his head. 'Wish I could. No, I've applied to BOAC. Not hopeful. Never played the Eton Wall Game. Still, I hear KLM are looking for pilots. If you'd like to meet their recruiting chappie . . . ?'

'No thanks, Peter.'

'No trouble, old chap.' He glanced around the packed bar. 'Should be around somewhere. This place may call itself a club. It's really the Dakota drivers' labour exchange. All looking for ways of staying in aviation. Legal. Or not quite.'

Ruskin came to the point. 'I hear you get blokes in here flogging aircraft?'

'Well, yes, but . . .' Witney's blond eyebrows went up in surprise.

'I'm in the market,' Ruskin said matter of factly.

Witney raised his glass. 'Well cheers, Mr Rothschild. I never knew you got on the German rackets.'

'I didn't,' Ruskin said. 'Too busy on the curry run.'

Witney indicated to the barman he wanted their glasses refilled. His glance picked out the heavy-weight in the chalk stripe suit. 'He's one of the big dealers, Jack. If you can get near him.' His nostrils flared in disapproval. 'Times are changing. You'd not get me fawning on the blighter. He's bought so much war surplus they call him Churchill's Antiques Limited. Jeeps, guns, tanks – you name 'em, he'll flog 'em.'

The penny dropped with Ruskin. 'That's not Ernie Cade, is it?'

'That's him,' Witney said.

Cade's name was getting into the papers. One of the widest of the wide boys, a superspiv in an era when they were breeding in Britain like flies, he stood as a symbol of commercial anarchy in a sea of official controls. Ruskin started across to meet him.

'Careful, Jack,' Witney warned.

'Careful?'

'He may have dodged the war with a dicky heart. He's healthy now. And rough.'

Ruskin joined Cade's circle who were in stitches at his open boastfulness. 'So where's the aeroplane market today?' he was saying in a Midlands accent. 'I've a nice few Junkers 52s if you want a Jerry souvenir for the backyard. I've . . .'

'How about Dakotas?' Ruskin's voice broke in. He was taller than Cade but no heavier.

Cade peered at him through small dark eyes. 'Dakotas?'

'DC3s.'

'I know what Dakotas are, son. Sure. Cash on the nail.'

'Where can I see 'em?'

Cade indulged a heavy chuckle. 'Where can I see 'em, the boy says. How many do you want?'

'Just one to start with.'

It was put-down time. 'I don't like kiddie winks deals, Flight Sergeant.' He sniffed. 'One, he says.'

The hangers-on laughed on cue.

Pushing through until he was face to face with Cade, Ruskin said, 'I flew 'em. You flog 'em. Do you want to sell me one or not?'

'Cash on the nail, I said,' Cade sniffed.

'I heard you,' Ruskin said. 'So where do I see your DC3s?'

'Keep this up, son, you'll have me splitting my sides laughing.'

'That's okay. You could always buy somebody else's demob suit.' Ruskin felt a dig in his back. It was Witney warning him to watch it. He turned back to face Cade. 'You can have mine for fifteen nicker.'

Cade was measuring him up, as if checking on Ruskin's capacity to punch his weight. 'Where did you get your money, son? Flogging your Naafi rations to hungry Germans?'

'No,' Ruskin said coolly. 'Whose rations did you flog?'

Cade had nearly had enough. 'Tell you what, Flight,' he said, condescendingly. 'I've a nice Dak up at Northchurch. It's at the end of the Tube line. So you'll not have to scrape up a taxi fare.' It brought laughter, but the note was uneasy. 'You go and have a gander. Able Victor. That's its name. You'll find a store basher there name of Dalrymple . . .' The laughter bubbled. 'I'm not kidding. That's his real name. Just tell him Ernie Cade said you could have a look eh?'

Ruskin nodded and turned away. Witney went with him and whispered, 'You bloody fool. He's got back alley artistes.'

'Hey, son!' It was Cade's voice. Ruskin turned. 'Flight Sergeant. Able Victor, remember!' And Cade burst out laughing. His cronies joined in, not sure what was so funny.

Ruskin and Witney went back to the bar to have one for

the road. 'OK, he's rough,' Ruskin said. 'He's also got Dakotas.'

It took them just over an hour to find Dalrymple at Northchurch. He was a thin-as-a-pole LAC in horn-rim glasses. His greased hair was parted down the middle and he wore overalls over his blue battledress. He was nearly thirty and obsequious to the point of self immolation. He drove Ruskin and Witney by jeep across the airfield, which was now little more than an equipment dump.

'Tell me, Dalrymple,' Witney said from the back. 'Whose jeep is this?'

'Mr Cade's, sir.'

'And that?' He leaned forward and pointed a finger at the hangar ahead.

'Mr Cade's, sir.'

'He *owns* it?'

'No, sir. He – er – uses it.'

'But the Ministry must still own it surely?'

'I suppose so, sir. I don't know much about these things.'

'And you, Dalrymple?'

'Me, sir?'

'You, Dalrymple. Who pays you?'

'I'm now employed by the Ministry, sir. Since I left the Raff.'

'I see. But you work for Ernie Cade?'

'I find Mr Cade a fair-minded man, sir.'

Ruskin was just thinking what a groveller he was when Dalrymple winked, making it abundantly clear that he knew how to cope with nosey squadron leaders.

Dalrymple drove the jeep into the neglected hangar, its graffiti-daubed walls a legacy of nobler days, and drew up a few yards from a much-flown Dakota. 'Able Victor,' he said, glancing from Ruskin to Witney and back, not sure why a flight sergeant was a squadron leader's superior.

Ruskin's face fell. Witney took off his officer's hat and tucked it under his arm as if he were at a funeral.

'Christ!' Ruskin murmured. 'No wonder they were laughing!'

'Able Victor?' Witney said. 'Able Vanquished!'

Able Victor, still in its camouflage marking of brown and green, was cranked up on maintenance crutching, the fuselage that is. One wingtip lay on the deck, the port undercart detached. Both engine cowlings, an aileron and the rudder were missing, and a hoist was attached to the port engine as if the engine were not properly in place. Only one propeller was to be seen. And a thick patch of oil smeared the concrete under the starboard engine.

Ruskin moved closer to the amputated bird. He saw that some earlier crew or crewman had rechristened Able Victor. The name stood out, in neat white paint, on the port side of the nose: 'Vera Lynn'.

'Vera Lynn?' Witney said. 'More like humpty dumpty. After.'

Ruskin said nothing. He began to move around the Dakota, patting it occasionally, knocking at the fuselage with his fist. The other two came after him.

Presently Ruskin walked a few yards back and surveyed Vera Lynn from a distance. 'Not bad, is she?'

'Not bad?' Witney thought he was joking.

Ruskin looked at Dalrymple. 'You got her log book?'

Dalrymple brought out the log book from his smock pocket. Ruskin checked it over as Witney tapped the starboard wing gently fearing it might fall apart if he used any force.

Ruskin smiled. 'Soon put her together again, couldn't we – er – ?'

'Dalrymple.'

'No, no, your first name.'

'Edgar, Flight.'

'Have a bit of fun, couldn't we?'

'A bit of fun? She's past it.' Witney was aghast.

'I don't know,' said Ruskin, appraising Vera. 'She's not old. She's only three. Built in '43. She was at Arnhem and the Rhine crossing. And Monty flew in her once. Couple of slight prangs. All she needs is loving care and elbow grease.'

'Not to mention wings, wheels and engines,' Witney said.

'The wheels ain't so good,' Dalrymple admitted. 'I got some nice new ones back there, though.'

'How much, Edgar? The wheels?'

Dalrymple was still casting a pained eye over Witney. He wasn't sure he was distanced enough from the Raff to be rude to a two-and-a-half ringer.

'Never mind him, Edgar,' Ruskin said, reading his mind. 'He's kosher.'

'A fiver to you, Flight,' Dalrymple said.

Ruskin threw him a wink and climbed into the Dakota. Most of the floor was up. Ruskin trod a narrow gangplank separating him from the control cables and electrics. He moved carefully to the cockpit. Witney came next, then Dalrymple. The control panel was open and some instruments were missing, including the IAS and the altimeters. A small battered doll hung grotesquely from a gap in the panel.

'The instruments are nearly all here,' Ruskin said, taking the captain's left hand seat, which also needed attention.

'Thank God for small mercies,' Witney sighed.

'In fact she's quite a girl,' Ruskin chuckled. 'I could start putting her together now, couldn't you?'

'Frankly, no.'

'Where's your sense of adventure, Peter? She's a beauty.'

Witney took the co-pilot's seat. 'You're not seriously thinking of buying it?'

'Oh I don't know,' Ruskin had his eye on Dalrymple. 'If Ernie Cade thinks I'm keen he'll up the ante, won't he, Edgar?'

There was nothing wrong with Dalyrymple's antennae. 'He'll not hear it from me, Flight.'

'How much does he want for it, for God's sake?' Witney was reluctantly manipulating the throttle levers.

'Dunno. He clearly thinks she's rubbish. That's why they were all pissing themselves back there, his glee club.'

Dalrymple touched Ruskin's shoulder. 'If it's any help, Flight, this is the last of a bunch. He flogged the rest.'

'See?' Witney triumphed. 'If this can take off pigs can fly.'

'Like to bet?' Ruskin said, moving the stick to and fro.

'With what? My gratuity against yours?'

'What else?'

'All she needs is a good flight engineer to look after her.' Dalrymple wasn't just sales-spieling either. He felt strongly that the Dakota deserved a better fate than to be left to rust into oblivion.'

Witney turned and asked, 'What's he asking for it, Dalrymple?'

Ruskin butted in, 'Anybody else likely to buy her today, Edgar?'

'I doubt it.'

Ruskin brought out two fivers from his pocket. 'One for the wheel. One to make sure nobody else sees her today. OK?'

'OK, Flight.' Dalrymple pocketed the notes and presently drove them to the Underground station.

They were halfway to central London when Witney said, 'You don't even know how much the bastard wants for it.'

'I want her.' Ruskin's mood was firm. 'That's all that matters.'

'I still don't see what you're going to do for dough?'

'I'll get it,' though he still hadn't a clue how. 'Peter. Use your loaf. How much do you think she cost to build. Eighty thousand quid? A hundred? A hundred and fifty? More?'

'Arithmetic gives me headaches,' Witney said.

An old lady opposite studied them through hooded eyes as the train rattled towards Piccadilly.

'She was an expensive lady,' the old lady overheard, and Ruskin gave her a winning smile.

'I'd rather fly it than buy it,' Witney said. 'And I'm not even mad about flying it.'

'I'll need a second pilot. If the rank doesn't rankle.'

'It's lunacy,' Witney pronounced.

'You can always booze yourself stupid in the Wings Club, yapping about yesterday's thrills. Shooting lines about Normandy and Arnhem and the Rhine crossing. And how you came back on one engine across the North Sea in zero viz.'

'I'll think about it, Jack,' Witney promised. He wasn't exactly thrilled at the prospect but the idea of going back to those law chambers was a real frightener.

'Not for long,' Ruskin warned. 'There are thousands in the queue.'

And for the first time Witney saw Ruskin's ruthless streak. They hardly spoke again until they reached Piccadilly and got out.

Cade wasn't expected back till late evening, and nobody in the Wings Club could tell Ruskin how to contact him. Rumour had it that he was at Gosport looking over some Government-surplus motor torpedo boats.

Ruskin decided to while away a couple of hours at the Windmill Theatre enjoying the flesh, and by the time he got back to the Wings Club Cade was in full spate with his usual clique. 'And there's this pint-size wog who says "I want rocket-firing Typhoons and never mind who for. With rockets".'

His clique laughed like a tame BBC studio audience. Post-war cynicism had set in early in the Wings Club, where arms disposals were a subject of humour.

Ruskin butted in. 'Could I have a word?'

Cade had an elbow on the bar. He straightened up. 'If it isn't the skytramp,' he joked. 'Mister Persistence himself. What can I do for you, son?'

'I've seen Able Victor,' Ruskin said simply.

Cade nearly choked. 'He's seen Able Victor,' he gloated, and laughter erupted.

'I don't know what this lot have seen.' Ruskin's voice was clinical. 'Except the end of the road.'

Cade was unused to challengers. He signalled the

barman. 'Set 'em up again, Eddie.' He pointed at Ruskin. 'And what's yours?'

'Not just now,' Ruskin said. 'I'd like to talk, first.'

'Nobody's stopping you, son.'

'Over there.' Ruskin pointed to the corner under the oil painting of a Sunderland flying boat.

Half-amused, his beady eyes shining, Cade collected his glass and led the way, pausing to call to his cronies, 'I'll yell if he assaults me.'

The clique did what was expected of them: they laughed.

'I don't like doing business on the Palladium stage,' Ruskin said as they reached the corner table.

'You might not be doing any business,' Cade said, sitting down with a view of his cronies.

'How much are you asking?' Ruskin said, having little or no idea of the going rate for Dakotas.

'Able Victor?' Cade said. 'Three and a half grand to you.'

'Two and a half.' Ruskin's reply was immediate.

'Son,' Cade said irritably. 'This ain't Petticoat Lane. It cost me more than that to get it out of the Ministry. Three and a quarter grand. And that's final.'

'No,' Ruskin surprised himself. 'Three's final.'

Cade was cutting a cigar. 'Cash?' he said without looking up.

'Now there's a slight snag,' Ruskin said.

Cade hesitated with his gold cigar cutter looking like a weapon in his hand. 'I thought so, son. So auf wiedersehn.' He began to get up.

'I need a couple of days,' Ruskin said.

'Where are you raising it?'

'My bank manager.'

Cade found it so funny he put his index finger to his temple to imply that Ruskin was loco.

'He'll back me,' Ruskin said with more certainty than he felt. 'I'm well known at home.'

'And what will you tell him you want all this ready for?'

'To start an airline.'

Cade clearly found Ruskin's naïvety harder to cope with

than the cunning of his fellow wide boys. 'Son,' he said presently. 'I will tell you – word for bleedin' word – what this office boy in the sticks will tell you. He will say – er – what's your name?'

'Ruskin.'

'First name?'

'Jack.'

'He will say "Jack, my son, aeroplanes is no good. An aeroplane is a mobile asset", he will say.'

'I'm not asking for predictions, I'm asking for two days.'

By now Cade was on his feet, signalling to his clique that he was about to rejoin them. 'Either you have access to three grand,' he told Ruskin, 'or you haven't. Me, I say you haven't. So listen. You raise the first grand and a half. I'll lend you the other one and a half. Catch? Sure. I ain't Father Christmas. And I'll have to know a helluva lot more about you from the day you left your Mum's womb. You'll pay me interest at thirty per cent and I'll own half the Dakota.'

'That means it's costing me double what we just agreed?'

Cade chuckled. 'You should be an accountant, son. You're missing your way. And Able Victor could appreciate, you know.'

'Twenty per cent and a quarter share,' Ruskin said. 'That's if I don't get the whole lot from the bank.'

'You're a hard lad,' Cade chuckled. 'Twenty per cent and a half share.' He began to cross to the bar. 'Pray for a miracle,' he called back. 'He'll still shake his head and moan about a mobile asset.'

As he left the club to catch the night train back to Yorkshire, Ruskin was overtaken by the sound of Cade's clique laughing. Presumably Ernie Cade was making him the butt of the gag. It didn't matter a sod, he thought. He could already see himself flying 'Vera Lynn', then buying more Dakotas. On the train out of King's Cross he found himself using the stop press column of the *Evening Standard* to draw the outline of a Dakota's fuselage. And across it he inked in the bold words, 'Ruskin Air Services'.

He'd get Jennie to decide on the logo and the colour scheme.

The odds were stacked against him and Ruskin knew it. He had known Geoffrey Lake since they were at school together, but only distantly as Lake was three years his senior. Now there was a new divide between them – he had been in the Forces and Geoffrey hadn't. And Geoffrey's promotion had come in the wartime absence of more able clerks who were out there flying bombers, manning destroyers or landing on beaches with tommy guns. Stocky, prematurely-balding, and with mean eyes behind thick lenses, he greeted Ruskin with one of those over-concerned handshakes Ruskin detested, using both hands. 'Good to see you home, Jack,' he enthused with more bonhomie than their remote acquaintance called for. 'Good to see you all getting back home.'

Liar, Ruskin thought, he can't relish the competition. They talked of mutual friends now back from the war, and some who would never be back. It was some minutes before they got round to Ruskin's request.

Lake held on to his glasses as Ruskin spoke of 'Vera Lynn'. Then he cleared his throat and played nervously with a paper clip. 'Trouble is, Jack, it's – er – a mobile asset.'

'I thought you'd say that,' Ruskin said, his dislike for the man mounting.

'I mean here today, gone tomorrow.' The sunlight streamed into the over-neat office with its mix of utility furniture and sepia photos of branch managers long dead. Lake let the blind down a touch. 'You could sell an aeroplane abroad, Jack. I'm not – er – saying you would. But you could. And then where's the collateral?'

'You'd be backing me not the aeroplane,' Ruskin said.

'But where would you be without it? And isn't the Government against you? I mean they don't want competition with BOAC and this new outfit they're calling BEA, do they?'

It was a bit too much for Ruskin. 'I always thought banks were here to help people like me, not to grovel to governments.' What was wrong with people these days? Now the war was over they all seemed to want the State to lead them by the nose.

'Jack,' Lake said, his voice dripping with sincerity. 'I'd do anything to help. You know that. But what guarantees have you got?'

'Nobody gave me a guarantee I'd not be shot down in the war.'

Lake coughed. 'Again, you'd be flying out of this country, wouldn't you?'

'That's where most of the work is.'

'If only you'd come to me about some reasonable business, Jack.'

'Safe, you mean? One hundred per cent stone bonk secure?'

'Reasonable,' Lake corrected.

Men like Lake made Ruskin want to hold his nose. 'Like manufacturing water wings in some clapped out woollen mill?'

'That's unfair, Jack.'

'Why's everybody so dead set on security? What's up with the country?'

Lake wiped his glasses with the blue hanky from the top pocket of his grey suit. 'I'd like to help, Jack, I really would.'

'But,' Ruskin said. 'Mobile asset.'

Lake nodded.

'Thanks for nothing,' Ruskin said.

Lake leaned over the mahogany partner's desk to shake hands. Ruskin merely gazed at him for a long moment and then went out.

He walked back to the Shaws' house through the hot narrow streets which seemed even meaner than he remembered them from his boyhood. He felt stifled. It was as if now the war was won people just wanted to lie down and hibernate. He couldn't see the town changing in his lifetime. It was like a jail.

Frank Shaw was dismantling the air raid shelter that took up about half the tiny back garden. He saw Ruskin come in from the back passage. 'He said no?'

Ruskin nodded. 'Johnny Caution. I doubt if the bugger's ever taken a risk since he struggled out of the womb.'

'What else could he say? Hare-brained scheme. I'm not knocking you, Jack, but who's going to put hard earned brass into old aeroplanes?'

'Hard earned?'

'People's savings.'

'Balls.'

Jennie came from the kitchen. 'So Mr Lake said no?'

'With creeps like him setting the pace now there's no point in having won the bloody war.'

Jennie reached up and kissed him. 'Love, he only runs a small branch, what do you expect? There are thousands more.'

'Yes,' Ruskin shot back. 'All like him, war dodgers from the fallen arches brigade, playing it safe now as they did then. It comes naturally.'

He felt angry. He started out past Shaw.

'Jack, where are you going?' It was Jennie.

'A walk.'

'Well, don't rush. I'm coming with you.'

She joined him, looking cool in a green linen dress, and they took a short cut down the back passage. Shaw followed them and called, 'Jack.' Ruskin turned.

'How much do you need?'

'Never mind,' Ruskin said.

'How much?' The voice was demanding.

'I'll get it.'

'How much?'

Ruskin grinned. 'I'll not rob a bloody bank in London if that's what's worrying you.'

'No, but you could get in with the wrong lot. How much are you short of?'

'Does it matter, for God's sake?'

'It's going to matter for our Jen, isn't it? We've – Mum and me – we've four hundred in savings certificates . . .'

It was preposterous, Ruskin thought. 'No,' was all he said.

'And a hundred in the building society.'

'No.'

'You can have it.'

'No!' Ruskin's voice rose.

And he went on his way with Jennie, holding hands. They were near the duckpond in the corporation park when Jennie said, 'He means well, love.'

'That's the bloody trouble.'

'He saw it as an investment.'

'He did not. He saw it as charity. A helping hand. A lift up.'

'And what's wrong with that?'

'Everything,' Ruskin said, studying the ducks and geese. 'I'll swim on my own.'

'No,' Jennie giggled. 'You'll swim with me.'

'What a word to use. Sounds like I'll come down in the drink.'

'With me!' Jennie enthused and put her arm round his waist.

'Not swimming,' Ruskin said, watching an eider duck diving. 'No rubber dinghy. No Mae West.'

'You go near Mae West I'll kill you!'

Under all the banter his mind was pinwheeling. All that mattered was that the Dakota became his property and that he got her airborne. He watched the ducks, and remembered standing at the same spot as a boy and going back to that two-up, two-down house with its outside privy. And he saw the officers fixing themselves in civvy street and the State airlines. His answer was simple. He'd get that Dakota and he'd fly his arse off.

'We should have brought some bread for them,' Jennie said of the ducks.

Ruskin leaned on the duckpond rail and kissed her.

Even Cade was impressed by Ruskin's persistence. It was the day after the bank manager's turn-down of Ruskin's plea for a loan, and at this rate Ruskin would be spending his entire RAF gratuity on rail fares to and from King's Cross.

They sat in the corner of the Wings Club under that oil painting of the Sunderland flying boat. The afternoon was hot and the weighty Cade mopped his brow with a blue-spotted hanky between mouthfuls of sausage roll. The place was less full than usual, and with no cronies to impress Cade was more confidential. 'I love you, I really do,' he said. 'You got nerve. You got dreams. You got no lolly. You want to buy an aeroplane with chat. I mean – Flight Sergeant – I mean I don't acquire DC3s by flashing an RAF uniform.'

'You never had one to flash,' Ruskin said, taking a long drag on his cigarette.

Cade's eyes were cold. 'Tuck your brevet in your pocket, Flight Sergeant. Forget thirty-nine–forty-five. That's yesterday's war. Ten sixty-six and all that jazz. Fly, or forget it. Get in business or take a nine-to-five job pen pushing. But don't come looking at my goods if you don't have the folding stuff. Like the jeweller said, son, if you can't buy the goods take your nose off my window.'

'So forget it,' Ruskin bluffed. 'If you don't have a monopoly of Dakotas I can go somewhere else.' He studied Cade. 'And if you do we'll put an end to it.' He got up and began to walk away, hoping to hell that Cade would call him back. He was halfway across the half empty bar when Cade's voice boomed behind him. 'Hey, Flight Sergeant, come here!'

Ruskin wanted to hit him, but there was too much at stake. He strolled back to their table.

'Put it down to Ernie's natural big-hearted ways, son. But if you can put Able Victor together again she's yours. Still three grand. Half of her's mine and I lend you the other half. Twenty-five per cent interest.'

'Twenty per cent.' Ruskin was trying it on.

'Twenty-five,' Cade insisted. 'You out to look a gift horse in the teeth?'

'Twenty.' Ruskin would have gone to thirty. He would have gone to any number for 'Vera Lynn'.

A small secret smile crossed Cade's heavy face. 'Haven't you a rich uncle somewhere, son?' His voice hardened. 'Twenty-five.'

'Don't do yourself, will you?'

Cade said, 'Who needs the deal? You or me? Deal?'

'You're on,' Ruskin said.

And they shook hands, limply.

CHAPTER 3

Able Victor, alias 'Vera Lynn', stood now on her own undercart legs. Her port engine was suspended from a hoist as Ruskin, Witney and Jock McEvoy, sticky and oil-grimed, worked to slot it into the nacelle. It was heavy, dirty work, and they had been at it now for more than two weeks. McEvoy was an engineer, better qualified than Ruskin. He held 'B' and 'D' licences besides the 'A' and 'C' for which Ruskin had qualified. These enabled him to certify an aircraft and its engines fit for flight after overhaul.

At first Ruskin and the doubting Witney had begun the job of restoring the Dakota. It was a bigger job than they had foreseen, and Ruskin had found his old oppo, McEvoy, in the Wings Club – 'lost' in civvy street. 'I can't pay you much to begin with,' Ruskin had said frankly. 'I'll pay you when I can.'

'I live a simple life,' McEvoy had joked. 'Where is she?'

Ruskin had taken McEvoy to Northchurch. One look at 'Vera Lynn' and McEvoy was hooked.

Now they were all three of them virtually living in the aeroplane. Ruskin had a camp bed in the cargo hold. They were living almost exclusively off corned beef sandwiches. McEvoy did much for their morale: he was such a pessimist he made the other two laugh. Even when deliriously happy, McEvoy would look fed up. But he worked with such expertise and energy that the Dakota's restoration owed more to him than Ruskin. She was still a long way from being in one piece though. And as they took a break now, Witney cast a shrewd eye over the still disembodied engines, the rudder lying on its side on the deck, and told Ruskin, 'You were done, chum, rooked, taken to the cleaners. She'll never make it to Hendon let alone Yorkshire.'

'I know what I'm doing,' Ruskin said, as he poured tea from an outsize flask into a chipped enamel mug. 'She's worth every penny and more.'

Witney's disbelief was clear. 'So how come Charlie Randall got one for less than two grand from the Ministry of Supply?'

For a brief moment Ruskin's sureness took a jolt.

'True,' Witney said.

Ruskin ran the back of his hand across his mouth. 'You can't believe any of the buggers when it comes to prices,' he said. 'And I'll certainly be on a loser if we don't get this finished.' The tone was critical as he made a point of studying Witney's gloved hands. Witney used gloves for all the dirty work.

'Hey up!' McEvoy warned.

They followed his glance to see a dapper civilian with an umbrella and briefcase approaching. He came into the hangar with some authority, looking around him, taking everything in. Ruskin thought, the man from the Ministry, and he wasn't far out.

'Good afternoon, Mr Ruskin,' the man said, addressing Witney.

'Not me,' Witney said. 'Him.'

'Ah yes,' the man said to Ruskin. 'Air Registration Board, Mr Ruskin. My name's Kellett.'

Ruskin felt his hackles rise. The last thing they could afford right now was a dose of bureaucracy. 'I hope you don't mind but we are a bit pushed.' He put down his mug and made for the hoisted engine. Witney and McEvoy got the message and joined him. Kellett had brought an official looking file from his flip-over briefcase in well worn brown leather.

He followed them to the Dakota, his face pallid and set. 'I was out this way talking to one or two of your competitors,' he said. 'Thought I'd drop in.'

Ruskin, Witney and McEvoy were now back with the hoist, guiding the aileron into its wing slot. Perhaps the little snooper would go away, Ruskin thought, if they ignored him long enough.

But Kellett primly set his briefcase on the ground at his feet, and flipped the folder open. 'We were notified that you'd purchased Able Victor,' he said stiffly. 'Just seeing what you plan to do with her, that's all.'

'Get her flying,' Ruskin said rudely.

'Some way to go, then, I'd say.' His tone was firm but friendly.

Exasperated, Ruskin rounded on him. 'You an inspector?' And he made the word 'inspector' sound dirty.

Kellett pursed his lips then said, 'We prefer to be known as surveyors, Ruskin. Awful police ring about the word "inspector". You – er – you do have a maintenance schedule?'

Ruskin indicated his brain. 'Only up here.' The gesture meant Ruskin having to take one hand away from the aileron. Kellett saw the problem, put down his folder, and joined Ruskin and Witney in their support of the aileron as McEvoy steered it into the nacelle slot.

'OK,' McEvoy announced, and they let go.

'I'll not ask you now for your maintenance plan, Ruskin.' Kellett was rubbing grease off his delicate hands. 'But we will require a signed certificate of airworthiness, of course. Signed by a qualified engineer.'

'I'm qualified,' Ruskin snapped. He resented snoopers. There were more of them about this summer than bluebottles.

'Oh indeed,' Kellett said. 'You have "A" and "C" licences permitting you to certify the aircraft fit for flight but not . . .'

'Mac's qualified to certify the aircraft and engines after overhaul,' Ruskin said tartly.

Kellett said primly, 'There will have to be an air test, Ruskin. And I shall need to be satisfied before I sign your certificate of airworthiness.' He fixed his gaze on Witney. 'Squadron Leader Witney?'

Witney nodded.

'I'm sure you will be able to remind Mr Ruskin that he will have to provide a certain amount of documentation. Load sheets, that sort of thing?'

It was a calculated slap in the face for Ruskin, meant to imply that two-and-a-half ringers were *responsible* people.

'I know what has to be provided,' Ruskin snapped, moving the hoist towards the port propeller, which was propped up on planks.

'Good, good,' Kellett smiled bleakly.

'And we'll be flying her,' Ruskin said. 'It's our necks.'

'And other people's heads, Ruskin.' His point made he put the folder precisely into the briefcase and made to leave. 'I hear you will be operating from Garton in Yorkshire?'

'That's the idea. Yes.'

Kellett smiled. 'Should be seeing quite a bit of each other. I'm being posted to that region. Well, jolly good luck, anyway.'

Ruskin outgazed him, McEvoy ignored him, and Witney put on a diplomatic fixed grin and said, 'Thank you, Mr Kellett.'

When Kellett was out of earshot, Ruskin muttered, 'God! Snoopers!' And he mimicked Witney's voice to imply what he thought of any crawling to authority. 'Thank you, Mr Kellett!'

'Hey, Jack!' McEvoy called impatiently. 'Should we finish this aileron job, like?'

'I suppose we need it,' Ruskin said, and he began to laugh.

The hangar was in darkness except for a light coming from inside the Dakota. Both ailerons were in place now and so was the port engine though its cowlings were missing. The rudder section lay a few yards away, where McEvoy had been working on it.

In the cargo hold Ruskin tiptoed along the catwalk spanning the open floor checking the cables below. Near the bulkhead a palliasse was spread laterally across the floor and, beyond it, the big flask and a stack of spam sandwiches. Ruskin let the cables slip from his fingers and went for'ard to the palliasse. He poured himself a coffee from the flask, took a sandwich, and sat down to read the manual on the Dakota under the light of an inspection lamp.

Presently he saw the reflections of a torch beam through the cockpit windows. He was puzzled. They had all been working so hard that he'd insisted on Witney and McEvoy having a break: Witney had gone to his parents' home in Kingston-on-Thames and McEvoy had gone no one knew where. Probably on a bender in Soho. Mac only enjoyed his loner's status up to a point: every now and then he needed the sort of company you found readily in Soho. 'It's sleazier than the Gorbals,' he'd once told Ruskin. And he'd meant it as a compliment.

Ruskin picked up the inspection lamp and went back down the aircraft. The night was so warm he'd left the hold door open. He was aware of footsteps. He reached the door and beamed the lamp at the visitor. It was Jennie.

'What the hell – ?' he began, surprise turning to annoyance.

'They said you'd likely be here,' she said, her pale face lit up by the glare. She shielded her eyes and Ruskin diverted the beam. 'I've heard of people eating and sleeping on the job. But this is ridiculous.' She was in the Dakota now, a slight figure in a pale blue mac and wearing brogues. 'Well aren't you going to kiss me?' she said, a note of mischief in her voice.

Ruskin obliged with a formal peck. 'I told you I'd be home this weekend.'

'You've been saying that for three weeks,' Jennie said, shaking her head at what she saw. The open floor. The cables. The palliasse. The signs of spartan living. The half finished spam sandwich in Ruskin's right hand. 'Have you eaten any proper meals this week? Even one?'

'I'm doing all right.'

Jennie's eyes fastened on what passed for the larder – a loaf of bread, an open tin of spam, three stale Naafi wads, a pack of margarine, a jar of sugar that had been spilled, two badly-cracked enamel mugs and a screwdriver evidently used as a spoon. Then she took in the palliasse with its untidy RAF blankets. 'Oh, Jack, for God's sake!'

His mouth was tight, his eyes flashed. 'You shouldn't have come. You can go straight back.' He was struggling a bit as she took an open food tin and sniffed at it.

'And that's gone off,' she pronounced. She found another can. 'And what's this?'

'Iron rations,' Ruskin said. 'Very nourishing.'

She shook her head in dismay.

Ruskin pulled a face. 'I suppose you'd prefer me standing in a flaming queue waiting for a State handout? I suppose you think this crate will put itself together again? Well I am not going to hang about waiting for *anybody*.'

'You can come out and we'll get you a square meal,' she said.

'I've had one,' Ruskin said stubbornly.

'What – this rubbish?'

'And you can cut out the nagging and go home.'

She was adamant. 'If you think I'm going to stay up there, muck out cowsheds and wait, you're dafter than I thought, Jack Ruskin. The war's over and all you want to do is stay in it.' She picked up the edge of a blanket with the tips of her thumb and forefinger and held it as far away from her as she could. 'And these are filthy. You can catch impetigo off them.'

'Impetigo?' Ruskin's voice rose.

'It gives you a nasty rash.'

'A nasty rash?' Ruskin was almost beyond words. 'Listen! Never mind nasty rashes. All I want is an aeroplane that flies.'

Jennie pressed Ruskin to go out with her for a meal. But he wouldn't leave the Dakota. And when he told her the blankets had only just come in that day from the laundry she chose to stay herself. He shut the Dakota's door and they made love. Three hours later Ruskin woke up and eased himself off the palliasse. He went through to the cockpit and began work on the throttles' mounting: everything he could handle freed McEvoy for more tricky engineering.

Jennie opened her eyes and saw 'Chad', the wartime joke face peering over a wall, looking at her from the fuselage. The graffiti caption said, in white paint, 'Wot – no Kilroy?' She saw Ruskin had gone, and heard him at work up front. 'Jack. You know what time it is?'

'Half past two,' came the reply.

'So you come back to bed.' She smiled to herself. 'You should be tired out.'

'I'll never get this crate off the deck if I hang about,' he called, and his voice brought metallic echoes.

'Come back to bed, love.'

'You think I'll never get her off the deck, don't you?'

Jennie smiled. 'I'd not be surprised.'

'Oh yes, you would.' Ruskin sounded as if he were fresh from a morning swim. 'Your old man thinks I'm certifiable. Your Mum hopes I'm not but isn't sure. And you'd like me in a steady job, nine to five, no risk, and a pension.'

'Stop your chunner.'

'Being a nice little prole, that's how you'd like me. Putting up with controls on everything. Christ! You have to go down on your knees to the Ministry of Food to run a fish and chip shop now.'

Jennie laughed. 'I can see you running a fish and chip shop.'

'So could your Dad,' Ruskin said, sorting out the throttle mounting. 'If it were nationalized.'

'I think he's right,' came Jennie's voice. 'I don't think you did vote Labour.'

'I did, heaven save us. But what for? To make civil flying a monopoly for group captains with . . .'

'Plums in their mouths, I know.'

'Silver bloody spoons.'

'Come back to bed, love,' Jennie urged. 'You'll be whacked in the morning.'

'I'm all right.'

'And stop feeling bitter.'

'I'm not bitter.'

'So come back to bed,' she giggled. 'You won't catch impetigo.'

He began to laugh. He lifted himself out of the captain's seat and snuggled in with her under the blankets. He could hardly tell her that for all he knew they'd never even been near a laundry.

Ruskin was on air.

Even Cade's being late could not ruffle him. He had come straight to the Wings Club from Northchurch, where two-and-a-half hours earlier he had seen the Dakota looking more like a flyable aeroplane.

At the bar now with a half of pale, he was idly aware of the two men standing near him – a sharply dressed, angular cockney with wavy greying hair and a cigar and a slow-spoken West-countryman in his late twenties. Ruskin vaguely knew the younger man. He was Tommy Skeel, who owned, or rented – no one was quite sure – two Dakotas. He was typically ex-Raff: thick tweed jacket, grey slacks, RAF tie. And the signet ring on his little finger had a small pair of gold pilot's wings moulded on it.

'I don't want to make life hard for you, Tommy,' the cockney was saying. 'But that stuff had best be in Lille tomorrow. Day after at the latest. Or I'm in breach of contract.' There was a hint of menace behind the high-pitched voice.

Skeel frowned. 'I'm flying Dakotas not magic carpets,' he said. 'One's held up in Rome with undercart trouble. The other's in dock with a duff engine.'

'Get another engine,' the cockney urged.

'Slight cash snag,' Skeel said. 'And I'm tied up for the next three days trying to fix something.'

'Hire another pilot,' the cockney said sharply.

Skeel saw that Ruskin could overhear. They moved to the fireplace the other side of the bar. They nodded to Cade as he came in.

At the bar Cade made no apology. 'I'm nearly always late, son. You'll get used to it. Just flogged a hundred jeeps sight unseen – even by me – like jelly babies to the infants school.' He drew a contract from his inside pocket. 'For you to put your monicker to, son. If you want your solicitor to look at it, OK.'

Ruskin put it in his pocket without even giving it a glance. 'Who's the one who thinks he's the greatest living cockney?' he asked, indicating the cockney and Skeel.

'Billy Ronson? You want to watch him,' Cade warned.

'I am,' Ruskin replied.

'War profiteer,' Cade smirked. 'Calls himself an air freight broker. Cheeky young devil. Just you take a squint at that contract, there's a good lad.'

But Ruskin was gone.

'Mr Ronson?' he said to the big cockney.

'That's me.'

'Quick word?' He paused. 'Confidential?'

They moved away from Skeel. Ruskin said, 'If you want a drop in Lille day after tomorrow I'm your man.'

'I didn't catch your name,' Ronson said.

'Jack Ruskin.'

'Well you ain't exactly famous like Bader or Group Captain Cheshire or Lord Tedder.'

'New talent crops up every day, Mr Ronson.'

'What are you flying?'

'A Dak.'

Ronson nodded. 'Thirty quid a flying hour. Not a penny more.'

'Thirty-five.'

'Thirty.' Ronson began to turn away.

'Thirty-two ten,' Ruskin said.

'Thirty, mate. I don't bargain.'

'And waiting time?'

Ronson chuckled. 'I wasn't born yesterday, brother. What waiting time? It's only bales of cloth. Nothing to break.'

'Plenty to rip, though.'

The big cockney's face lit up. 'Tell you what, comrade. You do the Lille drop. Carry on to Biarritz. Pick up some fruit and cheese for me. I'll pay you flying hours Lille and Biarritz and back. And you'd best be doing a hundred miles an hour minimum. But no waiting time.'

Ruskin worked it out. Fruit would need careful loading.

The cockney saw into his mind. 'It'll all be crated, sunshine. You're not in a seller's market. Snap my fingers now I could have ten bandits come running.'

'You're on,' Ruskin nodded.

In a voice down to a whisper the cockney said, 'And what's this with Cade? If he's trying to get you to sign a contract plead broken fingers. When you've got rid of him and me of Tommy we'll discuss. Right?'

Ruskin nodded and joined Cade, who said, 'You'll get us all a bad name talking to him. Now *you* read your contract, eh?'

'My eyes are tired,' Ruskin said nonchalantly, though his heart was running amok. 'I'll get my solicitor to look at it.'

'I thought you didn't have one?'

'Only when I'm dealing with sharp operators,' Ruskin said, raising his glass. 'Not honest geezers like you, Ernie. Cheers.'

Cheeky young bastard, Cade thought.

Witney and McEvoy were still working on the Dakota when Ruskin came into the hangar that night. He was eager as a boy scout and waving a piece of paper.

'Please don't wave it like that, Jack. It reminds me of Neville Chamberlain coming back from Munich.' It was still a sore point with Witney that any British Prime Minister should return from a meeting with a threatening dictator like Hitler grateful for a phoney deal and saying 'Peace in our time'.

'We're in!' Ruskin enthused. 'We're on! We're in business! Starting Friday!'

McEvoy stood dumbstruck with a spanner in his left hand and oil slicks all over his rugged face. 'Not this Friday, Jack. You must mean Good Friday.' That was about nine months off.

'Day after tomorrow,' Ruskin said in triumph.

'Not *flying*?' McEvoy queried.

'Lille. Biarritz. Where's your sense of adventure?'

'Mine's gone somewhere with my stomach,' Witney confessed. He thought Ruskin was more than slightly off his rocker, bearing in mind what still had to be done on the Dakota.

McEvoy ran a hand over his puzzled face. 'What will you be using for an aeroplane, Jack?'

'Deadbeats!' Ruskin laughed. 'Why do I surround myself with deadbeats?' He patted McEvoy warmly on the cheek. 'I thought they brought you up right in the Gorbals, Mac?'

'Ay, they never brought us up daft!'

Witney played it cool. 'You do realize, Jack, she's still short of a port propeller and a good deal of her tail section.'

'Not to mention one or two instruments,' McEvoy said.

Suddenly Ruskin's mood changed. His eyes were accusing. 'We can make it easily if we start now.'

'Never by Friday.' McEvoy was positive.

'Are you with me or against me?' Ruskin asked them.

It was Witney's turn to glare now. 'Oh we're against you, Jack. We're trying to wreck your chances. It's our life's goal to spoil your bloody fun. We're only here to get under your feet.'

'Enough!' Ruskin said, for all the world like some field commander in the war. 'Are you on or not? Mac?' He tried to hypnotize McEvoy into saying yes.

'Mad,' McEvoy muttered, shaking his head. 'Mad, that's what it is.'

'Peter?'

'I never swallowed that tale about the loaves and fishes either,' Witney said.

Ruskin hugged them both in turn in those bear's arms and leapt into the Dak. 'On with the dance!' he called and, with a wink at McEvoy and indicating Witney, he added, 'Chaps.'

'Jack!' It was Peter Witney.

Ruskin went back to the cargo door. He saw Jennie coming across the hangar with the flask and a packet of sandwiches.

'What's this then?' he called.

'For tonight.'

'There's not enough there for three midgets with a lazy streak,' he said.

She laughed. 'How much more do you want then?'

'Gallons, love. Gallons of coffee. Four times as much grub. In the Raff guard room the SPs have a flask the size of a bleedin' fuel tank. We could nick that.'

'You mean I could?' Jennie corrected.

Ruskin grinned. 'They'll probably take more notice of you.'

Jennie went off to find more victuals. And they worked all through the night, with only brief breaks, and most of the next day.

'If we're flying tomorrow, and I don't see how we can be, we should be getting some kip,' Witney advised.

It was seven o'clock at night. 'You go and get some,' Ruskin told Witney. 'And you, Mac.'

'How about you?' Witney said.

'I'll break when I'm ready.'

It seemed to Witney and McEvoy – and Jennie, who kept up the refreshment service – that Ruskin had the stamina of a carthorse. They tried to keep up with him, but by Thursday midnight all were dozing off. Ruskin himself fell asleep in Jennie's lap on the palliasse at three o'clock Friday morning. The other two were in the pilots' seats up front. By eight o'clock Friday morning they were all at work again. That dodgy port engine was run several times by McEvoy and the tail section was in place. The rudder and the ailerons responded to the controls.

At half past ten Ruskin told McEvoy there was no more time. They'd test-fly her. Witney was appalled. It was all too rough and ready for him.

'Peter,' Ruskin said. 'We can't faff about. The bloody load will be here any time now.'

Witney wanted to say it could stay on the ground till Doomsday but he hadn't the heart.

They took Vera Lynn out of the hangar, went through the pre-take-off drill, and Ruskin's delight was immense as each check showed everything working OK. The take-off was perfect, and the Dakota was like a new toy to Ruskin, responding as he took her into the climb and into port and starboard turns, then stalls and low-speed handling checks. They were on the second circuit of the airfield when they saw the pressure gauge for the starboard engine falling fast.

'Could be the instrument,' Ruskin said.

'Like hell,' McEvoy yelled.

'Chop her, Jack?' Witney said coolly.

It took Ruskin only a moment to decide as he took in the oil temperature gauge showing the starboard engine heating up. He chopped the engine and took them in on one, easily. He taxied the Dak gently to the hangar and shut down the port engine. They waited for his outburst of dismay. But all he said was, 'We'll put it right in no time, Mac.'

And McEvoy and Witney knew bloody well that was impossible.

'And you can authorize her fit for flight, Mac.'

'Jack, for Christ's sake!' Witney was appalled.

'That engine's losing oil like crazy!' McEvoy protested.

'You've an honest face, Mac. Sign it as OK. We can always get it absolutely right later.'

Ruskin and McEvoy set to work on the starboard engine right away. They had barely got the cowling off when the lorry arrived with the bales of cloth for Lille.

It took them another three hours before McEvoy patched up the flaw, and he wasn't even sure it was the only one.

Jennie sensed McEvoy's unease when she joined them late in the afternoon as the last of the cloth was put aboard. She took Ruskin aside. 'Love,' she asked outright, 'is she fit for flight?'

'Mac okayed her,' Ruskin said, poker faced. 'And Kellett from the ARB has signed her certificate of airworthiness.'

'Is she all right?' Jennie persisted.

'Of course she is,' Ruskin said.

'Then I'm coming with you.'

Ruskin shook his head.

'Why not?' she asked.

'There's no room,' Ruskin said, struggling. 'I mean there's no seat.'

'There's the navigator's place.'

'I said no and that's final,' Ruskin said. 'Besides you've got no passport.'

'I don't need one.'

'You might. The French get more bloody minded every day now the war's over. I'm taking no chances.'

Her eyes flashed. 'Oh yes you are. Aren't you?' He stood there, expressionless, conceding nothing. 'And I'm not hanging around here like some Naafi girl, just bringing you your tea and wads.'

'Oh, do what you like,' he finally blurted, and threw the remains of his coffee on the grass.

Jennie stayed for the take-off, all the same, watching from the shadow of the hangar where Ruskin could not see her from the cockpit.

Ruskin and Witney were halfway through their pre-take-off checks. 'Flaps,' Witney said.

'Quarter down,' Ruskin's response. 'Checked.'

'Gills.'

'Trail.' Ruskin set them to trail.

They went through the list. McEvoy's head came between them, his eyes on those starboard engine pressure and temperature gauges. Ruskin began to pile on more power.

'I don't like that engine,' McEvoy warned. 'We could have done with a bit more time on her.'

'It's a bit bloody soon to panic,' Ruskin snapped.

'He's not panicking, Jack,' Witney said with authority. 'Nor am I.'

'We got emergency strips between here and Lille,' Ruskin said.

Witney looked at him as if checking on his sanity. 'And a bit of Channel,' he said.

'I'll put it to the vote,' Ruskin smiled. 'And mine counts for three.'

From her place near the hangar Jennie saw the Dakota move off and pick up speed along the runway. A small black saloon drew up nearby. Adrian Kellett didn't get out. He just sat there watching Jennie watch the take-off. The Dakota climbed gently off the tarmac.

Ruskin's attention was divided between his airspeed indicator and the housing estate just beyond the peri-track, with St Mark's Church steeple dead ahead – and those starboard engine oil gauges. Both showed healthy readings.

Jennie saw the Dakota climb well clear of St Mark's steeple. Her hands trembled slightly on the handlebars of her bike. Only now did she notice Kellett as he came over from the car. 'Mrs Ruskin?'

'No,' said Jennie, suspiciously.

The pale little ARB man put on a toothy smile meant to reassure. 'I'm so sorry. I thought you were Jack Ruskin's wife. I thought I'd seen you – er . . .'

'I'm Jack's girl friend.'

'Ah yes,' he nodded. 'I don't think there's any need for anxiety, is there?'

She felt almost sick with worry, but she drew herself up and said, 'Oh no. No need at all. Jack's an excellent pilot.'

'They have to be,' Kellett said. He reminded her of a weasel. 'I mean one has to be to come through as he has.'

'You know him then?'

'Oh yes,' Kellett said. He spoke like a ventriloquist, almost without opening his mouth. 'We *have* met.' He paused. 'Unusual chaps these skytramps. Takes a large streak of independent spirit to take on what they're doing.'

Jennie took him to be an official snooper. She gazed at the sky and saw in the distance a flash of silver as the sun caught Vera Lynn's windscreen, and then got on her bike and rode off.

Kellett got into his car and made a note.

From the captain's seat, Ruskin set the Dakota in level flight. The oil gauges were still giving healthy readings. He turned to Witney and McEvoy and said cheerfully, 'I don't know what the panic was about. It's too bloody late now, anyway!'

And he began to sing snatches of a pop song, 'Don't Fence Me In'.

CHAPTER 4

The Dakota rode the endless white clouds.

Ruskin checked the magnetic compass, the airspeed indicator, indicating 160 knots, the altimeter showing 2,000 feet, and his wrist watch. It was just after half past four in the afternoon and almost a month since that first flight with the leaky starboard engine.

The engines were running fine now on this their fifth there-and-back to France with freight, but McEvoy was not happy with the W/T set. He had been a wireless operator before remustering in the RAF as a flight engineer, but signals still held mysteries for him. He was also, like the other two, showing signs of fatigue.

All through the last four weeks they had alternated between flying and putting things right on Vera Lynn. The engines alone had proved enough for one man, McEvoy, but he had also helped Ruskin and Witney with undercart and rudder problems, and several instruments had gone u/s on them.

Witney looked down at the thick cloud, ran a hand through his short blond hair, and said in that public school voice, 'Looks like ten tenths all over. It *must* be England.'

'Picked up that weather broadcast yet?' Ruskin asked McEvoy.

McEvoy re-tuned the set with oil-grimed fingers. 'We missed the last one, the next's not due for another four minutes.' The rugged little Scot had taken the brunt of the Dakota's technical troubles, with Ruskin having to spend so much time in London, the Wings Club in particular, hustling for jobs. Some skytramps, as they were known to Board of Trade snoopers, had already gone under. Victims of the over-competitive game, they had run short of both money and sleep. A few had even lost their lives in fatigued aircraft that were simply unfit for flight.

Ruskin was cutting corners to stay in business. He looked down at the cloud blanketing England. 'We'll have to get down into this before the next weather broadcast.'

Witney crossed the fingers of his right hand on the control stick and said, 'Now if we were really important and making for Croydon instead of our dump in the North we'd have a jolly nice beacon to beckon us in.'

After that first trip to France Ruskin had rented hangar space at Garton, a one-time RAF satellite airfield in Yorkshire, not far from his home town. It meant being handy for a bit of work to Ireland and Scotland, but also he could stay with the Shaws, though that arrangement had its snags.

He looked at Witney. 'They don't want bandits at Croydon,' he joked. 'Even if I could afford the landing fees. Or put up with all those Groupies and Wingcos who've run out of war to fight.' The State corporations' apparent preference for group captains and wing commanders still rankled.

He ran the rule over the instruments as they cloud-hopped north. The altimeter got most of his attention. He glanced at Witney and dipped the Dakota into the cloud. Over the W/T came the weather report in morse. 'That's it then,' Ruskin said. 'QBI conditions all the way.'

'And ten tenths down to three hundred feet,' Witney added.

McEvoy passed Ruskin a note on which he had written the barometric pressure setting of 30.59, and Ruskin adjusted his altimeter accordingly. Witney saw to the starboard altimeter. His alert grey eyes were worried. 'They're out of sync, don't forget,' he told Ruskin. 'Hundred and fifty feet difference.'

'I'd not forgotten.' He turned to McEvoy. 'Give 'em a good going over when we're down, Mac.'

McEvoy poked his rustic's face between them. 'You mean after I've mended the navigator's compass and the starboard rev counter and put in new shutter bushes in the port oil cooler and found out why the starboard engine's cutting and we're getting all this vibration? Not forgetting why the artificial horizon's sluggish.' The Dakota was that kind of aeroplane.

'Sounds like mutiny,' Witney said.

Ruskin grinned. 'And I want her OK for take-off at zero eight thirty tomorrow.'

'Would you mind,' McEvoy said impishly, 'if I get out sometime to go to the bog?'

'No,' Ruskin said, mock-solemnly. 'We also believe in high standards of hygiene.'

He dipped the Dakota gently down into the cloud. They didn't enjoy the luxury of GCA, the ground controlled approach in which a controller with radar guided them in like a guide dog for the blind. They were relying on dead reckoning, the straight maths of navigation. They began their descent, trusting that when they eventually broke cloud they would have the Garton landmarks in view. Ruskin ran his eye over the IAS, the compass setting, and his watch – and his altimeter. 'OK, Pete?'

They began their pre-landing checks. 'Hydraulic pressure,' Witney said.

'Check,' Ruskin said. 'Six five zero.'

'Six five zero P . . . S . . . I . . . checked. Brakes.'

Ruskin said, 'Brakes – on, off.'

'Fuel.'

'Check it, Pete.'

'Contents OK,' Witney said. 'Main tanks selected. Booster pumps on. Undercart.'

'Put 'em down, Mac.'

McEvoy saw to the undercart.

They went through the rest of the drill. And those altimeters were still at odds. A hundred and fifty feet difference. Ruskin had begun to sweat, Witney bit the inside of his mouth, and McEvoy's jaws worked faster on his spearmint. And still they were in cloud, not a break in sight. 'Never put your faith in weathermen,' McEvoy said dourly. 'Ten-tenths down to nine hundred and we're still in it.'

'Probably ten-tenths all the way to the deck,' said Ruskin, staring out at the wall of cloud.

Witney turned his alert gaze on Ruskin. 'You *are* taking the lower reading as the right one?'

'Correct,' he said. 'This one's right, the other's the duff one.'

Neither Witney nor McEvoy were reassured.

Vera Lynn continued the descent.

They all kept staring out. 'I was just thinking, Mac,' Ruskin said to relieve the tension. 'About you and the bog. We could stick an elsan in the hangar. Save us going over to the old guardroom latrines.'

'One in here right now wouldn't come amiss,' Witney hissed. They were all on edge with nothing but thick cloud and those contradictory altimeters. And still Ruskin kept the Dakota in the shallow descent. With Ruskin's altimeter showing 330 feet and Witney's 480, there was still only cloud. 'I hope we see the deck before we hit it,' Witney breathed.

And suddenly there was a stab of light through the cloud layer, the cloud thinned into wispy strands, and they were through. And the first thing Ruskin and Witney saw as the Dakota came clear was the church steeple pronging upwards dead ahead.

'Pull up!' Witney yelled. 'Pull up for Christ's sake!'

Ruskin had already reacted, however, his right hand at the throttles. There was a surge of power from the two Wasps as they were opened up.

'Undercart up!' Ruskin shouted. 'Raise flaps!'

Outside the Nissen hut near the hangar Kellett stood close to a shaken Jennie. Her eyes were closed and she was still biting her bottom lip as the Dakota rose and banked to clear the steeple and began a right turn to start a second approach. 'Looked a lot worse than it really was, I'm sure,' Kellett said consolingly. 'I have a tot of brandy in the car, if you care?'

Jennie shook her head and went back to the hangar.

It was relief all round in the Dakota cockpit. And then Witney blurted, 'Even Pilot Officer bloody Prune would know you always take the lower reading when the altimeters disagree. Always!'

Ruskin was not to be cowed. 'Our dead reckoning wasn't all that far out, though. Nearly spot on!'

'Yes,' Witney muttered. 'On that steeple!'

On the ground, Kellett saw the Dakota turn for its run into the airfield and then joined Jennie in the hangar where she was using a dope gun to spray a war surplus Hillman van. She had begun the job when Kellett had first shown up twenty minutes earlier. She had not made him feel welcome. But Kellett was used to cool receptions from bandits who saw him as just another snooper, even though he was from the Air Registration Board which had been started by the airline operators themselves before the war.

'Hello, Miss Shaw,' he'd said, spotting that all she was using as a mask to protect herself from the dope was a man's handkerchief over her nose and mouth. 'You really should wear a proper face mask,' he had said. 'Dope's the opposite of cough medicine.'

'I'll find an old gas mask,' Jennie had said, resenting his intrusion.

Kellett had tied a hanky round his own face, and given her a lesson in the use of the dope gun. 'You'd do better to use it from this side,' he advised. 'The prevailing draught, you see.' He handed her the gun with his steely little smile. 'There. Not just a snooper, Miss Shaw.'

'We don't look on you as a snooper, Mr Kellett.'

'Oh yes you do,' he'd laughed, his eyes studying the frail trestle table covered with oil-smeared documents, pilots' and engineers' notes on the Dakota, handbooks, copies of *Flight* magazine and spare parts. It was a picture of chaos. He had sifted carefully through the mass of paperwork, handling it with caution as if it carried the plague.

'No filing cabinets, Miss Shaw? No files on How Yoke?'

'I'm sorry?'

He had smiled coyly, showing those stained uneven teeth. 'You know her as Vera Lynn.'

'Oh Jack keeps things like that.' Jennie put herself between Kellett and the paperwork.

'Not in the aircraft?' Again that mincing smile.

'Probably.'

'What? Old log books? Old loadsheets? Maintenance schedules?'

Jennie had stayed vague and suspicious.

'Some of your competitors manage things rather better, Miss Shaw. They even meet their ETAs.'

She had been expecting Ruskin for three hours. 'We're not BOAC, Mr Kellett. And even they don't run to time.'

'No,' Kellett had said. 'Point taken.' And glancing at his watch had begun to stroll around the hangar, holding that briefcase in front of him with both hands.

Jennie had then taken up the dope gun and had a sudden urge to brain him with it.

It was another ten minutes before they heard the Dakota making its unseen approach. They had gone out to see the landing.

Now back in the hangar Jennie put her hanky mask back on and set to work on the van with the spray gun, working off her tensions and shock.

She heard the Dakota come in, and now the engines filled the hangar with sound.

In the cockpit Ruskin looked out and saw Kellett's Ford 8 parked by the Nissen hut. 'Official welcome,' he nodded, and Witney followed his glance. 'Got your pen, Pete,' Ruskin went on. 'He'll want to see our loadsheet maybe.' He turned to McEvoy. 'And you didn't do a fit-for-flight certificate, did you?'

'No problem,' said McEvoy, bringing out a fountain pen.

Witney couldn't even remember what they'd got aboard, he was so shaken by the steeple incident.

'You can smell the cheese,' Ruskin said easily. 'And there's fruit and Frog vino.'

Witney wondered what he should do about the loadsheet.

'Use your imagination,' Ruskin grinned. 'Make it just over four thousand pounds with an all-up laden weight of twenty thousand odd. Just put down a few numbers.'

McEvoy was already busy making out a fit-for-flight certificate.

But it was neither the fit-for-flight certificate nor a loadsheet Kellett first asked about. 'You did a flight plan before this trip?' he queried.

'Of course,' Ruskin lied. And turning to Witney he said, 'Give the gentleman our copy, Pete.'

Witney brought out the flight plan he'd just dashed off in the cockpit.

'Only there was no notification to the UK,' Kellett said.

'Those damn French,' Ruskin said easily. 'They can't even get their air traffic control right at Le Bourget, never mind the dump we took off from. They're all too busy digging up the gold they hid from the Jerries.'

McEvoy played the responsible engineer and handed Kellett the fit-for-flight certificate he'd just signed.

Jennie had made no move towards them. She was still at work on the van. 'Hey, love,' Ruskin called. 'It's me, remember?' She just kept spraying the van.

Kellett fixed Ruskin with a look and said quietly, 'She saw your first approach when you nearly took the top off St Michael's.'

Ruskin went over to her now. He took the dope gun, lifted the hanky away from her face, and kissed her. 'Fine way to welcome me back.' Her face was taut. 'Oh, Jen, it wasn't all that bad.'

'No?' she said tensely.

'No,' he said, taking in the slight figure under the spray-smeared overalls. 'And the last thing I want is a scene. I'm right up to here with today.' His attention was caught by two Customs officers who had drawn up in a small saloon and were now approaching the group outside. 'I'll not be a tick,' he told Jennie, and crossed to meet them.

'Customs,' said the older officer, who was in his late

forties with a florid face and ears with big lobes. He looked humourless and self-important. 'We have reason to believe this aircraft has just landed.'

Ruskin sized him up through hard eyes. 'We're just beginning to believe it ourselves.'

'Cargo manifest?' said Big Lobes. 'Ship's papers?'

'We have a loadsheet,' Ruskin said. Witney handed it over. Ruskin indicated the other Customs man, who was spruce and boyish and a touch in awe of the fliers. 'I should let him have it. He looks like the one who can read.'

'And being facetious will get you nowhere,' said Big Lobes. 'You heroes with wings cut no ice with me.'

Out of the corner of his eye Ruskin saw Jennie leaving the hangar. He said to Big Lobes, 'I've met shits like you. You'd make the walking wounded pay duty on their crutches.'

'This tells us nothing,' Big Lobes said sourly. 'Where's your cargo manifest?'

After all the pressures of getting the work, of flying the Dak in a far from fit state, of all those hours in the air and on maintenance, it was too much for Ruskin. 'Now listen, Himmler,' he said, facing the uniformed Big Lobes. 'If you want to see what we've brought in, just go aboard. But we've work to do on her, a lot of work, work that'll take us the rest of today and maybe all night.'

'I'd better warn you to be careful,' Big Lobes said, flashing a gold-braided cuff.

Ruskin's nose twitched as if he found the smell of Big Lobes offensive. He said to Witney, 'Show Heinrich over our ship, Pete. If he's airsick at the top of the steps make sure he vomits outside and not in. We've enough to do without mopping up after him.' And with a final contemptuous glare at Big Lobes he set out after Jennie. He called back over his shoulder to Witney, 'And don't let 'em waste our time. They're on salary and don't lose if they just hang about. We won the war to make Britain safe for these big noses.' He began to run, fearing that Jennie might be beyond catching up.

Witney brushed an imaginary speck off his flying overalls and put on a brisk smile for HM Customs. 'Right, chaps, let's now be practical. May we offer you some char and wads?'

A huge naive smile came over McEvoy's ruddy face. 'You see,' he said, addressing the Customs men, 'what all those years in the officers' mess did for him? Squadron leader he was.' And he very nearly sprang to mock attention as he met Witney's glance.

Outside, Jennie began to ride off on her bike.

'Jen!' Ruskin shouted.

She braked the bike and turned.

'What's this then?'

She looked troubled. 'Don't you know?'

'All I know is I get in after a dicey trip and . . .'

'Is that what you call it?' Her voice trembled. 'Dicey? It was bad enough in the war when I couldn't *see* what was going on. But this. You're going to break your neck sooner or later. And a lot of other people's.' She was badly shaken and intent on going home.

'Give me a few minutes to settle these buggers and I'll drive you,' he offered. 'I'll have to come back here right away, though, there's a lot to do on the Dak.'

Jennie was weary. 'So we're not going to the Rialto tonight to see *The Best Years Of Our Lives*? And you won't be staying for that special supper Mum said she'd make us. And we won't be able to just relax and not say a word about flying.'

'Just have to be another night, Jen.'

Jennie put her left foot back on the pedal ready to ride off. 'Mum's already done that supper. Hot pot with all our meat rations for the last three weeks in it.'

Ruskin cast an impatient glance towards the hangar. 'Listen, love,' he said with a hint of desperation. 'I don't think we're on the same planet. I have an aeroplane here that needs working on. The pictures can wait. Hot pot can keep.'

'But not Vera?'

Ruskin had run out of pleading. Jennie kept her eyes on his for a moment, and then she was away, pedalling hard. He tried to catch hold of the bike as he called, 'Jen! Don't be stupid! Jen!' But she was too fast for him. He stood watching her pedal hectically along the perimeter track, ran his fingers across his left temple, and went into the hangar.

Jennie was halfway round the track when a black Morris Minor drew up ahead of her. The driver, one of two youngish men in the car, waved her down. He leaned out, freckled and clear-eyed. 'Hello, Miss. You didn't by any chance come in on that Dakota, did you?'

Jennie was on her guard. 'No,' she said brusquely.

'Have you a passport?' the driver said.

'No.'

'Identity card?'

'Not more snoopers?' Jennie snapped. Spattered with that dope she hardly looked like a newly-arrived passenger.

The freckle-faced man smiled. 'We're immigration officers, Miss. Do you know if that aircraft has come in from the Continent?'

'You'd better ask the crew,' Jennie said coldly. And without waiting for immigration clearance she rode off. She could not get Ruskin's fraught expression out of her mind, and she felt she had no chance of winning this peacetime tug of war with his outsize ambitions.

The two Customs officers were checking the imported goods in the cargo hold when the Dakota began to move. They crossed to the door to see Ruskin, Witney and McEvoy on the end of a towbar attached to the Dakota's tail wheel section. Big Lobes peered anxiously down as if the Dakota were six thousand feet up instead of firmly on the deck.

'Sorry we've no parachute!' Ruskin yelled.

Big Lobes was angry. His young partner looked set to jump. The Dakota was swung into the hangar. And Ruskin's face lit up at the Customs officers' discomfort. He had no time for Government snoopers – and he put

Customs men firmly in that dreary league. But his smile went as quickly as it had come, his expression hardened at the sight of the two immigration officers leaving the Morris 8 in the hangar entrance. They came in smoking.

'Hey!' Ruskin yelled. 'You two! Can't you bloody read?' His glance led them to the big sign in red letters, a relic of RAF days. It read: *'Strictly No Smoking In Hangar'*.

'Immigration,' said Freckleface. 'We're IOs.'

Ruskin glared. 'I don't care if you're bleedin' IOUs. Get that overheated rattletrap out of here. Pronto. And stub those fags!'

The IOs' reaction was to look baffled about where they could douse their cigarettes. They got back into their Morris 8 and Freckleface started the engine.

'And cut that bloody engine,' Ruskin glowered, going right up to the car. 'We don't want ignition sparks in here.' And he tugged the driver's door open.

Freckleface said indignantly, 'I thought you wanted the car out?'

'Right,' Ruskin said brusquely. 'You can shove it.'

The Customs officers, Witney and McEvoy waited for the IOs to defy him, but Ruskin held the car door open and said, 'Out!' Big Lobes, who had little time for his old enemies of the Immigration service, who looked down on uniformed Customs men, beamed almost benignly. The two IOs got out and began to roll the Morris outside.

'Great!' McEvoy rarely enthused about anything but this moved him greatly. He placed an elbow against the Dakota's tail and chuckled. 'Makes up for a lousy day, that does.'

Witney came up and gave Ruskin a condescending pat. 'I like it, Flight Sergeant,' he smiled.

'Come off it,' Ruskin grinned. 'You're part of the Establishment like them.' He watched the Customs officers watching the IOs. 'What next?' Ruskin's voice was full of disgust. 'Health inspectors to see we've not brought in any Frog cockroaches? Treasury snoopers to see we're not flying currency? Social security nosey parkers to see I'm stamping your cards?'

Witney winced. 'Cards? What cards?'

Ruskin skipped the question, he was so full of fury. 'No wonder the papers are saying it's time we had a bonfire of controls. I'll personally donate the flaming matches.' He'd long had a feeling that having come out of one war he was moving into another – against the regiments of bureaucrats swarming over Britain.

Jennie was still getting over the shock of seeing what she thought was the near-miss over the steeple. Tight-lipped and drawn and looking older than her twenty-two years, she took the hot pot from the oven. Her mother was at the stove. Frank Shaw stood in the doorway between the kitchen and the living room scraping out his pipe. He saw the strain in Jennie's face. 'I said right along it'd never work out,' he said. 'Not with him. If he'd an ounce of common decency he'd have brought you back home.'

Jennie set the hot pot on a table mat with a picture of a medieval knight on it.

Mrs Shaw said, 'Oh leave her alone, Dad.'

'I'm only saying what's best for her. I mean he's never here. I don't think he's been to see his own Dad since his demob and it's only ten minutes' walk.'

Jennie picked up the hot pot dish with kitchen cloths and pushed past him. 'Mind out of the way,' she said. 'It's hot.' He watched her through to the living room where she put the casserole on another medieval knight on the dining table. She didn't even look at him as she said, 'You don't want him here anyway. Never did.'

Shaw turned in the doorway to lean on his right shoulder rather than his left. 'Since when have I not made him welcome? Ever since he came out with that George Raft demob suit I've bent over backwards to make him feel at home. Like he was my own.'

'You never stop telling him he'll never make it with his

background.' She'd told them nothing of the steeple incident. 'You're always on.'

'His own airline!' Shaw rasped. 'He knows we've nationalized civil aviation so he has to be contrary.'

Mrs Shaw joined Jennie at the table where they completed the place-settings for three. 'Stop it, Frank, and come and sit down,' she said.

Mrs Shaw helped them to plates of hot pot in silence. Only when they were eating did Shaw start up again. 'I mean where are you going to end up?' He was genuinely anxious. 'He's up to his neck in debt to God knows what sort of villains down there.' He always called London 'down there'. 'And he'll not even wed you.'

Jennie wiped her mouth with a napkin. 'If you mention that again I'm going,' she flared, the dark brown eyes flashing.

The threat worked – for a couple of minutes. Then Shaw said, 'If he's not flying that thing he's sticking it together with spearmint and elastic. Or he's down there with all those spivs and drones.'

'You don't know who he sees in London,' Jennie said, between mouthfuls.

'I've a good idea.' He put his fork down and ran a desperate hand across his bald dome. 'He's either going to wind up dead or in Dartmoor.'

There was the sound of the front door closing. 'I never knew our Alan was coming over tonight,' Shaw said. Jennie was already in the hall. Her eyes glistened, she put a hand to her mouth as much in surprise as to curb her emotions. Ruskin still wore his oil-grimed flying overalls, and there were oil streaks across his face, his hair was sticky with it, and he was red-eyed. She flew to him and they embraced, and then she led him by the hand into the living room, almost as if she were proud to show him off. 'Love,' she said. 'I'll run you a bath.'

'I'll manage,' Ruskin said, his eyes on Frank Shaw. 'You finish your supper.'

Mrs Shaw was on her feet wiping her hands on her apron. 'Can I put you some out, Jack?'

'Don't think there's time, Mum.'

Shaw jumped on it. 'You're not going back to that winged wonder tonight?'

'No,' Ruskin said, with a wink at Jennie. 'I'm taking Jen to the pictures.' Jennie's face came alive. She stretched up on tiptoe to kiss him and went upstairs to run his bath. Ruskin was aware of Mrs Shaw's eagerness to make him feel welcome and he told her, 'I'd love a bit of hot pot, Mum. There should be time. We'll only miss Mickey Mouse and the newsreel.'

Frank Shaw went on eating as if Ruskin were not there. He heard Ruskin taking the stairs two at a time and looked at his wife. 'I'll never see why she's so daft on him. He'll be no use to her if she lives to be a hundred.'

Mrs Shaw was already picking up Jennie's plate and going into the kitchen.

'What are you doing?' Shaw demanded irritably, knowing very well and implying that she shouldn't pamper the young.

'Putting this back in the oven,' she called back.

'How about the pot, then, if he's having some?'

'One thing at a time.' Mrs Shaw's voice was full of determination.

'Oh, all right,' Shaw said, beaten. He stood up, and tried to pick up the casserole. He burnt his fingers. 'Godalmighty,' he howled.

'Yes,' Mrs Shaw said from the doorway. 'He's been studying you.'

In the narrow bathroom Shaw had had put in just before the war when he was promoted to foreman, Ruskin began to scrub himself with a loofah. The bath was hardly big enough and he sat with his knees up. Jennie brought out a shampoo from the cylinder cupboard, poured water over his oil-greased hair and began to rub in the shampoo.

Ruskin sniffed suspiciously. 'God, it pongs,' he said. 'It's for birds, you'll be getting me nicked by the Raff police.'

'I can't see them fancying you,' she laughed.

'They could have me for trying to corrupt young erks. Did I ever tell you about when the Warrant Officer dug us out of our pits one dark night to surround a haystack?'

'It's going to be dirty,' Jennie said, rubbing in more shampoo in his hair. 'But go on.'

Ruskin rubbed shampoo out of his eyes. 'Corporal SPs were prodding the hay with sticks. And out came two poor erks.'

'Whatever were they doing, love?' Jennie asked with exaggerated naïvety.

'Oh, come on, love,' Ruskin said. 'What were they doing?'

'What happened to the erks?'

'Glasshouse.'

'Isn't that like prison?'

'Worse,' Ruskin said. 'If the poor sods had been squadron leaders it would have been different.'

'They wouldn't have been prodded in the hay?'

'In the what?' Ruskin laughed.

'You know what I meant.'

'Not with pitchforks they wouldn't.'

'What with, love?' Jennie asked, feigning innocence by fluttering her eyelashes like a girl in a silent movie.

'Feather dusters.' He pulled her to him and kissed her, making a play of pulling her into the bath with him. She threw another jug of water over him.

'Different now,' Ruskin contemplated. 'Every man for himself. No them and us. No King's Regulations bull. They've got to compete with the likes of me without my hands tied and my ankles in balls and chains. I want another Dak in six months, then another, and another. We'll fly our arses off to lick the bastards.'

She wondered why he got carried away like this. All the fun had gone, quite suddenly he was earnest.

'To lick who, love?'

'The State airlines,' Ruskin said matter of factly. 'BOAC. This new thing, BEA. Still beats me. The working class puts in a Labour government and it nationalizes the airlines and then gives all the best jobs to bloody group captains with plums in their mouths.'

Jennie thought she'd get him off his hobby horse. 'Are we going to see *The Best Years Of Our Lives* or not?'

'That's why I came home tonight.'

'We could always go to bed,' Jennie said, sitting on the edge of the bath.

'What? With your old man glowering down to his socks.'

Jennie knew what he meant but she chose to put a different face on it. 'I don't know why you two don't hit it off.'

'I'm the bloke who hasn't married his daughter, that's why. And who won't take a steady nine to five job with the council. He'll have to eat a lot of words one day when I'm running the biggest airline in Britain.'

He meant it. She poured another jugful of water to rinse out the shampoo suds. This time it was cold and he yelled in shock.

Downstairs the Shaws were finishing their supper. Frank had poured himself a bottle of brown ale. They heard Ruskin's yell. 'He could be a lot worse, Frank,' Mrs Shaw said persuasively. 'He could be cruel. And a drunkard.' She cast her gaze over his innocent beer.

Shaw leaned on the light oak table and said, 'He could have horns and a forked tail. He could also have some savvy and not fancy he's Colonel Lindbergh or Jim Mollison. He could think a bit more about our Jen and a bit less about that flying machine he calls Vera Lynn. I've a good mind to write to her.'

'If she's any sense she'll not reply,' Mrs Shaw said, raising her eyebrows at his cheek.

A few minutes later and Ruskin and Jennie came down.

'I'll get your hot pot,' Mrs Shaw said.

'No, sit down, Mum,' Ruskin said, pushing through towards the kitchen. 'I'll get it.'

Jennie was adamant. '*I'll* get it,' she insisted and went through to the kitchen as Ruskin took his chair at the table. He weighed up Shaw's mood. 'Thanks,' he said presently. 'That was very nice of you.'

Shaw was puzzled.

'That wardrobe,' Ruskin said.

'Tallboy, you mean,' Shaw replied.

Mrs Shaw looked at Ruskin. 'I told Frank you'd nowhere to put your clothes in your room.'

'No need, really,' Ruskin said, wondering if he'd ever get through to Jen's Dad. 'It's your tallboy and I can keep most of my stuff at the airfield. But thanks.'

Mrs Shaw beamed at this hint of reconciliation between them. 'Moved it out of our bedroom himself, didn't you, Frank. Nearly ruptured himself, didn't you?'

'It'd take more than a tallboy to give me a rupture.'

Jennie came in with the casserole and Shaw was fiddling with tobacco in his pouch. He was a bit worried that Ruskin might see him as a soft touch because of that tallboy gesture. He made a slight bow to Ruskin. 'Permission to smoke, sir?'

'If that's twist, no,' Ruskin smiled.

And it pleased Mrs Shaw that Jack Ruskin was able to stand up to her strong-willed husband.

When he and Jennie had finished their hot pot Ruskin even offered to wash up, his mood was so conciliatory. But the Shaws would have none of it and when they had the house to themselves and Mrs Shaw was over the sink with Shaw drying the pots, she said, 'You'll never change him, Frank. He's even more stubborn than you and that's saying a lot. Do you think I should try and get some carrots in?'

'Carrots?' Shaw's eyebrows shot up.

'Well, Jack's been flying that thing at night. The Air Force used to feed those night fighter pilots raw carrots to keep their eyesight sharp.'

Shaw nearly dropped a dinner plate.

'Don't you remember Cat's Eyes Cunningham?' she went on, and she was serious.

'Cat's Eyes Cunningham!' He couldn't believe his ears.

'They fed *him* raw carrots,' she said. 'He used to find those German bombers over the North Sea.'

'He did have a bit of help from radar.'

'All the same,' she said, sure that carrots would do Jack good.

'And Jack Ruskin's no Cat's Eyes Cunningham,' Shaw said firmly.

'No,' she replied. 'He's our Jen's lad and he's flying at night.'

Things weren't going well at the Rialto. Ruskin was not exactly riveted by *The Best Years Of Our Lives* and though he found the usherette's pretty legs a diversion in the aisle he began to feel he was wasting his life with so much work to be done on the Dakota. Earlier he had brought out a box of chocolates that he'd forgotten.

'Wherever did you get the coupons?' Jennie had asked.

'Storebasher at the airfield,' Ruskin had said offhandedly. 'He's rolling in 'em.'

'Black market?'

'Sure,' Ruskin said. 'And I forgot to tell Mum. He can get us all the meat we want and he'll have some Grade One salmon next week.'

'Dad won't approve,' Jennie had said.

'No, but he'll eat it.'

Now Ruskin was shifting about in his seat. And people in the row behind were having to change places. They didn't complain to Ruskin: his size made sure of that.

'It's only another hour,' Jennie whispered.

'I could just get the last bus to the airfield,' he murmured, and she turned sharply. 'You can drive home in the van.'

Jennie was appalled. 'You're not going back there now? Tonight?'

Ruskin said nothing. But his mind was full of images of the Dakota and those altimeters and the undercart levers and the port engine which had been sounding a bit out of sorts.

Jennie read his thoughts. 'Jack,' she said. 'You're not going back there tonight. And I'm not going home on my own.'

'I'll drive you then, and go on.'

There were mutterings from the seats behind and Jennie whispered, 'Why do you have to spoil it?'

He studied her for a long moment, then picked up his mac from between his feet and made his way out, stepping over people's legs. Jennie made as if to follow, then changed her mind.

She was aware of people staring at her. At least they couldn't see the tears in her eyes. And she couldn't see much of the film, either.

McEvoy was replacing the faulty altimeter under the light of an inspection lamp when a beam of light swept across the cockpit. He checked his watch, puzzled. Nine thirty. 'Pete?' he called.

Witney's voice came from the cabin beyond. 'Yes?' He was nearly through cleaning out the hold. Some of the fruit had got crushed and some bottles of vino had been broken and the place reeked of cheese. It had been mainly due to Witney that the Customs and Immigration officers had gone away satisfied. The load was fully covered by import licences and Witney was able to satisfy the IOs that no illegal immigrants had been landed. He'd got the impression they were looking for deserters from the European campaign who were slipping back into the UK.

Witney pushed through to the cockpit where McEvoy was peering out of the port window.

'I thought Jack and Jennie were going to the second house pictures and he wasn't coming back tonight?' Mac said.

Witney agreed.

'So who the bloody hell's this then?'

All Witney could see was the light of a torch coming towards them. And then another beam. He picked up a torch from the tools McEvoy had laid out on the co-pilot's seat and went back down the slope of the hold to the cargo door. McEvoy followed with a frown, noting the broom and the water pail lying in the bare hold alongside a loading crowbar. McEvoy picked up the crowbar. It was instinct. One of his Gorbals ways.

Witney was a couple of yards ahead of him and was suddenly on stage, held by a strong torch beam. McEvoy froze in the darkness, gripping the crowbar.

Echoing through the dark hangar came Cade's demanding voice. 'Jack Ruskin up there?'

'Who's that?' Witney thought he knew the voice.

'Is he up there?' The tone was insistent. A big man vaulted aboard and stood beside Witney, all menace. In the torch beam Witney could now make out Cade and another man, thinner than Cade, with a pug's nose. He was idly swinging what looked like a bicycle chain.

'Answer me,' Cade called. 'You're not dead yet.'

'He's not here,' Witney said quietly.

Pugnose climbed aboard now, and there was at least one other aide still with Cade below. McEvoy crouched in the cabin shadows, absolutely still, his right hand gripping the crowbar.

'Seen you somewhere, haven't I?' Cade asked Witney.

'The Wings Club.' Witney's throat had gone dry.

Cade climbed up now and ordered Pugnose to go forward in search of Ruskin. 'He's likely hiding in the cockpit.'

Pugnose only took three steps. His torch beam picked up McEvoy in the split-second it took McEvoy to head him off. McEvoy wielded the crowbar in both hands. His eyes were slits, his mouth was set. 'One more step I'll bloody brain you.'

Pugnose stopped, collecting links of the bicycle chain in his hand the better to swing it at McEvoy.

'Drop it!' McEvoy warned. 'Now!'

Cade summed up the scene. 'Drop it, Gabriel,' he

ordered, and the chain fell to the cabin floor. Cade turned to Witney. 'Now tell that young maniac to drop that bloody bar or you'll live to regret it. Or not, as maybe. I've a few more blokes out there.'

'Leave it, Mac,' Witney said, and McEvoy reluctantly tossed the crowbar aside.

Pugnose pushed violently past him and Cade asked, 'So where is the bugger?'

'He's not here just now.' Witney's chest had gone tight with fear. In the beams of the torches Cade's face had altered from that of the cynical, cocky spiv of the Wings Club. He was all malevolence now, calculating and rough. 'Skiving is he?' Cade said. 'Leaving it all to you two? He'll never be an aviation tycoon this way, he'll never pay off his debts, and mine's got top priority. So when's he back?' Another thug came aboard now as Cade took a grip on Witney's overalls near the neck. 'I asked you a question, son.'

'We've no idea when he'll be back.'

'Tonight?'

'Maybe.'

'Don't lie to me, son.' Cade's knuckles were taut under Witney's jaw. 'Name, rank and number won't do here. No Geneva Conventions. Got his home address, have you?'

'No.'

'I did warn you, son. Don't play dumb airmen with me. If you don't know where to find your boss in this racket you're the biggest mugs since Laurel and Hardy. His kind owe the money and run.'

Pugnose came back down the cabin. 'He's not there, Ernie.' As he came past McEvoy he jabbed his elbow in McEvoy's ribs, and McEvoy flew at him smashing his forehead into Pugnose's face. Blood spurted. Pugnose reeled and grabbed at the crowbar, and McEvoy's foot stamped on his hand. Witney made to join in, but Cade's other two thugs grabbed his arms and twisted them up his back.

'Gabriel!' Cade's voice was icy. 'Not tonight!' He glared at McEvoy. 'And that goes for you!'

Pugnose was set to butt McEvoy, who was preparing a karate chop. The moment froze. They moved away from each other. 'Now listen, Squadron Leader,' Cade growled. 'You tell Mister Civil Aviation to stop playing the invisible man, tell him Ernie called to collect overdue interest on his loan. And I don't keep the peace twice. He'll meet me in the smoke, usual place, 1200 hours tomorrow, right?'

'We'll be six thousand feet over the Midlands then,' Witney said.

'You'll be a bloody sight higher than that if he doesn't show, you'll all be halfway to meeting St Peter at the pearly gates. I've some spare Medical Corps stretchers I can't get rid of that can be put to good use.' He fixed Witney and McEvoy in turn with those hangman's eyes. 'Twelve o'clock spot on tomorrow. London. Without fail.'

Two torch beams pinned Witney and McEvoy. It was as if they were standing in the dock awaiting sentence. Cade briefly shone his own torch around the aircraft, sizing up its value as a piece of property he might confiscate. Then he indicated to his thugs it was time to leave. He got down from the cargo entrance saying to Witney and McEvoy, 'And you tell your Mister Big I don't reckon much of his airline's catering.'

The thugs got down. Pugnose turned to McEvoy and eyed him closely, as if taking a mental photo for future reference. Witney felt his hands shaking. McEvoy was on the verge of running amok with that crowbar. They'd been let off lightly.

Meanwhile Ruskin was on his way to the airfield at Garton in what had been a pre-war London taxi with a meter that didn't work. The driver was an ex-soldier who still wore his Tank Corps black beret – without the badge, of course – and he'd been full of chat about war and peace ever since Ruskin had got in. It had dawned on him that Ruskin must be one of those ex-Raff lads now flying clapped-out old Daks out of Garton. 'You know,' he said,

'I reckon your job's like mine. We can expand if we stick at it.'

Ruskin had been morose. He felt lifted by the stocky little optimist in front – one of those rarities in post-war Britain, a real independent who wanted more out of life than just cradle-to-grave security.

'I wouldn't have thought you'd get many people round these parts using taxis.'

'Don't you chuckle it, mate,' the little man said. 'Weddings. Christenings. Breeding like flies since demob. I could've come back and worked a cab for old Revidge . . . for a wage . . . but the old miser wouldn't part with the smoke off his exhaust. So I got this and started on my own. They keep saying most folk will have their own cars in a few years. I'll believe it when I see it. But if it happens I'll have an answer. I thought I'd take an embalming course at night school and branch out into undertaking.'

Ruskin got out laughing near the old guardroom.

'Five bob to you, mate,' the driver said.

'The meter would have shown a lot more,' Ruskin said, giving him a pound. 'Get some black market petrol with the change.' He walked across the airfield under the full moon, his mind full of his row with Jennie, and of the way his work relentlessly came between them. He was surprised to see lights on inside the Dakota. He had expected that Witney would have gone back to his digs and that McEvoy would be catching up on lost sleep on one of the old Raff palliasses they used on overnight stints in the hangar. An inspection lamp cast a beam from the cargo hold door towards the hangar entrance. It was dazzling, and Ruskin kept out of it.

He began to climb aboard.

Suddenly from above he sensed a quick movement. He looked up to see Witney poised with the crowbar in his hands. 'Christ!' Ruskin muttered. 'Put it down. The bloody war's over.'

Witney was white and shaking. 'I thought the bastards were back,' he said in relief.

McEvoy came down from the cockpit with an altimeter in his hands, solemn and angry. Ruskin was baffled.

'Time you got a new banker, Jack,' Witney said.

'Come on, for God's sake,' Ruskin protested. 'What *is* this? Nothing can be that bad.'

Their faces told him otherwise.

It was all very convivial in the Wings Club, but there was no sign of Cade.

Ruskin finished off his spam sandwich and kept an eye on the door. There were lots of new faces, newly-demobbed aircrews from Transport Command joining the queue for jobs in civil flying. Many, Ruskin thought, were too raw even to look capable of competing with the real bandits, of whom he now saw himself as one. Two smoothly-dressed men at the bar were taking everything in, and everybody, including Ruskin, who caught them weighing him up from time to time. Among those of special interest to them was an alert stockily-built man with a brown skin and black suit who sat alone drinking orange juice. Ruskin had seen him about the club from time to time. He was known as 'the Rabbi'.

Ruskin crossed to the bar and ordered another half of mild.

The barman sensed his impatience. 'Ernie must be the busiest bloke in town except for the government snoopers and the builders.' He leaned confidentially towards Ruskin and mentioned the two men at the bar. 'Them two have been asking more questions than a de-briefing officer.' The barman had been a rear gunner on Lancs. 'Can't make out whether they're Food Ministry snoops seeing how much spam we're getting through, or civil aviation inspectors. Or just CID.'

'I wouldn't serve 'em, Stan,' Ruskin said.

'They've got membership cards, Jack,' the chirpy Londoner said, frowning. 'And the council keep telling my old man they can't get round to repairing his bomb damage because there's not enough builders. We should make the snoopers train as brickies.'

The barman was summoned by the two men at the bar. Ruskin watched. It was clear they were asking about the rabbi, who now had company – a flight lieutenant on one side and a young civvy wearing a RAF tie on the other. They were clearly offering him a drink. Ruskin checked his watch. Cade was forty minutes late. Ruskin felt in his pocket for some paper, found none, and beckoned the barman. 'You got any writing paper, Stan?'

The barman passed his bill pad to Ruskin with a plea. 'Give him a few minutes, Jack. You've not even finished your beer.'

Ruskin began to write a note.

'He makes a rough enemy, Jack.'

'So do I, Stan.'

There was a stir in the bar, and Ruskin looked up to see Cade make his usual royal entrance. The big spiv was king here and Ruskin felt contempt for the ex-RAF aircrews who now formed his court. He looked on from behind his glass as Cade swept through with a sign to the barman that it was drinks all round for a group of cronies assembled under the picture of the Sunderland flying boat. Cade's eyes missed nothing. He gave a slight and nearly imperceptible bow to the rabbi, acknowledged greetings from right and left, saw Ruskin and ignored him.

Cade joined his cronies. He was his normal expansive self, too good to be true, Ruskin thought. The bluster was an act. His voice boomed through the large room. 'How long have you lot been propping up this plywood? Since you ordered your first drinks I've flogged eight tank landing craft and four thousand gas masks.' They laughed, as Ruskin knew they would, on cue. 'Now can I interest any of you heroes in half a million Army blankets, brand new, never sweated in, and Ernie Cade's personal guarantee they're flea free?' This brought the house down. Even the rabbi laughed. The only ones who didn't respond were Ruskin and the two mysterious members at the bar.

And Cade wasn't through with the funnies yet. 'Or I can offer three tons of Army blanco, twenty thousand gallons of whitewash to make your coal look good . . . when you can get it . . . and six thousand parachutes. Now think of the silk knickers that'll make.'

Even Max Miller at the London Palladium could not have had an audience in his hands like this, Ruskin thought, as he slipped his note to the barman. 'See our resident comic gets that, Stan.'

And Ruskin made his way very obviously to the door right across Cade's eyeline.

'Hey, Ruskin.' Cade couldn't resist the bait.

Ruskin turned, his hands stuffed in his pockets. 'You talking to me?'

'Now you mustn't be hurt, Flight Sergeant,' Cade chuckled. 'Ernie wants an important word, see. Don't run away.'

'You should know all about running away,' Ruskin countered, and he stood, feet apart, with his arms folded, facing Cade.

Cade turned to the barman, flashing anger. 'He gave you a note, Stan. Read it to me.'

The barman hesitated.

'All right, Stan,' Ruskin chipped in. 'Read it.'

' "You were late again",' the barman read. ' "Come and see *me* next time. And don't put your nose within a mile of my crew and my aircraft." '

Cade laid down his glass and crossed deliberately to Ruskin amid a chorus of shouts from his cronies. 'Come on, Ernie, it was only a gag' . . . 'He was only kidding, Ernie' . . . 'Forget it, Ernie.'

The Rabbi tried to move between Cade and Ruskin but Cade thrust him aside. 'There's no referee in this game, rabbi,' Cade snapped. The rabbi tried again, but this time Ruskin eased him away.

As Cade reached Ruskin he said, 'I said no running away. You'll swallow what you just said and have a drink on Ernie Cade.'

The bandits, the newly-demobbed RAF officers and NCOs and the rabbi, were forming a circle like a cock-fight pit in the middle of the room. Ruskin was rubbing his right hand over the clenched fist of his left. 'You go within a mile of my lads again, with or without your numbskulls, I'll put your eyes where your collarbone is.'

Cade's eyes shone, unblinking. 'Pint of mild, isn't it?' Their faces were no more than a foot apart now. The circle widened to make room for the heavyweight bout. 'Ernie Cade never runs away from anything, son. Nobody and nothing makes him run away. Isn't that true?'

'So what kept you out of the war, Ernie?'

That did it, as Ruskin knew it would. Cade's glassy control was gone. He snatched at Ruskin's lapels. His knuckles were white, his face was wild as an angry bull's. He made to tup Ruskin with his forehead. Ruskin evaded the lunge and brought up his right knee into Cade's groin, chopped his wrists and then got him by the throat. Two of Cade's gorillas among the crowd began to move in, but so did bandits and RAF fliers. Others began to pull the two heavyweights apart. And the club secretary, Squadron Leader Somes, burst in. His beery complexion lit up the strife. 'If you chaps must behave like ex-Commandos I will have you removed from the premises and blackballed for life. And I do mean life!' His presence was all authority and there were murmurs of assent.

Ruskin's self control came back. He needed the Wings Club. It was the main source of his bread and butter, the place where you got the work. 'We'd not like that, would we, Ernie?'

Cade's testicles were giving him hell where Ruskin's knee had gone in but he wouldn't let on. He looked set to resume the fight.

'Please, friends,' the rabbi said, thrusting his slight frame between the two. 'We are brothers. No violence. We have seen enough of violence.'

It was another half hour before the two had cooled down enough to hold their meeting. They pointedly bought their own drinks and found a remote corner of the club. 'You're not only hard up,' Cade said, more as an advisor now than adversary. 'You should be talking to Lord Beveridge not Ernie Cade. You should be coming out of the beautiful clouds. I buy you this aeroplane and . . .'

'She's mine!'

'Ruskin. Flight Sergeant. Jack. Half that lousy aeroplane's mine and you owe me interest on the other half. Payable monthly. And I want to know where it is, see?'

'You'll get your money.' In truth, Ruskin didn't quite see how just yet.

'This year next year sometime never,' Cade said. 'You remind me of my old feller. It'll happen, he said. It was always Christmas tomorrow. And he buzzes off and leaves me with my Mum and her gin and tonics. Now I'm definitely not Santa. It'd take me a lot longer to grow a white beard than it took the Japs to learn kamikaze was a bit short-sighted.'

'I said you'll get every penny.'

'Oh I will, son. I will. And sooner than you think.' The threat was back in his voice.

'I'll have your money in the post by . . .'

Cade's hands were linked across his paunch and he was cracking his knuckles. 'Not in the post, Flight Sergeant. In here.' He tapped his palm. 'Now.'

'Middle of next week,' Ruskin offered. 'Guaranteed.'

'You said that a week ago and I'm adding interest on the interest.' His look made it clear he had no confidence in Ruskin's ability to run a business.

'Listen,' Ruskin said. 'I've six jobs lined up.'

'You're under-pricing,' Cade snapped. 'All of you are. Every single bandit in the game.'

Ruskin ran off the jobs on his fingers – two runs to Biarritz and back, a load of wet fish from Grimsby to London with the chance of repeat trips, and three runs to Germany with newspapers for the troops.

'Wizard. Hotspur. Boy's Own Paper?' Cade jeered.

'Where's the lolly? Four hundred and thirty-seven nicker you owe me at the time of going to press.'

'I haven't got it right now,' Ruskin admitted with a gesture that implied Cade would have to wait.

'Ernie doesn't hang about, Flight Sergeant,' Cade warned. 'He doesn't stand in queues, he never stood in a queue once during the war.'

'That I believe,' Ruskin's voice was bitter.

'And he doesn't queue for a paltry four hundred and thirty-seven nicker.'

Ruskin asked him why he was squealing.

'You'll be the one to squeal if I foreclose,' Cade said. 'Heed some good advice, eh? Wet fish from Grimsby? Papers from Fleet Street to Germany? Where's the profit, son? You're not in a seller's market.' He pointed at the bandits crowding the bar. 'You're all under-pricing like you never heard of Carey Street.'

Ruskin stubbornly refused to look at the bandits. Cade beckoned someone from behind. It was the rabbi, who started over, watched by the two mysterious men at the bar.

'Rabbi,' Cade said, coming to his feet. 'You haven't got a drink.'

The rabbi shook his head. 'Thank you. One orange juice is enough.'

Cade indicated Ruskin. 'My friend would like to help you, rabbi. Flight Sergeant Ruskin. Mister Ruskin now.' Ruskin shook hands, wondering if the rabbi was really a rabbi. And Cade turned to Ruskin. 'Now, son, do you think that old crate of yours is capable of reaching the Middle East?'

'She went to India several times, which is a bit farther. And so did I. Eleven trips on the demob run.'

Cade's face sparkled. 'He's all right, eh?'

The rabbi nodded.

'Now, son, my friend,' Cade said to Ruskin. 'I have a way out for you. I have an offer. We, the rabbi and me, we have an offer.'

Ruskin was suspicious. He was also aware of the interest being shown by the two men at the bar. They were out of hearing range as Cade explained he had the exclusive agency for certain consignments. 'The rabbi pays me and I pay you,' he told Ruskin.

'Deducting what I owe you?'

'Sure,' Cade shrugged. 'Then we're all helping each other. Plus a bit of commission.'

Ruskin waited for the catch.

'We can discuss this later,' Cade said easily. 'The rabbi doesn't like to talk money.'

'How *much* commission?' It was no time for compromise or clouded deals.

'Twenty per cent.' Cade didn't even blink.

Ruskin made to leave. 'You'd leave me with enough for the fuel, would you?'

'Son.' The big spiv put on a pained air. 'You don't know when your bread is being buttered. With jam on. You'll wind up with forty-two quid a flying hour *net*. Fuel on top.'

It only inflamed Ruskin's suspicions. 'Danger money?'

'You could call it that.'

'So where to?'

Cade stalled. 'Get you another pale?'

'Where to?'

Cade studied the cool rabbi. 'Palestine, Mr Ruskin.'

'They're still shooting at us out there,' Ruskin said. The British were the pig in the middle of the age-old conflict between Jew and Arab, and were trying to get free of the nigh impossible job of governing Palestine. And British troops were being attacked by Jewish terrorist groups.

It was clear to Cade what was on Ruskin's mind. 'There's nothing for nothing, Flight Sergeant. If you're scared . . .' He let the words trail off as he took in the job-hungry ex-pilots around the club.

'Where's the cargo and when?' Ruskin had made up his mind.

'Cigarettes to Haifa,' Cade said, drawing on his cigar.

Ruskin knew what it was all about now. They were looking for a replacement for Johnny Staines, a bandit known to have been on the Haifa run. He'd come down in the Med and, so it was rumoured, his Dak had sunk like a rock he had so many guns on board.

'Deliver next weekend,' Cade whispered. 'Fly via Ciampino, Rome. Return load guaranteed. Bonus on completion.'

Ruskin asked about the return load.

'Citrus fruits,' the rabbi smiled disingenuously. 'Figs. Dates.'

The rabbi looked a gentle and inoffensive character, thought Ruskin, who said, 'I've a run to Biarritz, then one to Germany, before anything else.'

'You want the job or not?' It was Cade, leaning forward, hands on knees, his cigar between his teeth. 'Just say one way or the other, son. Gets you out of debt with a bit to go on with.' He took the cigar out with a flourish. 'Survival in this game means you have to fly your arse off. And there *is* a queue.' Again, that glance at the crowd of bandits. 'We'll give you two minutes.' He got up and crossed to the bandits, and said something which had them in stitches.

One of the mysterious men at the bar had Cade under surveillance. The other, Ruskin saw, was watching him.

In the hangar at Garton, Jennie helped Witney to supervise the stacking of bales of cloth in the Dakota. A war-surplus three-ton Army truck stood alongside the cargo door, and the driver and his mate were transferring the bales. Jennie was about to place a bale against the fuselage when Witney said he wanted it in another place. There were chalk marks on the floor. 'Centre of gravity,' Witney smiled.

'Good thing I took maths,' Jennie said. She could see McEvoy through one of the cabin windows working on the starboard engine.

'You'll be flying her next,' Witney laughed.

Jennie suddenly looked anxious. 'How do we know how much all this weighs?'

'Ssssh!' Witney hissed. 'You don't ask questions like that. Especially if Jack's here.'

'But he's not here, is he?' Her gaze was straight and accusatory.

It was some ten minutes later that Jennie had another surprise. Frank Shaw wandered into the hangar and stood looking at the Dakota as if it were a dangerous monster. It was much larger than he'd assumed, the first Dakota he'd ever seen on the ground, and it seemed too cumbersome to fly. Not only that, McEvoy had an engine exposed and the tyres looked too soft. He thought it was a dodgy piece of metal to be trundling over towns and cities. He ran a hand through the hair at the nape of his neck and saw Jennie as she came out of the Dakota. She had a scarf over her head but no gloves on her work-grimed hands.

It took Shaw some moments to get over what seemed to him a frightening reality. He shook his head and said, 'I never thought to see the day. My own daughter a doormat to somebody with a screw loose. Where is he, anyhow? Seems everybody round here works bar him. It's classic.'

'He's things to do in London,' Jennie said huffily.

'Not down there again? Not with that lot?'

'It's his backer wanting some money.'

Shaw sniffed. 'If he *will* get himself in with *them* what does he expect? They're not Primitive Methodists down there, you know.' He took in the loading of the final bales. 'You should be leaving this kind of thing to them who know all about it.'

Witney leaned out of the cargo door and gave the truck driver a thumbs-up signal. 'OK. When's the next lot?'

'Give us a couple of hours,' said the driver.

Shaw screwed up his face. 'They're not shoving any more in?' he asked, aghast. 'I suppose they'll leave room for the pilots?'

Jennie told him not to be silly.

Shaw was critical. 'You had anything to eat, have you?'

'I'm not hungry,' she said stiffly.

'You can come home now and have a square meal. Your mother's worried sick. You're looking like a scarecrow from a concentration camp. And all your colour's gone.'

The grimy lines on her face brought out the pallor and her dark brown eyes had lost their usual sparkle. But she said, 'I'm fine. And we've got to get this next load on.'

There was two hours, Shaw said.

She shook her head. 'I'm going over to the Raff cookhouse . . . unofficially . . . tea and wads for Pete and Mac.'

'And what about you?'

'I'll have something.'

'You'll come home,' he said, stepping back to let the truck out.

Witney emerged from the other side as the truck cleared them. He held out a hand and his smile was warm. 'You're Jen's Dad?'

'I am that, lad. And you're Peter?'

Witney nodded and took in Shaw's apparent state of shock. 'Not so bad as she looks, Mr Shaw. Always the same when you first meet an aeroplane. When I set eyes on my first Dak I thought no, it's just not on, we'd never get off the deck. But they're beauties really. And this one's a bit special. She has a pedigree all the way back to El Alamein and Arnhem.' Shaw raised an eyebrow. Nobody was going to con him. 'Come and meet her,' Witney offered, pointing to the cargo door.

'I'd rather not, thank you,' Shaw said, eyeing the Dakota with misgiving.

McEvoy came, saw what was going on, and winked at Jennie, who introduced him to her father.

'You're the engineer?' Shaw said. 'I've heard a lot about you. *You* must know how safe it is?'

'She's great, Mr Shaw,' McEvoy grinned.

'Wouldn't they give you more time to do all the checks if you were with one of the nationalized airlines?'

'Ay,' McEvoy said. 'Mebbe.' With that Glasgow accent and manner McEvoy could tell a whole story in one word.

'I mean,' Shaw insisted, 'you could get a job with them if you're a qualified engineer?'

'Sure,' Mac grinned. 'No problem.'

'So why?' It was totally beyond Frank Shaw that anyone should be working for a tatty little outfit like Jack Ruskin's when he could be with BOAC.

'I don't like them and us, Mr Shaw.'

The answer meant nothing to Shaw, and Witney was set on showing him over the aircraft.

'She looks a bit frail to me,' Shaw hesitated. 'Like she's made of balsa wood.'

Witney vaulted into the hold and looked down. 'She's a very tough lady, Mr Shaw. Come on. Have a gander.' He led Shaw up the aisle into the cockpit and invited him to sit in the captain's seat – 'Jack's chair'. The baffling array of dials and instruments dazed Shaw, who took the control column and moved it to and fro as he'd seen pilots operate in films. 'Beats me how you cope, it really does. Jack must be brainier than I reckoned.' His gaze travelled the instrument panel. 'But there's a helluva lot to go wrong, isn't there?'

'Aeroplanes talk, Mr Shaw. She lets us know when she's out of sorts.'

They went back to the hold where Jennie was checking the loading tethers on the bales. Frank Shaw gazed at the load. 'How do you know what it weighs?' he asked pointedly.

'We – er – we don't weigh the stuff here,' Witney replied noncommitally.

'Oh, they do that back at the mill?'

'Well, yes.' Witney struck an evasive note. 'Give or take a few pounds we know what the old girl can carry.'

It was all too haphazard for Shaw. 'When are you off with this then? In the morning?'

'Tonight,' Witney said with a glint. 'Mac permitting. And Jack being present.'

Ruskin's train had got in late from London. He sat in the back of the Tank Corps' man's taxi as they drove through the lanes to Garton. He had the rabbi on his mind, and Cade, and the Haifa trip he'd agreed to fly. He'd nearly had second thoughts on the train, which had been full of soldiers, sailors and airmen on their way home after demob. Across from him in the corner seat, Ruskin had faced an exhausted Army corporal, his kitbag and demob suit box on the rack. And there was a Raff sergeant air gunner, a Navy rating and two young soldiers who looked as if they should still be at school. He could hear their conversation now.

'Demob, Corp?' the blond young soldier had said.

'At last,' the corporal said wearily, running a hand across his scarred forehead.

'You as well, Sarge?' said the tall young soldier to the air gunner.

The air gunner had nodded.

'You, Jack?' the blond soldier asked the rating.

The rating put a thumb in the air.

The blond soldier indicated his mate. 'Our group's not due out for another ten bloody years, I reckon. We must be the only ones on the train on a posting.'

'India?' It was the corporal through sleepy eyes.

The blond soldier hesitated, wondering if he might be guilty of careless talk. The rating was tight lipped. The corporal smirked like a veteran. 'War's over, mate. It's not careless talk any more, except with the Russkis. India or Singapore?'

They studied Ruskin, the only obvious civvy with his old tweed jacket and flannel trousers. He raised a smile. 'Not long out myself.' It unlocked the moment.

'Bloody Palestine,' said the blond soldier. 'One lot over. Here we go again. Being knocked off by bloody terrorists.'

'Worse in India,' the corporal muttered through half closed eyes. 'Buggers can't wait to get at each other there.'

The sergeant air gunner, who blinked a lot and had a recurring twitch around the mouth, unbuttoned his blue battledress blouse and said, 'We should piss off out of everywhere. Leave the bastards to it and see nobody drops any more atom bombs anywhere.'

At that moment an elderly woman paused to look for a vacant seat in the compartment. She began to move on, lugging a suitcase. The sergeant gunner flung the door open. 'Hey, Mrs,' he called. 'You can have mine. I've been sitting down for days at the demob centre.'

She shook her head with a gentle smile.

The air gunner resumed his seat. But the blond young soldier went out into the corridor. 'Come on, love,' he coaxed the old woman. 'It's packed worse than a troop train. You'll never find anywhere.'

'You're very kind,' the old woman said graciously, and walked on, past the passengers standing at the corridor windows.

The blond young soldier sat down. And Ruskin couldn't keep his eyes off him and his mate. He felt he should have been the one to give up his seat. And he couldn't get it out of his mind that the two kids in khaki would shortly be in the terrorists' firing line in Palestine, where he would be flying for other purposes.

In the hangar, where the summer evening light was still good, Witney was supervising the loading of the follow-up truck load of cloth. The truck was plumb against the fuselage near the cargo door. McEvoy was still working on that starboard engine. Jennie stood with Shaw close by. 'It's not all that bad,' Jennie said, more in hope than in truth. 'Pete and Mac *are* being paid. Jack's a bit behind, that's all.'

'That's all.' Shaw spoke with quiet indignation. 'I tell you this, girl. That Peter, the squadron leader, the one with his head screwed on right, he told Mac to get back to his digs and get some sleep in. And what did Mac say? He said he'd only go with his rent money in his hand. He's living with some harridan, one room, use of kitchen and tin bath, and last time he was there she'd not let him use the kitchen. Your Jack's sailing too near the wind. He not only fails to pay folk what he owes, he flies black market cloth. I mean we don't even know it's not been thieved, do we?'

Jennie flared. 'Stop inventing things, Dad. Go home and leave us alone.'

But Shaw made no move. He lingered even after Jennie had gone back to help with the loading. And he was still there when Ruskin came up to him some minutes later.

'Hello, Jen's Dad,' he greeted Shaw with a boisterous slap on the back, glancing at the Dakota. 'So how about her, eh? Fancy a trip to faraway places?'

'You'd never get me up in that for a gold clock,' Shaw sniffed, the tip of his nose between thumb and forefinger.

'No seats yet anyway,' Ruskin grinned.

'You're not really going to fly people in it?' The very idea horrified him.

Ruskin nodded. 'Thirty-two passengers. When we've the money to buy the seats.'

'And pay the Prudential. I'd never insure you.'

Ruskin put his arm round Jennie's shoulders. 'See? All he thinks about,' he laughed. 'Insurance. Security. Never takes a chance. No wonder this country's on its uppers.' He gave Shaw no chance to reply. 'Why've they not finished loading?' he asked, suddenly serious. 'We've got to be off tonight and no messing.'

'They've all worked hard, Jack,' Jennie said.

'Using one truck?' he said critically. 'They should have used more.' He was alert now, jumpy, checking his watch. 'It's a six hour flight. If we get off around midnight we should make Biarritz just after dawn. Better not get there before. You can't expect the Frogs to have any landing lights on.'

Shaw scratched his dome. 'And how about the British then?'

The question puzzled Ruskin.

'Here,' Shaw said. 'It'll be dark when you take off.'

'Oh that,' Ruskin shrugged. 'I've a mate who'll see the Raff flarepath goes on. It's not only squadron leaders on the old boy net these days. It's our turn now.' His eyes were on the Dakota and he summoned McEvoy and asked, 'How's that starboard motor?'

'Another couple of hours,' said the oil-grimed McEvoy.

'Where've you been all day?' It was said with a smile. But McEvoy had made his point. Ruskin now asked if the complete load was aboard.

'Better be,' Witney said grimly. 'Unless you've a spare Lanc to take any more.'

Witney was pissed-off and McEvoy was at his most dour and Ruskin knew it wasn't just the money. All the same he brought out his wallet and gave a wad of notes to Witney and another to McEvoy. 'So that brings us to just one week adrift on wages.' His pale blue eyes were shrewd.

'Somebody coughed up,' Witney said. 'Who?'

'Moses,' Ruskin grinned. Nothing would have drawn from him the truth that the money came from the rabbi, via Ernie Cade.

There was a hint of relief on McEvoy's rugged face as he tucked the notes in his back pocket without counting them. 'I was going to kip down here tonight, but I'll go back to the digs and stick some of this under the old bag's nose.' He thought his landlady was a descendant of the Lancashire witches.

'We're leaving tonight, Mac,' Ruskin said firmly.

'Oh no!' McEvoy would have none of it.

Ruskin's face went taut. 'There's a technical reason why we shouldn't?'

'No.' McEvoy was adamant. 'A human one, Jack.'

'I'm with Mac,' Witney said. 'We all need some shuteye.'

'I don't,' Ruskin said.

'You probably kipped down on the train coming up.' Witney was alive to Ruskin's ruses.

But Ruskin shook his head. 'I don't spend my time dozing,' he said. 'I don't swan around in London. I don't loll about in the Windmill Theatre.'

'Well that's something,' Jennie said.

'This new job means no hanging on the other jobs,'

Ruskin explained. 'We do the Biarritz run tonight, get back for the Grimsby–London fish run tomorrow afternoon, and then it's overnight tomorrow with the papers for the troops in Germany.'

Witney played with the signet ring on the little finger of his elegant hand. 'We couldn't squeeze in a little trip to the South Pole, I suppose?'

There was the sound of an approaching car. They looked up to see Kellett park his Ford 8 outside.

'Our civil aviation snooper,' Ruskin said impatiently.

'Very necessary, I'd say,' Shaw murmured.

Kellett was careful to lock his car before he came in with that guileless smile Ruskin didn't trust. 'Ruskin,' he nodded. 'Miss Shaw. About to be off again, I see.'

'You want to see the fit-for-flight clearance, Mr Kellett.' Ruskin was at his most co-operative.

'If you don't mind,' the dapper little surveyor said.

'McEvoy can't very well sign it till he's finished the job.'

'No, indeed.'

Ruskin threw McEvoy a wink and the Scot took Kellett over to the Dakota, where they began to look at the engine from which McEvoy had taken the cowlings. Ruskin said, 'It's not his business but he just might ask to see the loadsheet.' Jennie found a blank loadsheet among the debris on the trestle table, and Ruskin began to fill it in from memory.

Shaw could hardly believe it. He stared at Jennie and said, 'He's not just making it up?'

'Dad!' Jennie said in mock reproof, as if it were in bad taste even to imply that Ruskin would get up to any such trick.

The starboard engine was giving Kellett pause for thought. 'Serious, was it?'

'Nothing to sweat over.' McEvoy spoke airily. 'It was only vibrating like a virgin in a dither.'

'And you've got it right?' He was putting McEvoy to another test.

McEvoy chose to prove he was a genned-up engineer.

'There was no gap at the contact points in the left magneto in the fully open position,' he said briskly. 'The cam follower was worn.'

'You have changed it?'

McEvoy nodded. 'I've changed the plugs on the other magneto. I found water in the leads and the contact breaker was oily.'

Shaw came over to them and found he was in another world.

'It will all be in your report?' Kellett urged on McEvoy.

'Ay,' McEvoy said. 'Along with the bit about the starboard rev counter reading less than the port. I changed the tacho-jennie. And one of the altimeters was out. I've replaced both.'

'Good, good.' The little surveyor could have been a schoolmaster.

'She'll be good as new by take-off,' McEvoy promised.

'Is that all that was wrong, Mr McEvoy?' Kellett said.

'No,' McEvoy said with a straight face. 'There were seventeen other faults.'

'You will make sure to mention them all?'

'Every one,' McEvoy said, pissed off. 'Every bloody one.'

Jennie came over with a cup of tea for Kellett, which let McEvoy off the hook. He got up on the inspection platform to resume his check on the engine, and Jennie went over to join Witney in securing the load in the hold. Ruskin was still fiddling his loadsheet.

If Shaw had little time for what he saw as the irresponsibility of the bandits he already had even less for the likes of Kellett. 'This is a full time job for you?' he sniffed.

'I'm sorry?' Kellett said, cup to mouth.

Shaw ran a quizzical finger over his left temple. 'You just spend your time checking on these lads who fly?'

Kellett nodded sheepishly.

'Seems like a bit of a doddle.' He put on his hanging judge look.

'I don't know who you are,' Kellett said primly. 'We've not been introduced.'

'Frank Shaw. Jennie's dad.' The pale, strong-jawed face was immobile.

'Oh I'm sorry,' said Kellett, and laid the tea mug on the servicing platform. 'There *are* statutory regulations, Mr Shaw. It wouldn't be in the public interest to have unserviceable aircraft flying in UK airspace, would it?'

'You mean it's all right if they crash on foreigners?'

'I didn't say that, Mr Shaw.' His manner was coy. He glanced towards Ruskin for support, but Ruskin was still fabricating his figures. They had weighed none of the bales.

Shaw was still in there. 'You keep a check on the big ones, do you? BOAC? BEA?'

'Indeed.'

'How many of you are there?'

'Ah, Mr Shaw.' The tone was confidential, as if they were into official secrets. 'Not enough.'

Shaw put him under scrutiny as if he were a specimen. 'We need more folk making things in this country, not watching other folk doing things.' And with that he went over to the cargo door, climbed aboard, and began to help Witney and Jennie with the strappings on the load.

It brought a lump to Jennie's throat to see him mucking-in, knowing how he felt about the game. Even so, he wasn't done with having his say. 'Ask me,' he pronounced after some minutes, 'there's enough on her for two aeroplanes.'

'I second that,' Witney murmured. His face was full of disquiet.

'I bet you two haven't eaten,' Mrs Shaw said as Ruskin came in with Jennie. Frank Shaw followed and bolted the front door behind them.

'They're full of corned beef sandwiches,' he said.

Mrs Shaw smiled. 'Bacon and egg, Jack?' she said

temptingly. 'I saved our ration. I've twelve ounces in the pantry.'

'If it's all the same with you, Mum,' Ruskin said. 'We're off at seven in the morning. Super contract. Return load. Cash on the nail. We'll need more aeroplanes if this goes on. Night, Mum.'

And he was already climbing the stairs.

Mrs Shaw was used to Ruskin's over-optimism in her presence. It was a sort of ritual now. 'He sounds like he's got the world at his feet,' she said, tuning the radio to the BBC.

'Round his little finger more like,' Shaw said. 'For the time being.'

Jennie wanted no more sermons. 'Night. I'm off as well.'

They heard her go upstairs and Mrs Shaw said, 'Surprises me you dragged him away from that aeroplane.'

'Treats it like a baby he does,' Shaw said, crossing to the wireless set and re-tuning. 'He'd breast feed it with aviation spirit if he could. He'd not have come back if one of the other two hadn't stayed all night with it.'

She studied him as he re-tuned the wireless. 'You'll never pick up Lord Haw-Haw, you know. You've never stopped twiddling that wireless since they caught him.'

His voice was scathing. 'I'm not trying to get Lord Haw-Haw.'

She put on a mimic's voice of Germany's wartime propagandist. ' "Jairmany calling. Jairmany calling." I sometimes think you wish the war was still on.'

In the congested bedroom with its small double bed and that tallboy Shaw had moved in for him, Ruskin set the alarm as Jennie slipped out of her clothes. She still had a young girl's body, he thought, taking in the neat firm breasts and the dancer's legs, shapely and elegantly muscled.

'You don't have to leave that early,' she said, with a bright-eyed glance at the naked Ruskin.

'We'll never leave the way we're going,' Ruskin countered. 'Six hours there, six back, with two for unloading and loading and formalities.'

'That's it then,' she said, taking off her pants. 'I'm coming with you tomorrow. We could have a day off in the sun.'

'I've a load of wet fish to pick up the day after,' Ruskin said, pushing under the bedclothes till his feet came up against the end-board.

'Ugh!' Jennie laughed. 'You're not going to come home smelling like a chip shop?'

'Put the light out, eh?' Ruskin said, watching her through half-closed eyes. 'I'm shagged.' She looked bloody marvellous but his mind was elsewhere.

She put the light out and he saw her form cross the shaft of moonlight stabbing through the join in the curtains and then felt her warm body beside him, her nipples against his shoulder. She put an arm round his groin and took hold of him and he was very nearly on the point of obliging when he remembered how the bed creaked, and thought of that loaded Dakota. 'No messing about,' he said. 'I'm away at six.'

She uttered a mock swear-word of frustration and snuggled against his warm back.

Neither found sleep easy. Ruskin's mind was alive. He would fly his arse off, take any jobs that were going, like the Haifa one. He might be crazy, but it was the only way.

Sensing his restlessness, Jennie sat up and leaned across to kiss him. 'Love. Stop worrying.'

'Go down and make yourself some cocoa,' he said.

'You want some?'

'No. Might make you sleep, though.'

'I don't want to sleep,' Jennie said.

And Ruskin half-turned, put his arms round her, then closed his eyes and began to snore. She knew it was only a pretence, he never snored when he slept. Snuggling closer to him she said, 'Wasn't it great of Dad to help?'

'Saving his conscience,' Ruskin muttered. 'He knew he'd spent too long running me down.'

'You're mumbling,' she teased him. 'I don't like men who mumble.'

'They can hear through that bloody plywood wall,' he said. 'Time we got our own place. Near the airfield.'

'If you think we're going to live in that Nissen hut, Jack Ruskin, you can think again. That's no home.' She was aware the idea had been tempting him for some time, and in some places families in desperation had chosen to squat in Nissen huts on Service camps. Jennie had other ideas. It might take time but they would find a place.

To Ruskin that Nissen hut had one prime advantage. It was handy for work. But he said now, 'It's not *very* draughty and it doesn't leak. I was thinking of digs, though, not a hut. There's a widow next door to Mac's billet. She'll let the front room downstairs, back room upstairs, use of kitchen and bath, thirty-five bob a week.'

She said nothing as she sat propped up on her elbow and looked to see if he opened his eyes. It seemed he'd gone to sleep but then he said, 'And it does have a privet hedge.'

She smothered him with a pillow. Ruskin fought her off and then they made love. And neither heard the bed creaking.

The airfield was deserted except for one cyclist riding round the perimeter track in the moonlight. Witney had volunteered to stay with the Dakota as security guard and had set his palliasse just inside the cargo door. He had dozed fitfully for a couple of hours but the load was on his mind and he had walked up and down the hold with an inspection lamp counting the bales.

He was relieved now to see some of the cookhouse lights still on. Most of the RAF had long gone from Garton. But there was still a skeleton establishment of RAF police and a Maintenance Unit.

Inside the cookhouse he found the duty sergeant cook, his stripes on an armband on his shirt sleeves, a beefy Geordie with droopy eyes that gave him the look of an amiable bloodhound. 'Evening, Sergeant,' Witney said cheerfully. 'Small favour?'

The sergeant eyed the switch of cloth Witney was carrying. He sniffed corruption. 'If you're saying will I swop eggs, meat, butter and sugar for that, you'd best do a bunk. You're in the wrong cookhouse.'

Witney bridled. 'I'm Squadron Leader Witney, Sergeant. I – er . . .'

The sergeant put his hands in his apron and studied Witney long and hard. 'I've seen you before, sir. Wait a minute. You're one of them bandits flying Daks?'

'Indeed, Sergeant,' Witney nodded, relieved. One of the awful things about the war being over was that he could no longer instantly command respect.

The sergeant felt at the cloth under Witney's arm. 'It's just that two of my erks were caught flogging tea and jam for clothing coupons, sir. In the glasshouse they are now. I had another, a corporal, nicked the best tinned salmon from the officers' mess, silly git. They caught him with it on King's Cross Station.'

Witney frowned. 'Glasshouse?'

'He's on his way,' the sergeant said.

Witney made it clear that all he wanted was to put the switch of cloth on the cookhouse scales.

The sergeant thought him barmy. 'You mean weigh it, sir? I thought they measured cloth by length, sir?' But he took the cloth and laid it on the scales after removing a sack of potatoes. Witney watched the pointer and began to do some mental arithmetic.

The sums added up to a seriously overloaded Dakota.

It was shortly after 9 a.m. and they were all set for take-off. The Dakota's propellers were turning at the runway start line, the weather was warm and mild with hardly a breath of wind and no cloud to speak of.

Ruskin threw Witney a sharp glance as they began their pre-take-off checks. Both were smarting over an early morning row in which Witney had asked Ruskin to think twice about carrying such an overload, and Ruskin had denied they had too much up.

'Very well,' Witney now said flatly. 'Check trim.'

'Elevator set,' Ruskin replied icily. 'Aileron neutral. Rudder neutral.'

'Mixtures.'

'Both auto rich,' Ruskin said, setting them.

'Pitch.'

And they went through the routine with Witney sounding more brassed off by the second. Suddenly he broke the routine and said, 'That bloody starboard motor's still vibrating.'

'Shouldn't be, not now,' McEvoy called as he peered over their shoulders at the engine's temperature and pressure gauges.

Ruskin glared at Witney. 'She's OK, Mac,' he snapped. 'If that's vibration I'm a Waaf.' He boosted the engines and shouted, 'Vibrating? What vibrating?'

'Chop her, Jack, and count me out.' Witney began to get out of his harness.

Ruskin ran down the engines till they were merely idling and faced Witney in the cockpit. 'Let's have it then. You've been tight as a virgin all morning. If you don't accept the motor's OK you're criticizing Mac.'

Witney's mouth was set. He rose to get out.

'Vibration?' Ruskin shouted. 'What do you think this is? The King's Flight?'

'It's not the engine.' He stooped to get through the space between the pilot's seats but Ruskin grabbed him by the arm. 'And don't be bloody stupid, Jack.'

'And don't you come the superior bloody two-and-a-half ringer with me. You nearly called me Flight Sergeant then.'

'Right.' Witney spat the word out. 'I like to stick to the truth.'

It went through Ruskin's mind to take off there and then. One look from McEvoy made him think better, and they taxied back to the hangar. The row flared again as they walked to the Nissen hut. 'And if you can't take it that I'm in command you know what you can do.'

'Don't think I've not thought about it,' Witney said.

'So I'll play duty officer,' Ruskin baited. 'Any complaints, Squadron Leader?'

'You know the complaint.'

'Old woman's objections.' The voice was full of contempt. 'We're in a bloody hard game, Squadron Leader, not playing pat-a-cake.'

'You didn't have the load weighed!' It was an accusation rather than a statement.

'And you weighed one switch and cocked up your arithmetic.'

'So what's our all-up weight then? You made out a loadsheet.'

'Give or take a pound or two, twenty-seven thousand pounds,' Ruskin said with conviction.

'Two thousand *inside* the limit?'

'The skipper's compliments on improving at maths.'

Unzipping his flying overalls, Witney said, 'I even minded dying for my country. I'm buggered if I'll die for the glory and profit of this tinpot outfit.' The look on his pale and tired face was scathing. 'Twenty-seven thousand pounds! And some!'

'Guess the lady's weight and win a coconut.' Ruskin had had a bellyful of Witney's bloody self-righteousness.

'Thirty-two thousand pounds,' Witney said instantly. 'Three thousand over the limit. We should have done it in two trips.'

They were near the open door of the Nissen hut now. Jennie was there, looking puzzled, against a background of the chaotic stacks of spares and mounds of manuals and paperwork.

Ruskin shot a look at Witney. 'This isn't Imperial Airways, old chap, old sport.' Even Jennie caught the sarcasm from ten yards away.

'No, it's bloody private enterprise,' Witney said tartly. 'No wonder Attlee nationalized the industry.'

'The bastard didn't nationalize me.' And Ruskin pushed past Jennie and poured himself a mug of cold tea from the big brown pot that stood among the jumble on the trestle table.

Jennie said nothing as she came in with Witney, who began to take off his flying overalls. McEvoy joined them and Ruskin said, 'We'll be going without our co-pilot, Mac.' He'd been thinking it over and he meant it. 'He finds our company a bit beneath him. Uncouth chaps we are.'

'I think we should all go,' Jennie said.

Ruskin would have none of it. 'You can stay here. That ARB snooper's bound to show up even if only for an eyeful of you. You can tell him I put in a flight plan. And give him a surprise by showing him Mac's fit-for-flight certificate. Which reminds me.' He threw a look at McEvoy who dug out a blank form from the oily bumph on the table.

Jennie thought she was in the way. Ruskin and Witney clearly wanted to have it out, and she sensed that Witney would feel freer to cope if she weren't present. He was a bit old-fashioned that way. 'I'll take this back,' she said quietly, picking up the teapot. 'Perhaps we can buy one of our own someday?' It belonged to the RAF Police in the Garton guardroom.

'We'll likely have gone before you get back,' Ruskin said pointedly. 'At least Mac and I will have.'

If he expected a farewell kiss he was left ungratified. She knew Ruskin well enough to recognize he would only use the moment to touch the strand of loyalty in Witney. He could have his fight with Peter, but not with her implicit support. She collected her old Raleigh bike and cycled off.

The row between Ruskin and Witney blazed again, with McEvoy trying to act as peacemaker. He was loyal to Ruskin but respected Witney's integrity. It wasn't good enough for Ruskin who leaned over the table, his palms pressed against its edge, and challenged McEvoy. 'You coming with me or not?' he said finally. 'If you want to stay behind with our saintly friend that's OK. I'll fly Vera by myself.'

McEvoy bit his top lip, then nodded. 'I'm with you,' he said, with a glance at Witney. 'Pity.'

Ruskin led McEvoy outside. They had only gone a few steps when Witney came out clutching his discarded flying overalls. 'You can't fly her on your own.'

'Wouldn't be the first time,' Ruskin said dourly, though he was secretly relieved that Witney had come round.

'And I'd rather not hear your Arnhem epic all over again, if you don't mind. Flying her on your own when your co-pilot bought it.'

The hint of a smile tinged with sadness crossed Ruskin's eager face. Nobody spoke again until they were close to the Dakota and Witney was having renewed doubts about Ruskin's ethics as a commercial flier. 'One more thing, Jack. This cash you coughed up? May we know where it's from? Only you did say we'd no more due on this cloth trip.'

Ruskin knew it was a try-on. Witney didn't like not being in the know, as he'd just demonstrated over the weight of their load. He'd better come clean. 'It's an advance on another job,' he explained. 'From a man of religion. A friendly rabbi who needs us as much as we need him.'

Witney had thought as much. He bridled now. 'Not one of these Palestine jobs, for God's sake?'

Ruskin nodded. 'The competition's queueing up for 'em.'

'But we've got no seats, Jack,' McEvoy pointed out. 'And I mean – stuffing her with illegal immigrants!' And though he was game for most jobs, McEvoy felt they should keep on the right side of the law when it came to cargoes, goods or people, that could be said to be against Britain's interests.

Ruskin felt their eyes on him. 'Who said anything about illegals?' he said easily. 'And even if they were, so what? People are sorting themselves out after the war, that's all.

And the displaced Jews from Europe have to live somewhere.'

'So what *will* we be flying?' Witney's voice was steely.

'Fags,' Ruskin said blandly. 'Well, we can't leave 'em to smoke fig leaves, can we? Whether they're Jews or Arabs.'

Neither Witney nor McEvoy wished to see the joke. 'You sure it's only cigarettes?' Witney demanded.

'Gospel truth.' And Ruskin smiled and levered his big frame into the Dakota hold.

Witney tossed his flying overalls aboard and put his hands on the edge of the fuselage to climb aboard and then paused, looking up at the towering Ruskin. 'I just compromised with you, Jack. But get this clear. I'll fly no weapons to Palestine that could be used by the terrorists on our chaps.'

'Weapons?' Ruskin called down.

'Weapons.'

Ruskin thought he'd never seen such iron in Witney's face. 'You think I'd do that?' He saw that they did. 'Anyway, let's get this stuff to France first. Haifa's not till the weekend. We can argue the toss about that later.' And he went forward to the cockpit, followed by McEvoy and finally Witney.

The delay had cost them an hour and a half. They ran through the pre-take-off checks again, and Ruskin began to roll the Dakota down the runway. While McEvoy's attention was on those starboard motor gauges, Witney's was on the airspeed indicator. The Dakota felt sluggish to him, and he'd more flying hours on Daks than any of them.

They had the throttles on full boost now. And still the needle moved too slowly.

'She's too bloody heavy!' Witney shouted against the din of the surging Wasps. He shot a look at the IAS needle: it was still hovering on 80 and they had less than a quarter of the runway left.

With his right hand on the throttles, Ruskin took in the looming perimeter and the housing estate beyond with St Michael's Church steeple almost dead ahead. He felt the sheer weight of the Dakota. His teeth were biting into his lower lip as he muttered, 'For Christ's sake, girl.' He began to sweat. It was too late to abort now. And still the IAS needle was below the necessary 100 knots needed for take-off. The end of the concrete was coming up, the houses and the prefabs dead ahead.

The needle hovered close to 100.

Ruskin pulled the stick back gently. For a crucifying moment the Dakota didn't respond.

Witney's face was screwed up as he braced himself for the crash. McEvoy stared petrified between the two pilots at the houses and church ahead.

The Dakota began to lift, imperceptibly.

'We'll never bloody make it!' It was Witney, eyes popping.

Ruskin's heart was pounding fit to burst and the colour drained from his face.

They were out of runway now and the perimeter fence flashed beneath them, and then the houses were right under the Dakota's nose.

The three men stared out, tense, expecting the undercart to strike a roof. But it didn't – and they were climbing.

'Gear up!' Ruskin yelled, and it was hard to find voice, he was in such shock. 'Up!'

Witney's hand was already shifting the undercart lever. 'And flaps?' Witney was close to panic.

'No, for Christ's sake!' Ruskin screamed. 'We'd stall!'

For what seemed half a day and was only moments they seemed to be flying level with the housing estate roofs. And then the Dakota began to rise.

Ruskin's hands shook on the control column, Witney felt he was about to vomit. McEvoy closed his eyes and breathed heavily through his mouth like an exhausted marathon runner.

'Christ!' Witney whispered. 'I thought we'd bought it!'

How near they'd come to a crash into the houses they didn't know. But Adrian Kellett was watching the incident through binoculars from the old vandalized control tower, and he reckoned that at the critical moment the Dakota's spinning wheels cleared the rooftops by no more than ten feet. His own heart racing from the excitement of the near calamity, he watched the Dakota as she now climbed well clear of St Michael's. He put down the binoculars, took out a notebook and began to write, logging and reporting on the incident. His hand was trembling so much the writing was little better than a scrawl.

In the Dakota they went through 1,000 feet now, climbing steadily. His head throbbing, his heart still in his mouth, Witney began to come round. He threw a quick angry glance at Ruskin. 'Jesus!' he exploded. 'Never again! Never! Not with me in this seat! She's like lead! Phoney bloody loadsheets!'

McEvoy had bitten the inside of his mouth so fiercely he could taste blood.

It was some time before Ruskin spoke. The flaps were up now and they rose steadily towards their cruising level of six thousand feet. 'That was a bit hairy,' Ruskin said, trying to compose himself.

'A bit!' Witney's anger was mounting.

'Anyway, we're OK now.' He took in the fuel gauges showing both tanks full. Their all-up weight could only fall now as the fuel was used up.

It was the nearest any of them had come to a major crash, and they fell silent as it dawned how near they had been to death and to what could have been a disaster on that housing estate.

Ruskin's mind was full of images of Dickie Marlowe's accident. He now felt the force of Witney and McEvoy's silent accusation. Then he said, 'No use brooding. We made it, didn't we?'

And Witney began to wonder what kind of man he'd chosen to fly with.

CHAPTER 5

The ageing London taxi – it had survived the blitz of 1940 – turned into the Mayfair street and drew up outside the Wings Club. In the back seats Ruskin and Witney had hardly spoken since leaving King's Cross, and even on the train journey from Yorkshire they had been ill-at-ease with each other. Ruskin felt Witney had made a bit of a meal out of their near-miss every day since, and Witney was set on having more say in the way they ran the business. 'If it's all going to be as hairy as that,' he'd said in front of McEvoy, 'you can count me out.' And Ruskin had shrugged and told him there were loads of pilots on the labour market. It didn't quite represent Ruskin's attitude. He valued Witney's experience and officer-class charm, even if he didn't like it much.

It was Witney now who had second thoughts. 'If you'd rather I didn't join in?' he said.

'Not join in?' Ruskin snapped. 'You bind on about it for days. As much as call me a liar. You wanted to see and hear for yourself, you said. And so you bloody shall – as we've come all this way.'

'I *can* put questions?'

'Ask all you like, Squadron Leader.'

Witney got out first and was about to pay, but Ruskin pushed him aside and winked at the driver. 'He'd only have been stingy with his tip,' he said.

The bar was packed with RAF fliers and civilian bandits, many of them now known to Ruskin as competitors in a cut-throat game. More squadron crests decorated the walls and some typical officers' mess furniture had been added. Maybe Ernie had supplied it after one of his auction raids on the Ministry of Supply. There was no missing him. He was at the centre of a gaggle of fliers, some still in RAF uniform, cracking his stale old spiv's gags, and indulging his usual boastful spiel about how he was beating the system and winning the peace.

Ruskin's eyes searched for the rabbi, who sat unobtrusively at a table in the far corner near the picture of the Sunderland flying boat. He took Witney over to meet their new client. 'Sorry we're late, rabbi,' he said. 'We came by rail.' That would explain everything.

The little rabbi put on his secret smile. 'I spent half the war waiting for people to show up,' he said gently.

Ruskin introduced Witney. He saw that Cade was watching. And he wasn't the only one. The two mysterious civvies at the bar were showing interest, too. They seemed to be permanent fixtures nowadays.

'I'm sorry,' Witney said inquisitively. 'Didn't quite catch your name. Rabbi—?'

'Just rabbi, that's all,' the little man said pleasantly.

'I mean you are a real rabbi?'

It was met by that smile. Ruskin took them off the hook. 'Another orange juice, rabbi? Or something stronger?'

The rabbi pointed a sun-browned hand at his half full glass. 'Jaffa juice,' he said. 'Any more would unsettle me.'

'Long time since I set eyes on a juicy jaffa,' Witney said jovially.

The rabbi's response was to bring out a large jaffa from the dark raincoat on his lap. He gave it to Witney.

'And you never grew this in Golders Green,' Witney joked.

The rabbi brought out a second jaffa. 'Take this for your son.'

'No kids,' Witney replied, noting that Ruskin had gone over to the bar for their drinks. 'No time. He's a demanding boss.'

'I'm told you fly with him?'

'And sometimes against him,' Witney said jokily, though he half-meant it. 'Or so he reckons.'

At the bar Cade joined Ruskin and asked, 'Who's your mate?'

'Could be a snooper from Civil Aviation,' Ruskin teased. 'Or Customs. Or Immigration. Or Scotland Yard.'

Cade took a long drag on his cigarette. 'Never use those words even in jest, son.'

'Eh?'

'Scotland Yard,' Cade said raising his eyebrows towards the two mysterious civvies. 'I reckon they're here already. So who's your friend?'

'He's here to see you don't land me in Carey Street. Or the Old Bailey.'

'This geezer I wish to meet.'

Witney was still quizzing the rabbi, who said, 'I like to keep in touch with my Raff friends, that's all.'

'You were in the Raff?'

'No.' Again that faraway knowing look, as if Witney were in no-man's-land.

'Thought you might have been a padre?'

'In a way I suppose I was.' The deep brown eyes met Witney's. And he indicated someone approaching their table, an extroverted and absurdly young-looking squadron leader named Alvin Richards.

'Pete, for God's sake . . . begging your pardon, rabbi,' Richards enthused, pumping Witney's hand and throwing an arm over his shoulders. 'Thought I might run into you here.'

The rabbi thought they were like schoolboys.

'No surprise,' Witney laughed. 'All the bad pennies roll this way. So they finally tossed you out?'

'They wanted me to stay on, old chap. But thought I'd have a bash at civil flying.'

'You get back in toute suite,' Witney advised, as if from painful experience.

'Oh, I don't know,' Richards said cheerfully. 'They tell me you're doing nicely trundling that flying trawler from Grimsby. Must say you don't smell of fish.'

'Eau de Cologne, sweetie,' Witney gagged. 'We've also been running to France.'

Richards grinned at the rabbi. 'Forgive my friend, rabbi.

He should have been in the Navy urging young midshipmen to find the golden rivet.'

Witney scratched his head.

Richards eyed him with pitying disdain at his naïvety. 'You must have heard of the chief petty officer leading the young midshipman to the bowels of the ship to show him the golden rivet?' He paused only to see Witney shake his head. 'And the midshipman bends over, you see?'

Witney began to nod, and the rabbi said easily, 'There were so many golden rivets in those days.'

Ruskin and Cade were with them now, and Cade had overheard some of the conversation. 'The rabbi is a man of religion,' he reprimanded Richards. 'He is not here to be insulted.' He caught Witney's look of venom.

There were introductions all round before Cade told Witney and Richards to make themselves scarce for a few minutes. 'We wish to get off the subject of golden rivets.'

Witney's look tested Ruskin, who said, 'We'll not be long, Pete, then you can join us.' And Witney went over to the bar with Richards, aware of the conspiracy they were leaving. They leaned on the counter facing each other and Richards was in a state of some alarm. 'Don't tell me you're flying for that bastard,' he said, meaning Cade.

'I'm flying with Jack Ruskin,' Witney said cautiously, aware of the two mysterious civvies over the other side.

'Ex-flight sergeant, I hear?' There was a note of disapproval at the post-war switching of rank that was going on.

Witney shrugged. 'Cade owns half the Dak. And Jack pays him interest on a loan for the other half.'

'So what goes on with the rabbi?' Richards showed concern.

'Chum,' Witney began in a worldly-wise tone, 'I know Cade's a rough bastard. Pretended not to know me just now, but we've met. Didn't actually flaunt the knuckle-dusters.'

Richards ran a hand over his mouth. 'Watch it, Pete. You think your flight sergeant knows what he's getting you into? I mean he didn't have our education.'

'No,' Witney agreed. 'But he's catching up fast.'

A frown crossed Richards' anaemic face. 'And you two aren't meeting Cade and the rabbi to discuss kosher rationing.'

'We know what we're doing,' Witney said, feeling sure they didn't.

There was a long silence as they took in the meeting between Ruskin, Cade and the rabbi on the one hand and the two interested civvies at the bar. Then Richards asked, 'You knew Charlie Plowden?'

Witney nodded. 'Flight lieutenant on Daks.'

Richards' piercing grey eyes held Witney. 'Ditched in the Med last week. Halfway between Malta and Haifa. His Dak went down like a stone. As if it were solid lead. And his loadsheet said he was only carrying one thousand eight hundred kilos of fabric. He had two other crew but they found fifteen bodies. Yet under "Passengers" the loadsheet said nil.'

'Illegal Jewish immigrants?' Witney felt that ache behind the eyes he always got when under sudden stress.

'They weren't ghosts,' Richards said with a knowingness beyond his apparent youth. 'You be careful.'

Witney studied the rabbi in the distance. 'I'm not against illegals,' he said presently. 'After what went on in Germany who could blame 'em? And what was it the Balfour Declaration said? Back in 1917?' He couldn't quite recall but it went something like 'His Majesty's Government view with favour the establishment in Palestine of a national home for the Jewish people'.

Richards wasn't to be put off. 'And it's not just illegals, Pete, is it?' He let Witney work it out and went on, 'There's a terrorist element among 'em knocking off our own kith and kin, our brown jobs. Where the bloody hell are they getting their Tommy guns and Stens?' His anger died as quickly as it had come. 'It's jail without the option if they catch the fliers, Pete. And Ernie Cade's a marked man.' He indicated with the slightest of looks the presence of the two bar civvies.

'Some good it'll do,' Witney said with some disgust. 'Cade could buy his way out of solitary on Dartmoor.' His eyes were on Cade animatedly talking to Ruskin and the rabbi and he wished he could lip read.

Cade was saying to Ruskin, with some finality, 'If you're scared, mate, if you want out, just give it me straight along with my advance. And we'll see about exercising my option to sell your kite if you fall behind with the loan interest.'

The rabbi looked pained at such blackmail.

Ruskin said, 'Who said anything about being scared?'

'That's how it sounded,' Cade blustered.

Ruskin's blood was up. 'You ever left the ground in your life, Cade? Ever? Except when you had your feet examined for fallen arches in the call-up medical?'

Cade wasn't to be taunted. 'And when I'm in lifts. Then I get claustrophobia.' He held up a hand to the rabbi. 'See, rabbi. No gratitude. You pick these brylcreem boys out of their peacetime gutter and all you get is lip.' His eyes fell on Ruskin. 'You on or not, son?'

'I said,' Ruskin replied grittily. 'My co-pilot has a few questions.'

Cade's nose twitched. 'You'll get nowhere in this game if you let committees make your decisions. That's what's wrong with BOAC. Ask 'em to fly a load and all you see is twenty sets of manicured fingernails drumming a mahogany table. If you're not on, just say so. I can get . . .'

'A hundred bandits to take the job,' Ruskin said as if bored. 'I know.'

Cade glared. 'And the rabbi's not here to be third-degreed by jumped-up ex-squadron leaders who won't accept the war's over, kaput.'

The rabbi got them out of it. 'I don't mind talking to his friend,' he said blandly.

Cade obliged. He raised a hand and snapped his fingers and called, 'Hey, Squadron Leader.' And when Witney got the message Cade wagged a beckoning finger.

'You're surely not going?' Richards asked Witney, appalled.

'Why not?' Witney was set on getting to the roots of whatever plot was being hatched. He went over, watched by the two civvies, took a chair, and began to question the rabbi about what was behind the Haifa job.

'I'm not anti-British, Mr Witney,' the rabbi said. 'Though I do wish they had handled the Palestine problem with more imagination.'

He made Witney feel guilty against all reason. 'Look, I'm with those who say the Jews should have a homeland. But don't expect me not to ask you questions when your lot are shooting British soldiers and police.'

'My lot?' It was the first time the rabbi's calm had gone.

'The terrorists,' Witney persisted. 'The Hagana, they're armed.'

The rabbi swirled the remains of the jaffa juice round his glass. 'An unofficial defence force, Mr Witney, not terrorists.'

'The Irgun Zvei Leumi?' Witney pressed. 'The Stern Gang?'

'I do not approve of *them*, Mr Witney.'

It was all too much for Cade. 'Get it clear, son. The rabbi's not here to be accused. He came through a rough war, rougher than yours.'

The rabbi raised a hand in a gesture of modesty.

Ruskin couldn't resist it. 'Let's not get on to what people did in the war, Cade. All you did was scoop up a small fortune with those flat feet.' He came near to provoking Cade, but now looked at the rabbi. 'When you say we'll be flying fags, you do mean cigarettes? Fags? Things you smoke? I mean it's not a code name for bullets?'

'Cigarettes,' the rabbi said simply.

'Nothing else? Like illegal immigrants?' It was Witney.

The rabbi's fingers drummed the edge of the table. 'I don't accept that those of my people who are going home to Palestine are illegal immigrants, Mr Witney. Just because some authorities say they're illegal doesn't make them so.'

'And we'll not find them in our aircraft?' It was easy to see why Witney had been destined for the law.

'You have my word,' the rabbi said solemnly.

Cade had had enough of Witney's caution. He pointed at Ruskin and said, 'Get yourself another co-pilot, son, or no deal. And you can watch me snap my fingers and see this lot come running.'

Witney's expression was glacial. 'Some of these desperate dans are less choosy about what they get into.'

It seemed Cade was about to snap his fingers and kill the deal, so Ruskin said evenly, 'I've already said yes to the job, haven't I?'

'So I'll dig you out another co-pilot,' Cade said, fixing Witney with a look of contempt.

'No need,' Ruskin said. 'I've got Peter.'

In the hallway of the Shaws' house, Frank Shaw leaned against the banister rail and Jennie sat on the second stair watching the GPO engineer installing their first telephone. And Shaw's expression told the story. 'I'm not even sure I wanted it in,' he growled, cupping his empty pipe in his right hand.

'Come off it, Dad,' Jennie laughed. 'You've never stopped wanting one since Billy Mannion got his. You said how smashing it would be to call the doctor without leaving the house.'

'Oh, in an emergency. But I never thought the day would come.'

The engineer, a red-haired ex-Signals Corps corporal of about thirty, was yet another of those registering disillusion with the new post-war Jerusalem. 'The way Attlee and Ernie Bevin and that lot went on you'd have thought every house would have its own privy and phone now. Still, I did put one in a place in Alma Street yesterday.'

'If they've started in Alma Street it's time we were on,' Shaw snorted.

'Mind you, the subscriber's on the Council.'

All Shaw's old class instincts, and his loyalty as a fully paid-up member of the Labour Party, now came to the front. 'We never put this Government in and turfed the Tories out to keep things as they were before the war. Everybody on the north side of Preston Road on, everybody south using phone boxes.'

The engineer got up off his knees and stretched, still holding the phone flex. 'In the Signals in Germany we all voted Labour. Even some of the officers did, I know that. Now a year's gone and did you see that bit in the paper about putting bread on the ration? Bread! All this talk about a new Britain.'

'It's not just us that's short of food,' Shaw said. 'It's the world. And a lot of it's a damn sight worse off than us.'

The engineer's war-weary face creased into a smile. 'Anyway, you must have a bit of pull getting this. If you lined up everybody who wants one in they'd stretch all the way from here to Blackpool.'

Shaw put on a modest look.

Jennie took it in and said, 'It was my boy friend who ordered it. He lives with us.'

Shaw was relieved that she hadn't said he lived with her, sharing her bedroom.

'What does he do, then?' the engineer asked. 'Work at the infirmary?' He was used to putting in phones for priority subscribers in the essential services.

'He runs his own airline,' Jennie said matter of factly.

'He what?' It was too much.

'He's like British Overseas Airways, only he's not quite as big yet.'

Enlightenment dawned on the engineer's thin cavernous face. 'He's not one of those ex-Raff blokes flying old crates out of Garton?'

'Not old,' Jennie said. 'They're not all that old.'

'I came home in a Dakota once,' the engineer said. 'On passionate leave.'

'Compassionate,' Shaw said.

'Passionate,' the engineer insisted with a shy grin. 'Made me glad I never volunteered for the paratroops, that trip. You'd never get me up in one again.'

Jennie sat hugging her knees on that lower stair. 'It's out of date to be frightened of flying.'

'I'll stay old fashioned,' said the ex-corporal.

'Everybody wants to fly now.'

'Except me,' the corporal said decisively.

'Makes two of us,' Shaw said. 'And there are only three present.'

'I'd fly any day and that makes it even.' It was Mrs Shaw who had just come through from the kitchen.

Jennie told the engineer, 'You'd be surprised how many people are asking when he'll take passengers.'

He was making the final connections now and he said, 'How's he been managing for a phone if he's so busy then?'

Jennie explained how they'd been using the kiosk at the airfield. 'No good, though. You keep looking at the people waiting outside and thinking they're all wanting to call the ambulance.'

Frank Shaw studied her through hooded eyes. They all knew damn well why she'd wanted the phone in: Ruskin was away so much it was about the only way she could keep any contact.

'All the same,' the engineer said. 'I reckon you're lucky to get it.'

'My prospective son-in-law's a very influential lad,' Shaw said, biting on his pipe stem. He was making it clear that no hanky panky was going on under his roof.

The engineer gave a final turn with the screwdriver and put in a test call. When the phone rang out Mrs Shaw put her hands to her face as if she were seeing a miracle. The engineer thanked the operator and put the phone back on its rest. Jennie pounced and dialled 'o'. The engineer had begun to pack his tool kit. He winked at Shaw and told Jennie, 'You could reverse the charge to him, love.'

Jennie pulled a face. 'You can't reverse calls to a public box, silly.'

In the Wings Club, Ruskin saw the barman point to the phone box. He went past the two mysterious civvies at the bar and Squadron Leader Richards and an elegant, prematurely grey civvy in his late thirties.

'Love,' he heard Jennie say. 'Guess where I'm calling from?'

'Home,' he said drily. 'You've got the line in?'

'Spoilsport. You could have sounded surprised.' Ruskin's mind was on Richards and that civvy. They were clearly talking about him and Witney and Cade and the rabbi.

'You're not going to be late tonight, are you?'

He brought himself down to earth. 'Late?'

'You've forgotten,' she said. 'I knew it.'

He was thinking fast. 'First thing I did in London was to get your present.' He'd thought of tying a knot in his hanky to remind him of her birthday, but had overlooked it. And he'd not had cause to use the hanky anyway.

'Tell me what it is,' she said. Her voice was full of eagerness.

He could picture the young optimistic face. 'You can wait,' he said, watching Richards and the elegant civvy.

'I don't believe you,' she said, in mock reproof. She paused. 'Isn't it great? You'll be able to work from here now. This can be the office.'

The idea didn't thrill him. He was more interested in what was going on between Richards and the civvy, and in the identity of the two men at the bar.

Jennie just wanted to hear his voice. 'The man who put the phone in wondered how you'd managed to swing it,' she prompted. 'They've got priority subscribers on the waiting list.'

'Words in high places,' Ruskin said trying to cover his impatience. 'Look, love, I'm in the middle of a meeting.'

'You'll not be late?'

'As long as the train isn't.'

'Only Mum's making you a super supper. Guess.'

'Black market black puddings,' he said, his eyes on those groups at the bar.

'One more try.'

'She's blown the family's points on some grade one salmon?'

'No,' Jennie said, letting the answer hang in the air. 'Your favourite honeycomb tripe.'

Ruskin promised to try to get home on time, then went back to Cade and the rabbi. He could see Witney had joined Richards and the civvy.

'Your oppo's left his drink,' Cade said of Witney. 'It's time you left him.'

Ruskin raised his glass to the rabbi. 'So we're on? Right?'

The rabbi was toasting the deal in jaffa juice when Ruskin was called to the phone again.

'What is this?' Cade smirked. 'If it's publicity, ten out of ten. The bandit in most demand.'

Ruskin nodded briefly to Witney as he thrust past to the phone kiosk. The elegant civvy was now known to Witney as a merchant banker lately with the RAF as an admin officer, a lanky money expert with a way of shooting his cuffs.

'Doesn't make sense,' Witney went on when Ruskin was out of earshot. 'If Cade can rustle up fliers so easily why does he hire Jack?'

'He's got a hold on him,' said Gerry Maynard quietly. 'Ruskin's in his debt. Like some others. Cade has a piece of Ruskin's Dak. He squeezes a punitive rate of interest on the loan. And he takes what? Twenty per cent of Ruskin's fees from the rabbi and from any other business he introduces. Profit every which way. Cade's building his own flying circus. And most of the risk-taking, physical and financial, is taken by the Ruskins.'

Witney couldn't wait to pass the banker's views on to Ruskin, who was clearly pre-occupied on the phone.

The caller had been McEvoy, who now shared the box at Garton with his visitor, a sharply-dressed operator named Bert Glover, who was to the North what Cade was to the nation. He was offering them the job, McEvoy had told Ruskin, of flying a load of eggs from Dublin.

Glover's voice had a nasal ring and a Manchester accent. Ruskin had an image of a sharp face under a flashy trilby and a well-fed body under a jacket with padded shoulders. He wasn't far out.

'Trouble is,' the nasal voice said, 'your oppo tells me you'll be nearer the Pyramids than the Liffey. And this is something that won't keep.'

'Fresh eggs, right?'

'Straight from the hens.'

With a look at his watch, Ruskin said, 'When can you have 'em ready for loading? I suppose they are already laid?'

'Ten in the morning,' Glover said.

'Make it eight and we have a deal,' Ruskin said. 'We'll go tonight and pick up first thing. But it'll cost you.'

Glover said they could negotiate.

Ruskin disagreed. 'You take it or leave it. Forty quid a flying hour and overnight expenses.'

'Overnight exes?' The voice sounded shaken. 'You'll not be lushing it at the Shelbourne?'

'Bed and breakfast in simple style, Mr Glover,' Ruskin said. 'But we won't put our heads down in a peatbog.' He could see Witney rapping the kiosk glass with his forefinger.

'Forty quid a flying hour?' Glover asked. 'How many hours?'

Witney pulled the kiosk door open. He wanted Ruskin to meet Gerry Maynard before the banker left.

Ruskin winked at Witney and told Glover, 'Three hours there, three back.'

'Is that going fairly fast?' Glover hadn't been doing his homework.

'Flat out,' Ruskin said earnestly.

Glover hesitated. And then he said, 'Okay.'

'With an extra hour for headwinds,' Ruskin added, pulling a face at Witney.

'Headwinds?' It was a bit much for Glover, whose fiddles

were not normally subject to the weather. 'You get head-winds over the Irish Sea?'

'Both ways, Mr Glover,' Ruskin said with a straight face. 'I could lose money on this job. And they'd best have the load ready by eight on the dot, otherwise I'll have to bring in a penalty clause. And they'd best load fast.'

Glover was on the defensive now. 'It's fresh eggs, Mr Ruskin, not powdered. They'll have to be careful with the loading.'

'Exactly.' There was a pause in which Ruskin felt he might have overdone it.

'They'll be there at eight,' Glover said. 'COD, right?'

'Wrong. Half in advance, the rest COD. Market price, Mr Glover. We're all flying our arses off.'

Glover agreed, and Ruskin asked him to put McEvoy back on. 'Well done, Mac,' he whispered. 'Don't let that bugger get run over, eh? We'll be back in about four hours. Tell him to make sure he's there with his wallet.'

And Ruskin hung up with a grimace of disbelief. 'I always knew somebody up there was seeing we were OK. A few more like this one and I can tell Cade to piss off.'

'Headwinds both ways?' said Witney, amused. 'He never swallowed that?'

Ruskin stepped out of the box. 'These spivs know less about the weather than they do about profit. They get dazzled by the glare from their own gold bracelets.'

Witney told Ruskin about Maynard. 'He's a merchant banker ready to back bandits.'

'Pull the other one,' said Ruskin. 'No bankers want to know. They talk about aircraft as mobile assets in a tone that implies you're indulging in sin just trying to fly one.'

'Not this one,' Witney said. 'And he wants a word about what we might be getting ourselves into.'

Ruskin had eggs on his mind, and they hadn't time to waste. 'Another time, Pete. We'll just make the train if we scoot. I want to make Dublin tonight.'

'We've got five minutes surely?'

Ruskin shook his head. 'I've a call to make on the way to King's Cross.'

It was a jeweller's Ruskin was looking for. The taxi driver found one in Gray's Inn Road and it looked more like a pawnbroker's. Ruskin darted inside to find a very old man with layers of flesh hanging from a bony face. He was peering through a loupe held in his left eye at a ring containing the world's smallest diamond. His fat and blousy assistant, a woman in her mid-forties with pierced ears and a doll's plump arms, ran the rule over Ruskin as if he were a thief who needed watching. Ruskin said he would like to see some bangles.

'What kind of bangles?' The blousy woman's voice was tired.

'You know – that go round the wrist.'

She thought he was being facetious. 'How much had you in mind?'

'Just let me see some, eh?'

And she brought out a stick of old worn bangles that looked like loot from some remote African tribe.

'Not second hand,' Ruskin said. 'New. Haven't you any gold ones?' He hated shops, and the fat woman wasn't improving his mood. Her full lips were blood red and he thought of vampires. She bent down to the safe and he thought her stays were going to burst. Her backside was as big as that on Low's carthorses. Presently she brought out a stick of gold bangles, counted them slowly, and laid them before Ruskin on the otherwise empty counter. Grandad managed a physiological miracle: he kept one eye on that ring under the loupe and the other, at quite an angle, on Ruskin.

Ruskin chose a bangle with a lacey design on each outer rim.

'You have taste,' the blousy woman smiled with nicotine-stained teeth. 'It's the best.'

'I thought somehow it might be,' Ruskin said. 'How much?'

She was asking thirty pounds and it was a bargain.

Ruskin got her down to twenty-two and then found he only had ten on him. He went out and borrowed the rest from Witney. He hoped Jennie would like it.

Frank Shaw came home for his midday meal and found Jennie and Mrs Shaw in the kitchen. They were talking about making the loft over the bathroom into an office, and Shaw thought of all the chaos and of Ruskin banging his head on the low slung rafters. There wasn't room up there for a midget, never mind Jack Ruskin. 'I heard that and the answer's no,' he said, leaning against the kitchen doorway.

'I knew he'd be against it,' Mrs Shaw said resignedly.

'They've got their phone in,' he said. 'And that's as far as I'm going. I mean what would he keep up there anyhow?'

'His papers, typewriter, that kind of thing,' Jennie said.

'Papers!' His tone was full of contempt. 'What papers? And every time the phone rings you'll have to come down, so you'd need a ladder on the landing.'

'You can hardly expect them to jump,' said Mrs Shaw scaldingly.

'So we'll have an extension line up there.'

'Oh will you?' Shaw said, his face set firm. 'He's using you, Jen. I mean he knows it's your birthday and where is he? Oh, I know he's an apprentice tycoon and all that. And I know who'll be paying the phone bills when they come in.'

'He'll settle up,' Jennie said.

'Or forget,' Shaw said. 'Like he forgets about you.'

This was too much for Jennie. She was seething as she thrust past him and went through to the hall and the telephone. 'Now see what you've done,' Mrs Shaw said reproachfully.

Unrepentant, Shaw took off his jacket and said, 'Saw Fred Arkwright this morning. Now there's a lad with his head screwed on. He wed Renee Darwen.' He raised his voice so that Jennie could hear. 'But it could have been her. And they're getting their own house in Blakey Street next week.'

Jennie's voice came from the living room. 'You'll not catch us living there,' she called.

'No, it'll have to be a country mansion to suit him.'

There was no reply. Shaw went through to the hall to find Jennie. She was dialling 'o'. 'So who're you ringing?'

'Jack.'

'London again?' He feigned shock. 'Another trunk call?'

Jennie slammed down the phone in anger. She found her handbag hanging on the banister post, brought out her small purse from which she took several coins, and tossed them on the Victorian hallstand.

'You've nobody to blame but yourself,' Mrs Shaw said when Shaw reported back to the kitchen. He looked deeply hurt and for once was lost for words.

Presently Jennie came in. Nobody spoke as Mrs Shaw put out the potato pie. The three of them were eating when Shaw said quietly, 'Not there is he?'

'He's likely gone to catch his train,' Jennie said distantly as if it were really none of his business.

Shaw forked potato pie into his mouth. It was rich in onion the way he liked it. Down to earth grub. That was the trouble, he thought. If only Jack Ruskin would come down to earth instead of living it up in that evil city down south.

It was around five o'clock before Jennie went to the phone again, and it was the first incoming call. Ruskin was in the kiosk at the airfield. 'Hello, love,' he began awkwardly. 'You're not going to like this but . . .'

'You're still in London?' Her disappointment came through every word.

'No, love,' Ruskin said. 'I'm at the airfield but we've an urgent job come up.'

Usual tale, Jennie thought. 'You're not coming back tonight?'

'I can't, love,' he said. 'We'll have to set off in half an hour if we're going to make Dublin before dark.' He tried to make a joke. 'And landing in the peatbogs means we need more than the moon for landing lights.'

Jennie was in no mood for jokes. She felt let down. And she chose to keep silent.

'Jen?'

'Go on,' she said emptily.

'I got your present.'

'I think you forgot all about it,' she said. 'You were going to Palestine the day after tomorrow. Now it's Dublin tonight instead.'

'Not instead, love,' Ruskin protested, and told her about the cargo of fresh eggs. 'Maybe we'll snaffle a crate.'

'Don't expect me to eat any.'

'Oh, Jen, come on.' Irritation was setting in.

'And then you're off to Palestine. So when do I see you?'

'Soon as we can.' He'd like to see her, but he wasn't going to lose this job. It was a right bonus.

There was a long dead moment before she said, 'Don't bother, Jack. Go to Ireland. Go to Palestine. Just don't come back here, that's all.' And she hung up, the temper in her throat, and went through to where Shaw sat in front of the empty grate, his back to the window the better to read the local evening rag. Jennie had promised to help her mother with the washing so she made for the kitchen.

'It's all done in there, Jen,' Mrs Shaw said sympathetically, having heard Jennie on the phone.

'I said I'd never do that,' Jennie said, biting her lip. 'Never. Never before he flies.'

Shaw turned over a page. 'Any road, it gave that phone a right baptism.' He caught the sad look on her face. 'He'll be back on, you'll see.'

'You don't know him,' she said harshly. 'You don't know Jack when he's like this.'

'I know the young bugger,' Shaw said, and his pipe was going like a chimney. And from the corner of his eye he saw Jennie go back to the hall. 'Don't tell me you're ringing *him*?' he called.

'I don't want him flying with this on his mind,' she said,

coming back into the room. The phone began to ring and she felt numb.

Shaw went past her to take the call.

'Oh, hello, Jen's Dad,' Ruskin struck a cheerful note.

'Just a tick, Jack,' Shaw said evenly, handing the phone to Jennie.

'That was silly,' she told Ruskin. 'I shouldn't have.'

It was brushed aside. 'Tell you what, love. We'll be back late morning and I needn't take off for the Middle East till early afternoon at the earliest, so I'll come over with your present.'

She smiled through tears. 'I know,' she said. 'You're getting it in Dublin.'

'I've got it now,' Ruskin said. 'Straight. Gospel truth. I got it in London.'

And she still didn't know whether to believe him.

Vera Lynn was on the concrete outside the hangar and the fuel bowser was pulling away when Ruskin got back from the kiosk on the pillion of an RAF dispatch rider's Harley-Davidson. 'Thanks, mate,' he said, dismounting. He went over to Witney and McEvoy who were busy checking the Dakota's undercarriage. 'We are tanked up?' Ruskin asked, alert to their concern.

'It's the undercart,' said Witney with a nod.

'The undercart-locked light keeps flashing,' McEvoy explained.

It made Ruskin cross. 'So is it the undercart or the electrics?' he snapped.

McEvoy frowned. 'I'll have to take out the panel and check the undercart mechanism to be absolutely certain.'

'Why've you only just spotted this?' Ruskin's voice was brittle.

McEvoy felt Ruskin was being unjust. 'There was two days' maintenance on her that I've done in one,' he flared.

'All right, Mac, no panic.' He knew he'd gone too far

with the over-tolerant Scot. He weighed up the Dakota through hard eyes. 'So let's go, eh?'

The silence was so long that Ruskin thought nobody would say anything, and then it was just one word from Witney. 'Go?' He was incredulous.

Ruskin was already climbing aboard. 'If we don't go now we've had it, we'll be over the peatbogs in the dark, and the Irish won't have anything to light our way in except bloody glow-worms.' He picked up his flying overalls from just inside the cargo door and began to don them. 'Come on, then,' he called. 'Fingers out.'

The other two stayed rooted to the hot concrete under the still-hot afternoon sun. It was McEvoy who moved first, vaulting aboard.

'Never again,' Witney was reminding himself. 'Never again.' Dodgy undercarts were like overloading. He kept looking at the undercart, those stilts, and the wheels. He turned away towards the Nissen hut, but it was only to collect his flying overalls.

Five minutes later he was in the cockpit with Ruskin and McEvoy going through the pre-take-off checks. The Dakota was in good shape except for that bloody undercart-locked light that kept flickering nervously.

'Probably the flaming bulb, that's all,' Ruskin said. 'I've known bulbs cock things up many a time.'

'The bulb's OK,' McEvoy said dourly. 'I checked.'

'Loose wire, then,' Ruskin said.

There were limits, Witney thought. He said, 'Or a one-legged undercart.' He had visions of them limping along the runway at close on take-off speed and the undercart suddenly folding like a three-ply fretwork.

Ruskin was bloody-minded. They were going, enough said. 'Mac signed the fit-for-flight certificate, didn't you, Mac?'

'No,' McEvoy murmured. 'Not yet.'

'Do it when we get back,' Ruskin said, with a sharp look at each of them. 'As usual.'

And he buttoned the two Wasp engines into life. He

chose to ignore that flickering undercart-locked light. And the take-off was perfect, though it gave Witney pains behind the eyes and McEvoy was having trouble with his breathing. Their evening flight across the Irish Sea with the westering sun in their eyes was the most pleasant trip they'd done together, and only the landing bothered them. That undercart-locked light was still flickering like a Victorian gaslamp. As Ruskin touched the Dakota on to the Irish soil, he was set for an awful crunch as the undercart buckled. He kept the landing speed high. As he felt and heard the tyres hit the deck, there was a slight bounce but no buckling, and he was aware of Witney's crossed fingers on the co-pilot's control column.

They were safely down. Ruskin felt like cheering. The other two were murmuring very secret 'amens'.

McEvoy spent that night checking the undercart and control panel connections while Ruskin and Witney slept. He found nothing amiss, but pointed out that more than one night would be needed to give the undercart a thorough going-over.

Ruskin and Witney had been given a room at a nearby farm, and McEvoy had joined them for bacon and eggs first thing. When they got back to Vera Lynn, they found a clapped-out ex-Army truck and a horse-drawn farm cart waiting with crates of eggs. Three Irish peasants, one a craggy old woman who must have been ninety, helped Ruskin and Witney load up in the bleak Irish dawn. One of the peasants, a farm labourer with a large moon face and shrewd amused eyes, preferred talk to work. He had a way of standing back in his torn US Air Force leather flying jacket to enjoy his gift of the gab. 'I wouldn't ride in this if it was painted green and personally blessed by the Holy Father,' he said, and Ruskin wondered why he was only a farm labourer. Maybe he wasn't.

'Neither would we if we'd any sense,' Witney said, stacking crates in the hold.

'I remember one o' them Flying Fortresses the Yanks was sending over to help you, and they kept coming down here as if they were happier in this neutral country. I remember the bang when one came in nose first in Paddy Linaker's field, you could hear it in Wicklow.'

'They must have been carrying windbags,' Ruskin said, exasperated by all the chat.

'Windbags?' The peasant didn't understand.

'He means, Paddy, we should cut out the chat and get on with it.'

The Irishman was a touch pained. 'I thought he'd be interested.' He handed up a crate of eggs. 'Is the British so hungry they have to send aeroplanes for eggs now?'

Ruskin was securing crates. 'We're bloody starving, Paddy, mate. We'll be after your peat next to keep us warm in the winter.'

'It's charity cases we are,' Witney said in a mock-Irish accent. 'The Aussies are sending Bundles for Britain.'

It was the signal for the Irishman to begin a long dissertation on the old British Empire, but Ruskin chipped in with a firm, 'Come on, Paddy.'

'And it's my second cousin you must be thinking of,' the Irishman said pleasantly. 'My name's Eamonn.'

'What I'm thinking,' Ruskin said, 'is these eggs will go off if you keep on.'

The Irishman said, 'We used to give 'em to the RAF boys who'd come over the border with raincoats over their uniforms in the war. They'd borrowed our raincoats. And we gave 'em eggs and silk stockings.'

'Silk stockings?' Witney queried.

'The good Lord and the little people between 'em saw to it we had our neutral comforts.'

'Eamonn, for God's sake!' Ruskin yelled, checking his watch.

'All right, Mister Captain, sir,' the Irishman said, passing up another crate. 'And would you be interested in taking a slice or two of bacon to help the eggs go down in your starving country?'

Even McEvoy who was up in the cockpit worrying his head off about that undercart burst out laughing.

Twenty-five minutes later they began the take-off from the grass airstrip. Ruskin and Witney went meticulously through the pre-take-off checks, with McEvoy's anxious face looming between them. They waved to Eamonn and his co-workers and began the run-up. It seemed the undercart was fine. The green light was steady and bright, no flicker.

It wasn't until they made their approach to Garton that they gave much further thought to it. They began the routine, running right through the check list as they came down through the clear morning sky with the flaps two-thirds down. It was then that Witney saw the first flicker of the undercart-locked light. As they watched, it went out, came on again, went out, and then began a near-rhythmic flicker. They heard the bang as the undercart went down. Ruskin caught Witney's anxiety. 'It was like this when we landed in Ireland,' he said with more confidence than he felt. 'The undercart stood up then.'

'Proves nothing,' McEvoy said dourly. 'I did change the bulb.'

'You never told us that, Mac.' There was alarm in Witney's voice.

'Changed it in Dublin.'

They were very near the airfield now, steeple-top height, cruising in at 95 miles an hour. There was no option but to try the landing, though it did go through Witney's mind that they might divert to an RAF station with emergency services. He knew that Ruskin would never hear of it. Besides, this load of eggs wasn't all that official. He saw the concrete ahead as McEvoy gave them full flaps, and they felt the braking effect. 'We've a fifty-fifty chance of breaking the world record,' he shouted. 'The biggest omelette since cooking began.' Neither Ruskin nor McEvoy seemed to hear.

McEvoy's eyes were riveted on that green light, flickering in a demented way. The vibration was causing three hams to swing from their hooks at the rear of the cockpit, and the crates of eggs were creaking and groaning in the hold.

It was then that Ruskin and Witney saw a Humber car turn off the perimeter for a short cut across the runway to the hangar. They were over the runway edge now, the Humber no more than a hundred and fifty yards ahead.

'Fucking idiot!' Ruskin yelled, pulling back on the stick as Witney gave them full throttles.

'Jesus God!' Witney yelled.

It seemed they couldn't miss the Humber. The twin Wasps roared, the horizon fell, and they were climbing.

They waited for the crunch. None came.

His heart was thumping so fast that Ruskin thought it would never get back to normal, and the pain behind Witney's eyes was blinding. The colour had drained from McEvoy's face.

Jennie had seen the incident from outside the Nissen hut. She closed her eyes. She could hear the Dakota banking away now to begin a new approach. It had cleared that Humber by no more than a few feet.

'Can I get you a coffee, Miss? Or something stronger?' It was the voice of one of the two Customs officers who, with two Immigration officers, had come on a tip-off to meet Ruskin's Dakota.

She shook her head, her eyes still firmly closed. She felt Adrian Kellett's small hand on her arm. 'Come and sit down, Miss Shaw.' His voice was gentle and considerate but he caught her in shock. And her reaction was to blame all these petty officials who lived in cotton wool and who made life so hard for Ruskin.

'Go away!' she said.

'I know how you feel, Miss Shaw.'

'Go away! Get out! You! All of you!' Her eyes were open now and on fire.

Kellett let go of her arm. The Immigration officers moved away and the young Customs officer. But the older one, florid and with an over-developed sense of authority, stayed where he was, a yard or so away.

'I said go away!' Jennie told him coldly.

'I understand how you feel,' the florid one said. 'But we do have our duty.'

She flew at him, slapping wildly, seeing in him the arch cause of the near-fatality. It took Kellett and the young Customs officer to pull her off. Kellett with an arm round her shoulders was trying to steady her, when they saw the Humber draw up.

Bert Glover got out and ran a handkerchief over his face. His hands were shaking, his eyes popping. He was in such a state he didn't notice the Customs officers' uniforms. Jennie just gazed at him with loathing, her clenched left hand pressed against her mouth as if to subdue her shock. It was Kellett who went to Glover. He was not more than half the size of the big spiv but he thrust his face under Glover's chin as if he were about to tup him. 'You bloody clown,' he snarled. 'You make a habit of that, do you?'

'Nobody warned me,' Glover said. 'They should have traffic lights. Or signals.'

'When was the last time you drove across a runway?' Kellett was livid, with colour rushing to his pale face.

'Oh I never stop,' Glover said, trying to conceal the fright he'd just had.

'You've stopped now,' Kellett said, in a voice of authority. 'I've heard of kamikaze pilots. I never heard of kamikaze drivers.'

'I like that,' Glover said, recovering. 'Give the gent a prize.'

Kellett held out a hand. 'You have a permit to be on this station?' he demanded.

'Hey, gumboil, remember your size,' was Glover's reply. 'They're not flying secret missions any more, didn't you hear? The war's over. And this is just a piece of public real estate. And I'm Joe Public.'

'You were nearly the late Joe Public,' Kellett said. 'And those lads might have gone with you.' He waggled his hand. 'Permit.'

An ex-Army Bedford truck rolled up now, and the two

Customs officers went over and began to question the driver. The florid man dropped the tailboard and peered inside. And Glover took in the uniforms, and the two Immigration officers. 'That truck's my business,' he blustered, but the Customs officers ignored him.

'Permit,' Kellett pressed.

'You never said who you are,' Glover said, eyeing Kellett up and down.

'No, I didn't.'

Glover tugged out a shiny leather wallet and brought out not a permit but a handful of sterling. He didn't even count it, but held it confidentially so that only Kellett could see it.

'If you know what's good for you, you'll put that away at once,' Kellett said, as a Hillman came up. A middle-aged man in a Harris tweed jacket and tailored grey slacks got out and took stock – the Customs officers, the Immigration officers, Kellett, Jennie and Glover. And it was clearly Bert Glover who was of most interest.

Vera Lynn was making a second approach now. They all turned to watch. Glover began to lose his nerve. He moved unnoticed to his Humber, got in, felt for the ignition key. It had gone. He looked out and saw Kellett staring at him and waving the Humber's keys.

The Dakota came in now, its wheels about to touch.

In the cockpit that green light was flickering like a doomsday warning.

Ruskin, Witney and McEvoy braced themselves, felt the judder as the wheels hit the deck, heard the screech of tyres on concrete, and prepared for the crunch. The Dakota bounced slightly, and then ran on firmly. Ruskin brought her round the peri-track, looking out at the activity near the hangar. Witney was first to spot the Humber. 'I'll kill him,' Ruskin swore.

'Like a rugger scrum out there,' Witney said questioningly.

'Kellett's there,' Ruskin said. 'Two Customs officers.'

'And Immigration officers,' Witney said. His eyesight

was paranormal and he could make them out as the two from the previous encounter.

'And that's Glover,' Ruskin said, seeing the big spiv move to the Humber. 'And that bloody Humber's his!'

'So who's the other bloke?' Witney pondered.

Ruskin didn't wait to ask. He pushed through the mill of officials at the cargo door and made straight for Glover, who was standing near his Humber with the young Customs officer keeping an eye on him.

'You bloody lunatic!' Ruskin blurted, snatching Glover by his lapels. 'You could have turned the lot of us into strawberry jam doing a bloody hare-brained trick like that!'

Glover tried to remove Ruskin's hands. He may as well have tried to shift a vice. He saw the violence in Ruskin's face. He began to climb down. 'I never saw you,' he said. 'I don't want to kill myself.'

'Never mind you!' Ruskin's voice rose. 'We're human!' For a long moment it looked as if Ruskin would kill him on the spot. But he just shoved him away and said, 'And now cough up.' He indicated the Dakota. 'There's your load. Not one broken.'

'I'll see them first,' Glover said with a nod towards the Dakota. 'If they've finished,' he added with sarcasm.

Ruskin threw a look at the young Customs officer. 'See he doesn't go anywhere,' Ruskin said of Glover, who was lighting a cigarette with a gold lighter.

'He can't go far or fast,' said the young Customs officer. 'The ARB bloke's got his car keys.'

In the Dakota, Ruskin found the senior Customs officer, the two Immigration officers, and the tweedy man nosing among the crates of eggs. Kellett was up in the cockpit with McEvoy. Witney was trying to cope with the posse of officials.

'I've just asked to see your loadsheet, Captain Ruskin,' said the Customs officer, eyes popping from that florid face.

'I told him that all we're carrying is what's here,' Witney said.

Ruskin nodded. 'We're not in from Germany stuffed with Leicas, Rolleis and Zeiss binoculars.'

'No, you're in from Ireland,' Florid said flatly, as if he knew a lot more besides.

'Dig out our ship's manifest for the gentleman,' Ruskin told Witney and gave him a wink on Florid's blind side. No manifest yet existed.

Kellett came down from the cockpit now. The near-miss with the Humber was burning in his mind. The bandits were to some extent a wild and irresponsible lot, but they were fliers whose lives had been put at risk by a greedy idiot. He had asked dutifully for McEvoy's fit-for-flight certificate and McEvoy had done his usual pretence about having mislaid it. Kellett knew that McEvoy would be writing it out in the cockpit now that his back was turned. He saw that Ruskin had problems with the Customs officer, who was making his way for'ard to the cockpit. And he blocked the Customs officer's way as if by accident, pointing to imaginary chalk marks on the hold floor. 'You did your C of G, Mr Ruskin?'

'Should be there somewhere,' Ruskin said, catching on. In fact there was no centre of gravity mark.

Kellett let Witney go past him, knowing he was going to cook up a cargo manifest, and told Ruskin, 'That spiv should go to jail without the option for what he did just now.' It all helped to keep the Customs officer's interest.

In the cockpit Witney found McEvoy busy hiding those three hams – one in his flying overalls, and another in his tool chest, another in a box of spares under the co-pilot's seat. 'Kellett suggested we should lose 'em quick,' McEvoy said.

Witney searched among the bumph and could find no blank loadsheets.

'No fit-for-flight certificates either,' McEvoy said. 'I made a few signs to Jennie down there, and she's gone back to the hut, but I don't know if she really got the message.'

Back in the hold Ruskin was doing what he could to cope with the invasion of bureaucrats – the Immigration officers, the senior Customs officer, Kellett, and the tweedy man. It went through Ruskin's mind that he must be from one or other of the security services. 'We're not carrying Brens, Stens or anything lethal,' he said edgily.

'I'm not Special Branch, Mr Ruskin,' the tweedy man said politely, with a nod towards the crates. 'Where did you pick these up?'

Ruskin stuck a finger on the stencilled shamrock stamps.

'Where, exactly? Who's the supplier?'

Ruskin shrugged. 'Near Dublin. And I don't know.'

'You flew them in.' The tweedy man was bolder now. 'Are you in the habit of not knowing your clients?'

'The hens aren't my clients.' Ruskin couldn't resist the jibe. 'My client's out there.' He threw a glance at Glover and his Humber.

'He has an import licence?'

'You'd best ask him.' Ruskin's tone was one of indifference.

'I'm from the Ministry of Food, Mr Ruskin,' the tweedy man said. 'You must be aware that my Department is the sole permitted importer of most foods and the prime purchaser of many other foodstuffs, including eggs.'

Jennie came in now, with the junior Customs officer carrying the big brown teapot. She went on past them to the cockpit, leaving the Customs officer to pour tea into the cracked enamel mugs.

'Any other food aboard besides eggs?' the Ministry man asked, sipping his tea.

His superior manner riled Ruskin. 'Well, apart from the caviare and the royal sturgeon and the crate of hot cross buns . . .' he began.

'Very funny, Mr Ruskin. We do have to see that food is fairly distributed and that there must be no undue rise in prices.'

'You get danger money, do you?' Snoopers drove Ruskin mad.

The tweedy man was moving for'ard. He pushed open the door to the cockpit just as Jennie was about to pull the pads of loadsheets and fit-for-flight forms from under her wool jumper. Ruskin also went for'ard, thinking of those hams. It was a relief to see no sign of them. The Ministry man's eyes roamed the nooks and crannies of the cockpit. He took in the overnight bags, the toolbox, the flying jacket in a heap on the floor. Like many another non-flier he was a touch overawed by the cockpit. And Witney saw his chance. 'Would you mind closing that door,' Witney said in his best squadron leader's voice. 'We're doing highly sensitive checks and you're creating a draught that affects the instruments.'

Ruskin felt proud of him. All that could be affected by the draught was McEvoy's fibrositis.

It worked. The Ministry man began to withdraw, with a final suspicious glance at the odd shape of Jennie's bustline. When he'd gone she brought out the pads of loadsheets and fit-for-flight forms from under her jumper.

Witney blinked. 'I'd kiss you if you weren't his bird.'

'Oh, don't let that put you off,' she said, pushing her face forward.

Witney kissed her.

'And you, Mac.' McEvoy gave her a shy peck and began to fill in a fit-for-flight certificate.

Ruskin left the snoopers rummaging and went over to Glover at the Humber.

'Who're the private army?' Glover said, trying to seem composed.

Ruskin held out a big hand, palm upwards, and laid it on the sill of the car window. 'Final stage payment,' he demanded. 'Not one egg cracked. Two hundred and thirty-five quid.'

'Hey, mate, I wasn't born in Barnoldswick yesterday. Two thirty-five?' He spoke with incredulity.

'Four hours' flying time at forty-five a flying hour. One

hour's loading – forty. Overnight exes – fifteen. As agreed.' Ruskin's hand was under Glover's nose.

'I don't know they're in there, do I?' Glover said with a nod towards the Dakota.

Ruskin invitingly opened the car door and stood there like some chauffeur.

'You never said who the snoopers are?' Glover hesitated. 'I'll wait till they've gone before I collect the eggs.'

'You'll come now,' Ruskin insisted. 'And cough up.' And he grabbed Glover by the lapels and began to drag him from the Humber. He was still seething over that near-miss on the runway. 'And another thing, dad. Don't ever try a dumb thing like that again. You must be clean gone, dicing across a runway. You nearly turned the lot of us into strawberry jam.'

The driver of Glover's Bedford truck came over now, glaring at Ruskin. 'Back in your cab, lad,' Ruskin ordered, his fists clenched. It took the driver less than two seconds to decide he'd need more than unarmed combat to survive a set-to with Ruskin. He turned away. 'Now, hike,' Ruskin told Glover.

As they went into the Dakota hold it was the tweedy man who spoke first. He ran a quick rule over Glover and said, 'Thought it might be you, Glover. Except that air freighting's a bit ambitious for you, isn't it? Eggs now? Change from cooking fats. Our fish and chippers have been missing your extras over the rations.'

Glover put on the pained look of the most misunderstood man in the world. 'I was going to offer this lot to the Ministry. Straight. Controlled price and all.'

'Very patriotic, Glover,' said the tweedy man. 'The more responsible citizens like you who try to stop the black market the better. But we're not buying, we'll very likely be confiscating.' He tapped a crate with a beautifully-manicured hand. 'So don't worry if a few are broken.'

'Hey, this isn't Nazi Germany,' Glover said.

Ruskin held out his right hand. 'Two hundred and thirty-five, Bert.'

'I said I'd settle the same day,' Glover dodged. 'Not right on the button.'

'COD.' Ruskin's face was impassive.

'If I had the lolly with me . . .' Glover began. Ruskin was about to grab him to remove his wallet. But Kellett held out the car keys under Glover's nose, then let them fall at Ruskin's feet. Ruskin put a size 10 shoe on them. Glover got the message and brought out his leather wallet with his initials embossed on the outside. 'The Nazis were no worse than this,' Glover complained, his plump face flushed. 'And I've not seen the condition they're in,' he said with a gesture towards the eggs.

'You've not seen the condition you'll be in,' Ruskin said. 'Cut out the guff.'

Glover had a habit of hunching his shoulders forward as a gesture of aggression. 'And if they're confiscating, *they* should pay,' he said with a glance at the tweedy man. But the tweedy man was too busy searching for other concealed items of illicit food. Ruskin put a hand against the fuselage, his arm acting as a bar between Glover and the open door. Glover began to feed crisp fivers into Ruskin's other hand.

Witney came down from the cockpit now and handed Kellett the fit-for-flight form and the tweedy man the loadsheet. 'They'd got lost under one of the seats,' and Kellett smiled, because there were fresh ink smears on Witney's fingers.

Two newcomers came aboard now. Nobody had heard them drive up. One was tall and lean with thinning silver hair brushed straight back without a parting, the other a younger man of thirty or so, stocky and built like a door. They knew Ruskin and Ruskin knew them. They were the two mysterious civvies he had seen in the Wings Club watching Cade and the rabbi. They nosed casually among the crates of eggs, waiting for Glover to complete his payment to Ruskin.

It was now three hours since the posse of bureaucrats had

left, along with Bert Glover and Kellett – and the eggs. They were loading crates labelled 'Cigarettes' now. Jennie was helping to stack and her gold bangle was evident on her left wrist. McEvoy was doing instrument maintenance in the Nissen hut, and Ruskin and Witney supervised the transfer of the crates from the 3-ton Bedford truck into the hold.

The two mysterious civvies were suspicious. The stocky one was opening random crates and checking while his older colleague went through export documents with a blond young man of no more than twenty-five, who had brought the consignment with the truck driver. The older man made notes from what he read in the documents.

'Customs found them in order,' said the blond young man easily.

'You the exporter named? Dawson?' said the older man, looking more like the plain clothes policeman they now knew him to be.

'He's my father,' the blond young man said. He was very calm and self-controlled.

'Is he about?' the plain clothes man said.

'He's at home,' the blond young man said. 'I can answer all your questions.'

'I'd rather ask him.' The plain clothes man's earlier veneer of amiable charm had gone.

'He's in a wheelchair,' the blond young man said. 'He copped it in the Rhine crossing.'

The plain clothes man weighed him up, aware he was on sensitive ground. 'But is he – er – is he Jewish? I mean you don't look Jewish.'

The blond young man was unruffled. 'He's a Jew,' he said easily. 'So am I. We're trying to set up trade with Palestine.'

'Cigarettes?' said the plain clothes man, unconvinced. 'You'd think they'd need more important things than fags.'

'Oh I don't know. I'm just out of the Raff in Germany and they made welfare number one priority over there after the mutiny in India over slow demob. Now it's Ensa shows and gift shops selling Leicas and Rolleis and silk stockings.'

'Holiday camp,' the plain clothes man sniffed, still perusing the documents.

'The Government daren't risk a mutiny over there, with the Red Army facing us.' He was doing his share of weighing up now. He had it worked out that the plain clothes man had not been in the Forces during the war. 'Have you been there?' The question was gently put.

It caught the plain clothes man to the quick, 'No – and I don't see what it has to do with it.'

Witney laughed at the easy way the blond young man had established the plain clothes man as a wartime non-com.

The plain clothes man gave him a hard look.

And the blond young man took him off the hook. He tapped a crate and said, 'Tobacco's a drug. It calms people down. We have a lot of calming down to do in Palestine.'

Kellett drove up now, and he went to Ruskin near the cargo door. He was flaunting a fit-for-flight certificate he had just collected from McEvoy. 'That's better, Ruskin,' he said amiably. 'You see it's not all that difficult to complete your documentation as the law requires, is it?'

'I always do, Mr Kellett,' Ruskin said in wide-eyed innocence.

'But not always in advance,' Kellett said, with a look over his glasses.

'No nit-picking, eh?' Ruskin said. 'We are a bit busy.'

'It is my job to see you observe the rules, Ruskin. So no more last minute docs, eh? I mean it's like filling in your pools coupon on Saturday evening and getting someone to give it a Thursday postmark.'

Ruskin told him he should be running Littlewoods.

The silver-haired plain clothes man, having failed to find much wrong with the blond young man's papers, was now examining the flight plan as if it might be incriminating evidence. 'I see you plan to break in Rome?' he asked Ruskin.

Ruskin nodded.

'Why Rome?'

'Ground facilities,' Ruskin shrugged. 'Juice.'

'Why not somewhere else? I mean I'm not an airman but . . .'

Ruskin was running out of patience. 'So what are you?'

'I'm a police officer. You know that.'

It was too much for Witney. 'He's Special Branch,' he called. 'They got so used to throwing people on the Isle of Man under Regulation 18B during the war they're feeling a bit lost for someone to push around.'

'I should be a bit careful,' the plain clothes warned.

Ruskin put on a solemn look and told him, 'You mustn't address a squadron leader like that.'

Plain clothes surveyed Witney, drawing himself up to his full six-foot-three. 'I'm surprised someone with your background can talk like that.'

'The war's over, chum,' Witney said. 'We're entitled to keep our eyes on you lot a bit now.'

It was clear the policeman was being drawn into a tendentious row. He turned to Ruskin. 'So why Rome?'

Ruskin withered him with a look. He'd had a bellyful of bureaucrats. They seemed to be in the national woodwork. He resumed the loading and said, 'If you'd like to make yourself useful?' Witney, Jennie, the blond young man and the truck driver made a point of getting stuck into the job. Plain clothes and his assistant snooped around for a couple of minutes, and then left without a further word. They had found nothing to justify their visit.

'So why Rome?' Ruskin asked the blond young man. 'We could make Malta first leg.'

'Maybe next time if you prefer it,' was the bland reply. He still had another truckload of crates to bring. McEvoy and Witney agreed to hang on to protect the cargo already loaded while Ruskin and Jennie went to the Shaws for an early supper.

It was a balmy summer's evening. Jennie would have

loved to go walking in the dales, but she drove them to the town.

'Why all that fuss about Rome?' she presently asked.

'The only thing he ever flew was a kite,' said Ruskin, still irritated by the Special Branch man.

'Anyway, you got me a super present,' Jennie said, aware that Ruskin was near snapping-point. 'How long have we got before we have to come back?'

'Two hours,' Ruskin said. 'And you can stay at home. No need for you to come back.'

'If I come back it'll not take as long to load and . . .'

'Blast!' Ruskin snapped. He'd just remembered. 'We forgot that bloody ham!' he said.

Jennie did a U-turn.

An hour later they were sharing the ham with Jennie's parents around that veneered walnut table in the back room. Shaw was not in the best of humour. It still rankled that Ruskin seemed to be in with folk who weren't one hundred per cent law-abiding. He was critical of those who got more than their fair share of scarce food.

'So you'd rather I didn't bring back any more black market grub?' Ruskin was being provocative.

'Nobody said that, Jack,' Mrs Shaw said.

'No, but he's going on about it like some preacher.'

Shaw would not be drawn. He seemed to be enjoying the ham and eggs.

'You'll not make me feel guilty,' Ruskin said, tucking into his own plateful.

Shaw wiped his mouth with his handkerchief. 'That's it, that's just the trouble. No sense of right and wrong any more.'

'He's not a hypocrite,' Jennie said tartly.

Each in turn got a look from Shaw. 'You want me to stop eating, do you? Is that it?'

'Only be a waste of good grub,' Ruskin grinned. 'And that's immoral with half the world starving.'

'It's nowt to be cynical about,' Shaw muttered.

'Cynical?' Ruskin winked at Jennie. 'Listen. I had a

vegetarian navigator once. On the Rhine crossing he gave his emergency rations to a red beret bloke to give to the first hungry Jerry he met. Now that's not being hypocritical.'

With a flourish, Shaw pushed his plate away. 'That's it,' he announced. 'I'll not have it.'

'Don't be silly, Frank,' Mrs Shaw said.

'Our Alan would never.'

'No, well he's very pure,' Ruskin said. 'He was a conchie.'

'And they're making him pay. The war long done with and they'll not release him from that farm job.'

It almost provoked Ruskin. He had no time for those who had stayed at home during the war. He knew it was unreasonable, and he could be wrong about their motives. But resentment burned.

It was Mrs Shaw who kept the peace. 'Lovely bit of bacon, Jack. And the eggs are as fresh as if they were laid today.'

Ruskin nodded towards Shaw. 'He'd prefer powdered egg off the ration book.'

Mrs Shaw pushed Shaw's plate back in front of him. 'Get on with it and don't be silly.'

'I'll promise not to look,' Ruskin said, his blue eyes bright with mischief.

Shaw got up from his chair now, and went over to the wireless, and switched it on, making a point of not eating his ham and eggs.

'Dad!' Jennie reprimanded him.

'We're missing the news,' Shaw said, in case he was tempted to resume his ham and eggs.

'Don't know why you bother with the news,' Mrs Shaw said. 'It's all bad.' And indeed the news was about the start of bread rationing in Britain and attacks on British troops in Palestine as they tried to frustrate illegal immigration and confiscate illegal caches of arms.

Ruskin took it all in about Palestine but chose to keep

Shaw off the subject by indicating the loaf on the table. 'You got plenty in, Mum?'

'No more than we need,' Mrs Shaw said stubbornly.

'The way they're rushing to buy it all up.' Shaw shook his head in dismay. 'Greed. And they'll only hoard it till it's stale and make things worse.'

Ruskin was mopping up the remains of his ham and eggs with a piece of folded bread. 'Who's to say we need it rationed, anyway?' he said. 'Even if there's no shortage they'll invent one to get another control on. They're strangling us with controls.' He saw Shaw being tempted to finish his ham and eggs, and Ruskin's eyes shone. 'And Labour's going to lose the by-election next Monday.'

Shaw had quietly begun to finish his meal. As a diversion he told Ruskin, 'You need your head seeing to, flying to Jerusalem.'

'Haifa,' Ruskin said, still mopping up ham and eggs.

'Palestine, anyway,' Shaw said. 'I just hope you'll not be giving any aid and comfort to those who're fighting our lads out there, that's all.'

Ruskin's nose twitched. 'How about that egg and bacon then?' The old devil wasn't going to get away with it that simply.

'I'd not want anybody from this house helping terrorists,' Shaw said dourly.

It failed to upset Ruskin. 'Most of 'em aren't terrorists,' he said. 'The Jews have a right to a place to live. I mean nobody rolled out the red carpet for 'em on the Continent in the last few years.'

'I don't dispute that,' Shaw said, making it seem he was finishing his ham and eggs as a duty. 'All the same we should clear out. Leave 'em to it – Jews, Arabs, Yanks, whoever. We've done enough. We should bring the lads home, and from India.'

'You didn't say if you liked your ham and eggs,' Ruskin smirked.

'They were all right, I suppose,' Shaw shrugged.

Mrs Shaw came in now with what was left of a small

birthday cake she had made herself. 'We started it last night but it wasn't like Jen's birthday without you here, Jack.'

'I bet you used up all your points on it,' Ruskin said. He liked Mrs Shaw's unselfishness, and he'd only known her when there was rationing.

'Very nearly,' she said self-effacingly, cutting a large slice of cake and handing it to Ruskin.

Shaw wondered why Ruskin should be treated as a guest of honour. 'What are you taking to Palestine anyhow?' he asked.

'Cigarettes,' said Ruskin. 'Terrific cake, Mum.'

'All that petrol to fly cigarettes?' It was Shaw again. 'I'd have thought the world could find better uses for its petrol.' And he waved aside the offer of a piece of cake and began to fill his black briar pipe.

Mrs Shaw didn't want any more arguments. 'Anyway,' she said reassuringly, 'Mr Strachey says bread rationing won't last long.'

Ruskin took another bite of cake and said, 'The way this Government's going on we'll have him and Ernie Bevin begging rice from the Burmese.'

'And you'd do better flying rice than fags.' Shaw liked to have the last word, and it was nearly time for Ruskin to set off back to the airfield.

The Dakota came down the morning sky in bright sunshine. It had been one of their smoothest trips and conditions were perfect. Clear blue sky. A gentle tail wind. And the Dakota running as if she were brand new.

'Should see Rome any minute,' Ruskin said.

Witney threw him a quick look from the right hand seat. 'If we'd any nous we'd go and see the Coliseum, watch the bints on the Via Veneto, find a spaghetti joint, pick up a crate of Chianti, and scarper back home.'

Ruskin turned to McEvoy, who was staring ahead from between them for a first glimpse of the eternal city. 'Our gentleman flier's been ruined by the lush life of the officers' mess, Mac. I always said two-and-a-half ringers and above should stay as penguins. Safe on the deck where they can do least harm.'

'Bints on the Via Veneto?' said McEvoy, daydreaming.

'See?' Witney winked at Ruskin. 'Some of us know what's important.'

As the banter rambled on they saw the city in the morning sun and began their approach. The sun's reflections glared at them off the hot concrete. Ruskin brought Vera Lynn in to a perfect landing and as arranged sought the south-west corner of the airfield. It was remote and deserted. Nothing moved. And Ruskin's mind went back to that first landing in India when the erks were on strike. The south-west corner of the airfield was hot, sand-coloured, and without any obvious signs of life. Ruskin brought the Dakota to a stop and they went down through the hold and pushed open the door. A wave of hot air greeted them, but nothing else. Witney raised his arms as if he were about to make a speech and called, 'Friends, Romans, Countrymen . . .'

'Can't be the sun,' McEvoy said to Ruskin. 'He's had none yet.' He jumped down, laid the palm of his left hand on the concrete and said, 'If we'd kept a few eggs we could have fried 'em.' In the distance the eternal city shimmered in the heat haze and the three men scanned the empty landscape for signs of movement. It was some moments before Witney was the first to spot a small dustcloud which gradually took the shape of a jeep skeltering towards them. It was sand-coloured like everything else, and it contained only the driver, a flustered Italian of about thirty wearing Italian Army desert kit stripped of its insignia. His hair was jet black and his arms and legs deep brown from his service across the Med. He had a wide scar on his right forearm where a bullet had picked a track and there was oil on his hands. His olive eyes were large and round and nervous.

'Captain, I am sorry,' he apologized to Witney. His basic

English had an American accent. 'I am on the other side. Of the field. Is mistake.'

'He's the skipper,' Witney indicated Ruskin.

'I am sorry again,' the Italian said, this time to Ruskin. 'Please. You come.' He gestured towards the battered, dust-filmed jeep. Ruskin looked unsure.

'Is OK.' The eyes were uneasy and urgent.

'Is not OK,' Ruskin said firmly, with an eye on the Dak. It would be the height of daftness to leave a valuable load of cigarettes in an open dump like this.

'Is much OK,' the Italian pressed, pointing to another dustcloud coming their way. This one took shape as a clapped-out US Army truck with a faded white star on the bonnet. Its canvas top was ripped and holed and when it stopped hot water dripped from its radiator onto the concrete. It came right up to them as McEvoy, with a skin too sensitive to take hot sun, took shelter under the port wing. A lithely-built man in khaki shirt, shorts, ankle socks and sandals jumped down from the passenger's side. He wore a smile and his right hand was outstretched in greeting.

It was the rabbi.

He reassured Ruskin that it was safe to leave the Dakota. They piled into the jeep and the rabbi took them to a roadside spaghetti house amid the rubble of war. Their table was already laid with two bottles of Chianti and plates and forks and glasses, two of them chipped.

The rabbi had a kosher dish while they had the spaghetti.

Ruskin was still suspicious. 'I'd still have gone for Malta,' he said. 'I know Luqa.'

The rabbi was in high spirits. His smile disclosed a row of white teeth that Ruskin thought were so perfect they might be false. They were the rabbi's own. 'No refuelling snags here, my friend,' the rabbi said. 'We have friends.'

'Mine are at Luqa,' Ruskin said. 'We'd have had no problems with a fill-up.'

Again that secretive smile. 'I'm buying the fuel, remember. And I have a nice arrangement here.'

All this time Witney had been studying the rabbi, and he was jumpy. 'Rabbi?' he said. 'Couldn't it be a bit dodgy in Haifa for us?'

'You will be well cared for,' the rabbi said, flashing a glance at Ruskin. 'As I've assured Captain Ruskin.'

He had a way of making Witney feel guilty when all his instincts told him he had no need to be. 'Let me make it clear, rabbi,' he said. 'I'm not anti-semitic.'

'No, nobody is,' the rabbi smiled.

'Believe me,' Witney said. 'But how can you justify your people murdering our lads out there?'

The rabbi shook his head solemnly. 'I can't,' he said. 'I can't. It's a terrible problem. It is my people's homeland.'

'I mean our lads who're being knocked off, they've been in a war for your people,' Witney said. His pale face was full of suppressed anger.

The rabbi impaled Witney with a stare. '*Both* my peoples. I'm as British as you are, Squadron Leader.'

Nothing broke the silence except the sound of the unshielded fan and the ex-Army generator stuttering away outside. It was some time before the rabbi opened a zip satchel and brought out two creased photographs. He handed one to Ruskin, asking him to pass it round. It showed a young RN rating who, on closer inspection, turned out to be the rabbi. On his rating's cap was the tag, 'HM Submarines'. The other photograph was of a Royal Navy submarine, grey and sinister, as it began to dive in a heavy sea.

'Your sub?'

The rabbi nodded.

'I never knew they had padres on subs,' McEvoy said, peering at the portrait photograph.

The mysterious smile played round the rabbi's lips. 'I made one condition when I joined. Submarines – or I'd volunteer for the Army. So they took me.'

'As a padre?' McEvoy asked in surprise.

'Torpedoman,' the rabbi said simply. And he poured

them more Chianti. Ruskin planted a hand firmly over his glass as he checked his watch.

'Let's get back,' he said on impulse, feeling uneasy. 'I want to see that refuelling.'

'They'll nearly have done it by now,' the rabbi said confidently. 'Seven hundred gallons. Main tanks full. Auxiliary tanks a hundred and fifty each. You'll make Haifa on five hundred and fifty.'

They were surprised to find him so genned-up. He carefully put the photographs away and tugged a wad of lira from his breast pocket. He checked off several of the notes without actually counting and left them on the table. He insisted on driving them back to the Dakota. He drove hard, his foot down the whole way across the rubble and the pitted concrete.

An ex-Italian Air Force bowser was pulling away when they got back to the Dakota. The truck had already gone leaving a large oil smear on the concrete. As they left the jeep the rabbi went round with Ruskin as he made his external checks. He then shook hands with each of them and wished them a good trip.

From the cockpit Ruskin and Witney saw him take the wheel of the jeep and, with a final hectic wave, drive off. 'OK,' Ruskin said, and they were about to begin their cockpit checks when there was a shout from McEvoy behind them.

'Hey, hold it!' McEvoy yelled. He had been on his way back to the cockpit after shutting the cargo door when he saw that the freight distribution marks he'd chalked on the fuselage floor were no longer where they were in relation to the load. He'd then taken a closer look at the crates. They weren't the same. 'Come and have a shufti,' he called to Ruskin and Witney. He pointed a finger at the chalk marks. 'My loading marks are nearly covered. They weren't before. And those crates are made of heavier wood.' His face was a question mark. Ruskin nodded. McEvoy picked up a crowbar wedged between the crates, brought out a hammer, and forced one of the crates open.

It was stuffed with neatly-packed Sten guns and Sten parts and magazines. There was a whiff of fresh oil and new metal. Ruskin made quickly for the cockpit and looked out through the windscreen. All he could see was a receding dustcloud thrown up by the rabbi's jeep. He went back to the hold, where Witney and McEvoy had cracked open a second crate. It was a mix of second-hand Bren guns and more new Stens. Ruskin felt the sweat run down his chest and upper arms. Witney's pale face had gone white. McEvoy felt choked.

Witney made a helpless gesture towards the crates. 'I say we turf out the lot fast and beat it back home.'

Ruskin said nothing. His eyes were on those Stens.

'Our all-up weight was only a couple of thousand pounds inside the limit with the fags,' McEvoy said. 'But this stuff.' He took out a Sten as if weighing it in his hands.

'Don't touch the stuff,' Witney warned. 'Fingerprints.' And as McEvoy wiped the Sten with an oily rag, Witney gazed accusingly at Ruskin and added, 'I'm not having our lads' blood on my hands.'

If Ruskin had harboured doubts in those first few moments, he had none now. There was nothing to say the Brens and Stens were for use against British forces. He'd heard of a defence force being formed by some Palestine Jews, and nobody was saying they were in the same league as the terrorist gangs. He put this to Witney and McEvoy.

'If you believe that, you'll believe Jews are Arabs and this lot only fire blanks.' Witney sounded bitter.

Ruskin ran a check on McEvoy. The little Scot stayed impassive. He'd stay loyal, Ruskin was sure of that. He went up for'ard and brought Witney's overnight holdall and placed it on one of the crates under Witney's nose. 'We'll pick you up on the way back,' Ruskin said as if he were addressing a lower mortal. 'That's if you've not scrounged a lift from the flying nannies.'

Witney made no move to pick up the holdall. He just fixed Ruskin with a look of glassy disapproval.

'You didn't bring mine,' McEvoy said.

It shook Ruskin, but he covered up. 'Never thought you'd want it, but all right.' He turned towards the cockpit.

'Shouldn't we think it out, Jack?' McEvoy urged.

'I've done my thinking,' Ruskin snapped. 'You with me or not?'

'I don't like it,' McEvoy said.

'Who does?' Ruskin was in no mood for compromise and gave McEvoy a few moments to see sense.

Presently McEvoy shrugged. 'OK,' he said. 'But I still don't like it.'

Ruskin turned to Witney. 'If you'd jump down, sir, we'll pass your luggage. Sorry we can't supply a batman. Or chaperone.'

Witney came close to hitting the towering Ruskin. His eyes were icy. 'If we were still in,' he said, 'I'd have you put under close arrest.'

'That's your trouble,' Ruskin said with contempt. 'You can't believe we're the masters now.' It was a phrase Ruskin had heard some Labour MP use after the election. He urged Witney to move to the cargo door and told Mac to shut it after Witney had got out.

Witney jumped down and Mac tossed him the holdall.

'He could be right, Pete,' McEvoy said. 'And who's to say this stuff's not going to be used in self-defence by the Jews. Not against our lads? And the Jews have had a bad enough time these last few years.'

Witney took in the inhospitable sandy landscape, the distant strange city in the heat haze. He had not much more than five pounds on him and he was too proud to ask for a loan from McEvoy. He stood under the hot sun for a few moments as McEvoy kept the door open.

'What's keeping you?' It was Ruskin, yelling from the cockpit.

Witney threw his holdall inside then climbed back.

'Just this time,' McEvoy said. 'We'll not let him make a habit of it.'

Witney went po-faced back to the right-hand seat in the cockpit. Ruskin eyed him coldly and said sardonically, 'Pre-take-off checks, Squadron Leader?'

And Witney led them into the routine.

They took off into that innocently blue sky, got to their cruising height of 6,000 feet and said not a word to each other the whole way across the Mediterranean.

Jennie leapt to her feet when the phone rang, but Shaw said, 'It's not him, it's for me.' All evening she had hoped against hope for a call from Ruskin. She wasn't sure he'd even reached Rome let alone pressed on for Haifa. His long absences made her edgy. She had planned to go for a walk in the park and take advantage of the warm June evening, but had stayed in on a hunch that the call would come through. She looked into the fire in the grate – Shaw wasn't happy even on summer nights without a fire – and heard him on the phone in the hall. 'Four three one six . . . Oh hello, Tom. Can you make it then? . . . That's grand . . . Certainly, lad, any time. I've a bottle of pale in the sideboard . . . Yes, that's grand. Bye.'

Jennie had an idea what it was all about. She went through to the kitchen where her mother was washing up at the old sink with its stone basin, and plugged in the iron ready to do some of Ruskin's shirts.

Shaw came in, smugly stuffing his pipe with that scented tobacco. 'Tom Harwood,' he enthused with a glance at Jennie. 'The lad who was with me at Austin's and then went to work for the council markets department. Got demobbed this week. Came to see me yesterday. Specially. Fine lad, head screwed on right, could be running the market in a few years. Or maybe bigger ones. Manchester or Bradford, I shouldn't wonder.' He paused and tucked the tobacco firmly into the bowl. 'You know what? He finished up a lieutenant in the Navy. Had his own ship.'

It was too much for Jennie. 'It must have been very small,' she said.

'It was a tank landing craft. He'll make a good catch for somebody, if you ask me.'

Mrs Shaw was no less irritated than Jennie at Shaw's clumsy attempts to deflect Jennie from Ruskin to some more orthodox lad. 'Nobody is asking you,' she said, going over a dinner plate with a dish rag.

Shaw ignored her and looked straight at Jennie. 'Used to know him once, didn't you?'

'Vaguely,' Jennie said, bored.

'I asked him round for a glass.'

'Not tonight?' Mrs Shaw said disapprovingly. 'Not now?'

'He'll be round in half an hour.'

'Oh Dad,' Mrs Shaw scolded. 'The front room's not tidy.'

Shaw lit his pipe and spoke smugly through his clenched teeth. 'He'll not mind taking us as he finds us.'

Mrs Shaw's hand went to her mouth in consternation. 'But if he was a lieutenant . . . ?'

Jennie's eyes blazed at Shaw. 'You could always meet him in the backyard,' she said.

Less than twenty-five minutes later, Harwood turned up – a fresh-faced and modest 24-year-old with a shy manner, very correctly dressed in the best demob suit Shaw had so far seen, even if it was a chalk stripe. Shaw made a big fuss of him and showed him through to the living room and poured him a pale ale. 'Mum . . . Jen,' he called.

In the kitchen Mrs Shaw carefully wiped her hands while Jennie took no notice. 'We'd best go in,' Mrs Shaw whispered.

Jennie shook her head and stayed ironing as Mrs Shaw went through.

Shaw was raising his glass to Harwood. 'Cheers, lad, you're safe back and that's what counts.'

The fresh face cracked into a big innocent smile. 'I'd not have minded another year or two in the Navy, but there it is.'

'You know Mrs Shaw, don't you, Tom?'

'Oh yes, we have met.' He offered his hand. 'Mrs Shaw.'

'It was in Frank's office,' Mrs Shaw remembered, weighing up the lad. He did look very eligible. 'You've grown up so much.'

Jennie couldn't take any more of the selection committee. Either she could stay where she was, and hear the over-polite chat, or she could nip out through the backyard, or she could go and put a jumper on and take a walk. Why shouldn't she go through? She put the iron off and went through.

Tom Harwood's face lit up, all interest, taking in the dancer's legs and the small firm breasts and the sexy walk.

Shaw got the wrong message. 'Our Jen,' he said with a hint of modest pride. 'I know you two have met.'

'The bride was given away by her father,' Jennie thought, and the very idea made her mad. 'Hello, Jennie,' she heard Harwood say, and she caught a glimpse of his mouth, and she thought he was a bit like a ventriloquist's dummy. 'Glad you're safe back, Tom,' she said, gliding past him.

'Jen?' It was Shaw, all reproof.

She turned on her way to the door. 'Can't stay,' she said. 'I'm late already.'

'Late?' Shaw said.

'Very.'

And she went out, closing the door behind her.

The airport at Haifa was all shadows. Men worked hectically in the half-light from the moon. Ruskin had never seen men beaver away like this, not even in the run-ups to the drops in Normandy and Arnhem and across the Rhine. And these were men whose faces he could hardly make out. They merged with the night. He could make out the vague shapes of the crates as they were swiftly transferred from the Dakota to a procession of small trucks, mainly 15-cwts and also a few jeeps.

It was creepy and chilling.

They had brought in the Dakota by dead reckoning, without any radio aids and by the light of the half moon and torches held by unseen people.

Now the anonymous hosts were everywhere, buzzing like night-ants, unloading the crates from the Dak, loading them into the vehicles which rolled in one by one as if from nowhere.

And those who weren't working carried arms.

Ruskin stood with a swarthy thickset Jew of early middle age in an open-necked shirt who gave a stream of orders in a calm voice in Hebrew. Nearby was his signalman with an infantryman's signals pack and a headset. Witney was inside the hold supervising the unloading and McEvoy kept a beady eye on the unloaders to make sure no damage was done to the Dakota in the rush.

The middle-aged leader shot a glance at his radio operator, who gave him a thumbs-up sign. 'No sign yet,' said the leader. He had been counting the crates as they came off. 'Another three.'

Witney jumped down and stood by Ruskin. 'I don't know about you, but it's making me feel ill.'

'There's some bicarb in the first aid box,' Ruskin said, less controlled than he tried to look. His nerves were on edge. He expected the British Army to pour in any minute. He had visions of the Dakota being left absolutely u.s. with some idiot going berserk with a Sten gun. There was a Wild West feel about the scene. And yet there was this efficiency, this control. Ruskin couldn't work out why the leader had said there were only three more crates to shift. There were about ten still aboard. The third was coming off now and Ruskin could see McEvoy inspecting the interior of the hold for damage to the fuselage. One of the unloaders – dark and bright of eye with biceps rippling under his bush shirt – threw McEvoy an understanding wink as he guided a crate of Brens down to waiting hands.

It went aboard a 15-cwt truck.

The leader's shadowed lips parted into a very white smile. He shook Ruskin's hand with both of his, and Ruskin noticed he wasn't even sweating. His eyes flashed with gratitude. 'Our many thanks,' he said. And he was gone into the night. A jeep revved in the darkness, and the remaining unloaders, silent shadows, climbed into jeeps and trucks. And they too disappeared.

'Hey, for Christ's sake,' Ruskin yelled, and his voice shattered the silence in this busy and bizarre landscape. 'What is this?' One truck was left, and it reversed up to the Dak's cargo door. The driver and the three unloaders shone inspection lamps on the Dakota and its hold. Then the unloaders, one middle-aged Palestinian Jew and two youngsters, casually unloaded the remaining crates.

Ruskin and Witney went back into the hold, where McEvoy was minutely peering at the fuselage. 'They've not been all that careful,' he pronounced. 'But there's nothing serious.'

'And they've most of 'em pissed off and left us holding the baby,' Witney said. His voice shook, and so did his hands. It was eerie. The three unloaders went on with their work as if they had all the time in the world. One threw Ruskin a knowing look, another winked at McEvoy.

And then there was the sound of vehicles approaching at speed and the sound of British voices. Very British. 'Hold everything and stay just where you are,' was the first intelligible call. Ruskin reckoned it came from a British Army major. He was right.

Two British Army sergeants leapt into the hold with Sten guns. The major – dapper, pale and with a bully's face – climbed up after them. 'Hold everything and don't move,' he commanded. He picked on Witney. 'You the captain of this aircraft?'

Usual bloody class-error, Ruskin thought, as Witney pointed a finger at him.

'Ah yes,' said the major. 'Now, Captain. What have we this time?' He was working out Ruskin's status in the class set-up. He hadn't quite made up his mind whether he was a pukka chap or a prole. And only now did Ruskin see that the major had a classical moustache – blond.

Ruskin was sweating like hell but his reply was measured. 'This time? It's our first time.' He could brazen it out. 'Cigarettes,' he said.

'I'll see your ship's papers,' the major said, having decided that Ruskin was a beer rather than a whisky man. 'Loadsheet. Cargo manifest. Flight plan. Etcetera. Usual bumph.'

'Fetch the major our docs, Mac,' Ruskin told McEvoy. He wanted Witney to hang about. He might be useful in the presence of this class lunatic.

As McEvoy went for'ard, Ruskin saw that the two sergeants had been joined by two more who were prising open the remaining crates with bayonets.

'So who are you flying for?' the major purred.

Ruskin put a finger into his own chest.

'I mean who are your employers?'

The sergeants foraged on. And Ruskin had an idea there were a lot more soldiers around the Dakota. 'I'm an independent,' he said without a blink. 'I run it.'

The major had him sorted out now. A Northern prole. 'Oh dear,' he scoffed. 'One of our bandit chappies, eh?' His narrow eyes twinkled. He ran a chubby hand over his moustache. 'Put two behind bars last week. Always had doubts about the Raff. Rum lot they recruited. Can't face an honest day's work in civvy street, so they'll do anything to keep flying. And by anything I do mean anything.'

A right gauleiter, Ruskin thought, as the posse of sergeants went on prising open the crates. Close by, a bayonet went into a crate and the sergeant prised the top off. They all looked now – Ruskin, Witney, the sergeant and the major – and the crate was full of cigarette cartons. The sergeant opened one. Out spilled cigarette packs. Players. In twenties.

Ruskin gulped in relief and wondered if his Adam's

apple had disclosed his let-off. Witney was enduring that pain he got behind the eyes. And McEvoy, who had just come up with the documents, murmured a silent prayer of thanks. Sweat was pouring off him, though the Haifa night was cool.

The sergeants prised open two more crates to disclose nothing more – or less – lethal than cigarettes.

Ruskin fixed the major with his cold look. 'Help yourself, major,' he invited. 'On the house.'

The major pointed a warning finger at Ruskin.

'Don't do that, Major,' Ruskin said, and exaggerated his northern accent. 'It's supposed to be rude to point. I wouldn't know. I'm just a lad from up north.' The major's blood pressure was on the point of hitting danger level, but Ruskin couldn't resist. 'What's the daily rate for a major these days? Sir?'

'We've not finished yet,' said the major, though his confidence was slipping.

'Help yourself,' Ruskin said, grandly sweeping his hand over the remaining crates. 'But make it quick. Time's money. And we're not on Army pensions.'

Even Witney had to marvel at his nerve. And the major was getting so much on his tits that he didn't care a sod just now about those weapons that had been so swiftly moved into the night.

Ruskin was standing at his full six-foot-two with his arms folded across his chest. He dwarfed the podgy major. 'I mean we want to get back home and you've some catching up to do in the Mess, no doubt . . .' He made a drinking mime. And he knew the major would like to put him in handcuffs and daren't.

The Dakota's hold was full of cool night air as the major finally nodded confirmation to the sergeants that they need do no more prising.

Ten minutes later crates of jaffas were being put aboard.

It was a relief to Ruskin, Witney and McEvoy when they got Vera Lynn off the Haifa airfield and over the Med. They set course for the UK via Malta this time. They were all eating jaffas over Northern France with the Channel in sight when McEvoy picked up a news broadcast over the radio. The main item was about an attack by Jewish terrorists on the British HQ in Jerusalem. Thirty-nine people were dead and fifty-three missing.

They flew on, stunned.

CHAPTER 6

The white-out was total.

Snow blanketed the landscape as they began their approach into Garton. Ruskin stared out through the melting driven snow on the windscreen. He felt a bit queasy from the stench of the fish they had taken from Grimsby to London. One box remained aboard full of fresh herring which they aimed to share on landing. They loathed the fish run. But it was important to take any jobs that were going, though Witney had long ago won his point about trips to Haifa. They had been to Palestine twice since the arms run, re-fuelling in Rome, but their cargoes had been innocent machine parts and other goods on the outward run and fruit on the returns. Witney had also prevailed on Ruskin, after a near-disastrous return from France in nil visibility with a duff radio, to take on another crewman. Alby Clarke was at the radio now. Alby was not short for Albert but Albino. He had prematurely white hair. He'd done twenty-eight bombing trips over Germany and nothing would induce him to talk of it. A very private man, able and stubborn, he was logging a weather report.

Witney gazed at the frozen landscape below and the scurrying snow. He shivered and said, 'Our timing's a bit short of perfect. We spend half last summer on runs to the Med, the old girl hot as an oven, and now we play eskimos at angels six.'

'Stop binding,' Ruskin said easily, trying to pick out landmarks in the white desert. 'It's Rome tomorrow.'

'That's if the fuel bowser can get through,' McEvoy said pessimistically. It was the worst winter of the century and the country was paralyzed.

'Right,' Witney agreed. 'The miners can't even get to the pits, so how do the bowsers get to us?'

'We're an essential service, didn't you know?' The irony tickled Ruskin that at least some of the bandits could move stuff across the nation. They'd had a lousy deal from the Labour Government since the war ended.

'Mr Attlee doesn't,' Witney shot back.

McEvoy recalled that in the pub in Grimsby the night before he'd heard people saying the Government aimed to ground all independents.

'They've enough on their plates with the pits they've just nationalized,' Ruskin said. 'And they're going to need all the snoopers to see folk don't use electricity in the home in restricted hours.'

'Makes you think,' McEvoy said. 'A hundred quid fine or three months in clink just for lighting a fire.'

Ruskin chuckled. 'Who won the war, daddy? They'll have us for breathing next.' He could make out St Michael's steeple now and the village and the hangar.

They began their pre-landing checks.

In the Nissen hut Jennie heard Vera Lynn on her approach. She poured coke into the mouth of the stove watched by Ernie Cade and his driver-bodyguard, an ex-commando with tattoos on the backs of his navvy's hands.

'Harold would have done that,' said Cade, nursing an enamel mug of tea and trying to avoid contact between his lips and the rusted rim. He was wearing a British Army officer's warm and ex-RAF flying gloves and wool-lined boots against the Arctic conditions.

'I never heard him volunteer,' Jennie said.

'Harold.' Cade snapped his fingers and the bodyguard made to take the big scuttle from Jennie.

'It's done now,' she said. She had no time for Cade or his henchmen, and she had a clear idea of why he had come.

He studied her through those small sharp eyes. 'You always keep an eye on things while Jack's away, Mrs Ruskin?'

'There's always someone here, Mr Cade.' Anything less than that would have invited theft. 'And my name's Miss Shaw.'

'What, still?' Cade smirked as if shocked. 'They put up with that sort of thing north of Watford, do they?'

She ignored him and began to make up the metal-framed standard RAF bed.

'He doesn't make you sleep here as well?' Cade was only stirring.

'He doesn't make me do anything,' Jennie said. 'But there's always someone here on watch.'

Cade feigned dismay. 'Last time you were here you gave me the royal treatment. Sugar in my char.'

'We're short of sugar,' Jennie said formally. 'And milk. And tea. Everybody is.'

'You should've told me,' Cade said. 'I'd have brought you enough to last the winter.'

'I've no doubt.' She thought the big spiv should be in jail.

'Off your high horse, miss. I didn't invent the black market.'

'No, you just run it.'

The din from the Dakota's twin Wasps drowned any further talk.

Ruskin eased her down on to the packed snow, held her slight skid and brought her round the peri-track. He went into the Nissen hut leaving Witney, McEvoy and Alby to tuck Vera into the hangar. Jennie kissed him formally as he took in Cade and the ex-commando. He'd seen Cade's big Humber, an ex-Army staff car, outside. 'Some for us, the rest for the lads,' he said, with a glance at the box of fish he'd brought in.

'I heard you were doing the wet fish run,' Cade said, working out just how hard up Ruskin was. 'Some of the other bandits reckon it doesn't pay.'

'I knew you'd be here,' Ruskin said.

Cade smiled. 'And you pong a bit, son. I was told you'd be here two hours' back. So we'll get on with it, eh?' He moved his head to indicate Jennie. 'I don't mind if she stays. Not the others, though.'

'Oh, she stays,' Ruskin said firmly. 'You bet your last

miserable fiver she stays.' He moved to the door and held it open, inviting Cade to talk outside.

The blast of freezing air had Cade buttoning up his officer's warm. 'Not out there?' he protested. 'In that?' The snow was falling heavily.

'We can go in the hangar.'

'That's worse than a fridge in a prefab. And I never do my best thinking in the cold.'

'Great,' Ruskin said. And he insisted.

They crossed to the hangar, muffled against the fierce cold. Witney and McEvoy were kicking the heavy towbar into place on the Dakota's tail wheel strut.

Cade was irritated by the cold. 'When I came here I was all set to pull you out of your nosedive. Now I've a mind to let you crash.'

Ruskin took in Witney and McEvoy heaving on the towbar. He turned to Cade's ex-commando who was following some steps behind. 'Hey, Muscles,' Ruskin called. 'How about some light training?' He pointed to Witney and McEvoy and the towbar.

The ex-commando wanted to crown him.

But Cade said, 'Why not, Harold? Help keep you warm.'

And as the ex-commando joined Witney and McEvoy in moving Vera Lynn inside the hangar, Ruskin faced Cade and said, 'I told you. I'll settle inside a week.' He hadn't a clue where he would find the money. Cade would have to wait perhaps much longer than that.

'You haven't got a week, son.'

They went into the hangar and stood by the trestle table on which lay loadsheets and fit for flight certificates and greasy manuals with Dakota spares as paperweights.

'We all need cash flow, son,' Cade said, his gloved hands deep in the pockets of the khaki warm. 'Even Ernie Cade needs cash flow. And I'm having to spend too much time chasing you heroes with empty wallets. And what happens? This.' He meant the icy weather. 'I miss thirty thousand Army surplus paraffin heaters and that makes me feel unwell. I'd have been on three hundred and fifty per cent profit and I'd have flogged 'em in a day. So do me a favour, son, before I am compelled to put you in the hands of the receiver. And I don't mean the Great Receiver in the Sky.' He was running an appreciative eye over the Dakota as it was towed into the hangar. Alby had joined the other three now. 'I'll say this. You've looked after the old bird.' He managed to say it with menace. 'So I'll give you a price you can't refuse.'

'I just refused.'

'And don't be cocky with me, son. You're deeper in than you think. I hear tell you've not been paying your crew. And I see you got one more and that's not businesslike in your circumstances.'

'Wireless op,' Ruskin said.

'You got one already,' Cade said of McEvoy, who was busy on the towbar swopping vicious looks with the ex-commando.

'Mac's an engineer. He remustered and never finished his training as a Wop.'

'You're an engineer,' Cade said.

'Not in Mac's class.'

'You've not recruited a wet nurse as well,' Cade sneered.

'Listen,' Ruskin flared. 'You weren't up there when our rudder cables broke and we were in ten-tenths and needed radio nav *and* repairs at the same time.' He was pissed off with spivs who had never flown but had money.

'I'm not in the thrills and spills game, son,' Cade purred. 'That's for you boy scouts. And it ain't Baden Powell you have to please, it's Ernie Cade.'

Ruskin sized him up, sensing his capacity for destruction. 'I'm making sure the Dak stays in one piece and that should please you. I mean she is half yours.'

Cade took off a glove and began to pick his teeth. 'You looked at our agreement lately?' he asked.

'I'm a bit busy to be going over old bits of bumph.'

'Do yourself a favour,' Cade urged.

Ruskin brought out his wallet. 'I owe you three hundred and fifty quid. A hundred for now, OK?'

Cade shook his head. 'Where've you been, son? I know you don't go in for lawyers' bumph, but if you still have a copy of our agreement in here . . .' He pulled over a cardboard box on the trestle table. 'There was one in here, I know.'

'It's in the office now,' Ruskin said.

Cade leaned with his backside on the table. His eyes were colder than the weather. His voice was deliberate and precise. 'I, Ernie Cade Limited, retained the option to change the rate of interest on your loan, without notification, after six months. I exercised that option, son. I know you're flying your arse off, and not quite with us, but you can forget twenty-five per cent.'

'So you upped it to twenty-seven and a half. Thirty?'

'No, son, I made it a nice round hundred per cent. So you get down to the public library and take a look at *Mathematics For The Million*.'

'What's your middle name?' Ruskin said. 'Shylock?'

Cade tut-tutted. 'I could stomach you bandits if only you'd get the message. It's a cold world, son. Only fit for men with balls.'

The Dakota was safe in the hangar now. Witney and Alby moved off to the Nissen hut for tea with Jennie. McEvoy, with an eye on Cade and the ex-commando, chose to stay until the ex-commando also moved out. Cade got the message, gave his blessing with a sweep of the hand, and the ex-commando went out with McEvoy just behind him.

Cade was taking in the Dakota spares Ruskin had picked up over the past six months. 'You've been acquiring. Buying for the Christmas tree. What with?' He paused. 'I'll give you three thousand cash for your fifty per cent share in the Dak, and cancel all interest on the debt. How's that?'

'They should have called you Nuffield. Vera's worth ten grand on the market today. And about a million to me.'

'You're dicing, Ruskin. And you dice with Ernie Cade at your cost.'

'I never gamble. They couldn't get me in a game of brag in the Raff and I rate all bookies as vampires.'

'I'm giving you one minute, son.'

Ruskin rode the threat. 'Your chauffeur's waiting outside,' he said of the ex-commando. 'And I'm not leaving this hangar before you do.' He was clenching and unclenching his strong fists.

Cade thought it prudent to leave.

Ruskin and McEvoy watched him driven off by the ex-commando, who seemed to be taking mental photographs of McEvoy. Back in the hut they rejoined Jennie, Witney and Alby round the stove where Witney was asking Jennie how bad was the financial position. 'Cade doesn't come out of London in this weather except to collect.'

'He knows the weather's grounded a lot of the bandits who owe him money,' she said. 'He's foreclosed on three operators from round here alone.'

'Pound of flesh time?' Witney asked Ruskin.

Ruskin brushed off the crisis. 'You look like a bunch of erks on sick parade,' he joked.

'It's certainly not pay parade,' Witney replied.

On the instant Ruskin brought out his faded wallet – a present from his mother on his twenty-fifth birthday during the war. He took out its entire contents and laid the notes on the RAF bed. Witney, McEvoy and Alby found the moment too embarrassing as Ruskin threw a look at Jennie that made it clear that there was not nearly enough money there. She fetched her gas mask case, which she used as a handbag, and got her purse out.

It was all too much for Witney. 'Don't be silly. I don't know about Mac and Alby.'

They shook their heads in rejection of the cash.

'My grasping landlady's away at her sister's till Tuesday,' McEvoy said. 'And if we're away again first thing tomorrow I need nothing for beer tonight, either.'

'We are,' Ruskin told them.

'In this muck?' Witney was looking at the heavy snow beyond the caked windows.

They were ignoring the money.

Ruskin knew what it meant to Alby, who had a wife and kids. 'Come on, Alby. I know Betty gets upset about asking shopkeepers to put it on the slate.'

'We owe nothing to anybody,' Alby said simply.

Ruskin would press them no more. There was work to fix. Their load for Rome should have been with them by now. It had clearly been held up on the snowbound roads. Jennie explained that the client had phoned to say it would be with them in another hour or so.

'I should have written a penalty clause in the contract,' Ruskin said. 'If there'd been a bloody contract.' He turned to Alby. 'What was that last weather forecast? Or weren't you tuned in?'

'Frost today and tonight,' Alby said. 'Light snow. Very cold.'

'So don't any of you go using electricity in restricted hours,' Ruskin said as a joke.

'We burn logs,' Witney said in his best accent.

'Landed gentry,' Ruskin said.

'I have a gas fire,' McEvoy said. 'A wee one.'

They all looked at Alby and Ruskin asked, 'You don't just get between the sheets with a hot water bottle?' He wondered how the hell they were coping.

'An old pot one,' Alby said, straight faced. 'Fawn coloured with a brown top on.' There would be no more from him on the subject. He turned to check a W/T set.

'OK,' Ruskin said with finality. 'O-eight-hundred in the morning, even if you all have to get here on skates.' He peeled off his flying jacket and helped himself to another mug of tea, making it clear he was staying.

'How about the loading when the stuff comes?' Witney asked.

'Clients' blokes,' Ruskin said.

'And the overnight guard on Vera?'

'All fixed,' Ruskin said with a sharp glance at Jennie.

'Who?' Witney insisted.

'Go easy with that electricity,' Ruskin advised. It was clear he had made his mind up.

'You mean you're not coming home?' Jennie had much to discuss with him.

'I'll get some grub sent over from the Raff guardroom,' Ruskin said, as if food were all that mattered.

Noting Jennie's dismay, Witney offered to drive her home.

'No thanks,' she said stiffly, and on impulse she put on her Land Army coat and set out.

'Jen?' Ruskin appealed. She paused in the open doorway with the snow flurries spotting her hair.

'I told Mum and Dad we'd be in for supper,' she said emptily. 'That's what we told them.'

Ruskin had the look of a wounded bear in a trap. 'I could get the Raff blokes to keep an eye on Vera and drive you home,' he struggled. 'But I'll not be able to stay to eat. I'll have to get right back.'

'I'll drive myself, thank you.' And Jennie's face was so full of hurt that Witney, McEvoy and Alby all volunteered to stay on guard over the Dakota.

She was having none of it. In spite of a final plea from Ruskin she went out to the car. It wouldn't start in the cold. Ruskin came out and got it going. She kissed him briefly and drove off with a lump in her throat.

McEvoy and Alby went off to their digs to get some sleep.

Witney hung about.

'Time you were off for some kip,' Ruskin said.

Witney fixed him with a stare. 'Cade using muscle, is he?'

'He doesn't even make me sweat.'

'He will. He's putting blokes like you out of business and collecting.'

'Not from me. Go and get some kip.'

Witney would not be put off. 'He's got you out on a wing and a bloody prayer, mate.'

'Your wages will be paid, Squadron Leader,' Ruskin said

dismissively, making a sign towards what McEvoy and Alby had left of the notes on the bed. 'Even if the Bank of England's pipes freeze up.' It was all bluster and he knew it.

'He's got you over a barrel, Jack. How much?'

'I'll see him away. We'll fly our arses off.'

'I'd rather we didn't.' The tone was very responsible.

'This isn't Group HQ, Squadron Leader. It's the bloody front line in Mr Attlee's socialist Jerusalem.'

Witney used a crowbar to clear heavy ash from the base of the stove. 'I could come in with a few smackers.' The offer was cautious. Ruskin took offence easily over such things. 'I have an aunt. Nice old girl.'

'God!' Ruskin said. 'Spare us.'

'She's not rich,' Witney went on. 'She's comfortable, and she'd like to set me up with a small house in Kingston, near where she is. There's one she has her eye on. It's going for two thousand quid. But she'll let me have the cash to find my own castle, if I prefer.' He stopped for a second. 'Or aircraft.'

'Aircraft?' Ruskin said. 'She never said that?'

'Not in so many words, no.' His eyes met Ruskin's. 'Cade'll bust you, chum. He's the biggest shit since Hitler.'

Ruskin was shaking his head.

'I can put in two-and-a-half grand now and get us all off the hook.'

On guard, Ruskin said, 'You're not trying to buy me out?'

'No,' Witney said. 'But I'd like a share in Vera.'

'When we first saw her you said she'd never get off the ground again.'

'Mistake,' Witney conceded.

Ruskin waved him away. 'Go and get some sleep, chum.'

The moment had come for Witney to lay it on the line. 'I know what you're planning. Overloads. Short cuts in maintenance. Fit-for-flight certificates that should never be signed and . . .'

Ruskin bridled. 'I brought in a wireless op at great expense to ease your mind.'

'After that trip you had no option. The greatest navigator since Columbus you may be, but you got us lost because we had no contact with beacons.' He hesitated, measuring the effect of his words. 'We'll do this Rome trip in three trips, not two. And I'll put up the ante to stall Cade.'

'I see the snag,' Ruskin said, dropping into the tatty chair with its torn fake hide and its stuffing hanging out.

'Right,' Witney said. 'I want a say in the way this business is run.'

Ruskin feigned sleep, cupping his head in his right hand.

Jennie drove the Standard 8 past the black Victorian villas on Highfield Road and parked outside one with a doctor's plaque on the sooted gatepost. She didn't get out right away. The surgery always filled her with trepidation, though she had not been near the doctor since she'd had a spell of migraine during the war.

She got out of the car, locked it, pulled her Land Army greatcoat together and made her way up the narrow dimly-lit drive, bent against the driving snow. The afternoon was barely over, yet night had set in, and it was bitter. She pressed the heavy white bell button and waited a while. A shadow appeared beyond the stained glass window of the door, which was opened by a middle-aged woman in a fair-isle cardigan. She had an enormous bosom and a spot on her chin from which sprouted a cluster of greying blonde hair.

Jennie gave her name.

The receptionist gazed at her over horn-rimmed glasses. 'Well, come in,' she said irritably. 'You're going to let the cold in.'

A grandfather clock in teak dominated the poorly-lit hall and gave the wrong time, and there was a tiny mahogany desk strewn with papers, a telephone and a diary which the receptionist began to check. 'I don't know the name,' she sniffed.

'I phoned from home first thing this morning,' Jennie said. 'The doctor answered himself.'

The receptionist looked up and a note of caution came into her crisp intolerant voice. 'Oh, you're on at home, are you? You must live this side of Preston Road?'

'No,' Jennie said. 'The other.'

The woman aimed an imperious finger at a door opposite. 'Wait in there, will you?'

Jennie remembered the room. Ill-lit, with a gas-fire popping on its lowest setting, it had dark mahogany chairs round the walls, a central table full of very old copies of *Punch* and *The Tatler*, and an unread copy of the *Daily Telegraph*. On the walls were old oil paintings, dead behind their aged varnish, and a bracket clock, its face unreadable, ticking away like doom. One step before the funeral parlour, Jennie thought, her eyes roving. the cowed and respectfully quiet people who spoke in whispers. These were the valiant Britons who'd just won World War 2, the war to end all wars, who had gone through hell to survive, and were now in the post-war Jerusalem. Some Jerusalem! They coughed and sneezed and there was snot on two of the kids' faces, and there was a young man with a crutch between his knees and a green beret on his lap sans its commando badge.

An anaemic-looking mother edged her child off a chair and beckoned Jennie. 'Here, love,' she offered. An elderly man further from the door frowned. 'She'll not jump the queue, will you, love?' the mother said to Jennie.

The elderly man said, 'We could all move up one then.'

And so they went through the motion of musical chairs, keeping their strict places on the rota. Jennie took the final chair at the end of the queue. She took in the snotty kids, the gas-fire, the shivers of three elderly patients, including the man who'd been worried about his place. Facing her on the brass-handled sideboard stood a notice which read:

NO SMOKING
NO SPITTING
NO ANIMALS
CHILDREN TO BE KEPT UNDER CONTROL

Jennie could not keep her eyes off that awful gas-fire as the doctor's class-riddled voice drifted in from the hall. 'No, Mrs Bradley, but you can come here if you have any more trouble.'

The mother said quietly, 'You've got to be half way to the cemetery before he'll visit.'

'Things will improve when they bring in the National Health,' said the elderly man.

Jennie was obsessed by the gas-fire. The mother leaned over and whispered, 'Irma Grise out there said it had to stay on low.'

Jennie went over and stooped on one knee, turning the tap up. The burners stuttered into greater life. Jennie came to her feet just as the door opened.

'Next now,' the receptionist ordered. And then she saw Jennie and the gas-fire on high. 'And what might you be doing? Turn it down at once.'

Jennie had met a battleaxe or two in the Land Army but none as nasty as this one. 'If we've not all got pneumonia now we soon will have,' she said, making no move to turn down the flame.

The receptionist brushed past her, only to find her path blocked by the ex-commando's crutch. She flounced out after the next patient, glaring at Jennie.

'How long have you been waiting, then?' Jennie asked the young mother.

'An hour, hour and a half.'

Jennie studied the pathetic creatures with all their ails and then made her mind up. 'Goodnight,' she said, and went into the hall, past the bad-tempered receptionist and out into the freezing night.

Back at home, Shaw was on his knees blowing his lungs

out to get the coal fire going in the grate as Mrs Shaw polished the table.

'You sure you're not lighting it in forbidden hours?' she asked.

'Forbidden?' The voice was indignant. 'We use less than most.'

'All the same, I don't want to see you in convicts' gear just for lighting a fire.'

'I've always wanted to see what it's like in Strangeways,' he said, striking another match. He burnt his forefinger. 'Damn!'

'I bet Stafford Cripps isn't going cold,' Mrs Shaw said, getting at Shaw's stolid loyalty to the government.

'He believes in austerity,' Shaw replied. 'And we'll have a good fire on when our Jen gets in.' He reckoned she hadn't looked too well lately. 'Going out to the aerodrome a day like this, she must be barmy.'

Mrs Shaw thought they were lucky to have Jen and Ruskin still staying with them after the way he'd told them to get out over all that flying to Haifa and giving what he called aid and comfort to terrorists.

'I didn't tell them to leave,' he said, still trying to get the fire going. 'I told him to.'

'Same thing,' Mrs Shaw said. 'Our Jen would never stay without him. Just to think. They might have been freezing in that dreadful Nissen hut if I'd not told Jack you never meant it.'

He tossed her a black look. 'Can't you see I'm trying to light this.'

Mrs Shaw liked to bait him. 'It said on the news it's back to the blackout tonight. The war over nigh on two years and they're making us go through that again.'

'You can hardly blame Mr Attlee for the worst winter this century.'

'Excuses,' Mrs Shaw pronounced. 'Anyway, thank God they're letting our Alan off the farm at last. He's paid his price for being a conchie.'

It was a taboo subject for Shaw. 'They were lifting

parsnips with pneumatic drills today,' he said as a diversion.

The fire came to life.

It was really blazing with Shaw sprawled out in front of it reading the evening paper when Jennie came in. 'I'd have thought he'd have had the decency to drive you back a night like this,' Shaw said.

Jennie warmed her hands at the fire. The last thing she wanted was another war of words over Ruskin.

'Did you hear me?'

'Yes, I heard,' she said resignedly and went through to the kitchen where Mrs Shaw was setting up the ironing board.

'You had us worried, Jen,' Mrs Shaw said. 'You think all sorts of things with these icy roads.'

Jennie pecked her on the cheek. 'Stop fretting, Mum.' She moved back to the door, saw that Shaw was deep in his paper, and closed the door slowly. Shaw noticed, but said nothing.

'I went to see the doctor, that's why I'm late,' she told Mrs Shaw.

'Whatever's the matter?' Mrs Shaw said. And when Jennie didn't reply, she added, 'Don't tell us you're pregnant?'

'I think I am,' Jennie said, taking her coat off.

'What does the doctor say?'

'Never saw him.' Her mood was defiant. 'I couldn't stand that waiting room. We treated cattle better in the Land Army. And that old faggot he's got for a receptionist.'

'Jen, for goodness' sake you should never be in this cold kitchen.' Mrs Shaw's face was a picture of worry. 'And what does Jack say? I mean we'll have to get the banns read.'

'No banns, no banners,' Jennie said, and her mouth was firm. 'And I don't want him told yet. Not that I know for sure myself.'

Mrs Shaw clapped a hand to her face as the gravity of the news sank in. 'God knows what your Dad's going to say. He'll have a fit. And he's at an age where anything could happen.'

'So we don't tell him,' Jennie said. 'He'd only start getting at Jack anyway.'

Mrs Shaw privately thought it was high time somebody did get at Jack. 'You'll have to see the doctor, love.'

'Not that jumped-up quack.'

'Jen, don't talk about our doctor like that.'

'He's not my doctor. Not any more.'

'I overheard that.' They whirled to find Shaw in the doorway, his paper under his arm. 'I always know when you two are up to something.' He tapped the door. 'You close it slowly. You always do just before my birthday. But unless I'm getting senile I think this is February and I'm not fifty-one till May.' He was weighing them up and they weren't sure what he'd overheard. 'Well, I've reckoned that doctor's got a bit above himself. Not like Doctor Nolan who brought you into this world.' He watched her. 'You ailing, lass?'

'I'm going down with the 'flu,' Jennie lied.

'Then you should have a mustard bath and get to bed with two hot water bottles.'

'I'll have some supper first,' Jennie said, opening the pantry door.

'Mum will see to that,' Shaw insisted. 'You'll come through and keep warm.' The phone had begun to ring and Jennie rushed past him to the hall. 'And if that's His Lordship I'll have a word. It's high time he started looking after you.'

Jennie felt excited as she took the phone and heard his voice. 'You can get back after all,' she said, relief all over her face. 'I'll bring the van over and pick you up.'

'You know I can't leave this place, love,' Ruskin said, his tone a touch spiky. 'I just wondered if you can dig out my tropical gear and bring it over first thing?'

It made Jennie suspicious. 'It won't be hot in Rome this time of year.'

'We're pushing on from there,' Ruskin told her. 'After

we've dropped the machine parts. Nice extra job.' He'd so far kept it quiet from all of them.

'Where to?'

Ruskin spread out his long legs either side of the stove as he lolled in the torn armchair. 'Oh, just over the Med.'

'Not Palestine, love.' Jennie was appalled. 'Not Haifa. You were lucky not to end up in prison last time, you were lucky to come out of it alive.'

Ruskin was suddenly alert. His head spun round. Witney had come in and was standing behind him as Ruskin collected himself and told Jennie, 'Luck's got nothing to do with it, love. See you in the morning, OK? I'd like to get off around O-nine-hundred at the latest.'

'I won't be there,' Jennie said, hurt and fearful. 'I won't.' And she hung up and saw Shaw with his elbow against the banister rail.

'So the silly young bugger's back gun-running?'

'He didn't say that,' Jennie said.

'You know very well. Running guns for those terrorists to use against our lads. No wonder he'll not put his head round our door.'

Jennie looked desperate. 'He's not running guns, so don't say it.'

'You don't know he's not.'

'Any more than you know he is.'

'You must be daft as well as blind.' Shaw was trying to make her out. Things were going on beyond his ken.

Jennie went past him through the living room to the kitchen. Her heart was thumping and she had lost her appetite.

In the Nissen hut Witney stood with his backside to the stove like some prosecuting counsel at the Old Bailey. 'So I'll ask again,' he persisted, his forehead lined with concern. 'Haifa?'

Ruskin tried again to put him off. 'You should be back at your digs in bed. I want you flying Vera most of tomorrow. I'll be half-knackered.'

Witney would not be moved. 'Change of plan on our

side, too,' he said with finality. 'Mac and Alby are coming back now as well. We'll all help with the loading and then we'll spread guard duty through the night, three hours apiece.'

'I see,' Ruskin said through a tight mouth. 'You've had a meeting? The National Union of Second Pilots and Allied Fliers?'

Witney folded his arms. 'That's it.'

'Your idea?'

Witney nodded, his pale face iron-hard.

'Our born leader, eh?' The voice was all scorn. 'Well, get this. I don't need your silver spoon contribution. You don't own this outfit, you don't own half of it, you don't own one bloody rivet.' The idea that they'd got together behind his back stung him.

Witney wouldn't give way. Gazing down at Ruskin he said, 'And we're not going to Haifa.'

'Off home now,' Ruskin said dismissively. 'And wrap up warm. I've some loading to get on with.'

Witney did not go home. He hung around until McEvoy and Alby had come back from supper and they joined Ruskin stacking crates into the Dakota. It had become almost a ritual now, this pre-flight battle between Ruskin and Witney, with Ruskin offering Witney his freedom and Witney refusing to go.

In the hold now Ruskin was checking each crate and its marked weight and making notes on a clipboard. It was so unlike him to be fussy Witney made a point of it to McEvoy. 'If he's being fussy about weights we must be near the bloody limit.'

'Beyond it, I reckon,' McEvoy said, his shrewd eyes missing nothing.

Witney went down the sloping hold to Ruskin and pointed to the clipboard. 'Kellett been reading the Riot Act?'

'I had a dream,' Ruskin taunted. 'I've become a law-abiding bandit. We must observe the regs.'

'You wouldn't observe a regulation if they held you down and put it in six foot letters in front of you.'

'You think nasty thoughts,' Ruskin said, checking another of the machine crates marked 'Rome'.

'You had a dream,' Witney said. 'I have a theory.'

'There's a marble statue of a bloke like you. The Thinker. Elbow on his knee, chin in hand. Squadron Leader Thinker.'

The bastard's good at insults, Witney thought, but he won't duck out of this. 'You're planning this drop in two trips not three,' he accused.

'I'm doing my arithmetic.' It was as if Witney weren't even there.

'And three into two will go.'

'Give a kilo or two.' He went on coolly checking the crates. 'And, Peter. You're the co-pilot not what they call a participating shareholder. Your job is to fly this, not work out policy.'

Witney snapped, 'You charge for three trips and do the drop in two. And then settle a bit off what you owe Cade.'

Ruskin idly murmured something about making Witney financial director of the one-plane airline.

'And then you work in a third run on the outward leg?' The question hung. 'A dirty job to Haifa?'

It was nearly one in the morning when they secured the last crates. Alby was first to take his turn on guard while the others went back to the hut for some kip before the morning start.

Witney was still sick with worry when he and Ruskin made a final check on the load just after breakfast. 'You don't seriously think we'll get off with this load in these conditions, do you? I had a good squint at it last night while you slept. If you're telling us our all-up weight's inside twenty-nine thousand pounds I say you're a liar.'

'Did I tell you that?' Ruskin asked, all innocence.

'No,' Witney replied. 'But you'd better say it soon.' And

he shut up abruptly. Kellett was coming aboard. Ruskin turned to see the slight Air Registration Board man brushing dust off his trousers where they'd touched the hold floor. He was all charm and morning-bright goodwill as he spoke of their luck in being bound 'for warmer climes'. Even his first hard comment sounded like an uncle's advice. 'No more of this Haifa nonsense, I trust?' His snooper's eyes had already picked up Ruskin's tropical gear on its coat hanger near the cockpit door. Jennie had brought it down first thing, having ironed it before going to bed.

'Haifa?' Ruskin would have made an actor, Witney thought. 'Hell. Can't stand the flies, Mr Kellett.'

Kellett already had McEvoy's signed fit-for-flight certificate in his hands. He was happy that for once it had been ready. 'McEvoy's worth his weight in gold to you, Ruskin,' he said.

'That's what he's probably hoarding, the money I'm paying him,' Ruskin joked. Anything to keep Kellett in good humour.

But Kellett was aware of the weight of their load. 'I'd say you're at the limit?' he suggested.

'Maybe take a couple more crates.' The hangar seemed full of them.

'If the fuselage was elastic,' Kellett said.

'You know very well, Mr Kellett,' Ruskin said. 'Bandits have been going out of business like flies in a blitz because they've been flying with half loads.'

The real reason, Kellett pointed out, was that they'd been borrowing at extortionate rates of interest. 'I've lost five clients this week through having their wings clipped by sharks.'

It was hard to tell sometimes whose side Kellett was really on. Maybe it was part of his semi-official game. 'If the ARB ever fires you, Mr Kellett,' Ruskin said with a broad wink at Witney, 'you can always find a job here. With an engineer like you we'd never be grounded.' He picked up the theme later when they had the loaded Dakota on the hardstanding and Ruskin let Kellett run the engines as part of the check. As Kellett chopped them and agreed they were running like Rolls Royces, Ruskin said, 'One thing, your busted clients won't be blaming you. It's different with some of your civil aviation oppos. You've only got to mention their names to make the bandits spit. You at least don't make life hell for us.'

'Am I supposed to?'

'I didn't spend five years in the Raff to make the world safe for bureaucrats and pilots with posh manners.'

Kellett knew all about the chip on Ruskin's shoulder. 'Putting it a bit strong, isn't it?'

'The smell's a bit strong,' Ruskin said. 'You might say civil aviation here's a touch like ripe Camembert.' He put on his schoolboy grin. 'I'm on a south of France next week. Like me to bring you some back?'

Kellett sniffed corruption. 'Very kind of you, Ruskin,' he said shaking his head. 'My wife and I prefer Wensleydale when we can get it.' He peered out through the windshield at the snow-blanketed airfield and the flakes hitting the glass. 'I trust you're not seriously thinking of trying to get off in these conditions.'

Suddenly the schoolboy was the hard man. 'My decision, Mr Kellett, as captain. You're only here to approve the Dak.'

'Quite so,' Kellett said, miffed.

The snowclouds seemed to hang right on the hangar roof as Ruskin made his way along the slippery trail to the hut. Jennie was paper-pushing on the filing system she was trying to establish. Alby worked on a W/T set, McEvoy tinkered with an altimeter, and Witney stood like the leader of the revolution, hands on hips, near the stove. Ruskin got the mood right away. He had an instinct for sensing blokes' moods. 'What's this?' he asked. 'United we stand?'

'We're not going, Jack.'

Even Jennie winced at the directness, knowing it would upset Ruskin, who now took in McEvoy's and Alby's reactions, knew he had a fight on, and implied with a look that Jennie would be better out of it. She put on her Land Army coat, pecked him on the cheek, and went out.

'Jen,' Ruskin said. 'Don't hang about round here. Get home.'

She said nothing and presently they heard her Standard 8 being started.

'It's a bit cold for revolutions,' Ruskin said, warming his hands over the top of the stove.

'And too cold for flying,' retorted Witney.

'If this was the Raff, today would be a write-off for flying. And you know it.' McEvoy had a point.

'OK,' Ruskin said. 'It's too cold for brass monkeys besides. But we aren't brass monkeys.' He shot appeals to McEvoy and Alby that might set them against Witney.

Witney saw the trick. 'It's too cold for bloody aeroplanes never mind monkeys. We'd have a draggy run. We don't even have de icers on the wings and we'll be collecting hoar frost by the yard. And with a blasted overload, too.'

'You don't know we've an overload,' Ruskin shot back. 'But all right.' His look was accusing. 'I'll do the bloody trip myself.'

'If you're tired of life . . .?' Witney began.

'I'm tired of bloody cowards who'll find any excuse to stay on the ground and can't wait to grow old and draw their pensions.' His eyes withered them.

'Below the belt, Jack,' McEvoy said. 'I mean Pete's right. Snow, ice and an overload.'

It wasn't in Ruskin's nature to compromise. But he had to make a move. 'What are you saying, Mac? If we spread the job over three trips, not two, you'll accept the conditions?' It was a politician's throw.

'Something like that, aye,' McEvoy said, caught on the hop.

'Alby?' Ruskin asked.

'It lowers the odds against us,' Alby said.

Ruskin faced Witney. 'Comrade Lenin?'

'I don't like compromise,' Witney replied.

'I'm the one who's doing the compromising, chum. Three trips not two is some climbdown.' He had a notion that beyond the overload risk Witney was really on his guard about the Haifa trip.

But Witney agreed.

They took out nearly a third of the machine parts' crates from the Dakota's hold and Ruskin said, 'We'll be nigh on empty if we go on much more.'

Witney wanted to put out two more, but Ruskin would have none of it. 'Enough,' he said firmly.

They took Vera Lynn through the packed snow to the runway start line.

Even as they taxied Witney saw the hoar frost forming on the starboard wing. 'Still don't like it,' he said, just before they began the pre-take-off checks.

Then they were off, picking up speed on the treacherous snow, the wipers clearing the flakes off the windshield. The Dakota bumped over the snow, with Ruskin keeping her to an invisible line under the snow cover. There were groans and squeals and the engines soared on full power. And Witney felt tense as he saw the hoar frost piling up on the wing. The Dakota felt draggy. The throttles were on full boost. It went through his mind to call Ruskin to abort. But they rolled on.

It seemed the Dakota would never reach take-off speed as Kellett watched through his binoculars from the upper floor of the vandalized control tower. Snow blew in through the broken windows and he was covered in it. He could almost feel the weight of the stuff on the slow-moving Dakota as it consumed runway.

There was very little of that runway left. Ruskin moved the column to lift her off. There was no response. She felt like lead. And then, with only a few yards left before the wall of snow that covered the perimeter fence, the tyres came off the snow, spinning like black pinwheels. They cleared the snowbank by a few yards.

Ruskin kept them in a shallow climb. His chest was pounding. He'd thought a few seconds earlier that they'd never make it. Witney was grim and going through those agonies of pain behind his eyes. McEvoy thought he'd be lucky not to vomit. Alby had seen nothing of it, but he'd felt the danger and the nearness of a crash.

They got to their cruising height and Ruskin eased down the Wasps. The Dakota still felt sluggish. And hoar frost lay thick on both wings. Witney knew it would put up their stalling speed by fifteen knots. 'Bloody crazy!' He could find no other words for a few moments.

'There was some drag, I admit,' Ruskin said.

'We'll have to call you lucky, Jack,' McEvoy said.

Ruskin was busy dousing his own terror now. 'Luck?' he blustered. 'The only guys I knew who carried four leaf clovers on raids bought it. Never trust to luck. It's just a four letter word.'

They were holding their cruising height in comfort now. The twin Wasps were on song and they'd known worse vibration and all the gauges were behaving. But even Ruskin cast an anxious glance at that ice on the port wing. And Witney knew what was going through his mind. He ran a check on the ice on the starboard wing. He wished to God they were over the Med with the sun melting it.

Jennie was back among the infinitely tolerant patients in that Victorian waiting room. Some of the pale faces were known to her from her first visit. A baby screamed. The ex-commando limped in using a single crutch. The gas-fire popped on low. Jennie had put up with it this time. But now she'd had enough. She was next to go in to the doctor. She bent over the fire and raised the flame. And the ex-commando threw her a thumbs-up sign.

The battleaxe receptionist pushed the door open, her bosom filling the space. 'Next,' she said. And as Jennie got up, the receptionist saw the gas-fire. 'I warned you last time. I'll have to report this to the doctor.'

Jennie's face was set in an expression of combat. 'Well, you see,' she said, her eyes flashing, 'I've a bad temper and

I don't like folk much and I take it out on the weak and the sick and those least able to fight back.'

It brought some alarm to the receptionist's craggy features. She indicated the door to the doctor's room.

Jennie went in to face the plump middle-aged doctor who wore glasses halfway down his nose and a Rotary badge on the lapel of his jacket. Jennie only vaguely remembered his face. And she thought even this might be from his photographs in the local papers. He was prominent on what they used to call the 'Home Front' during the war. In other words he never became an MO with the Forces. He sat at a large rolltop desk with every cubby hole stuffed with papers and letters. He was making copious notes. He told Jennie to sit down without even looking at her. Presently he swung his chair round.

'Yes, now,' he said condescendingly. 'Miss Shaw, isn't it?'

'Jennie Shaw.'

He examined her over his glasses. 'You came before and left without seeing me?'

She crossed her arms and put a hand to her chin.

'Why was that?'

Jennie had never even as a child liked him. Memories flooded back. He was a pompous twit. 'I'd have thought Cinderella's auntie out there on reception might have told you. Poor sick folk shouldn't be left to shiver in the cold.'

'There is a national fuel emergency.'

'It's warmer in here,' Jennie said. 'And I've not read anything about saving gas.'

He was losing and knew it. 'So what do you think is wrong with you, Miss Shaw? I've not treated you before.'

'You have. You sent me to the infirmary to have my tonsils out.'

He rifled through some papers trying to unearth her record. 'So tell me what you think is wrong now.'

'I'm pregnant. I think.'

'Better have a look at you then. Then you can get on

with the wedding.' He indicated the curtain behind which stood an examination couch with its heavy mahogany legs.

'I didn't know this was the vicarage,' said Jennie.

'One thing I know, young woman. You have a fine old chip on your shoulder.'

'We're not back in the Thirties,' Jennie called from behind the screen. 'We never came through the war to be treated like peasants. That's all done with. You should feel privileged to have those people out there as your patients. This country's not the same any more. And the sooner you and your kind realize it the better.'

'Now, if you've finished, we'll have a look at you, shall we?'

Jennie had begun to undress. She put her skirt back on now. 'No, not you,' she said. 'Never.'

And she went out.

Ruskin rolled spaghetti round his fork and took a mouthful. They were back in the cafe that wasn't much more than a shack in the middle of nowhere near the south-west corner of the Rome airport. The padrone had done it up since their last trip and the war damage was almost invisible. Only when you looked close could you see the pitted stonework where the bullets and shrapnel had struck.

The atmosphere was sullen.

'We agreed, all of us,' Witney said, sipping at his vino blanco. 'No more Palestine runs.'

Ruskin just munched at his spaghetti.

'I don't like being called the Israeli Air Force,' Witney said. 'And that's what they're saying in the Wings Club.'

He'd gone over the top, Ruskin knew. 'Come off it. Half the bleedin' members are doing this run now. They get good bonuses.'

'Blood money.' Witney was scathing.

'And they always see the lads get return loads.'

'Tell that to our blokes who're getting knocked off and

maimed by the bloody terrorists. Tell them how well the bandits are doing.'

McEvoy and Alby tucked into their spaghetti saying and seeing nothing, just listening.

Witney was getting steamed up. 'They unload crates of Stens from our Dak and stencil them with a polite reminder, "Please don't use against the British troops". '

Ruskin was deaf to such sarcasm. He went on eating and enjoying the vino. Witney tried twice more to push the issue. In the end Ruskin wiped his mouth with an oil-grimed handkerchief and looked at Alby and McEvoy. 'Coming or not?'

They were both unsure.

'Why not start with me?' Witney asked.

'OK.'

'I'm flying no more guns into Palestine, not for you or anybody. I'm for getting right back to the UK and not flying on to Haifa. I'll walk back if need be.'

Ruskin stared him out. 'Oh you'll never need Shanks's pony. Not your sort. You can always hitch a lift from Colonel Blimp of the British Control Commission.' His eyes fell on McEvoy. 'Mac?'

McEvoy shifted uncomfortably in the reed chair. 'You'll not find another engineer in this dump.'

It shook Witney. He rounded on him, 'That's not what you were saying in the latrines just now.'

'Don't get me wrong,' McEvoy said. 'I was saying Jack will have to fly without an engineer.'

'I am an engineer,' Ruskin said defiantly.

'Well – er – yes.' McEvoy didn't want to make anything of the fact that he was better qualified than Ruskin.

'Alby?' Ruskin didn't even look at the wop. He just spaded into that spaghetti.

'You've not got a brother still in the British Army,' Alby said.

'Fair vote,' Witney smiled. 'Three against one we don't go.'

'You're forgetting the fine print of our agreements,' Ruskin mumbled over his spaghetti.

'Agreements?' Witney scoffed. 'We have none.'

'I have four votes,' Ruskin said easily, tucking into the spaghetti with one hand and shielding his eyes against the sun with the other. It was really bright. Perfect flying conditions. The same all the way across the Med, very likely. He twisted a large roll of spaghetti round his fork and grinned. 'You can see why the Italians screwed up the war.'

The jeep in which they'd been driven to the spaghetti house came back now to take them back to the Dakota. They found the second jeep still there, under the wing edge, with the jowly Italian who had stayed to guard it. A fuel bowser was pulling away.

'The quicker you pick up your kit the better,' Ruskin told the other three as they made for the cargo hold door.

Ruskin climbed up and couldn't believe his eyes. The hold was completely empty. The crates had been unloaded and nothing put in their place. The air was pungent with the fumes of aircraft fuel.

Witney came up to stand by Ruskin. The sight pleased him. 'That's it then,' he said. 'No load, no run.'

McEvoy and Alby joined them, baffled.

Then they were aware of a movement in the cockpit. A man emerged from the seats. It was the rabbi. 'Sorry about this, Captain Ruskin,' he beamed. 'Slight, ever so slight, cock up. I do hope you enjoyed lunch.'

Ruskin summed it all up. The load was late, and the three others had made up their minds not to fly on. 'OK,' he told them. 'Pick up your gear.'

The rabbi was baffled.

'We're not going on, rabbi,' Witney said decisively.

'You're afraid?' the rabbi said, his eyes wide with wonder at such a revolt.

'No, rabbi,' Witney said, moving for'ard. 'It's not fright.'

'Simon Pure talking,' Ruskin said harshly.

The rabbi looked lost.

From outside came the sound of an approaching vehicle. Ruskin and the rabbi looked out across the sand-coloured landscape with its azure background. Out of the sun lumbered an old Italian Army truck like others they had seen before. Relief, then doubt, crossed the rabbi's face. Witney, Alby and McEvoy had all gone for'ard to pick up their gear. They came down with their holdalls now just as the truck swept round in a half circle to bring its tailboard near the cargo door.

The rabbi spoke to Witney, Alby and McEvoy. 'Would you mind not leaving for a moment?' He jumped down as the truck driver vaulted from the cab and went round to the tailboard. They took the pins out and the tailboard came down with a bang. There was silence for a long moment as if an unspoken order had gone out for caution.

Then on a signal from the rabbi men and women and some children began to jump and scramble down from the truck. The rabbi and the driver waved them to Vera Lynn. Some held pathetic bundles of minor possessions. Others had nothing but the clothes they wore, and these were mostly tatty and in rags.

Ruskin, Witney, McEvoy and Alby stood shaken in the door to the hold.

'Jewish illegals for God's sake,' Witney murmured.

Ruskin for once was lost for words. McEvoy and Alby were just as dumbstruck as the European Jews, tired and drawn but with highlights in their eyes, pulled themselves and each other into the cargo hold.

Witney moved his holdall from the doorway to make more room for them to climb through. McEvoy and Alby dumped their holdalls in the lee of the doorway.

Ruskin felt a lump in his throat. 'People, Peter,' he told Witney. 'People, not guns. Europe's been kicking 'em in the crutch for years and they see this as going home.'

An old woman tried to prise herself aboard. McEvoy and Alby leaned down and lifted her inside.

Witney watched them pile in. They hadn't a clue where

to put themselves, and stood or sat along the steep slope of the fuselage. 'Can't we dig up some safety harnesses?' he asked Ruskin.

'And a couple of stewardesses?' Ruskin rasped. 'And a first-class section?'

Witney knew it was a daft suggestion.

'And now that it's people,' Ruskin said, 'I'd just as soon have a co-pilot.'

The rabbi heard this as he joined them near the door. The immigrants were forming themselves into rows now along the floor of the hold as if they were in a cinema. 'No, for Christ's sake!' Witney suddenly yelled. 'You'll be safer along the sides.' And he got in among them, sorting them out, setting them along the sides like paratroops. None understood a word he said. He mimed his orders.

'You flew a few paras in your time, Alby,' Ruskin said. 'How about it?'

And Alby joined Witney, and so did McEvoy. And they settled their passengers who filled each side of the hold. Witney picked up his holdall and went for'ard to the cockpit without a word either to Ruskin or the rabbi.

Ruskin chuckled. 'Seems he didn't fancy walking back, rabbi.'

Ten minutes later Ruskin and Witney went through the pre-take-off checks and rolled Vera out of Rome into a perfect sky. Many of the immigrants prayed. Others held hands. Children were gripped between outstretched legs. There was no panic. Just the most extraordinary silence. Even as the Dakota vibrated and bumped a bit in those early moments on leaving the ground the only murmur was from a small child.

Ruskin's hands were relaxed on the control stick. 'Undercart up,' he said.

McEvoy saw to the lever. 'Travelling up. Locked,' he confirmed.

'Light OK,' Witney said.

'Flaps up,' Ruskin said.

'Travelling up,' McEvoy said.

And the flaps came up on a perfect take-off.

When they got to their cruising height Ruskin went back to see his passengers, but only after changing into the crisp tropical gear Jennie had ironed for him. He threw out smiles and winks and good cheer and took their proffered hands as he went slowly down the hold. He put on a confidence-boosting swagger and saw the anxiety fall away from many of their faces. He'd once or twice behaved like that with the paras and later with the erks he flew to India and the veterans he brought home for demob. He felt like an airline captain.

An elderly Jewish woman held out a gnarled hand on which the veins stood out. 'Thank you, captain,' she said with feeling. 'How long before we're home?'

Ruskin grinned. 'Couple of hours, love. A little more maybe.' He saw the tears well in her eyes. And he thought he could do with a bit of a cry himself.

They used dead reckoning to make the airstrip near Haifa. No radio contact with anyone. The night was dark with clouds scudding across the moon as they made their approach. Landing lights with long spaces in between flickered into momentary life to give them a kind of flarepath. And even as the Dakota's tyres touched, lights were being doused, leaving only those ahead of them, and some of those were moving.

As they taxied along Ruskin was aware of the shadowy movements of men and vehicles. Jeeps took shape, and 15–cwt trucks. Yet even as he pushed the side window open Ruskin could hear little. Then men were everywhere giving thumbs-up and V-signs. They wore open-necked shirts with wool jumpers and most were armed. Lights flashed and in the reflections Ruskin and his crew began to make out the dark, open-air faces of the reception committee.

'Must be a no-go place for the British,' Witney said. He was apprehensive and half expected a convoy of British troops or police to invade the scene.

There had not been a sound from the passengers. But

now, sure they were 'home', they burst into wild cheers and singing.

Some prayed.

Ruskin led the way back down to the cargo door. The immigrants crowded every port window, gazing down at the ground which for them was a miracle. Now and then a hand would stretch out to Ruskin, Witney, McEvoy and Alby.

They opened the cargo door and the passengers spilled down excitedly into the arms of the men who were to spirit them away. There were vague lights in the distance as if men with torches were ringing the area. And an eerie quietness engulfed the scene as men and women embraced and were hustled into trucks, which moved off as if their engines were muted.

Even Witney was moved. 'I don't know what the bloody hell we're still doing in Palestine,' he said, shaking his head. And he didn't mean himself and Ruskin and the others. He meant the British Government and its mandate problems of reconciling Arab and Jew.

There was a sweet smell of olives on the night air as they stepped down to stretch their legs. An immigrant saw them and insisted on kissing each in turn. Others followed suit. The crew were overwhelmed with gratitude and affection. And a bowser drove up and men who were shadows began to refuel Vera.

'Glad you came?' Ruskin asked Witney.

'We're all bloody mad,' Witney said, anxiously scanning the dark landscape. Any moment now he expected to hear the rat-tat of Stens and see the British Army pouring in.

It was bitter outside and Shaw was pokering the fire into life. Jennie brought in four mugs of hot chocolate on a plywood tray as Mrs Shaw began to tune the wireless set.

Shaw noticed. 'I'll never know why you want to listen to him,' he said, and knelt and blew hard at the underside of the grate as if he were a bellows. 'He can do all the praying he likes it'll not make a ha'porth of difference. I don't remember Winston saying we'd win the war anywhere but on the beaches and the landing grounds. Even in the streets. Never in the churches.'

'Frank!' The note was one of reproof. 'You know I don't like you talking like that. And can't you stop that hammering a bit.' She was on about the din that was coming from upstairs where they had a burst pipe.

'I'm not getting the wrong side of Harry Whitaker,' Shaw said firmly. 'Not in this weather. Finding an honest plumber's worse than finding an honest millionaire.'

'They reckon he's minting it out of the freeze up,' Mrs Shaw said, struggling with the radio dial.

'He can mint it till putty comes of his ears for all I care,' Shaw said. He glanced at Jennie and nodded towards upstairs. 'You made one for him, have you?'

Jennie indicated the fourth mug on the tray. The fire was livening up now and Shaw went to collect the mug. A BBC voice came on to announce the Archbishop of Canterbury and 'a special prayer for our time'.

'It's Attlee and Bevin and Cripps he should be talking to,' Shaw cracked.

'They can't bring snow and ice,' Mrs Shaw said.

Shaw chuckled. 'We don't want it brought, we want it taken away.'

And he went off with the plumber's hot chocolate as the Archbishop began his prayer. 'Almighty God, who has ordained that men should serve Thee in serving one another by their labour; have regard, we pray Thee, to this nation, oppressed at this time by many burdens . . .'

The phone was ringing in the hall. Jennie ran to get it, telling Mrs Shaw to turn the Archbishop of Canterbury down a bit.

'Oh, Jack, love, when did you get in?'

Ruskin had brought in the Dakota two hours before. They'd been busy unloading fruit and he didn't want to hang about on the telephone because the Nissen hut was like an icebox. He said he was on his way.

Jennie, thrilled, went back into the living room where Mrs Shaw was switching off the wireless.

Frank Shaw came in from upstairs. 'I never heard you give him the news,' he said disarmingly.

'News?' Jennie asked.

Mrs Shaw knew what he was leading up to, and didn't like it. 'And I never heard the Archbishop.' It was a diversion.

'You missed nothing,' Shaw said.

'What news?' The truth was dawning.

'I'll get Harry a biscuit to go with his hot chocolate,' Shaw said, making to go into the kitchen.

'He knows,' Jennie accused Mrs Shaw. 'You told him?'

Shaw faced her. 'And what's wrong with your own father knowing you're expecting.' He was calmer than she'd expected.

Mrs Shaw broke in. 'I've not minded keeping your little secrets all these years. But he is your father. He has a right to know.'

'Not if I don't want him to, and I didn't.'

This upset Shaw. 'It's not as if I'm just some nosey Herbert down the street.'

'I don't want Jack worried,' Jennie said. 'He's enough on his plate as it is, and I won't stand for anybody, anybody, making things worse for him.'

Shaw held her with a look. 'It'll make him feel worse knowing he's about to become a father, will it?'

'He's not about to become a father,' she said. 'It takes around nine months usually.' He'd made her angry. She stormed out into the kitchen.

Mrs Shaw eyed her husband balefully. 'Some things are best left alone,' she said.

It was almost an hour later when Jennie looked out of the front room window and saw Witney drive up in his Morgan with Ruskin next to him. The two men sat talking with the windscreen wiper still going against the driving snow.

'All I'm saying is we'll wind up in the drink if we keep this up, and no sleep,' Witney was saying.

'You're getting some in tonight,' Ruskin said. 'You were wrong about that load to Haifa, you're wrong about this.'

They got out now, and Ruskin brought out a cardboard box from the back.

'I knew it,' Mrs Shaw said in some alarm. 'He's coming in. Mr Witney.'

'Well he's not the King,' Shaw said.

It was Jennie who opened the door to them. Ruskin kissed her and planted a jaffa in her hands. He put the box on the dining table and said, 'Pete's just staying for some hot chocolate.'

'Not something stronger, Mr Witney?' Shaw asked.

Witney declined. 'We're flying again first thing, Mr Shaw.' He gave away none of his own doubts about the way they were flying their arses off.

'Not Palestine again?' Shaw's face clouded over.

'What do you mean – again?' Ruskin asked, as Mrs Shaw went through to make hot chocolates.

'I wasn't born the day before yesterday.'

Ruskin flopped down on the sofa. 'We've been in Rome, Jen's Dad.'

Shaw looked at the box of jaffas. 'They don't grow jaffas in Italy.'

Ruskin grinned as Jennie leaned over and kissed him. 'You'd not know a jaffa from a Cox's orange pippin.'

Ruskin and Jennie went to bed early in the small back room. Jennie was already between the sheets when Ruskin came in from the bathroom. 'Come on, hurry up,' she laughed. 'I've got the electric blanket on.'

'You be careful,' Ruskin joked. 'You'll end up in Armley Gaol using electricity in Mr Attlee's paradise.'

'And I've something to tell you,' she said as he got into bed beside her. 'Want to know?'

'In three words at most,' Ruskin said, making the most of a yawn.

'We're getting a prefab.'

He closed his eyes. 'We're what?'

'A prefab. One of those –'

'I know what prefabs are,' Ruskin mumbled, as if already half asleep. 'Peasant hovels meant to tide the proles over the next ten years. But, you see, they'll be around in the year two thousand.'

'Anyway, we can have one,' Jennie said, propped up on one elbow gazing at him. 'Dad's in with the man who's second to the boss of the housing department, and he says we can have one on the Newley Estate.' Her tone became conspiratorial. 'And we don't even have to go on the waiting list.'

'Your old man's getting naughty in his old age,' Ruskin said sleepily. 'I must speak to the National Union of Spivs about him.'

'Jack, most people would give anything for a prefab.' She ran a hand across his chest.

'I'm not most people.'

'They've got their own bathrooms, fitted baths, inside lavs. And fridges.'

'You'd not catch me dead in a prefab.'

Jennie plucked a hair on his chest to rouse him. 'You do nothing but say how much you want to get out of here.'

Ruskin opened one eye. 'If your old man was in with the number one in the housing department instead of his deputy we'd get one of those requisitioned houses on Manor Road. But I don't even want one of them. I don't want anywhere in these parts. We'll have to move south one day for what I want to do.'

She kissed him. 'What do you want to do?'

He had both eyes closed again. His nose twitched. 'Knock the hell out of BOAC and BEA.'

'There's something else, Jack.'

'Mmmmm.'

'If we had a prefab our baby could have his own room.' His face was in repose and he was breathing steadily. 'Jack?' She knew he was really asleep and not just feigning it. Otherwise he would have snored. 'Rotten devil.' And she kissed him and snuggled against him.

The Dakota cockpit was like a fridge as they went through the pre-take-off checks. Alby and McEvoy had been badly snowbound on the way to Garton and it was after eleven o'clock now. Ruskin had wanted to get off as soon after eight-thirty as possible to make Rome before dusk. Now they'd be lucky.

'Pitch,' Witney continued.

'Max R . . . P . . . M,' Ruskin said.

'Fuel.'

'Contents OK. Main tanks selected. Booster pumps on.'

'Flaps.'

'Down. Checked.'

'Gills.'

'Trail.'

'Superchargers we don't have. Oil coolers.'

'Set.'

'Autopilot. None.' And Witney added one to the routine. 'Ice,' he said.

'Ice!' Ruskin knew what was coming.

'No bloody de-icers and we try to get off in this. We must be candidates for the hatch.'

'We did it before,' Ruskin said calmly.

'Only bloody just. Look at it. Look at the bloody frost and it's colder now than last time.' Hoar frost was building on both wings.

'And stick to procedure,' Ruskin said, boosting the twin Wasps. The windshield wipers were busy, and beyond them was the white-out with a snow-laden sky that seemed to meet the distant rooftops. Even Ruskin was having secret second thoughts.

From the hut Jennie watched Vera move ponderously over the packed snow, making new tracks to the perimeter, and then to the runway start line, now invisible.

In the cockpit Ruskin ran up the engines. The brakes

came off. And Vera began to move over the invisible runway. Again there was that feeling of immense weight, though they knew she was slightly under-loaded. Snow swirled into the windshield and over the wings. Ruskin and Witney – and McEvoy, from his vantage just behind and between them – saw the speed indicator show a slow rise. Witney had his left hand near the throttles to prevent creep and Ruskin's hands were tight on the control column.

They were running out of runway. And they barely had enough speed to make a take-off. The moment the needle touched 90, Ruskin eased the tail off the ground and saw a little more speed added and then began to lift the Dakota. She didn't respond at once, then she was off the ground, and then the wheels touched the snow again.

Jennie watched in horror as the Dakota again lifted, her engines roaring on full boost. She looked ponderous and seemed almost to hover for a second or two.

Fear spread in the cockpit now. Witney's knuckles were white on the throttles as he tried to squeeze a bit more thrust out of the Wasps. Ruskin's face was taut. McEvoy's hands were already pressing hard into the pilots' seats as he braced himself.

'She's not lifting!' Witney yelled. 'She's not! The ice! The bloody ice!'

They had a sense of slow-motion as Vera bumped off the packed snow again, shuddering and groaning. She gained some thirty feet, but Ruskin could really feel the weight of that ice on the wings now. She gave a slight lurch and Ruskin corrected it. The horizon shifted again beyond the frenzied wipers on the windshield and Vera stalled sickeningly to port.

'Christ!' Witney screamed.

'We've bought it!' McEvoy yelled, raising his hands to his face.

Ruskin's grip on the control column was now so tight he tore his fingernails. And then the port wing dipped sharply. Vera careered briefly to the left. Ruskin's hands flew to his face even as they struck. The crew's screams were drowned by the racing engines and the din of the impact as Vera's port wingtip sliced through the snow. The wing snapped like a twig and the port propeller dug into the ground. The port undercarriage crumpled.

In spellbound horror, Jennie saw Vera spin and skid laterally towards the perimeter fence beyond the end of the runway. She made for the phone, shaking, wanting to vomit, and called the civil ambulance and fire services from the emergency list she had put up on the wall.

Buffeted, their safety harnesses taking the strain, Ruskin, Witney, McEvoy and Alby felt they were in a ghost train to hell. They knew they would die as Vera skidded through the snow, breaking up. And then there was the heart-stopping sudden stop. Crates came crashing through the cabin door from the hold.

Ruskin had a sensation of being hit from behind and in front at the same time. He lashed out, fighting his way through a sort of pea-soup fog, and then being sure he had no legs any more. And the fog turned into a wall and everything went dead. He wasn't sure how long it was before he came round. His whole body seemed to be in a vice. His head raged. He imagined he could hear the crackle of flames. 'Get out for Christ's sake!' he heard himself screaming. And then his vision cleared, his senses recovered, and he could make out Witney wrestling with his seat harness.

'Pete?' Ruskin murmured, his voice shaking over the one word.

'Nothing broken,' Witney said. 'I think.'

Ruskin turned to look for McEvoy and Alby amid the chaos of splintered crates and machine parts. Alby was squirming out of his harness, blood pouring from the side of his face. McEvoy looked dead.

They got clear of their harnesses and began to lift out the unconscious McEvoy.

Jeeps and trucks from the nearby RAF maintenance unit raced up ahead of Jennie's Standard 8. A party of RAF

Police broke open the cargo door as other RAF men peered into the smashed cockpit.

'I think they've bought it,' said a young LAC, and Jennie overheard. She felt numb, as if she were under some strong anaesthetic.

She was aware of the RAF men throwing out boxes and machine parts from the hold. And then Ruskin appeared through the jumble and let himself down to put one foot on the snow. His face and the collar of his flying jacket were red with blood. Witney and Alby came out now, both dazed and in deep shock. And the RAF men were handing down the still body of McEvoy.

Jennie ran to Ruskin and kissed him and then they bent to the motionless McEvoy.

An ambulance came through the snow and they lifted McEvoy inside. Witney went, too. He had concussion and fractured ribs and was coughing blood. Alby's head cuts were superficial. As the ambulance men gave him first aid, Ruskin stood forlornly looking at the stricken Vera. Suddenly he put his hands to his face as if he could not take another moment of the nightmare.

Jennie had often wondered if Ruskin could ever be less than buoyant, ever feel despair. This was as near as she had ever seen him come to breaking point. She took his right hand and felt the sticky blood. And she could feel him shaking.

'Anyway, love, nobody was killed,' she said inadequately.

'No,' he said. 'And life's too bloody short for this kind of thing to happen. I'll get her right again. I'll get Vera right. And I'll get another Dak while we're doing it.' Then, oddly, he told Jennie it was a long time since he had seen his father, and it was time they took him out for a meal.

She looked at him through eyes that were full of relief and bewilderment. No, he wasn't beaten. And the future wouldn't have anything to do with cradle-to-grave security.

It was another hour before he would let her drive him to the hospital outpatients' department for treatment.

Ma oys
in Wood

Charles H. Hayward

Updated & Revised by
Gill & Alan Bridgewater

HarperCollins*Publishers*

Metric Equivalents

INCHES TO MILLIMETRES AND CENTIMETRES

MM—millimetres CM—centimetres

Inches	MM	CM	Inches	CM	Inches	CM
1/8	3	0.3	9	22.9	30	76.2
1/4	6	0.6	10	25.4	31	78.7
3/8	10	1.0	11	27.9	32	81.3
1/2	13	1.3	12	30.5	33	83.8
5/8	16	1.6	13	33.0	34	86.4
3/4	19	1.9	14	35.6	35	88.9
7/8	22	2.2	15	38.1	36	91.4
1	25	2.5	16	40.6	37	94.0
1 1/4	32	3.2	17	43.2	38	96.5
1 1/2	38	3.8	18	45.7	39	99.1
1 3/4	44	4.4	19	48.3	40	101.6
2	51	5.1	20	50.8	41	104.1
2 1/2	64	6.4	21	53.3	42	106.7
3	76	7.6	22	55.9	43	109.2
3 1/2	89	8.9	23	58.4	44	111.8
4	102	10.2	24	61.0	45	114.3
4 1/2	114	11.4	25	63.5	46	116.8
5	127	12.7	26	66.0	47	119.4
6	152	15.2	27	68.6	48	121.9
7	178	17.8	28	71.1	49	124.5
8	203	20.3	29	73.7	50	127.0

This edition published 1995
for Link House Magazines Ltd by arrangement with
HarperCollins*Publishers* Ltd
77–85 Fulham Palace Road
Hammersmith, London W6 8JB

Revised edition first published 1993

ISBN 0 583 31990 4

Printed and bound in Great Britain

Contents

Introduction

IT WAS WITH some trepidation that we accepted the task of revising Charles Hayward's book – for in the eyes of so many, *Making Toys in Wood* had become the toymaker's bible. However, our natural reluctance to tamper with a classic was balanced by the knowledge that, with the passage of time, the original edition had come to seem somewhat dated.

We haven't altered the substance of Charles Hayward's book – the character of the projects is unchanged – but we have updated many of the products and added some safety precautions. We have also updated the introductions to the projects in light of the current understanding that there are no such things as boys-only or girls-only toys.

If you are a modern toymaker who appreciates the value of fun, timeless, well-built toys, we're sure you'll enjoy these projects.

ALAN & GILL BRIDGEWATER

Toymaking Techniques and Tips

A VARIETY OF materials can be used in making toys: wood, cardboard, particleboard, and even plaster. All irregularities, such as nail holes, splits, bad joints, and rough wood, are best filled with plastic wood and, when dry, rubbed down perfectly smooth.

Painting. Toys should be well finished and brilliantly colored, with strong contrasts. There should be the fewest possible sharp corners, and the paint should dry completely hard so that it will not only tend to keep clean but will allow for easy cleaning if it becomes necessary. With regard to the paint, we favor the use of acrylic paint rather than oil-based paints because acrylics are so easy to use. There are pros and cons, however, for both kinds of paint. On the one hand, with acrylics, the paint dries very quickly, the brushes can be washed in water, and the colors are bright. But, on the other hand, although gloss enamels do take 24 hours to dry and the brushes do need to be cleaned in spirits, the colors have a special full-bodied quality. If you are a beginner, it would be best to start with acrylics and then experiment with other kinds of paint. *Warning: For toymaking, it is vital that the paint be nontoxic.* If in doubt, ask your supplier.

When you are using acrylic paints, lay on two coats and then, when the paint is completely dry, apply a couple of coats of clear high-shine varnish.

Various difficulties come up in painting toys, such as how to hold a small article while you are painting it, how to arrange to paint the whole piece at one sitting, and finally how to station it for drying without causing damage. It is often a good idea to paint part of the toy and allow it to dry before painting the remainder. Another plan is to rest the partially painted toy on some upturned brads or thumbtacks and to complete the painting in that position. Sometimes a nail can be tapped in, in an out-of-the-way spot, which can hold the toy while it is being painted and for suspension for drying. You could also drive a number of nails through a piece of plywood so that the painted articles can be rested gently on the points.

Some pieces have a hole into which you can drive a large screw a few turns to provide a temporary handle (Illus. 1). In other cases, you may have to drive in three or four nails, not only to enable the article to be handled but also to keep it up from the table while drying. It is usually possible to insert these nails in unnoticeable places. This is shown in Illus. 2.

As to suitable marking and colorings, the beginner toy painter would be well advised to take a walk through the toy department of one of the big stores and note schemes adopted by the professionals. Remember that children are not interested in finicky detail; they like striking effects and lots of bold primary colors.

When several colors are being used in close proximity, it is wise to use the lighter tone first to avoid any difficulty in covering. For example, when painting a "Donald Duck" character, it would be better to paint the white eyes and the yellow parts first and allow them to dry before putting on the surrounding colors and the black segment in the eyes.

There is no particular necessity to adhere to natural colors on toys for very young children. But common objects, such as railway engines, horses, dogs, cats, and birds, should be painted close to the real thing for older children.

Brushes for toy painting should be of good quality and not too large. Ordinary paint brushes will do for some work, but for the smaller toys it would be best to use watercolor brushes. For defining clear-cut edges and for small work, it would be best to obtain special lining or fine-point brushes. Always clean brushes immediately on completion of a painting session.

Old toys can be brought to life by repainting. The most important

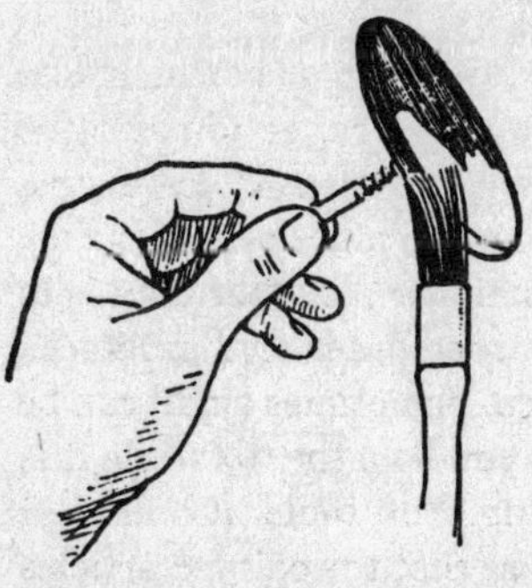

Illus. 1.
Screw used to hold work while being painted.

Illus. 2.
How pins or nails can be used to support work while drying.

part of this work is the preparation. Every part of the toy must be thoroughly washed to remove all dirt, grease, and oil. After washing, the old paint should be well rubbed down with fine sandpaper to provide a grip for the new paint. Before second-coating, rub down lightly with fine sandpaper.

You may want to repaint a rocking horse. The traditional color is known as dapple-grey. Contrary to a fairly common belief, it consists of light patches on a darker ground, and not vice versa. The general tone is a light dove grey, occasioned by a grey background being spotted with a much lighter grey, almost white. Here and there the white spots are more pronounced, being laid over a somewhat darker patch of grey. To paint a rocking horse then, you would need three tones of grey, made from white, black, and perhaps a touch of blue or yellow. The lightest tone should not be much removed from white, the middle tone should be a dove color, and the darkest tone a slate. Paint a convenient section with the middle tone and blend in a large patch here and there with the darker grey. While the color is still wet, take a sponge and mottle with the light tone. Blend well with a dry brush to avoid any harshness. Over the darker patches, the light spots can be somewhat larger. The mouth and nostrils are usually painted red, the eyes white with a black segment, and the hooves black.

One point to remember is that, although paint covers up the wood beneath, it cannot change its surface. That is to say that, if you leave the surface rough or uneven, the paint is going to be rough or uneven too. Therefore, always finish off the wood well before beginning to paint. A cabinet finish may be unnecessary, but it should be reasonably good.

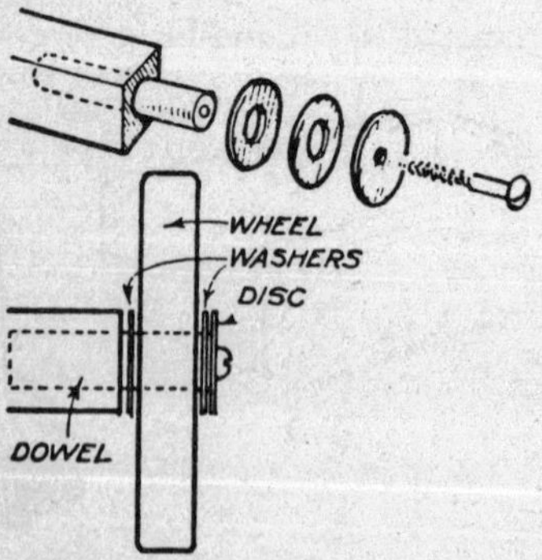

Illus. 3.
Dowel used as axle for large wheel.

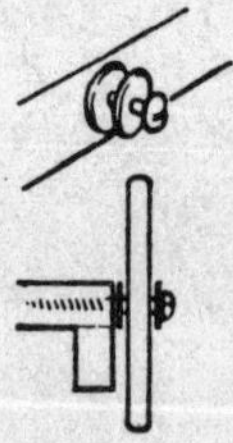

Illus. 4.
Small wheel pivoted on screw.

As mentioned before, any nail holes or other blemishes should be filled in with plastic wood. Allow plenty of time for it to dry before cleaning up. If the hole is large, put in one layer and allow it to set before finishing off. Otherwise, the outside is liable to dry, leaving the inside soft. Pile the plastic-wood filling above the hole because it is liable to shrink as it dries out.

Rounded corners. In all toys, all sharp edges and corners should be rounded over. The plane can be used for long edges and when a generous round is required. Otherwise, a file or even sandpaper will take off the sharpness. Attachments with sharp corners should also be avoided. If necessary, they can often be filed. Screws should be countersunk below the surface. Nails should always be hammered in, and care should be taken to see that there are no points projecting right through. Try as much as possible to use glue and screws rather than nails.

Incidentally, a nailed joint can be strengthened considerably by "dovetailing" the nails—that is, driving them in askew in alternate directions. It's also good to be aware that nails always have a stronger grip when driven in across the grain rather than with it. This applies as well to screws.

Wheels. These are always something of a problem. Various types can be obtained in both plastic and metal, the latter being either of the pressed-disc type or with spokes. We favor using plastic wheels.

When the wheel is fairly large and has to withstand substantial strain—when the child has to ride on the toy, for instance—it's best to arrange an axle in the form of a fairly large dowel, as shown in Illus. 3. A washer at each side reduces wear, and a disc at the outside held with a round-head screw prevents the whole arrangement from coming off. For smaller wheels, the shank of the round-head screw can serve as the axle (Illus. 4).

1. Two-Seater Toboggan

MOST PEOPLE ENJOY a run on a toboggan. The one presented here measures just over 5′ in length and will hold two adults or three children in a pinch.

As the main runners are bent to give the curvature, they should be made in a suitable hardwood such as beech, which bends well. Alternatively, ash or birch could be used. The nose piece to which they are attached should be in a hardwood, which is not liable to split. Elm is excellent in this respect, though other hardwoods could be used. The sides and seat slats could be in softwood.

The entire toboggan is painted to protect it from dampness, but it is inevitable that the runners will become exposed with friction, even

Illus. 1.
You can have a great run on this toboggan.

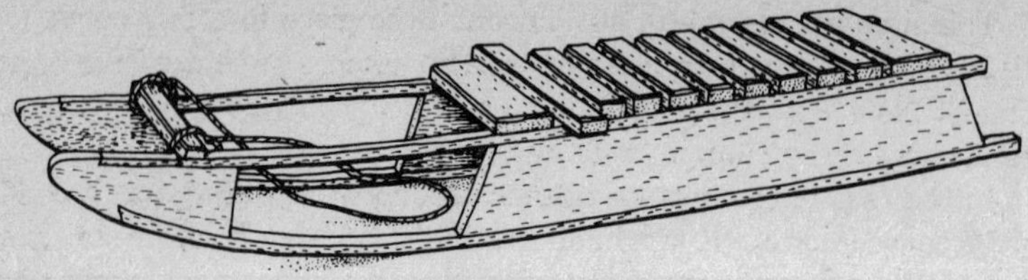

Illus. 2.
Completed toboggan. Both hardwood and softwood are used. The overall length is just over 5′, though this could vary somewhat.

when metal facings are added. Therefore, it is advisable to wipe them dry and keep the toboggan under cover when not in use.

Runners. Illus. 3 shows how each pair of runners fits into notches cut in the nose piece. They are screwed in, but it is also advisable to use a water-resistant resin glue. They are screwed to the sides. Cut the sides to size, and prepare the two nose pieces from 7/8″ wood. Note that the runners, which are 1¼″ wide, are thinned down at one side only, towards the front, so that they finish flush with the nose piece, whereas they overhang the sides. They can be made straight and trimmed flush after they are attached.

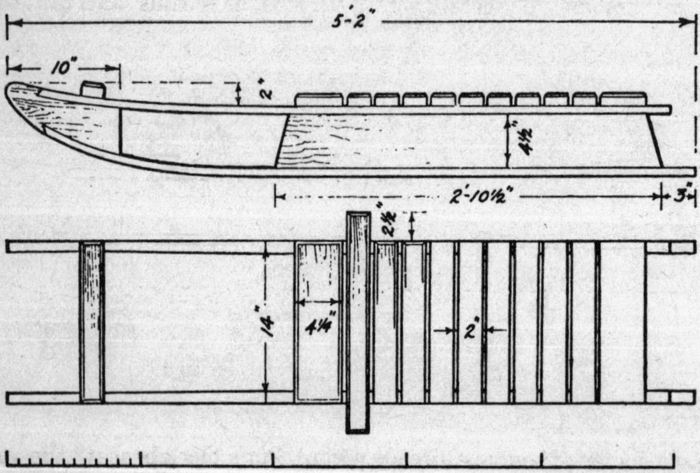

Illus. 3.
Scale elevations and plan with main sizes. The runners must be of hardwood.

The simplest plan is to cut out one nose piece to a fair curve (see Illus. 3) and mark the other from it. The notches are cut with saw and chisel. Note how the end is cut at an angle so that it resists any tendency for the runner to fly out.

In the case of the bottom runner, the notch is slightly curved. If it were curved more, the strain on the holding screws would be too great unless the runner were steamed first. It is better to give a *slight* curve and rely upon a certain amount of shaping after attachment. This necessitates the screws being well countersunk.

At this stage, the runners point outward and are straight. You need to attach them to the sides, and a certain amount of improvising is necessary in arranging methods of holding the work. Attaching them is greatly simplified if a steaming chamber is used. The wood should be left in for about an hour and bent around pegs or held with clamps. An exact curve is not necessary. If steaming is not possible, the bending can be facilitated by pouring a kettle of boiling water over the wood beforehand. In both cases, no glue should be applied over the damp wood. The simplest way is to steam (or dampen), screw the runners to the nose piece and side, and leave to dry. The whole workpiece is then taken apart, glued, and assembled afresh.

Assembling. Various methods can be used. One is to screw both runners to the nose piece and attach the side to the lower one. The top one will probably lie loosely across the side, as in Illus. 4 (it depends

Illus. 4.
How the runners and sides are assembled.

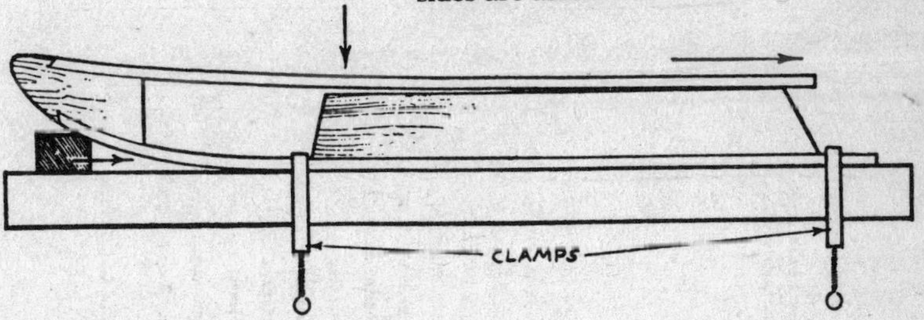

on the degree of bending already given). Put a block beneath the nose and fasten two clamps to hold the lower runner to the bench, as shown. It is then a matter of adjustment, pushing the block inward and clamping down the top runner until the degree of rise is correct. The latter is not critical, but both sides must be alike. It may be necessary to pull the top runner outward, as shown by the arrow. When correct, the screws can be driven in.

The seat slats can now be attached. They should be chamfered around the top edges, and the screws should be well countersunk. Note that the second slat from the front projects so as to form a footrest for the rear passenger (see Illus. 2). The front and rear slats are wider than the others, and if they have two screws each, there is no risk of the entire workpiece working out of truth.

If metal runners are used, the screws must be countersunk. They should extend up to the nose and be bent around to the top edge. A thickness of about 1⁄16" is suitable. Brass doesn't rust but is expensive. Iron is cheaper, but it needs to be wiped dry after use and given a wipe over with oil. It's best to use curve-section aluminum.

CUTTING LIST

	Long		Wide	Thick
	ft.	*in.*	*in.*	*in.*
2 runners	4	10	1⅜	¾
2 runners	5	1	1⅜	¾
2 nose pieces		10½	5½	⅞
2 sides	2	11½	4¾	⅞
2 slats	1	2½	4½	⅞
9 slats	1	2½	2¼	⅞
1 slat	1	7½	2¼	⅞

2. Clock Face

THIS CLOCK FACE provides children with a great deal of fun, while at the same time being instructive. The figures are painted on, but if you doubt your skill in painting them, you can use transfers or rub-on type or you can draw little circles around the figures of a large almanac and cut them out and glue them on.

The exact size of the clock is not important. The clock shown in Illus. 1 measures 8″ × 8″, but it might easily be an inch more or less. It

Illus. 1.
A useful teaching toy.

depends upon the material available. If possible, use plywood, but it is not essential. A good way to make the clock is to draw the face on white cardboard and stick the whole piece to the wood.

The face. Fasten the cardboard down with two thumbtacks, and with compasses put in the various circles. The large band in which the figures appear can be painted blue, red, or any other bold color. If you are going to cut out figures from a calendar, they should be pasted on after painting. In the case of transfers or rub-on type, they are best applied before you varnish the surface.

To mark out the hour divisions, a 60° set-square provides the simplest method. All 12 can be marked with it. For the minute divisions, mark off between each hour with dividers. If nursery rhyme transfers are available, they can be applied at the corners, as shown.

Hands. It's best to fret out the hands from thin wood or metal. Their length should suit the dial. It is advisable to paint them black. To enable them to remain in any position in which they are placed, use either a spring washer or a small spring. Use a rivet that is long enough to pass through all the thicknesses, and drill holes in the dial and hands. Thread on the hands, putting washers between each and at both ends of the rivet. Pass on the spring washer or spring, and burr over the back end of the rivet. A little adjustment will probably be needed to provide the required amount of tension.

Strut. This is a plain piece of thin wood hinged at the top, as shown in Illus. 2. To prevent it from opening too far, a piece of cord can be tied to screw eyes in the strut and at the back of the dial.

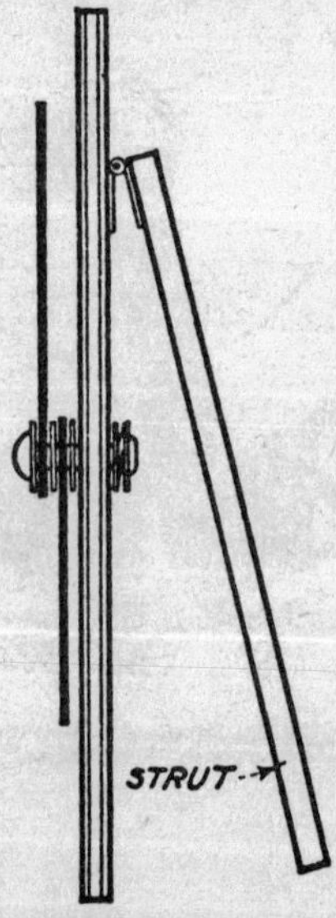

Illus. 2.
Side view of clock, showing strut.

3. Engine and Tender

ENGINES OF ALL kinds are always popular with children, but one on which a child can actually ride has particular appeal. That shown in Illus. 1 has proved a great success. One point to note is that all sharp edges and corners are rounded over.

Although the parts shown in Illus. 2 were arrived at chiefly in accordance with what seemed good design, they were to an extent influenced by the material that happened to be available. You can therefore adapt them to suit whatever wood you are using.

A few points should be noted at the outset: The wheels are cut from

Illus. 1. Well made, this toy will last for years.

solid wood and are permanently attached to axles of ¾″ dowel. These revolve in holes cut in the main framework, bearing pieces that enable them to be attached and removed if required. The boiler is built up cooper fashion, since it was found that a solid one is too heavy.

Framework. This consists of two side pieces joined by three cross pieces fitting in notches. Glue and nail the whole workpiece together, dovetailing the nails to give maximum grip.

The small wheels are fitted level with the bottom edge, and bearing pieces are fitted to contain them. Screw on these pieces and bore the holes, inserting the point of the bit exactly on the joint. Bore in from each side; then allow the bit to pass through to the far side to make sure that they are in alignment. Mark the position of each bearing so that there will be no difficulty in replacing them.

In terms of the driving wheels, they are fitted at the top, as shown in Illus. 2. Here again, the holes are bored level with the joint, which is ⅝″ down from the edge. To prevent the wheels from scraping against the framework, little pieces of 1/16″ wood are glued and nailed at the outside, as shown in Illus. 2. Prepare each pair in a single piece, cut the hole, and attach level with the hole in the frame. You can then cut

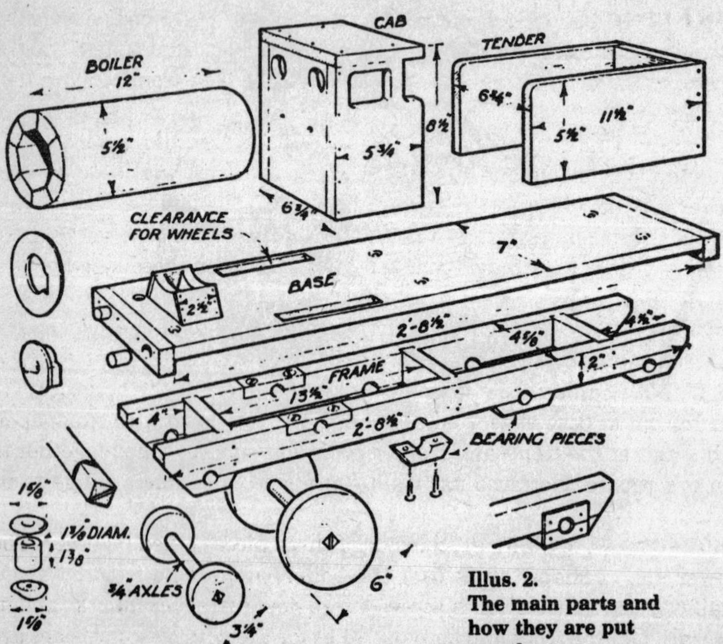

Illus. 2.
The main parts and how they are put together.

along the joint with a knife, thus enabling the bearing piece to be removed.

Wheels. Mark out with compasses, and cut with the bow saw, cleaning up with the spokeshave. Cut a square in the middle of each to take the square that will be formed at each axle end (Illus. 2). Note that the shoulders cut when these squares are made should allow generous clearance outside the frames.

To mark the shoulders, wrap a piece of thin cardboard around the axle and draw a pencil around this. Make four saw cuts and ease away the waste with the chisel. Pass the wheels over the ends and wedge as shown. Note that the wedges are at right angles with the grain so that there is reduced risk of splitting the wood. Candle wax can be used to lubricate the bearings, but it should not be applied until after the toy has been painted.

Base. Trim the main board to length (exactly equal to the frame) and screw it to the frame. Mark the clearance for the driving wheels and the slots. When attaching the ends, place the nails so that they clear the buffer holes, which are ¾″ in diameter. Nail the end pieces to the base only, not the frame.

The saddle consists of two pieces of ½″ wood cut at the top to the curve of the boiler and joined by two pieces of 3/16″ wood. Assemble, level the joints, and attach with a few nails driven in at a slight angle. Later it is held by a screw passing through the base from beneath into the boiler.

Boiler. This consists of eight pieces put together like a barrel. The simplest way is to plane all eight pieces to the same width and then to bevel all the edges to the correct angle (67½°) using an adjustable bevel. Glue them together in sets of two each, let the glue set, and put these together to form two complete halves. Fasten these together and finally glue up.

Fit in the two ends, shaping them octagonally to fit against the flat sides of the pieces. There should be a 2″ hole cut in the front end, but fit it first and mark the middle so that the circle of the boiler can be struck out at both ends. Plane to shape and rub down with sandpaper. Fit a disc at the front, and make a door of two pieces glued together to form a rebate. Note the flat right-hand side to enable a hinge to be fitted.

The funnel, or chimney, consists of three pieces glued together. The lower disc is shaped to fit over the boiler, and a hole is bored about halfway down the dowel. A screw driven down attaches it to the boiler.

Cab. Cut the front and bore the holes for the windows. The sides are shaped and glued and nailed to it.

Tender. This is simply three pieces glued and nailed together. The lower edges should be glued, and the whole workpiece clamped down to the base. Nails can then be driven upwards through the base.

Attach the boiler with a screw through the saddle, and fasten the cab to the end with two screws. Clamp down to the base and nail upwards. Doors can be hinged to the back of the cab to open inward.

CUTTING LIST

	Long		Wide	Thick
	ft.	*in.*	*in.*	*in.*
Frame				
2 pieces	2	9	2⅛	¾
3 pieces		3¾	2⅛	¾
10 bearings		3¼	¾	¾
Wheels				
8 wheels		3½	3½	¾
2 wheels		6¼	6¼	¾
5 axles		6½	¾ dowel	
Base				
1 base	2	9	7¼	¾
2 ends		7¼	1⅝	¾
4 buffers		1¼	¾ dowel	
2 saddle pieces		3¾	1⅞	½
2 saddle pieces		2¾	1⅞	3/16
Boiler				
8 pieces	1	½	2½	¾
2 ends		4¼	4¼	¾
1 disc		5	5	3/16
1 door piece		2	2	½
1 door piece		2½	2½	3/16
1 funnel		1½	1⅜ dia.	
1 funnel rim		1¾	1¾	⅛
1 funnel base		1¾	1¾	⅜
Cab				
2 sides		8¼	6	⅝
1 front		8¼	5¾	⅝
1 top		6	7	⅝
Tender				
2 sides		11¾	5¾	¾
1 back		5½	5¾	¾
2 doors		6	2¾	¾

Allowances have been made in lengths and widths; thicknesses are net.

4. Block Truck

PAINTED IN BRIGHT and varied colors, a truck with blocks always appeals to toddlers. Any remnants can be used.

Truck. As a general guide, a length of 9″ × 6″ is about right, but the exact sizes are unimportant, as long as the blocks will have an easy fit. Cut the opposite sides to the same length and nail them together. A base of plywood is nailed underneath. Note that all corners and edges are rounded over. Fasten two square axles beneath by screwing downwards through the bottom, allowing a slight projection at each side. The wheels are wooden discs pivoted on round-head screws.

Blocks. All the blocks should be cut to the same size. Square up the wood in lengths and round over the edges. A stop attached to the cutting block enables any number to be cut to the same size. Round over the remaining edges and all corners. Finish with varied colors. To avoid the difficulty of handling when the paint is wet, stick three brads into one side. You can then hold them while painting, and the blocks can be supported on them while they dry. Allow to dry thoroughly before use.

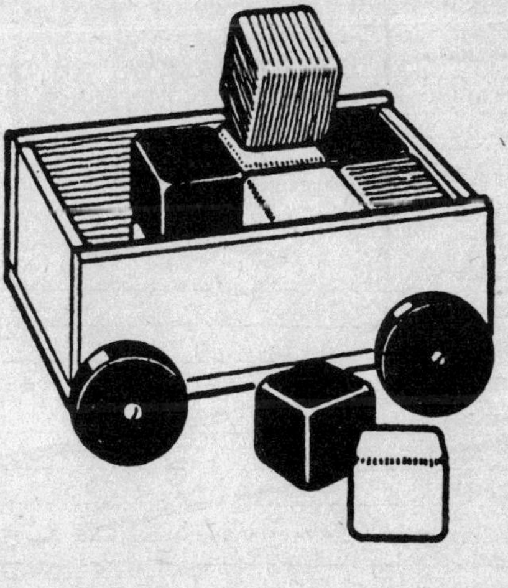

Illus. 1.
The blocks can be cut from any standard size of timber, and the truck made to suit.

5. Sand Motor

THIS TOY IS popular owing to its dual capacity: For the young child it provides all the joys of the sandbox but on a smaller scale, and it is a source of power for the older child to attach and animate small models. For example, the cranked handle could be used to operate a pivot-jointed figure. Or a grooved wheel could be fitted directly to the axle, and an elastic band fan/drive belt used to turn small secondary wheels.

Construction is simple. It can be made of plywood, and it consists of the body, or carcass, into which the rotor is fitted. The axle upon which the rotor revolves is formed into a small crank at one end, and from this point the movement is obtained to work models. Above the rotor is a hopper into which sand is loaded to trickle through the central orifice into the buckets formed in the rotor, thus operating the motor. A tray that can be made to any desired dimensions contains the complete unit, thus keeping the toy clean and suitable for a table game. To manipulate the sand, you can make a small scoop from plywood remnants.

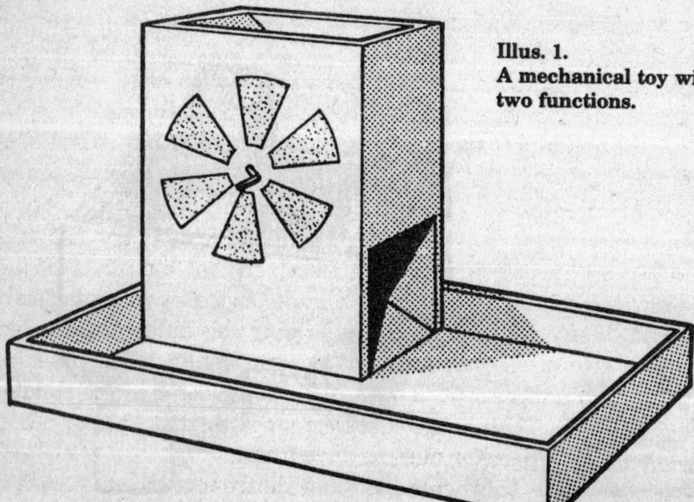

Illus. 1.
A mechanical toy with two functions.

The rotor. Mark out and cut two circles of plywood about 1/8″ thick, the centers being clearly marked and bored out a tight fit on the axle. This part should be made accurately to ensure that it revolves truly when mounted. A good plan is to thread the circles upon the axle, press both together, and mark around the outer edges eight equal divisions on the inner faces of the circles. From the marks made on the edges, draw radial lines, which will be used to locate the buckets when gluing up later.

Now cut off and prepare the material for the buckets. You might use 1/8″ ply. See that the length is accurate, as otherwise a fair joint cannot be made when erecting the rotor. Glue up as a subassembly each back and bottom, keeping the ends flush and level. Put aside to dry. Assemble the buckets upon one circle of the rotor sides. Lay this upon a flat surface, inside face upwards, and glue each bucket well, with the bottom of each bucket lying exactly upon the radial lines drawn on the circle and flush to the outer edge. When this has set, glue the end joints of the buckets standing uppermost and place the remaining side in position, taking care that the edges are flush and true.

If this work has been carried out carefully, the rotor should spin true when the axle is pushed into position. Should it wobble a little, however, do not attempt to alter it, as a certain amount of latitude has been allowed in the hopper feed to accommodate this possibility.

The carcass, or body. Plywood is the best material for this part. Cut out and square up, and, placing the two sides together, locate and drill a hole that will allow the axle to rotate freely. You might also want to cut perforations in the sides, as shown in Illus. 1, and paint the faces of the rotor.

The better method of fastening the frame is with small wood screws bored through the faces of the sides and secured to the ends. The back is dry-screwed only to facilitate removal of the rotor if required at any time. Having prepared these parts, it is necessary to prepare the axle (F) and spacing collets (E) before assembling. For the axle, obtain a straight piece of 1/8″ galvanized iron wire and fashion one end into a crank having about a 1/4″ throw. This is not critical, but if it is too large it would probably cause the motor to work sluggishly when models are attached. If any difficulty is met in forming this axle, make the wire red hot so that it will bend easily with a pair of pliers. The collets can be made from a piece of 1/2″ dowel, a hole being bored in the middle to accept the axle. Their lengths are arranged so that the rotor has a little end play. The rotor must revolve freely.

To assemble the body, glue and screw the front to the ends, push the axle through the bearing hole, and place a collet in position. A touch of two-tube resin glue will secure this to the axle. Now push the rotor on the axle, again securing with a touch of adhesive, and finally fasten the remaining collet. The back can be placed in position, and, if everything is correct, the rotor should revolve centrally and truly in the frame. Note: In the interests of child safety, you could glue wooden beads on the ends of the axle wire.

Interior. The position of the plywood sides forming the hopper is shown in Illus. 2. There is nothing special about them other than a little neat fitting. They only require securing with glue. The outlet should not be too large or the sand will run too quickly.

The deflector board at the base can be closely fitted and glued, and, if desired, a small shelf can be fitted to form a base to any model being operated (see side section). To obtain movement for a model, various methods can be used. But, generally, if a slot is used, it is possible to obtain either vertical or horizontal movements, either being governed by the direction of the slot in the model, the model being pivoted always in the line of direction of the slot. This is shown at D.

Illus. 2. Sectional side and end views, and small details.

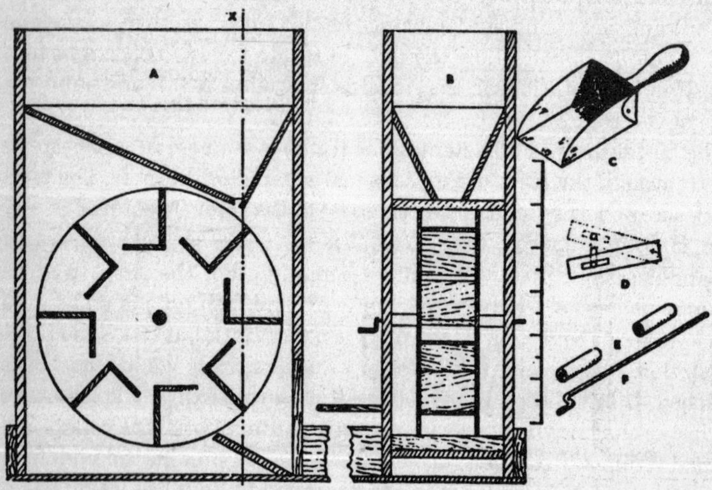

6. Toy Scales

WITH THIS TOY, children can have a lot of fun comparing the weights of various objects. For the twin uprights (A), take two lengths of ⅜″ wood 8″ long. The width at the base can be 1¼″, tapering to 1″ at the top. Cut tenons to enter the base. These uprights are placed ⅜″ apart and are supported at the foot by the piece (B), 2½″ × 1¼″ and ⅜″ thick, which is glued to them.

Base. The base (C), to be firm, should be ½″, squared up to 10″ × 4″ and finished with chamfered edges. Toes are optional; if used, they can be 1″ square, cut from any scrap of thin wood.

The bar (D), of ¼″ wood, is 7½″ long × ½″ wide. Mark the middle and drill a fine hole. By passing a wire through this hole, the balance can be tested and any necessary adjustment can be made. To fit the bar, drill through the uprights about ¾″ from the top and pass in wire 1⅛″ long and 1/16″ in diameter. The balance bar (D) is slipped onto this wire with a thin metal washer on each side. On the uprights, stop up the holes drilled for the wire.

Discs. Discs (E) can be 3″ in diameter. Use ⅛″ plywood, painting the edges, and suspend with stout cotton thread. Any adjustment in the balance can be made by gluing pieces of cardboard to the underside of the lighter disc.

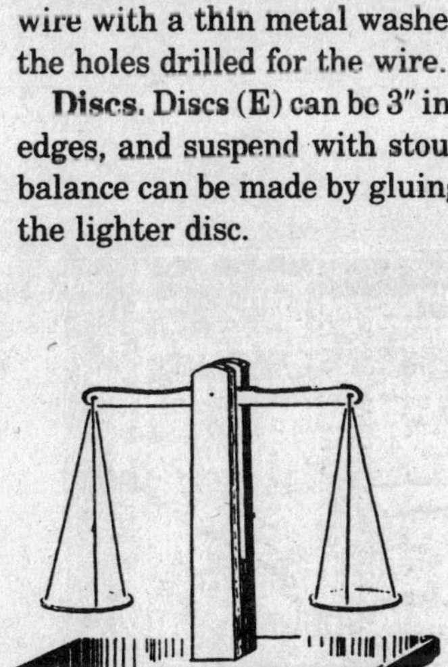

Illus. 1.
Completed toy.

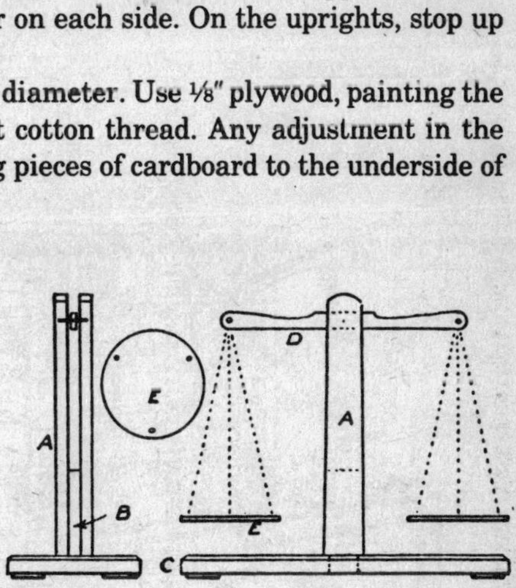

Illus. 2.
Elevations with scale.

7. Toy Shop Counter and Shelving

OF TODDLER TOYS, few are more satisfying than the make-believe shop, especially when made to a fair size. If desired, an altogether larger toy shop could be made, say, 3′ long × 2′ 6″ wide to 2′ 9″ high.

Counter. For a useful counter of the size suggested, the following parts are required (the lettered parts are shown in Illus. 2).

	Long		Wide	Thick
	ft.	*in.*	*in.*	*in.*
(A) two ends		6	4¼	½
(B) front	2	3	6	⅜
(C) shelf	2	2½	4¼	⅜
(D) two partitions		4¾	4¼	½
(E) top	2	3¼	5¼	¼

Illus. 1.
Toy shop for toddlers.
The display case is
27″ × 18″; the counter
is 27″ × 6″ high.

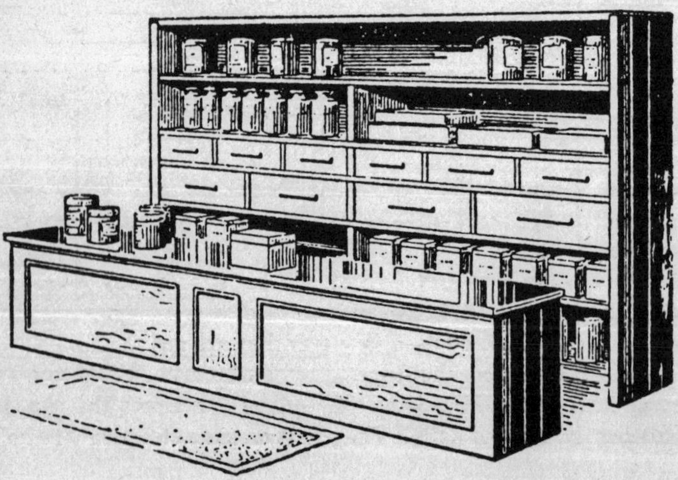

The ends (A) are trenched for the shelf (C), which will be glued in. The front (B) is glued on and additionally held with a few nails. It can also be glue-blocked at the corners and under the shelf. The two partitions (D) are housed to the shelf, and the top (E) is glued down and either nailed or blocked; all nail holes should be neatly stopped.

If you are going to paint it, you can paint lines on the counter front to represent panelling. Or the panelling can be effected by means of narrow, say ¼", strip detail. A pair of toy scales, with weights, should be obtained.

Drawers. Toy drawers can be made in the simple manner indicated if you have facilities for clamping up small glued work. Using ¼" for fronts and 3/16" for sides and backs, the parts can be glued together. Thin 1/16" plywood will serve for the bottom, also glued on. If all parts have been correctly gauged and are well clamped in the gluing, they will stand constant wear. The actual front is, of course, a dummy, and later a thin overlay of plywood is glued over everything to hide the joints. Wood handles or knobs will be added.

Display case. This, in detail, may vary slightly, but it is wise to follow the general dimensions given below (lettered parts shown in Illus. 2).

	Long		Wide	Thick
	ft.	*in.*	*in.*	*in.*
(F) two ends	1	6	5⅛	½
(G) bottom shelf	2	3¾	5⅛	½
(H) partition	1	1¼	5⅛	½
(J) five shelves	2	3	5⅛	¼
(K) two drawer divisions		2½	5⅛	¼
two drawer divisions		2	5⅛	¼
(L) top	2	3¼	5⅛	½
(M) back (ply)	2	3¼	17¼	3/16

For the drawer fronts, allow one length 26" × 2" × ¼" and one length 26" × 1½" × ¼". These lengths allow for fitting, but all the thicknesses are net.

As the display case and counter will be painted, any wood can be used. For lasting wear, however, it is wise to select a hardwood. Plywood may, of course, be used for parts that are not prominent.

For the ends, bottom shelf, and top, it is wise to use ½" material. The bottom shelf (G) is housed to the ends (F), whereas the top (L) is rebated on, glued, and nailed. The partition piece (H) should be housed

Illus. 2.
Scale elevations and details of counter and

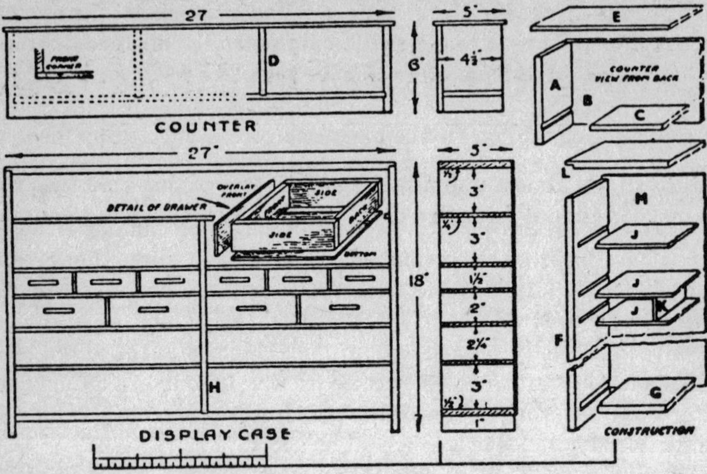

to the bottom shelf and nailed to the upper shelf (J). If drawers are to be introduced, it is well to house them in the intermediate shelves (J) to both ends and the partition. Shallow grooves should also be run in these shelves for the division pieces (K), the little extra trouble being worthwhile if the drawers are to run smoothly. The work should be carefully gauged, as it is an advantage (to children, at least) if the drawers can be interchangeable.

Many dummies can be made up to resemble boxes, tins, and bottles. They can be mostly cut out of wood and, when painted, look very realistic. A box of model maker's acrylic colors is handy for this.

8. Toys on Wheels and Stands

THERE IS AN almost unlimited variety of toys of this kind that you can make. A glance through a child's picture book will give you many suggestions.

Animals on wheels or stands. For these, you can either saw the shape out of a single piece of wood, say ½ or ⅝", as for the zebra, or you can use two pieces of ⅜" wood, as for the lamb. The advantage of the latter method is that you can show four legs in a realistic form. Plywood, ¼" or ⅜", has the advantage of being considerably stronger. The shapes can be cut with a fret, coping, or scroll saw, and the corners rounded over. Where the feet join the stand, holes to receive them can be cut. The coloring, though based on nature, should be bold and bright and convey a touch of humor. Screws serve as axles for the wheels, which arc cut from wood.

Wriggling serpent. This is best made in a single length, as shown in the diagram. After the joints have been cut, the parts are held

Illus. 1.
Animals on wheels and stand.

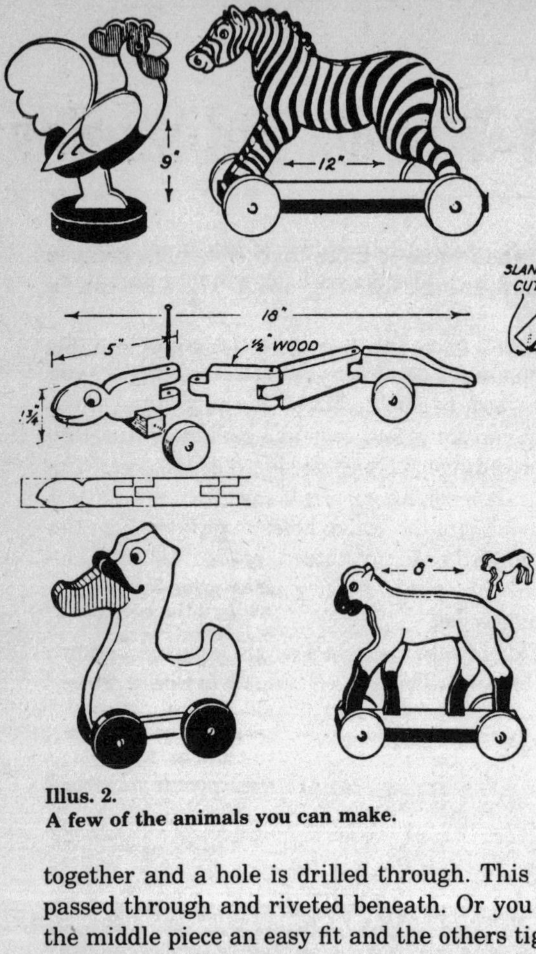

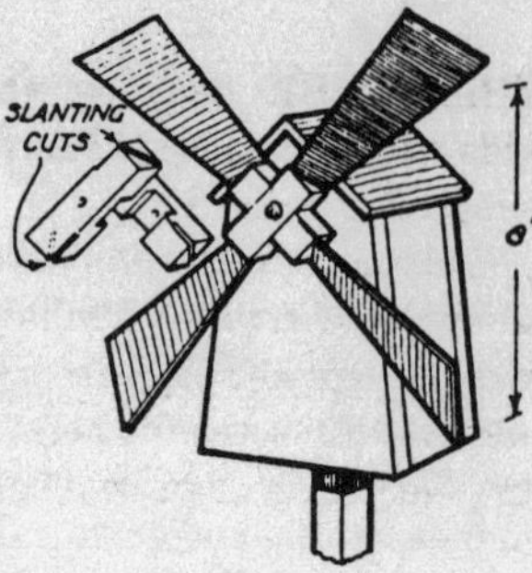

Illus. 3.
Revolving windmill.

Illus. 2.
A few of the animals you can make.

together and a hole is drilled through. This enables fine nails to be passed through and riveted beneath. Or you could make the hole in the middle piece an easy fit and the others tight. This saves riveting.

Windmill. This calls for making a simple box with one end pointed and the roof pieces being nailed over it. The sails consist of two little central blocks 1½ or 2″ long halved together. At both sides of each, slanting cuts are made with the saw (make sure that all slope in the same direction) and a piece of thin plywood is glued in. The whole mechanism revolves on a brass round-head screw. If the wood used for the house is thin, a little thicker block can be glued inside to provide a bearing for the screw. At the front, another block is needed to enable the sails to clear the roof or, alternatively, several washers can be used. The sails will revolve freely if the toy is placed in the wind. It could be used to frighten away birds in the garden.

9. Boat-on-Wheels Riding Toy

THIS IS THE ideal toy when there is more than one child, because kids will have a lot of fun pushing each other about. The sizes can be adapted if desired.

Top and bottom. These can be cut out of any wood of suitable thickness—½ to ⅞". Probably two or even three pieces will have to be jointed together in their width to enable the shape to be cut out. It is advisable to screw battens beneath to strengthen the joints. To mark out the shape, draw in a central line with a straightedge and mark in

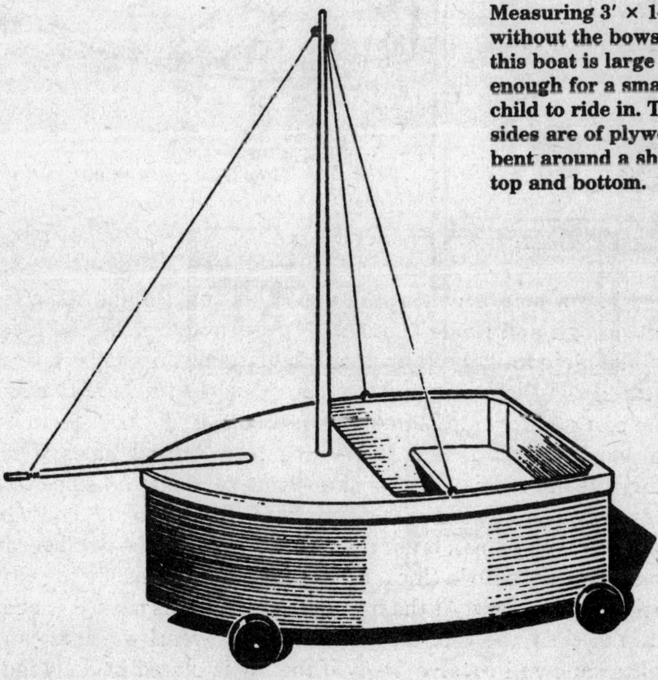

Illus. 1. Measuring 3' × 14" without the bowsprit, this boat is large enough for a small child to ride in. The sides are of plywood bent around a shaped top and bottom.

the line of the stern square with it. Pencil in the length and the greatest width (which occurs about 14″ from the stern), and drive in nails at the bow and the stern width. Bend a thin lath of wood so that it reaches to the greatest width, and hold it in position with a nail driven into one side. Mark around the lath with pencil, and repeat for the opposite side.

Cut around with a bow saw or keyhole saw, and smooth with the plane. Trace around the shape to mark out the top. Note from Illus. 3 that a cross batten is attached immediately beneath the mast.

Back and sides. A thickness similar to that of the bottom can be

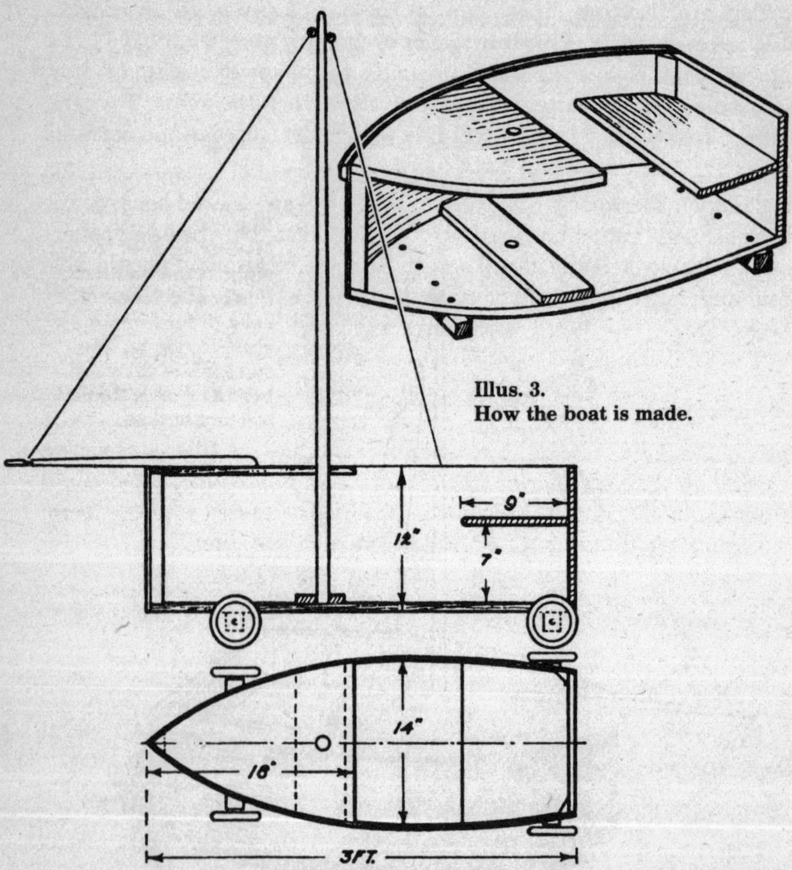

Illus. 3.
How the boat is made.

Illus. 2.
Elevation and plan with sizes.

used for the back or stern. Fasten with nails or screws, and prepare the seat to the same curvature as the bottom, rounding over the front edge. An upright to be fastened at the bow must be planed to a triangular section; the angle is obtained easily by placing the wood in position on the bottom.

Cut out the sides in 1/8 or 3/16" plywood, the grain running vertically to simplify bending. It is advisable to allow a slight overlap for trimming. Begin the erection by fastening the bow upright between the top and bottom and nailing on a couple of temporary struts at the middle to steady the parts while the sides are attached. Start at the front, attaching the ply with countersunk screws and glue. Bend the ply gradually around the sides, gluing and nailing as you proceed. When you reach the back, trim off the overhang at both the bow and stern and then deal with the other side. A 1/4" lath about 1 1/4" wide is attached to the top edges all around.

Triangular blocks glued in the back corners strengthen the back joints (Illus. 3). The seat is nailed in all around. To give a suitable bearing for the wheels, squares of about 1 1/2" are screwed beneath the bottom. Long round-head screws serve to pivot the wheels. Washers are advisable on both sides. The wheels could be either of plastic with plump tires, or they could be cut out of 3/4 or 7/8" wood. The diameter is about 4 1/2".

The addition of the mast and bowsprit completes the boat. Ropes attached to screw eyes could be added, as well as sails, at any rate, at the front. Back sails and ropes are best omitted as they will get in the way of the child. You could also add a rudder, with a tiller screwed on at the top. Two screw eyes in the stern and two in the rudder could serve to pivot it, a dowel rod or long bolt being passed through them. Alternatively, ropes could be fitted instead of the tiller.

10. Home Pinball

YOU CAN BE fairly certain that this game will keep children absorbed and amused for quite a while. The pinball table in Illus. 1 has the added attraction of allowing for the balls to be fed one after another to the table for play, and, unless the feed wheel is removed, they cannot be taken from the table, so there is no chance of the balls getting lost. For a woodworker with average skill and some woodturning ability, making the table should not be difficult, but considerable care should be taken to see that the holes in the side of the case align with the pockets in the feed wheel, otherwise the wheel will not function properly. It is also important for the surfaces on which the balls roll to be as smooth as possible.

The sides of the case can be put together with lap joints, but before assembly the top edges require rebating for the plastic covering. Use

Illus. 1. Pinball is a game that people of all ages enjoy.

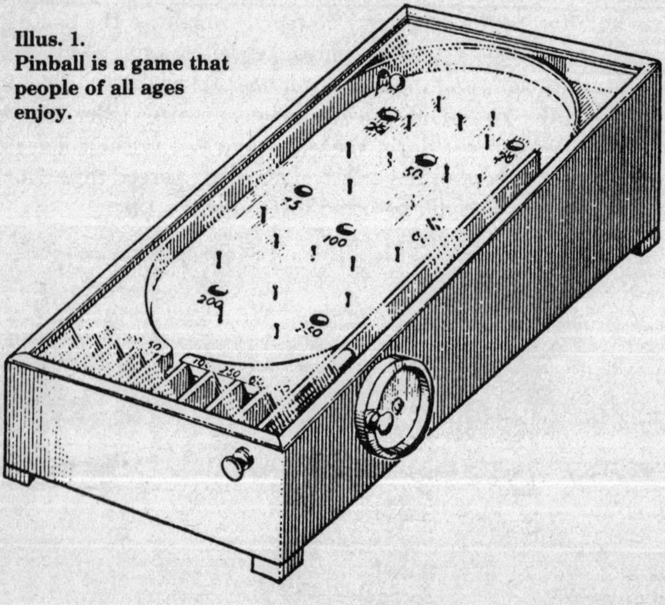

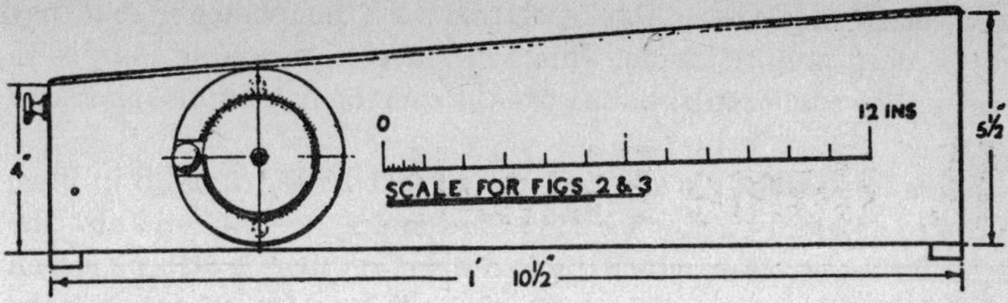

Illus. 2.
Side elevation.

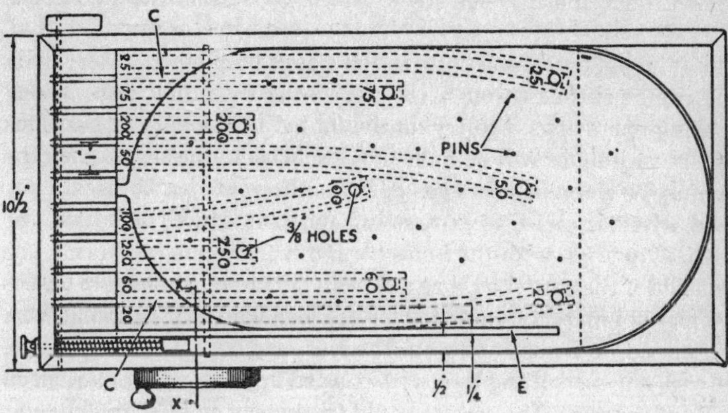

Illus. 3.
Plan.

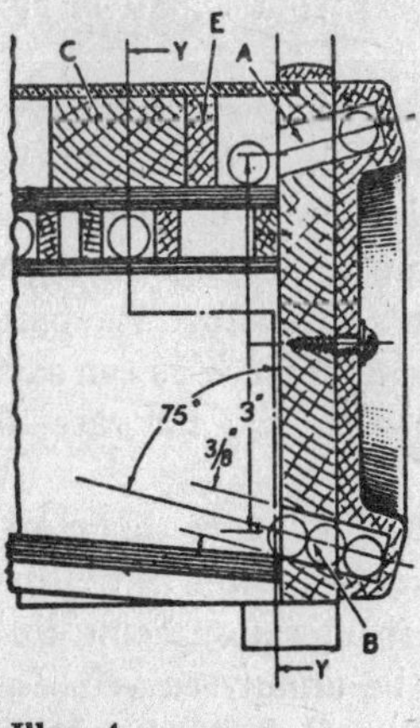

Illus. 4.
Section on X-X.

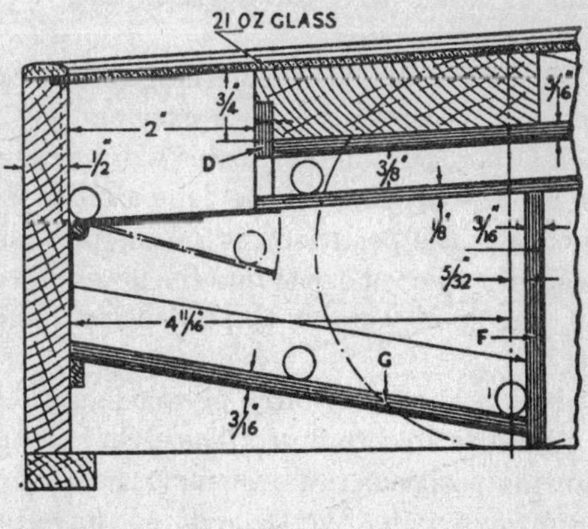

Illus. 5.
Section on Y-Y.

clear plastic sheet in 1⁄10″ thickness, and work the rebates so that they are 1⁄8″ deep and 3⁄16″ wide. This will leave an adequate margin to receive the veneer nails that secure the capping holding the plastic in place.

Holes for balls. It is advisable to bore the holes (A and B in Illus. 4) before assembly. After locating the centers carefully and also the center for the screw on which the feed wheel revolves, a drilling jig can be made. This can comprise a strip of wood, say, 1″ × 5⁄8″, through the thickness of which a 3⁄8″ hole is drilled at an angle of 75° approximately to the surface. The screw center is also marked on the strip, and a nail driven through and into the screw center marked on the side of the case.

Using the jig, one of the holes in the side is then bored, after which the jig can be turned through 180° for boring the other hole. During the boring operations, the jig can be nailed to the side at positions where the nail holes will be hidden by the wheel. As the holes for the balls must be clean, it is suggested that a Forstner bit be used.

Feed wheel. Since it is extremely important for the pockets in the feed wheel to align with the holes (A and B), it is suggested that the drilled side of the case should be used as a jig for boring the blind holes in the piece of material intended for the feed wheel. This should be a close-grained wood such as beech. The piece can be fastened to the side of the case during drilling by a screw turned into the center marked on the side of the case. The screw should be slightly smaller in diameter than that which will be finally used. The table has been designed for 5⁄16″-diameter ball bearings, and, when drilling for the pockets, care should be taken that the depth of each is such that a ball is just accommodated.

If the pockets are too deep, a ball behind the one in the lower pocket will partly project into the pocket and obstruct the turning of the wheel. Other, but smaller, holes will be required to be drilled in the case, but the drilling can be done after assembly. You can see from Illus. 5 that the partitions of the compartments into which the balls pass after play are housed into the lower end of the case. You can save some trouble if you cut these housings before putting the case together.

Table. Best-quality-birch plywood should be used since this material permits a smooth finish. The eight holes can be located as in Illus. 3, but the positions are arbitrary, the only consideration being that the runways under the table do not have to be unduly curved. The nails are driven in after the board has been enamelled. The two lower ball guides (C) are cut so that the grain runs obliquely in order to

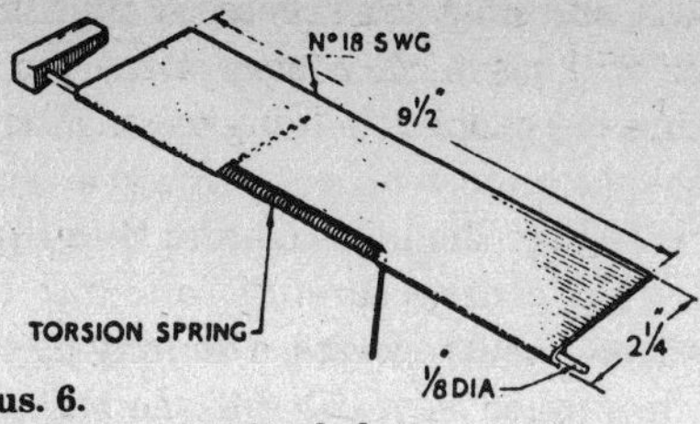

Illus. 6.
Detail of spring-loaded closure.

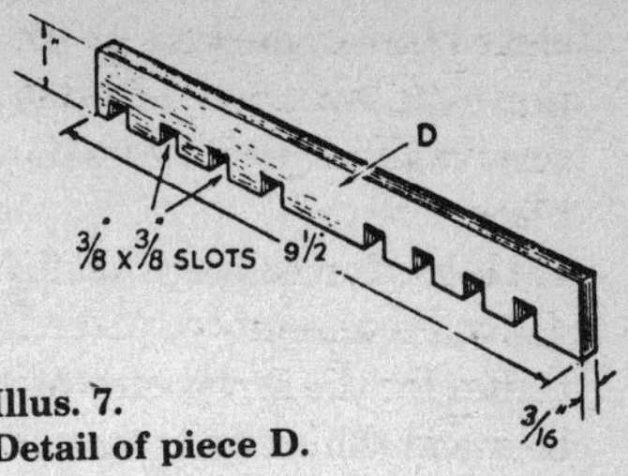

Illus. 7.
Detail of piece D.

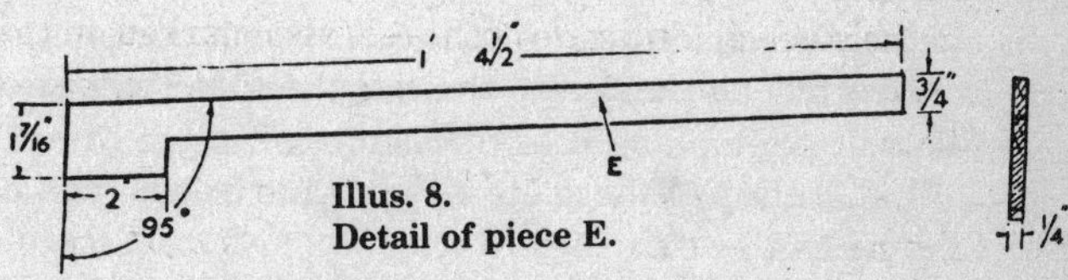

Illus. 8.
Detail of piece E.

avoid short fibres at the tapered ends. These guides will require rebating to receive the slotted piece (D shown in Illus. 7).

It is advisable to form the walls of the runways from 3/16″ ply, since this will allow nails being driven through the thickness of the walls to hold them in position after gluing. This cannot be done satisfactorily if hardboard is used. You can now prepare the partitions of the ball-receiving compartments. It should be noted that one partition of the compartment designated "20" is formed by a projection on the piece (E, Illus. 8). The partitions are attached by the housings and by veneer nails driven through the piece (D).

Having prepared the guides (C), you should then glue them to the table and secure them by a few veneer nails from underneath. You can see from Illus. 5 that the lower edge of the table is flush with the bottom of the rebates in the guides (C). In attaching the piece (E), it is advisable to prepare a small block ⅜″ wide and to use this block as a gauge when attaching the piece. This will ensure that the passageway along which the balls are propelled is uniform in width.

When these parts have been attached, the table is inverted and packed up so that a solid support is provided. The positions of the runways are then marked, and the walls glued and pinned in position. The gauge previously used can again be employed to obtain uniformity in the width of the channels. Where the runways are curved, it is best to drive a few nails into the board to retain the curve of the walls while the glue is setting. When the runways are completed, the slotted piece (D), with the partitions nailed to it, can be glued and nailed into the rebate provided for its reception. The floors of the runways are formed from a piece of ⅛″ plywood of adequate width to cover all of the runways. You can see from Illus. 5 that the floor projects over the lower edge of the piece (D) so that no obstruction is caused to the passage of the balls. The slots should align with the runways. You may find it necessary to slightly trim the openings in order to secure proper alignment.

The parts now assembled constitute a unit, which is inserted in the case, and the table is rested on fillets glued and nailed to the sides of the case. Note that one of the walls of the runway from hole "25" is against the adjacent side of the case, which prevents the attachment of a fillet, but adequate support for the table will be provided by the fillets at the top and the other long side of the case. The semicircular wall at the top of the table will have to be attached after the table is in place.

Spring-loaded closure for ball compartments. This is cut from aluminum sheet of the gauge specified in Illus. 6. A satisfactory alternative to the use of snips for cutting is to make deep scores where the metal is to be cut and then insert the waste part of the metal in a saw kerf up to the score. If now the metal is bent first one way and then the other by applying pressure through a piece of wood held against the metal, it will soon fracture along the scores. The bead retaining the ⅛″ closure pivoting rod can be formed by clamping the closure between two pieces of iron in a metal vise with the edge to be bent over projecting. The rod is then laid against the projecting edge and the latter hammered over, the blows being applied to a piece of iron placed against the edge.

To finish the bead, the workpiece is removed from the vise and laid on a flat metal surface, when the partly turned-over edge can be further hammered to embrace the rod. Obviously, the space for the spring is filed out before forming the bead. The rod will have to be withdrawn to allow the insertion of the spring, and, when replaced, it should be a tight fit in the bead so that it moves with the closure. The operating lever can comprise a piece of brass, which is drilled to receive the end of the rod, the end being sweated in the hole.

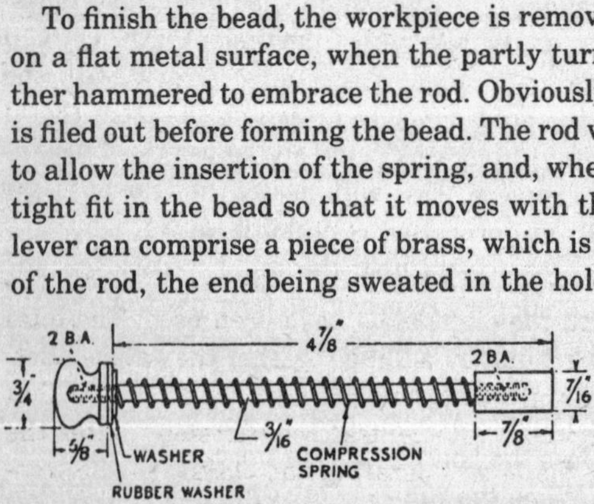

Illus. 9.
Detail of ball impeller.

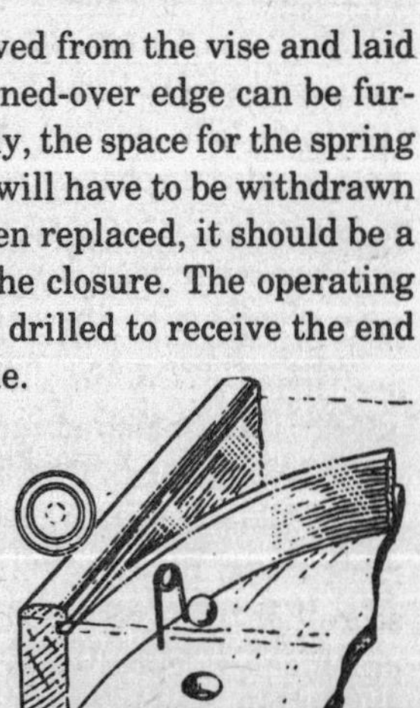

Illus. 10.
Detail of spring.

Shoot. This is formed by a partition (F) extending across the width of the case. Abutting against the partition is an inclined floor (G), which, with the partition, forms a valley that slopes downwards towards the hole (B, Illus. 4). The slope of the floor should be such that the valley has the greatest possible incline in the space available. The floor rests on fillets, as indicated in Illus. 5.

Ball impeller. The 3⁄16″ rod can comprise a 6″ wire nail filed clean in the lathe and cut to length. The ends are threaded 2 B.A. to receive the knob and head, which are drilled and tapped accordingly. Boxwood is very suitable for these parts since this wood can be tapped satisfactorily.

When the impeller is in position on the board, the metal washer abuts against the inside of the case, the rubber washer being outside. This latter washer cushions the knob against the case when the impeller is released.

The scores allocated to the holes do not necessarily have to be followed. It is suggested that before the plastic is attached, a number of games should be played and the aggregate score noted for each hole. From the results obtained, the values of the holes can be suitably accessed. Before driving the nails into the board, it may be worthwhile pressing in some ordinary dress pins so that the best positions can be found.

You can see from Illus. 1 that where the upper curved wall flows into the side wall to the left of the table, a spring abutment is provided. On striking the spring, a ball bounces back and rolls down the board. The path to be taken by a ball can be more or less determined by carefully adjusting the speed of the ball and consequently the amount of rebound. A safety pin with the guard removed can serve for this spring.

Finish. As the pinball table is largely intended for use by young people, it is suggested that the table be enamelled a bright green color.

Playing a game. Assuming that the balls have been discharged into the shoot, a player operates the feed wheel to raise a ball to the position for play on the table. When the ball has been played, the operation is repeated until the eight balls have been used. The total score obtained can then be found by adding together the values allotted to those compartments in which the balls are found. Those that have failed to score will occupy the central compartment. After the score has been recorded, the lever operating the closure of the compartment is depressed so that the balls are again returned to the chute and will be ready for the next player.

11. Miniature Train

COMPARE THIS WITH some of the crude toys offered at high prices. It not only has a realistic appearance, but it is very strong. Incidentally, the engine only took two evenings to make, the woodwork being completed in the first and the finishing in the second.

There are many additions you could make to this train: carriages, locomotive with tender, station, signal box, and so on. It's best to draw them in full size so that you maintain the correct proportions.

Engine. The construction is obvious from Illus. 2. Cut out the various parts to the sizes given, trim where necessary with the plane, and rub down any roughness with sandpaper. This latter should on no account be neglected because the toy relies very largely upon the finish for its effect. Rub off any sharp angles and corners. The rounded top of the cab can be chiselled and finished with sandpaper. Use dowels for the boiler, wheels, funnel, and dome. To ensure the wheels being all alike in thickness, you can fasten a stop to a mitre block having a square cut.

To assemble, nail the cab to the boiler, keeping it centered and the right height up from the bottom. Note that glue should be used throughout as well as nails. The strength is thereby increased enormously. SuperGlue answers the purpose very well. The base, which is $\frac{3}{16}$" thick, is now nailed to the cab, and the saddle prepared to fit beneath the boiler. Its top surface can be hollowed with a gouge or file. It is attached at the same time as the frame block to which the wheels

Illus. 1.
Tiny engine and trucks that can be cut from standard material.

Illus. 2.
The parts and their sizes.

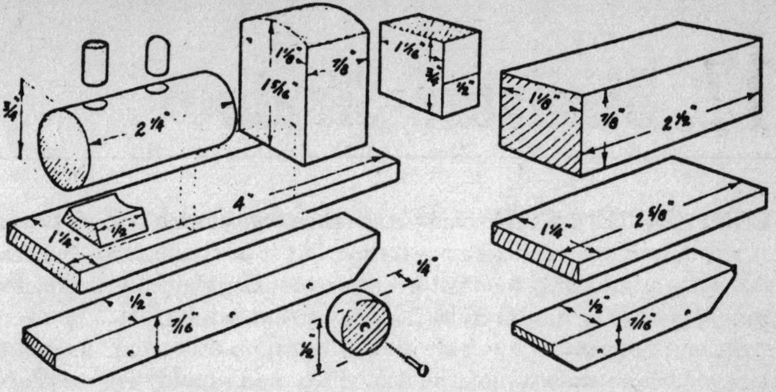

are screwed. Having glued the parts, fasten the base with a couple of nails to the cab. Drill a hole right through the frame block, base, and saddle, and knock a nail right through into the boiler. This way, you avoid splitting the saddle piece.

Bore ¼" holes along the top of the boiler, and glue in pieces of dowel to form the funnel and dome. The coal bunker is attached at the rear, and pieces of 3/16" material are cut to form the side tanks. Glue both the bottom edges and the sides of the side tanks, and nail through into the boiler.

Having cut off the wheels, drill a hole in the middle of each large enough to enable them to revolve freely on the round-head screws to be used. Use ¾" fine-gauge screws and stagger the opposite wheels slightly so that the screws do not foul each other in the thickness of the wood. You will find that if you use ¾" screws, they will pass nearly through the frame block.

Finishing. The simplest finish is with acrylic paints. They are ready for use as they are, but they can be mixed with water if necessary. Acrylic paints come in vivid colors and cover well. They dry very quickly. Follow with a coat of clear varnish. If you use spirit or shellac varnish, it will dry rapidly. Oil varnish takes much longer to dry but is probably more durable. Details such as the windows and cab door can be painted in black. Complete all painting before varnishing.

Trucks. From the instructions given for the engine, you can easily make the trucks. A solid block can be used for the truck portion itself, this being mounted upon a base and frame block similar to that for the engine. For the oil tank, a piece of dowel can be used. The guard's van is a solid block and a separate end piece, with a piece of veneer or even cardboard bent around the top and glued down.

12. Backyard Sandbox

MANY CRUDE ARRANGEMENTS are often used for a children's sandbox, and the roughest contrivance will serve the purpose if no objection is taken to a structure that may be unsightly. Here, we present a form of combined box and table that can be folded up overnight and removed to a storage shed in winter. Later, when the child is beyond the sandbox age, the box will come in handy for seedlings and the like.

The design for this sandbox need not be followed in detail, the size depending on your own requirements and the construction largely on the material available. The material, if bought rough, can be planed just sufficiently to prevent a child's limbs from encountering splinters.

The sandbox presented here was made about 3′ 6″ square, being built of four sides, 3′ 6″ × 9″, nailed together and additionally held by heavy steel trunk corners. The floor was of tongued-and-grooved boarding, nailed on. Below, two 4½″ × ⅞″ battens were screwed across, as shown. These are desirable not only for strength but also for raising the floor off the grass.

The hinged tops, apart from acting as lids, serve either as tables or seats when folded back. This, of course, adds greatly to the usefulness of the box, which, without being filled with sand, provides (in the size indicated) a playpen that will accommodate as many as four toddlers.

Illus. 1. Children's sandbox—the double-top folds back to form tables or seats.

Illus. 2.
Sandbox construction.

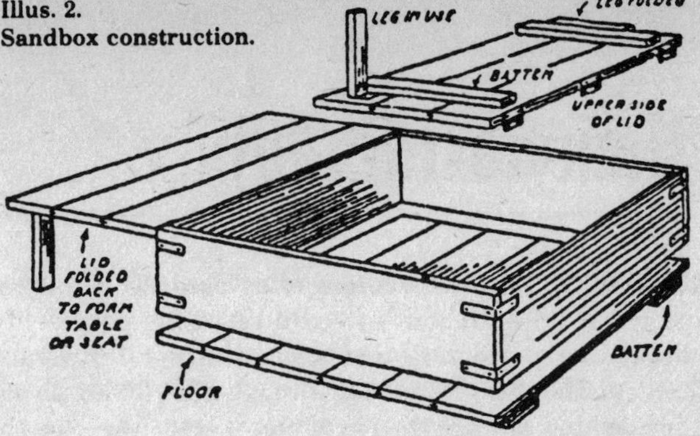

The tops, or lids (Illus. 2), are approximately 3′ 6″ × 1′ 9″, each being made up of tongued-and-grooved matchboard with 2½″ × ⅞″ battens screwed on. (Note that these battens are screwed on the *upper* face when the lid is *closed.*) Each lid is fitted with three stout hinges, which, of course, will necessarily show on the outside.

To provide legs for the lids when opened back, you can use four short lengths of 2″ × ⅞″ material. The length will depend on the width of the box sides. The legs may conveniently be fitted to lie alongside (and outside) the lid battens and should be hinged with stout back-flap hinges.

When the lids are open and in use either as tables or seats, there is little chance of the legs bending inward. Any risk of this can be obviated by very slightly bevelling the hinged end of each leg so that it shows a gentle outward splay when on the ground. Turnbuttons can be screwed to the battens to keep the legs in position when down.

As already stated, the box can be any size; however, 2′ 6″ square is about the minimum and 3′ 6″ is a useful average. Alternatively, it might be oblong, say, 4′ × 2′ 9″.

13. Hammering Toy

CHILDREN LOVE TO hammer, but they can do quite a lot of damage. However, here is a toy with which they can hammer away without doing any harm. The pellets are knocked into the hole at the top and are driven out at the end. They pass through an interior channel, lining up one behind the other, the pressure from the last pellet knocked in driving out the first one.

The accompanying drawings show how the toy works and how it is made. A channel is cut in the main block and a plywood side screwed or nailed to it to enclose the channel. A metal spring is screwed into a little recess in the top of the channel to offer a slight resistance to the pellets, otherwise they would pass through too easily. It is raised by the pellets as they pass through.

Construction. Plane up the main block to the sizes given, and cut the channel. Much of the waste can be removed by boring a series of holes along the length. A gouge is useful to follow, and finally a chisel. It is a good idea to prepare the pellets—say, half a dozen—to make sure that they pass through without jamming. A chip removed here and there will ease matters.

The spring can be cut from an old clock spring, or any other suitable metal can be used. Two holes must be drilled through it to take the screw. To drill the holes, heat the end of the spring to a cherry red and allow it to cool naturally. This will soften the steel. Hold the spring with a damp rag to prevent the heat from travelling and taking out the temper along the entire length.

Nail on the plywood side, and cut out the two ends and the top piece. The latter fits in grooves cut across the ends. Before fastening, cut a hole in one end to line up with the end of the channel. When complete, put the whole workpiece together with glue and nails. Drive in the nails and fill in the holes with plastic wood. Level down the joints and take off all sharp angles and corners with sandpaper. Finish with oil paint.

For the pellets, you can use short lengths of ¾" dowel rod. It is necessary to chamfer the ends as shown in the illustration so that the pellets pass around the curve easily.

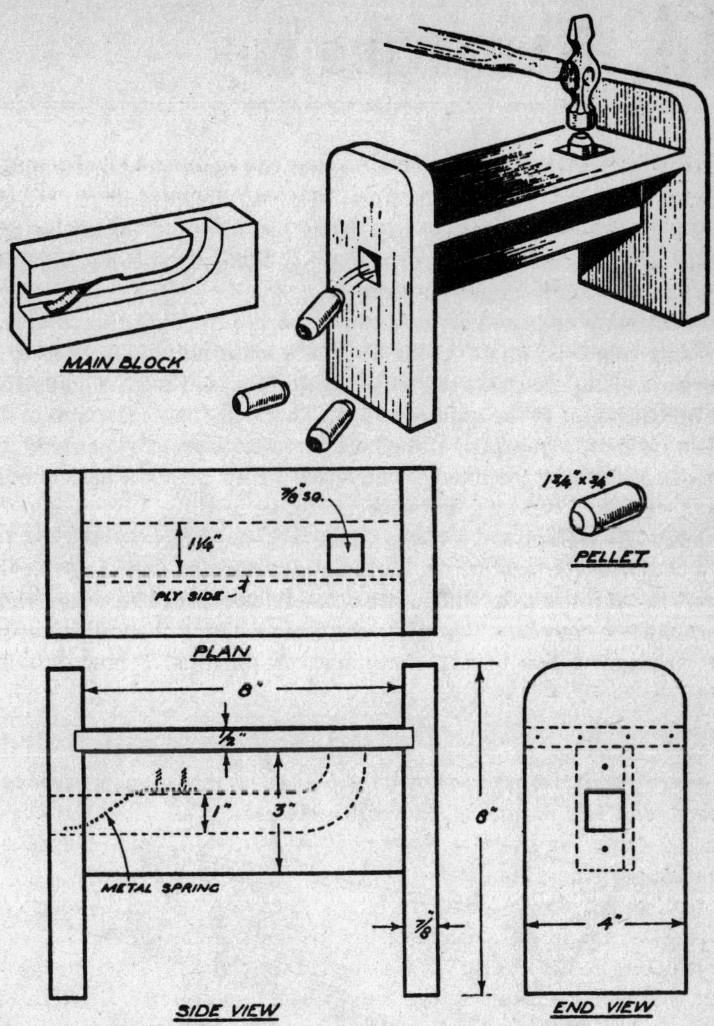

Sizes and construction of hammering toy.

14. Wheelbarrow

A WHEELBARROW IS an ever-popular toy among children, and, if painted in bright colors, it has an even stronger appeal. If you can get a ready-made wheel, wood or iron, by all means use it. Otherwise, it is quite simple to make one from solid wood, laminating two pieces with the grain at right angles for strength.

Practically any kind of wood can be used, providing that it is reasonably free from knots. Using 1″-square material, make a frame, as shown in Illus. 2. Draw the shape in full size so that the adjustable bevel can be set to the required angle. This will enable the ends of the cross rails to be marked; also, the shallow notches in which they fit. The ends forming the handles can either be left straight and rounded over, or pieces can be glued on beneath, as in Illus. 4, to enable the shape to be worked.

Put the parts together with glue and nails, and bore holes at the front to take the axle. Judge it as closely as possible and bore right through the one piece. Repeat on the other rail and then allow the bit to pass right across to correct any inaccuracy. Illus. 5 shows how the

Illus. 1.
The dimensions of this popular toy are 24″ long over the frame by about 12″ in width.

wheel is made from two ½″ thicknesses, the grain at right angles. Bore a hole halfway in from each side to take a tightly fitting iron axle rod, and add a ½″ circular block at each side, as in Illus. 5, to stiffen it. Illus. 5 also shows how the ends of the frame rails are cut away to enable the axle to be fitted afterwards.

For the body, use wood about ½″ thick. Prepare the bottom to the sizes in Illus. 3 to fit on the framework, standing in a trifle. All edges will have to be bevelled, but this is best done after the sides have been added. The angles at which the ends of the long sides are planed are not important. Since the bottom edges are a little over 12″ long, the top edges might be about 18″. Cut to shape, and bevel the bottom edges of both to give the required slope. They must be alike.

Fasten to the bottom with glue and nails, and fit the front end, as in Illus. 6, noting that the edges must be at an angle. Cut the top to a curve, and fasten again with glue and nails. Follow with the rear end. Level the edges and either nail or screw to the frame.

The legs are notched to fit over the rails and are taken off at an angle to line up with the slope of the sides. Fasten with a screw through each rail, and nail through the body at the top.

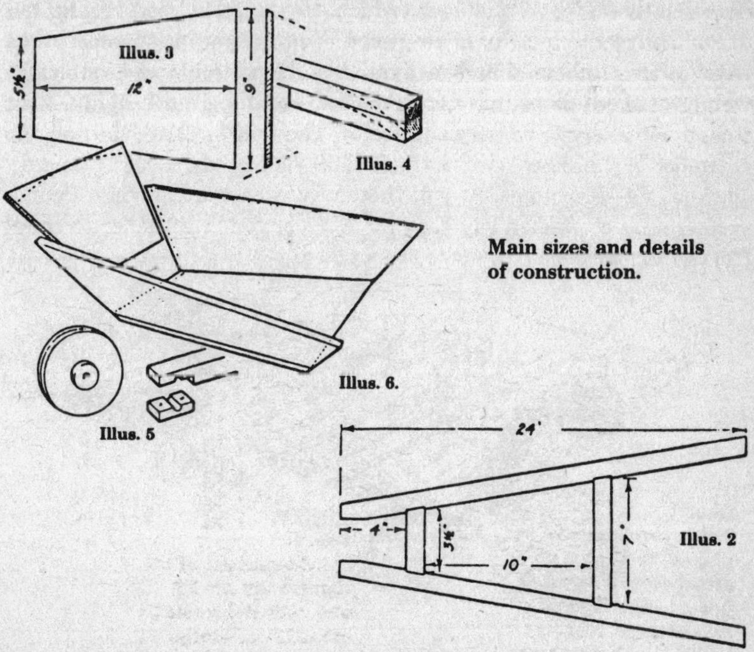

Main sizes and details of construction.

15. Xylophone

THE XYLOPHONE HAS become an extremely popular instrument in recent years, and the work involved in making it is most interesting. The one presented here consists of 27 notes, ranging from G to A. If carefully made of suitable wood, a practical instrument is possible with good tone. There is nothing difficult about the work, though you need a good ear for tuning. We are greatly indebted to Messrs. Boosey & Hawkes Ltd., manufacturers of musical instruments, for much of the information in this section.

Easily the best wood for the keys is Honduras rosewood. It has a ring about it that no other wood seems to possess. This wood may, however, be difficult to obtain. Should that be the case, try to find a timber of comparable weight and quality. The instrument presented here has notes of purpleheart, which yields quite good results but doesn't have the quality of rosewood. You may want to experiment with other timbers that are available. Honduras rosewood has a weight of about 60 pounds per cubic foot; anything much lighter than this is not likely to be very successful. The following are the weights of timber of a similar class: satinwood 59–64 pounds, cocus 74 pounds, boxwood 54–70 pounds. Any of these would be worth trying, though professional craftsmen say they have never found a timber to equal Honduras rosewood.

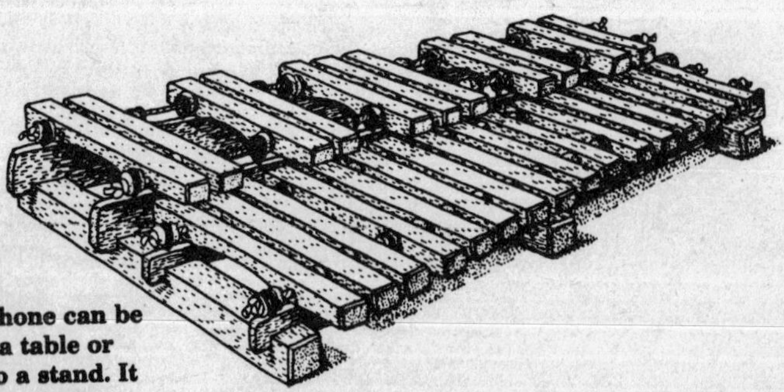

Illus. 1.
This xylophone can be played on a table or attached to a stand. It has a range of over two octaves. Middle C is the fourth note from the left in the front row.

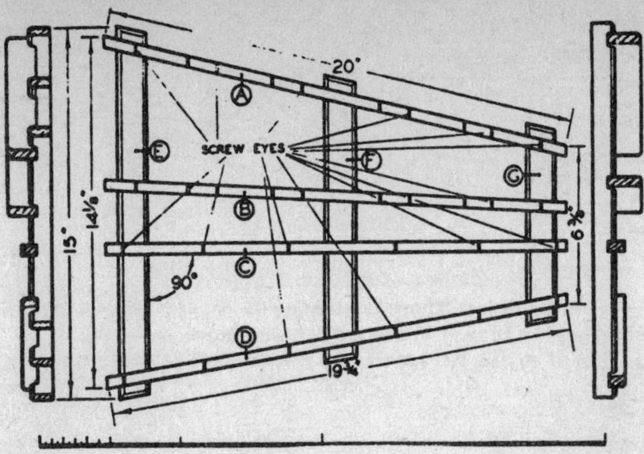

Illus. 2.
Construction of frame. Note that only the C member is at right angles with the E, F, and G cross pieces.

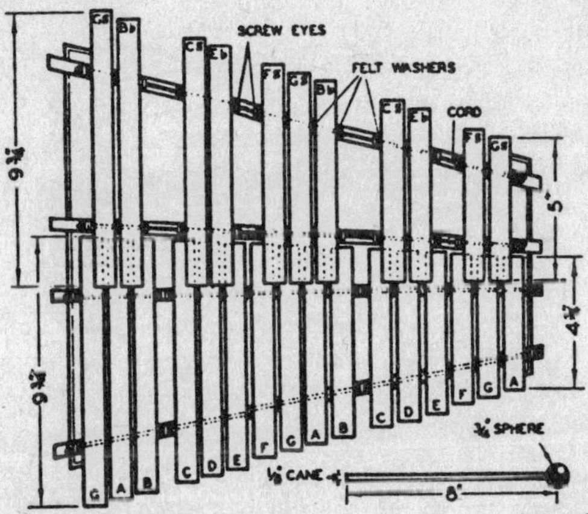

Illus. 3.
Position of keys on the framework. They are not fastened tightly; the cord with spacing washers holds them in place.

The stand can be made of any straight-grained timber. The one in this project is of Parana pine. The converging members fit into notches cut in the three cross pieces and are held with screws driven in from beneath. Strips of felt glued to the top edges provide a suitable bed for the keys to rest on.

Stand. Dimensions for the stand are given in Illus. 2. It is helpful

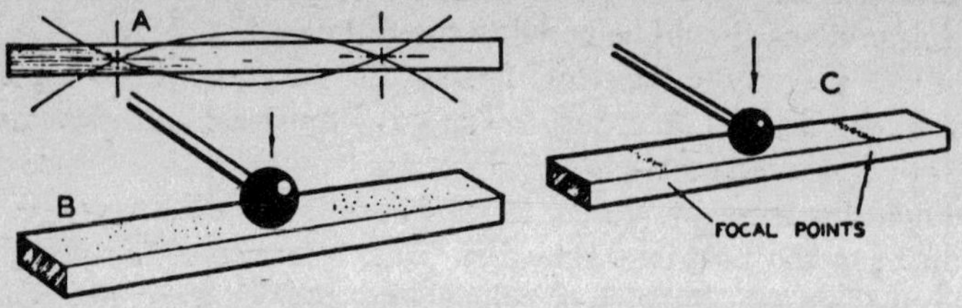

Illus. 4.
How the focal points can be found. There is no need to test each note this way if you follow the sizes in Illus. 3. When drilling the holes, some slight variation is permissible to enable the keys to be placed in alignment on the frame.

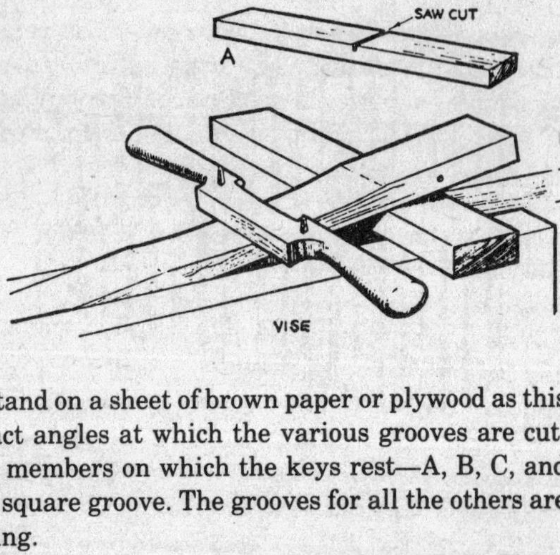

Illus. 5.
Trimming the note for correct pitch. Hollowing the underside has the effect of flattening the note; trimming the ends sharpens it.

to set out the entire stand on a sheet of brown paper or plywood as this will give you the exact angles at which the various grooves are cut. Note that of the four members on which the keys rest—A, B, C, and D—only C requires a square groove. The grooves for all the others are at an angle, all varying.

Plane up the four pieces (A, B, C, and D) to finish ⅜″ thick. Those that support the black notes (A and B) are 1¼″ wide, the others (C and D) ⅝″ wide. In this way, the black notes stand up above the others.

By placing the cross pieces (E, F, and G) on the full-size drawing, the exact positions of the grooves can be marked; also, the angles. Note that each set of notches is at the same angle. Thus, all those to hold piece A are at the same angle, and so on.

Since the grooves are cut with the saw and chisel, all the grooves in the cross pieces are drilled for the screws. The latter should be of fine gauge so that they do not split the thin wood, and, for the same reason, the thread holes should be bored to the full depth.

You can use any of the usual finishes for the stand: French polish, varnish, or cellulose. It is best to apply the finish when the parts are separate and to assemble later.

To hold the cords on which the notes are threaded, screw eyes are driven in in the positions shown in Illus. 3. Strips of felt are glued between them, any varnish or polish being scraped away beforehand. Felt can sometimes be obtained in strips, but it may have to be cut from a wide sheet.

Keys. All of the keys are ¾″ wide × ½″ thick. The length varies according to the note; the shorter it is, the higher the note. You can follow the sizes in Illus. 3, though you should realize that each has to be tuned afterwards. Plane up the wood in strips and cross-cut to the lengths given. Mark on the back of each the note it is supposed to be: A, C sharp, and so on.

Each has to be drilled in two places to take the cord, and there are ideally exact positions, known as the focal points, for the holes. The holes should certainly approximate to these, though anything like micrometer accuracy is quite unnecessary. A variation of as much as ⅛″ or so will not affect the note much. If the positions in Illus. 3 are followed, they will not be greatly off.

These focal points represent positions in the keys where there is practically no vibration. When a key is struck, it vibrates, as shown in great exaggeration by the curved lines at A in Illus. 4. The points where the curves cross each other are the focal points. You can test this for yourself by putting some fine dust on a key, as at B in Illus. 4, and striking with a hammer. The dust will tend to concentrate in the region of the focal points, as at C. The effect is more noticeable with a metal key than a wood one.

Tuning. Having drilled the holes—noting that, except those opposite strip C, they are at an angle, which follows the slope of the pieces (A, B, C, and D)—the edges and corners are rounded and finished with sandpaper.

If you now make a test, all the notes will appear sharp, possibly by a tone or even two tones. To lower the note, reverse it and take shavings from the middle with a spokeshave, as in Illus. 5. The amount to be removed can soon be ascertained by trial and error. Tuning against a piano is the simplest method. If, by any chance, too much is removed so that the note is flat, it can be corrected by taking shavings from the end of the note to reduce its length. This, however, should be unnecessary.

An alternative to flattening the note by shavings is to make a saw cut across the lower surface, as at A in Illus. 5. When you complete the tuning, give the keys a coat of clear varnish or clear cellulose. Each is marked with the note it represents. Paint on the marks at the ends, where they are not normally struck with the beaters.

Fitting. Tie a knot at one end of a length of cord and thread a felt washer onto it. Pass it through the end screw eye, put on another washer, and thread on the first note. Continue the process until you reach the next screw eye. In the case of the black notes, it is necessary to tie knots in the cord so that there are wide spaces between B$\flat$ and C$\sharp$ and E$\flat$ and F$\sharp$.

Beaters. These can be spheres of boxwood or hard rubber about ⅞″ diameter mounted on cane handles.

16. Toy Roller

CHILDREN WILL ENJOY playing with this indoors or out. You can make the roller portion of a size to suit any remnants you may have on hand.

Roller. If you have no suitable round wood (such as an old curtain pole), plane a piece of wood square to the nearest size and mark the circle at the ends. Plane away the corners to form an octagon, and then reduce these corners until the whole piece is rounded. Finish off with a file, using a rocking and sideways movement to take out lumps. Follow with sandpaper. Bore holes at the ends in the circle centers to take the pivoting screws.

Handle. To make the handle and other parts strong, a wedged tenon should be cut at the top and bottom of the shaft. The corners of the forked portion should be dovetailed. An alternative is to cut out two pieces of strip iron, bend them to shape, and screw them to the shaft. Note that washers are inserted between the arms and the roller itself. It's a good idea to paint the roller with a bold, definite design so that the child can easily see it turn around.

Larger roller. If you want to make a much larger roller, you can cut out three discs in ⅞″ wood, say, 6 or 9″ in diameter. These are fastened together by two or more squares of ⅞″ wood let into notches cut in the diameter. They should be glued and nailed in. A sheet of thin plywood is wrapped around the whole thing. The grain should run along the length so that the ply will bend easily. Start at one of the square pieces, allowing the ply to overlap about halfway. Work gradually around, gluing and nailing as you proceed. When you reach the starting place, trim the edge if necessary and complete the attachment. Trim the ends when the glue has set. Use screws for pivoting the roller in the same way as shown in the illustration for the small roller.

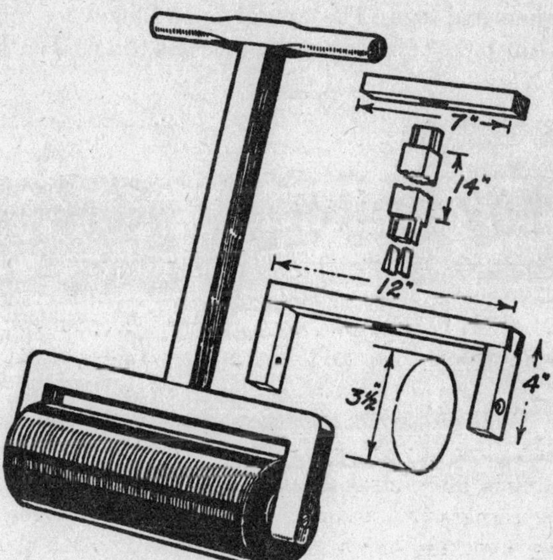

This toy can provide endless fun.

17. Blackboard and Easel

CHILDREN NATURALLY SEEM to like to draw, and it's far better to encourage a budding artist by providing something to draw on—as opposed to the house walls. The blackboard and easel presented here are inexpensive and easy to make, and can be turned over for use as a child's table.

Board. It's best to use a 3/8″-thick plywood or laminated board with rounded corners and edges. The sizes given in Illus. 4 are only offered as a guide. Any piece of board near to the sizes will do. For the black-

Illus. 1.
Blackboard in normal use.

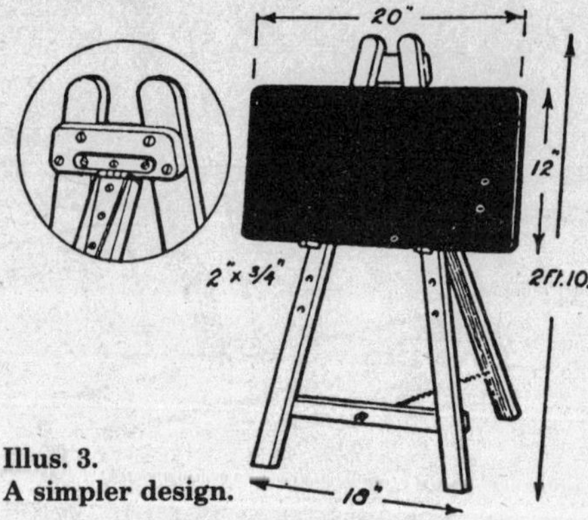

Illus. 3.
A simpler design.

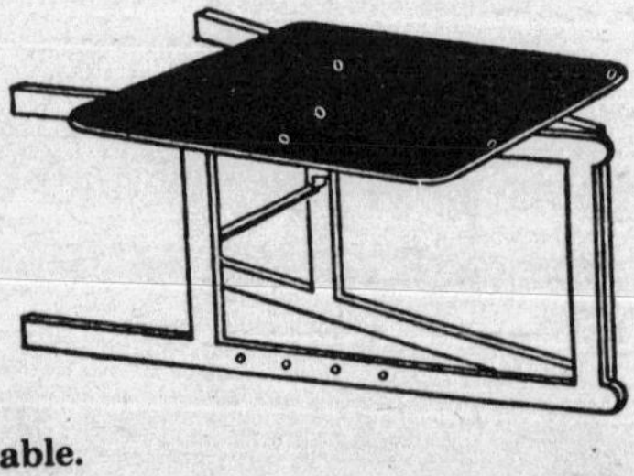

Illus. 2.
In use as a table.

board, use the special blackboard paint made for this purpose. For a board for a painting easel, stain the board with an ebony water stain.

Easel. This structure is made from 2″ × ¾″ pine or beech and, when finished, painted and enamelled a cream or buff color. The cross rails are tenoned to the uprights, the tenons being about 1″ long. For extra strength, the tenons could be pegged with dowels driven through. The front uprights are semicircular at the top, while the rear uprights are cut square with the upper edge of the top rail.

Holes for the pegs are drilled through the front uprights a suitable distance apart, and the two frames are then hinged together at the top with a pair of 2″ brass butt hinges. The 12″ rule-joint stay, shown in Illus. 4, keeps the easel steady when opened so that there is little danger of its being knocked over. The same applies to the pegs. They are shown in Illus. 4, with a large-diameter disc to the front, which prevents the board from tilting forward. These discs should be well wedged to the pegs.

As it is sometimes difficult to obtain rule-joint stays with two bent ears, a method is shown whereby the flat ear can be screwed to a small

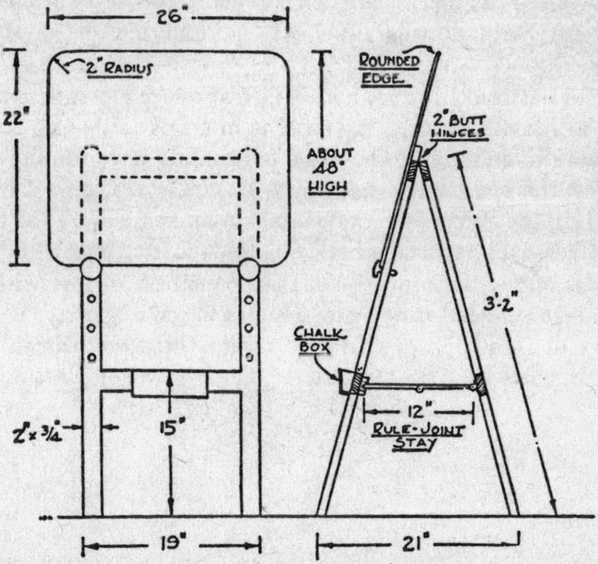

Illus. 4.
Front and side elevations.

Illus. 5.
Details.

CUTTING LIST

	Long		Wide	Thick
	ft.	*in.*	*in.*	*in.*
2 front uprights	3	3	2	¾
2 back uprights	3	2	2	¾
4 cross rails	1	5	2	¾
1 board	2	2	22	⅜

All sizes are net.

block that is in turn screwed to the cross rail of the easel. If you are able to obtain stays with two bent ears, then the block is not necessary (see Illus. 5). For the blackboard, a small chalk box in tin or plywood will be useful. For a painting easel, a larger container for paints is a good idea.

A simpler pattern that does not require any special joints to be cut is shown in Illus. 3. In this, the easel is in tripod form. Cut out the parts to length, and mark where the horizontals cross the uprights. Round over the ends where necessary. At this stage, do not bother about cutting the ends of the horizontals at an angle. Bore the screw holes and fasten all parts together, two screws to each joint as in Illus. 3. The ends of the horizontals can then be cut off in line with the uprights and levelled. A hinge, preferably of the cross-garnet "T" type, is used to hinge the back strut. A piece of cord threaded through holes prevents the easel from opening too far. The legs can be plain dowels.

18. Table Bowling

THE DISADVANTAGE OF floor bowling, where children are concerned, is that the ball is likely to cause damage if the game is played in a room. This cannot happen with the table game since the ball is anchored to a cord. In the game presented here the pins are connected by cord to a yoke, which can be pulled against the action of a spring to set them up again after having been knocked down. The added advantage of this feature is that the pins cannot be separated from the board and lost.

The board is best made from 9-mm. birch plywood since this material will remain level, and, as it has a close grain, a nice finish can be obtained if enamelled. As the pins receive rough treatment, they should be turned from a hardwood, such as beech or birch. In all probability, you can purchase a wooden ball about 1¾" in diameter,

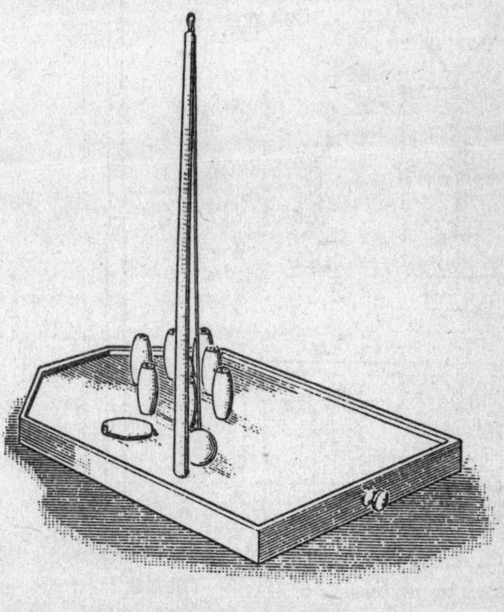

Illus. 1.
With this amusing indoor game, the pins themselves have cords attached to the underside. To stand them up after play, it's only necessary to pull the handle at the front.

Illus. 2.
Side section through board.

Illus. 3.
Plan view with main sizes.

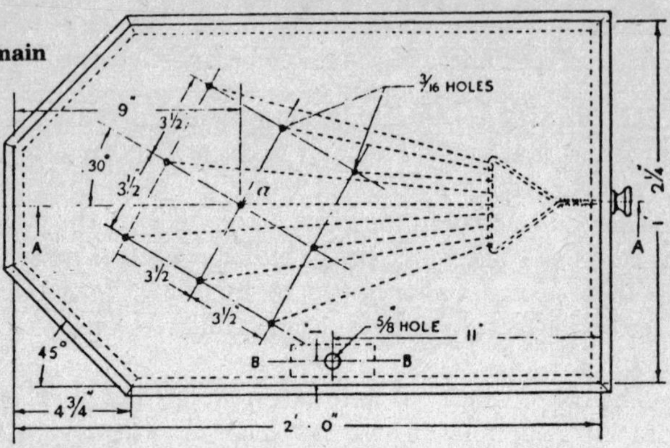

Illus. 4.
Wire yoke.

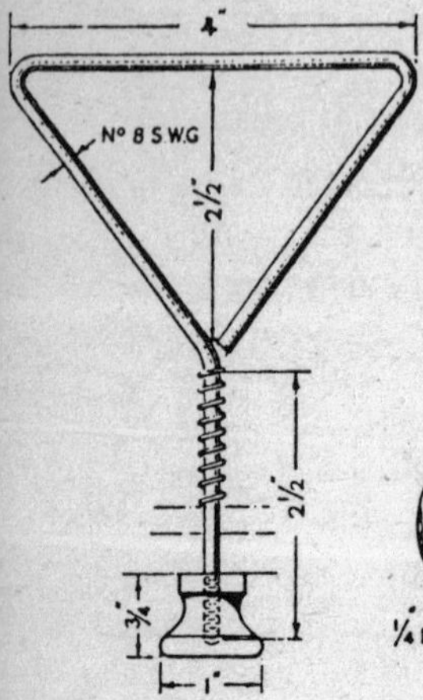

Illus. 7.
Ball section.

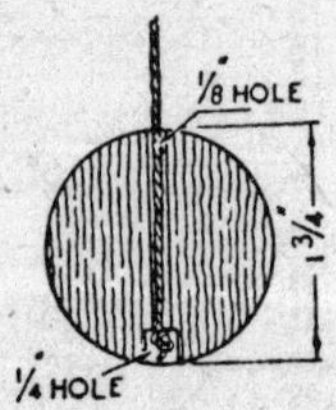

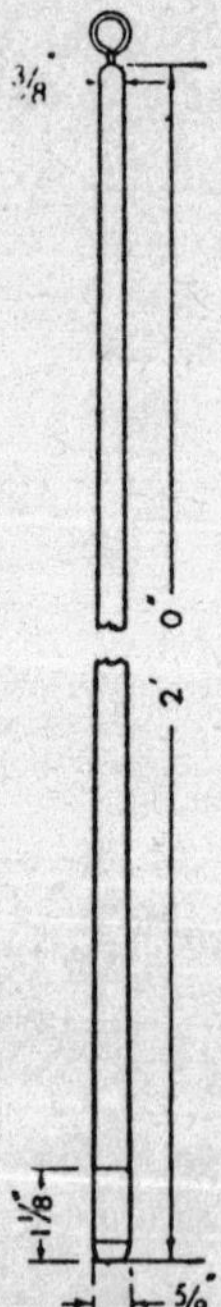

Illus. 8.
Post detail.

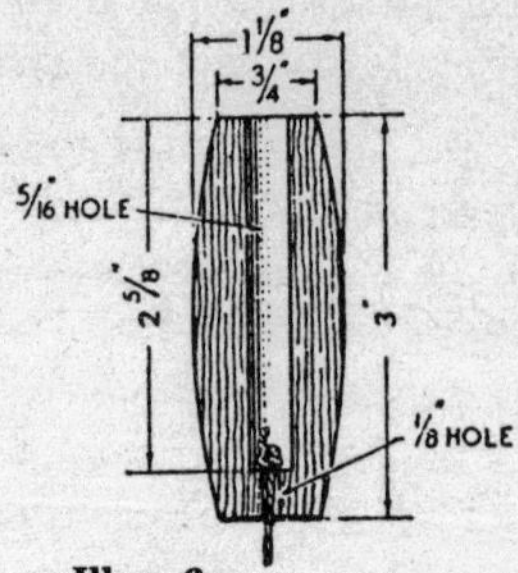

Illus. 6.
Section through pin.

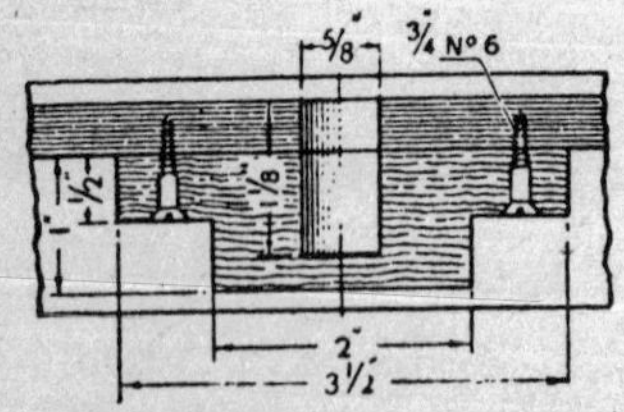

Illus. 5.
Block on underside to support post.

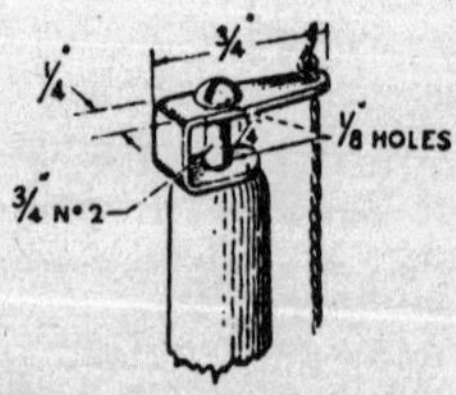

Illus. 9.
Effective attachment for cord at top of post.

but if you have to turn one, it need not be perfectly spherical. For the post, ⅝″ dowelling should be satisfactory.

A suggested material for the yoke is ¼″-diameter galvanized iron wire, since it can be bent cold in the vise and an adequate thread can be worked at the end to take the knob. You may have a suitable compression spring on hand, but, if not, you can purchase one from a firm that specializes in the manufacture of springs. If you can obtain a piece of boxwood or ebony for the knob, so much the better, since the knob will have to be tapped in the end-grain to take the yoke. The grain of beech is hardly dense enough to permit threading.

Construction. Referring to Illus. 3, you will see that the dimensions are given for the board excluding the edging, as it is believed that this will simplify setting out. If you first locate the central hole *a*, you will find that it is an easy matter to set out the positions of the other holes. In order to prevent the cords chafing when they pass through the holes, they should be countersunk, as indicated in Illus. 2. The particular arrangement of the holes enables the cords to be clear of each other, and the spacing permits the pins to be knocked over without fouling each other. By avoiding the alignment of three pins with the length of the board, the game is made more difficult and interesting.

As the post must stand firmly upright, it is made a tight fit in the ⅝″ hole indicated in Illus. 3. The thickness of the board does not allow a blind hole of adequate depth to be bored for the post, and therefore the piece shown in Illus. 5 is screwed and glued under the board before boring the hole.

So that a good attachment for the 1¾″ × ⅜″ edging can be provided, a fillet *b* is glued and nailed around the edges of the board. When this is attached, the edges should be cleaned up and carefully tested for squareness. The edging is glued and nailed to the fillet, the abutting ends being mitred. It adds to the appearance of the board if the top edge of the edging is rounded as shown. An 11/64″ hole will have to be drilled to receive the shank of the yoke, and this hole should be so positioned that the yoke will be just clear of the undersurface of the board but allowing free movement of the spring.

You will find that a 15″ length of ¼″-diameter galvanized wire will suffice for the yoke. You should have no difficulty in bending it to shape in the vise, but you should take care to see that the shank part is straight and central with the triangular part. An adequate thread can be cut with a die to enable the attachment of the knob.

Pins. A 2′ 8″ length of hardwood, such as beech or birch, about 1⅜″ square is required for the pins. The length is cross-cut to provide nine pieces, each about 3½″ long. After marking the diagonals at the ends of each piece, central ⅛″ holes are bored to a depth of ½″ at both ends of each piece. At one end of each piece, the ⅛″ hole is counterbored 5⁄16″ in diameter, as shown in Illus. 6. A mandrel is next turned to fit the 5⁄16″ hole in each piece so that each can be turned between centers. The back center of the lathe will, of course, be centered in the ⅛″ hole left for the cord. The lower end of each pin should be slightly dished as indicated so that the pin will stand firmly.

You can turn the ball in a similar manner as that employed for the pins, but you don't need to get the ball absolutely spherical.

Attaching the cords. In connecting the cords to the yoke, allow sufficient slackness so that the pins will be free to fall over after having been struck by the ball. But this slackness should not be such that the yoke has to be fully pulled back to set the pins on their ends again. The spring acts to return the yoke to its original position so that there is always the right amount of slackness to permit the pins to fall.

The cord from which the ball is suspended is shown attached to a screw eye fastened in the top of the post, but an alternative method of attachment can be seen in Illus. 9. The fitment shown comprises a piece of strip metal cut to the shape indicated and mounted on the post by a screw, which passes through clearance holes in the fitment. Made this way, the fitment is free to pivot about the screw and any tendency for the cord to wind around the post is prevented.

To make the completed table game look attractive, apply a couple of coats of acrylic paint, followed by a coat of clear high-shine varnish.

19. Play Shop

A MAKE-BELIEVE SHOP large enough for children actually to play in is always popular. Although it runs into rather a lot of material, it's best to use plywood or particleboard. The sides are hinged so that the whole structure will fold flat, and the shelves and counter are detachable. Any kind of trade can be represented; in fact, you can prepare two or three boards, such as BAKER, BUTCHER, and GROCER so that the children can change games.

Construction. Cut out three pieces of plywood or particleboard—or whatever is available—to the sizes given in Illus. 2, and mark out the position of the door and window. Actually, the exact sizes do not mat-

Illus. 1. This play shop is made from plywood or particleboard and applied strips. The suggested size is 4′6″ long × 2′6″ deep × 4′6″ high.

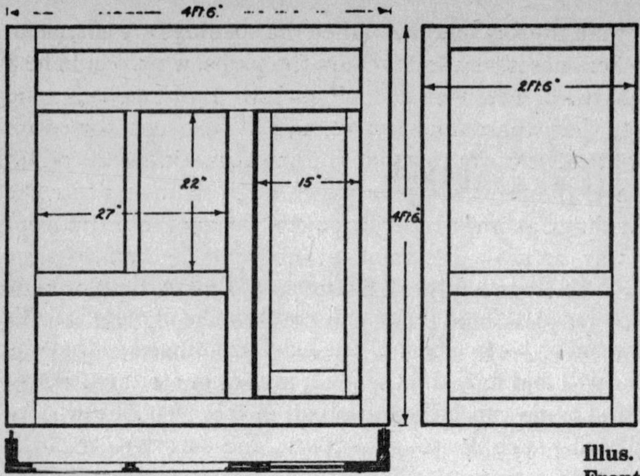

Illus. 2.
Front elevation with sectional plan, and elevation of side.

ter a great deal, but those shown can give you an idea of what are good working proportions. The door could be about 3′ 3″ high × 15″ wide, and the opening can be marked out and cut to this size. In the case of the window, however, the clear plastic sheet needs to fit in a rebate, and, since this is formed by allowing the front battens to overlap the edges, the openings in the main board must be cut about ⅜″ full all around. This is shown clearly in Illus. 3.

To cut the openings, it is necessary to bore holes to enable the keyhole saw to be started. When it has sawn a few inches, the handsaw can be substituted. The handsaw cuts more quickly and keeps to

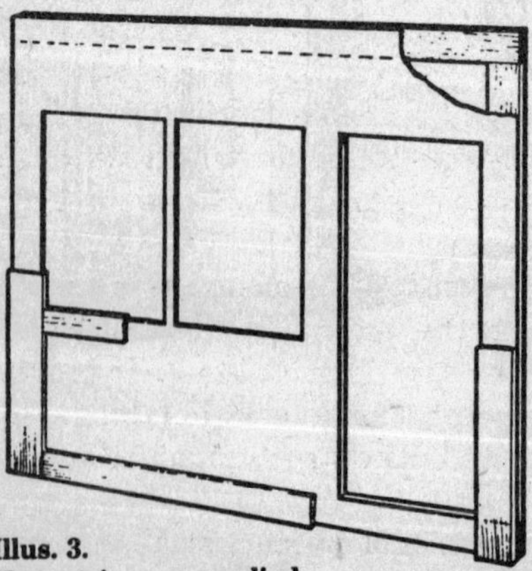
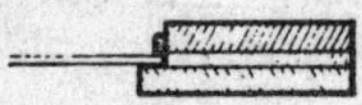

Illus. 3.
How strips are applied to the main board.

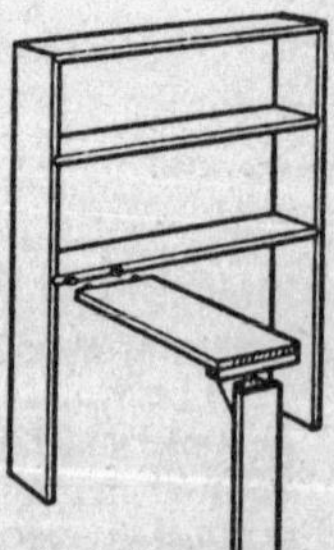

Illus. 4.
Shelves and counter.

the line better than the keyhole saw. When the openings are cut, clean up the edges where necessary and prepare the strips, which could be 3 to 4″ wide × ½″ thick. You need enough for both front and back, and you should note that where a joint is vertical at the front, the corresponding one at the back is horizontal. The one thus stiffens the other.

Fasten those at the front first, nailing through the board into the strips. Nail on the back ones right through the panel into the front strips. In this way, no nails are visible at the front. Before fastening, however, it is advisable to apply the finish, as it is much simpler to do when the parts are separate. Paint can be used throughout, or the main panel can be painted or distempered and the battens stained.

Hinging. A provision has to be made for hinging the sides to the front, and, to enable the whole structure to be flat, a batten as thick as the total thickness of the sides is screwed on at one side. This is shown in the plan section in Illus. 2. Thus, when the left-hand side has been folded in, the other side can close over it. The method of allowing the front battens to overlap and thus form a rebate in which the clear plastic sheet can fit has already been mentioned. Illus. 3 and 4 show this detail clearly. The plastic is held by beads fastened at the back with nails (see section at top of Illus. 4).

The door can be made similarly to the main front and sides. Battens are nailed to each side of a sheet of ply or particleboard. After levelling the edges and fitting, it is hinged to the right with three 2″ hinges. If possible, avoid driving the screws into the joints. The addition of the trade board completes the exterior. It can be fitted with two screw eyes at the top to engage hooks driven into the battens. Thus, another trade sign can always be substituted.

Interior attachments. These are shown in Illus. 4 and consist of a shelf fitment, the size of which is arranged to agree with the window, and a counter. Put the shelves together with simple grooved joints. Grooves are cut across the uprights, and the shelves are glued and nailed in them. At the top, simple rebates are cut to hold the top shelf. The whole attachment merely stands behind the window, though you could add hooks and eyes for security.

The counter is held in position with hooks that engage in screw eyes entered into the bottom shelf. At the free end, a cross batten is fastened underneath and an upright strut is hinged to it. To prevent it from closing by an accidental knock, a triangular strut is hinged to the underside of the counter. Thus, the entire structure can be folded flat when not in use.

Goods to sell in the shop can consist of ordinary small cartons and packets in which goods are actually sold, but many additional ones can be made in wood, such as loaves, cakes, and fruit. When painted, they look very realistic. A container of sand can be used to represent sugar to be weighed out.

If preferred, this project could be made in the form of a house rather than a shop. The general construction and sizes could be similar to those shown here. The windows, of course, would be considerably smaller than for a shop. The interior could be painted or covered with remnants of wallpaper. On one of the side walls, you could construct an imitation fireplace with a mantel. Another popular item is a dresser fitment consisting of a series of shelves. If you have the time, you could make a few small pieces of furniture—say, a table and a couple of chairs. Add as many realistic touches as possible. Such details as a mailbox, knocker, and lock take little time to make, and they always appeal to children. Window curtains, preferably to draw, should be provided. You might also want to add a window box containing a few flowerpots.

Generally, these miniature houses are placed against a wall. If this makes the interior somewhat dark, an electric light can be arranged to hang within. But be careful not to have wires trailing on the floor.

20. Handy Cart

THIS CART IS great for carrying bricks or for generally helping out in the garden, and it can be made from remnants of timber. Make the main box portion from ½″ softwood. Trim the ends to size and round over the top edges before assembling. If the sides are made about ¼″ deeper than the ends, there will be no complications at the joints. Put the parts together with glue and nails, using resin preferably as it is highly water-resistant. Drive in the nails and fill the holes. For the bottom, ⅜ or ½″ plywood is advisable. Glue and nail from below.

An axle tree is screwed on beneath. In the middle of it is a notch to take the end of the rear support (see illustration). The wheels, which can be cut from solid wood or ply, are pivoted on round-head screws with washers at both sides.

The rear shaft is tenoned at the top into the handle, being taken right through and wedged. Note how the handle ends are rounded over

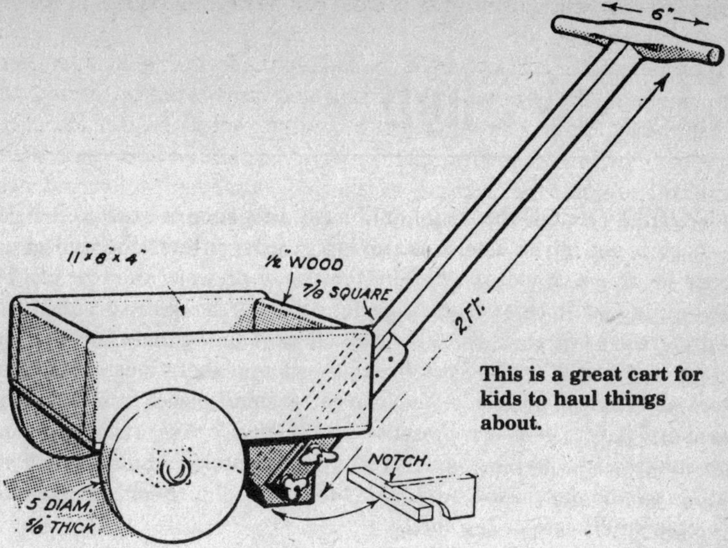

This is a great cart for kids to haul things about.

with the chisel and finished with sandpaper. At the lower end, a piece is planted on at each side to form a fork. This cnables it to be held to the support with bolts and thumbscrews.

Paint the entire piece with oil paint, both inside and out. Note that, as the wheel screws are entering end-grain, they cannot have maximum strength. They should therefore be as long as possible, and the axle tree itself should be in hardwood.

21. Toy Shop

A VARIATION OF the usual dollhouse, this shop is sure to delight both boys and girls. The construction is most interesting and gives scope for much ingenuity, and by the use of plywood the cost can be kept quite low. In this design, the shop occupies the entire ground floor and there are two rooms on the second floor. The premises can be fixed up for any sort of trade. Portable counters and shelves can be added, stocked with items for sale. You can carve small pieces from scraps of wood and paint them to represent boxes, loaves, cakes, and so on. You can make joints by the same means for a butcher shop. Miniature bottles can be purchased. And little tables and chairs could be used to set up a small café or tea shop.

Illus. 1.
This toy shop is approximately 20″ high and 15″ wide, including the base.

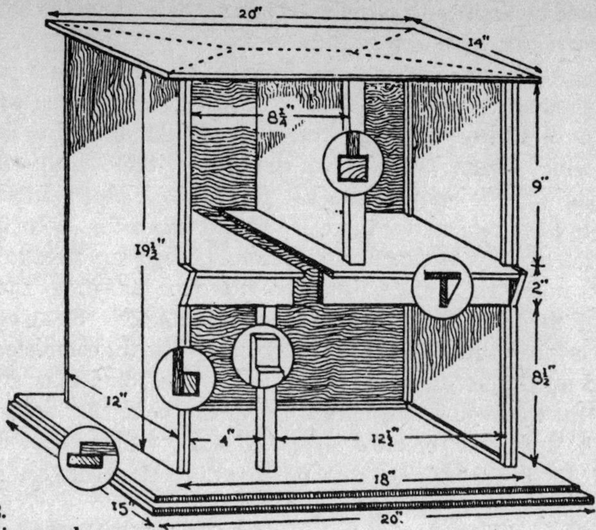

**Illus. 2.
Main sizes and
construction details.**

Main construction. This is clearly shown in Illus. 2, and, although sizes are given, they can be altered to suit any special requirements. But be sure of keeping good proportions. Plywood of 3/16 or 1/4″ thickness can be used, although it should be strengthened where necessary with small fillets. The ends are 1′ 7½″ high × 11¾″ wide, fillets ½″ wide × ¼″ thick being nailed at all the edges. The top is 1′ 8″ long × 1′ 2″ wide, nailed down to the ends to overhang 1″ all around; the bottom is 1′ 8″ long × 1′ 3″ wide and is nailed to overhang 1″ at the ends and back and 2″ at the front. Fillets ¾″ wide × ¼″ thick are used to thicken the edges of the bottom. They are mitred at the corners and overhang ¼″. The floor is roughly 1′ 5⅝″ long × 1′ ½″ wide. This width permits it to overhang the ends ¾″ at the front. Fillets should be nailed across the ends for support, and the floor is nailed in place. A piece of wood 1′ 7½″ × 1′ 6″ is used to cover in the back. Two small, shaped triangular pieces 2″ long × ¾″ wide at the top are fastened to the front edges of the ends level with the floor, and a strip 1¾″ wide is attached across underneath the floor, level with the edges of the ends, the fillets being cut away for its reception. The doorway of the shop is formed by fitting an upright ½″ square. It runs up behind the strip under the floor to stand level at the front, and it is glued and nailed. A division of plywood is fitted midway across the floor to form the two rooms, and a ½″ upright is fastened at the front edge. The shop fascia is completed by nailing a strip of wood across the edges of the floor and triangular pieces, as shown in Illus. 3.

Fronts. As shown in Illus. 4, the fronts of the rooms are 9″ × 8¼″, strengthened at the edges with ½″ × ¼″ fillets and pierced with an opening 5″ × 4″. Plywood of ⅛″ thickness should be used to cut the overlaid window frame (Illus. 5), which is 5¼″ × 4¼″ overall, with the main parts ¼″ wide and the rest ⅛″. The frame is glued outside the opening to form rebates for the clear plastic sheet that is held with fillets, while a sill is attached outside. Small hinges are used to hinge the fronts to the ends, and buttons are fitted for fastening. The shop door (Illus. 6) is 8½″ × 4″, pierced with an opening 5″ × 3″; an overlay (Illus. 7) is glued outside and plastic is fitted, while the completed door is hinged on the left-hand side. You could fit modern mantelpieces (Illus. 8) in the rooms, the upright members being 2½″ long × ¾″ wide × ½″ thick, and the top 4″ long × 1″ wide, with the ends shaped as shown. Small slips of wood chamfered at the bottom edge could form picture rails.

Roof. Illus. 3 shows the construction of the roof. The ridge piece is 6″ long × 5″ high and nailed through the top, while four shaped rafter pieces (Illus. 9) run from it to the corners. Plywood jointed over the rafters and nailed down is used to cover the roof. Chimneys (Illus. 10)

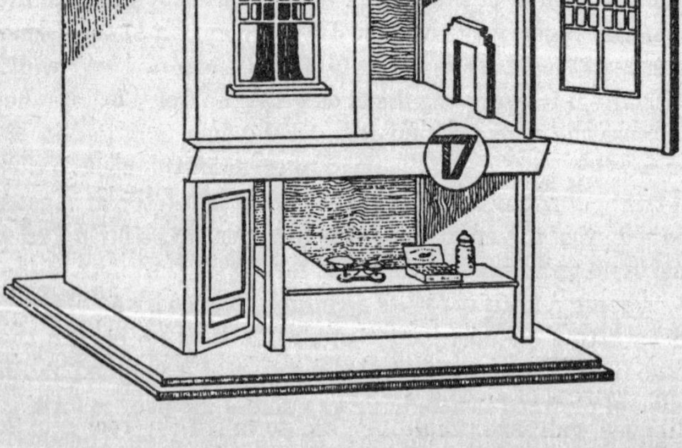

Illus. 3. General view, showing roof supports.

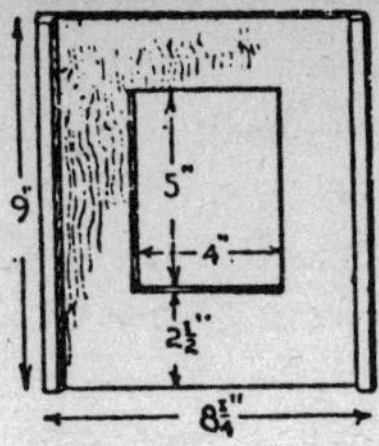

Illus. 4.
Upper front.

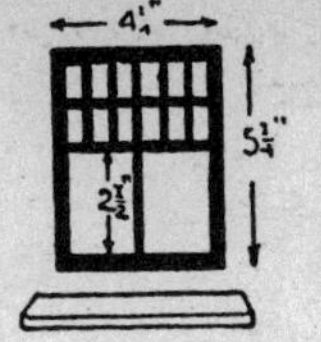

Illus. 5.
Window frame.

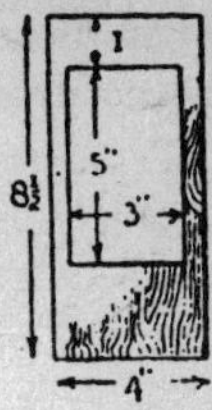

Illus. 6.
Door.

Illus. 7.
Door overlay.

Illus. 8.
Mantelpiece.

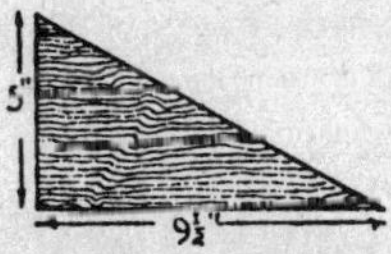

Illus. 9.
Roof support.

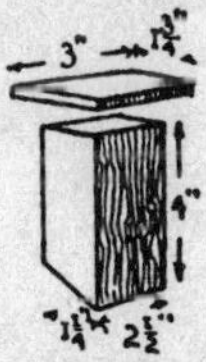

Illus. 10.
Chimney.

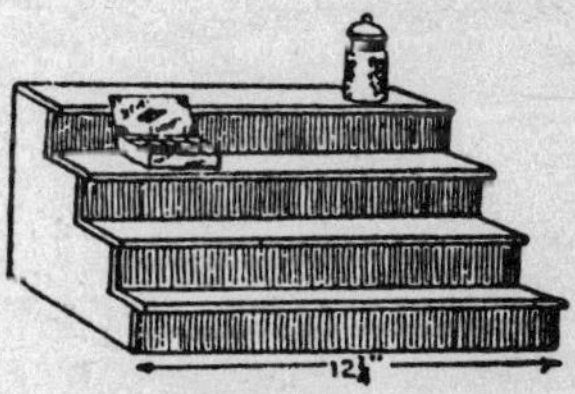

Illus. 11.
Display stand.

attached at each end of the roof are very effective. They are made with a shaft 4″ long × 2½″ wide × 1¼″ thick, having the bottom end cut to the slope of the roof and completed with a thin capping 3″ × 1¾″.

The shop could be fitted up with shelves at the back and end. It is not advisable to enclose the front with glass or plastic, but a portable counter made in an L-shape to run across the front and towards the back is an excellent idea. A set of stages or sloping shelves (Illus. 11), which can be substituted in its place, offers a change in stock and will hold the interest of a child.

Dollhouse wallpaper could be used to finish the rooms at the top.

22. Hobbyhorse

WHAT TODDLER WOULDN'T enjoy galloping around the house on a hobbyhorse? The construction of this one is obvious from the diagrams. The head can be fretted out of plywood or solid wood about ¾″ thick. It is fastened with screws to the main shaft. The latter is about 1¼″ wide at the wheel end and tapers to 1″ at the head. It is through-tenoned and wedged to the axle tree, and struts are added at each side, being notched in and glued and nailed. The wheels are pivoted on round-head screws with washers at each side.

Construction details.

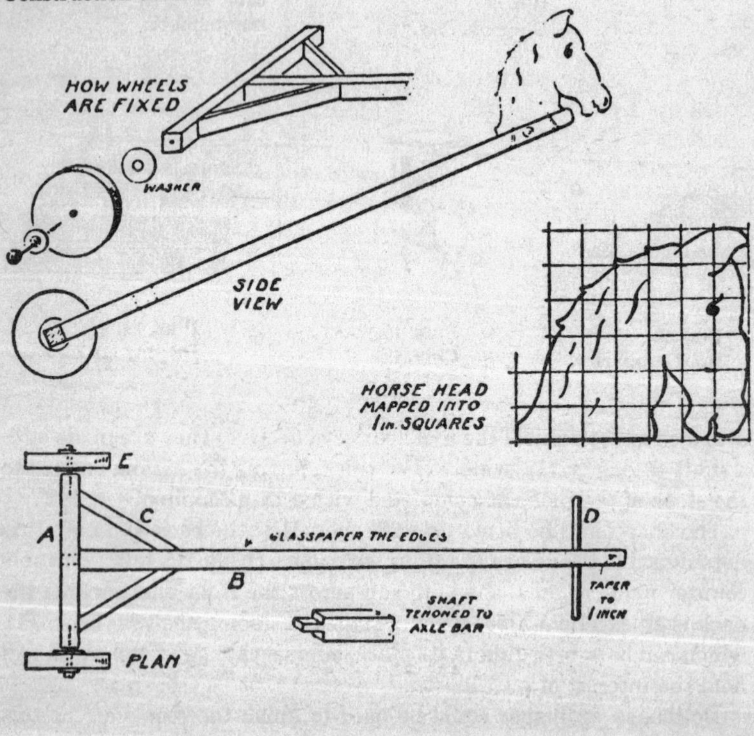

23. Penguin Tic-Tac-Toe

THIS LITTLE GAME is fun for children—and adults as well. The aim is to get three penguins in a row either across, down, or diagonally before your opponent does. You need 10 penguins—five for each player. The first player to get three in a row is declared the winner.

There is, of course, no actual construction. You will need a piece of ⅝″-thick plywood, 7¼″ square. This is subdivided into nine squares (shown in Illus. 2), and the top edges should be well rounded. The dividing lines are V-shaped grooves cut into the block about 1/16″ wide × 1/16″ deep, and here a parting tool or V-tool is invaluable. A countersunk hole is drilled in the middle of each square to a depth of ⅜″ to take the ⅜″-diameter dowel peg that is attached to the foot of the penguin.

The pattern for the penguin in Illus. 3 is actual size so that you can mark out from it. It is of ⅛″-thick ply, inserted into a slot, cut into a piece of ⅜″ dowel, glued and tapered off, as in Illus. 3. An easy way to handle these short pieces is to get a length of ⅜″ dowel about 6″ longer than the actual required length. Slot and taper it off while it is held in

Illus. 1.
This game is played like regular tic-tac-toe.

a vise; then cut off the required length. Repeat the process until you have 10 pieces.

As already mentioned, 10 penguins are needed, five colored in black and five colored in light grey. The cross-shaded areas on the beak and feet are orange in both cases. The penguins are, of course, painted on both sides.

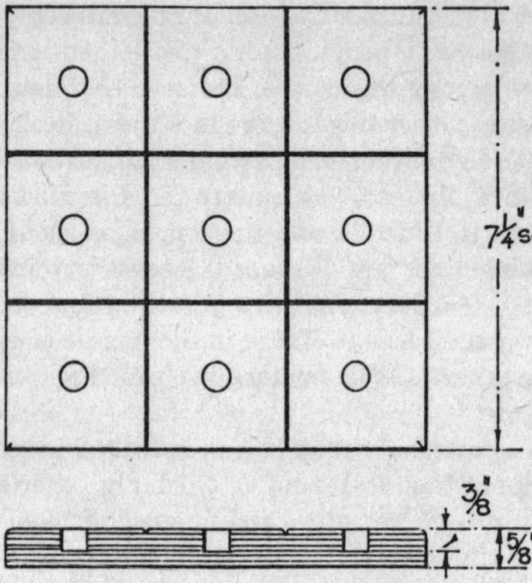

Illus. 2.
Plan and section of board.

Illus. 3.
Full-size pattern of penguin. You can trace over the pattern to get a correct outline. The beak and feet are colored orange.

24. Doll's Crib

WHETHER FOR A doll or teddy bear, this toy will give children hours of pleasure.

Joints throughout are mortise and tenon and should present no difficulty. The drop side rails (C) can be grooved throughout their length to take the tenons on the slats. Ply panels (D) are nailed and glued to the outside of the end framing, part B being shaped after the framing has been assembled but before the ply is glued on. The drop side rails (C) are also grooved at each end (Illus. 2) to slide up and down a bead attached to A. Illus. 3 shows the method employed to operate the sliding drop side, and either one or both sides can be made to drop, the block being attached to either the outside, as shown, or the inside. The "mattress" could be either upholsterer's webbing or even rubber webbing. If the latter is used, do not strain it too tightly or the frame will be distorted.

Illus. 1.
Crib for dolls or stuffed animals.

Colored lacquer or gloss paint could be used as a finish, with decorative transfers.

Illus. 2.
Method of construction and lettered parts.

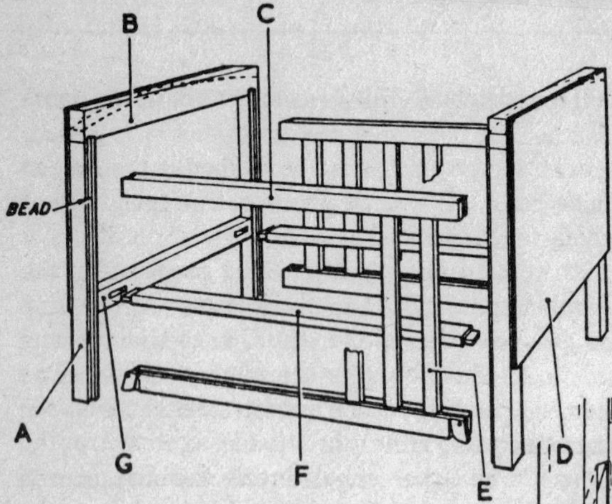

Illus. 3.
Detail of drop-side device.

CUTTING LIST

	Long		Wide	Thick
	ft.	*in.*	*in.*	*in.*
(A) 4 legs	1	7	1	7/8
(B) 2 top end rails		9½	2½	3/8
(C) 4 drop side rails	1	6½	1¼	5/8
(D) 2 end panels	1	3	9½	3/16
(E) 16 slats	1	2	1	3/8
(F) 2 side rails	1	8	1½	5/8
(G) 2 bottom end rails		9½	1½	5/8

Blocks from odd material. Allowances have been made as to lengths and widths. Thicknesses are net.

25. Dump Truck

DUMP TRUCKS ARE especially fun for kids to play with in the sandbox. The chassis (A) is the main section of the truck, to which the cab and body are fastened. The cab is constructed by attaching the seat to the back (B) and fastening the latter to the chassis. The back edge of B should fit flush with the shoulders on the chassis, marked C.

The engine block (D) is fitted to the chassis and strengthens the front of the cab. The dashboard (E) forms the shape of the front, and the front (F) and sides (G) are attached to it. The entire piece is attached to the engine block. The sides (H) fit into the recessed sides of the back (B) and can be attached to the end of the seat for added rigidity. Piece G fits behind the front.

The roof (J) is fastened down temporarily to enable the shaping and fitting of its supports (K), the tops of which are shaped to a dowel on the back edge, as can be seen in Illus. 3. Holes of the equivalent size are drilled into the underside of the roof to accommodate them. The bottom ends are nailed down to the dashboard. These should be quite steady and well fastened to give support to the front of the roof.

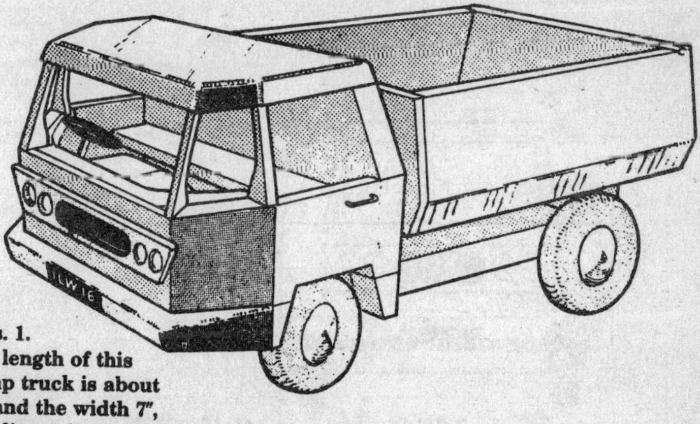

Illus. 1. The length of this dump truck is about 12″ and the width 7″, but dimensions can be varied.

The radiator and headlamps are incorporated in one piece (L). The lamps are drill holes, and a groove is cut or a shape painted on to indicate the radiator grid. It should be noted that the underside of the chassis tapers at the front to form the bumpers or fenders, to which a license plate is added.

The body consists of the base (M), two edges of which are tapered in slightly to give the slope of the sides (N). The bottom edge of the sides should be shaped before attaching them to the base. The end piece (O) is attached to the ends of the base and sides. The back edge of the body (P) fits inside the side pieces (N). A piece of dowel is fastened on the top edge, with ¼″ protruding at each end to engage in the groove cut in the sides. When the body is tipped up, the back will automatically swing open for unloading. A strip of wood is attached to the back of the cab, upon which the body rests, as can be seen in Illus. 2. Another strip

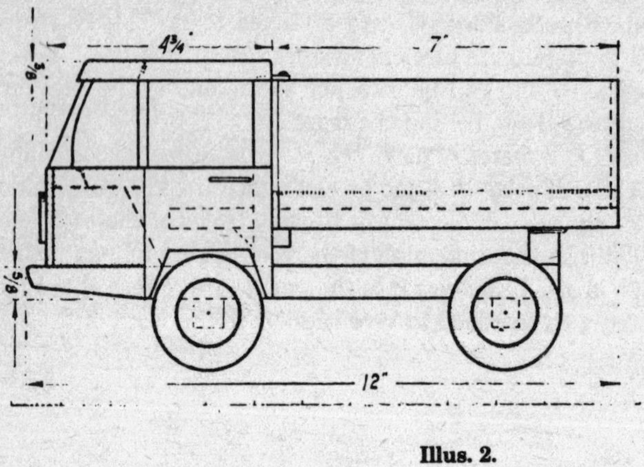

Illus. 2.
Side elevation with scale.

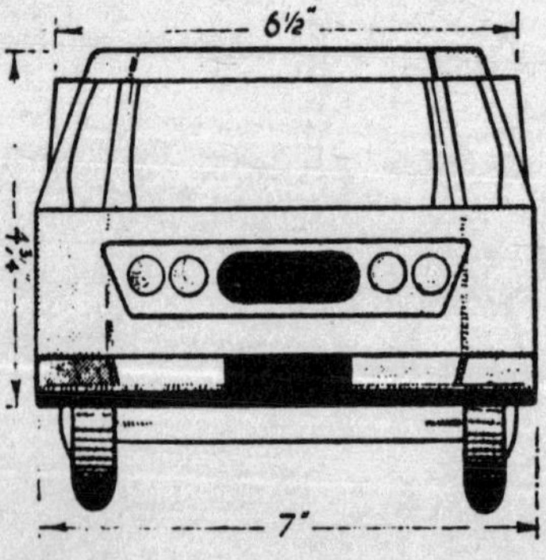

Illus. 3.
Front view.

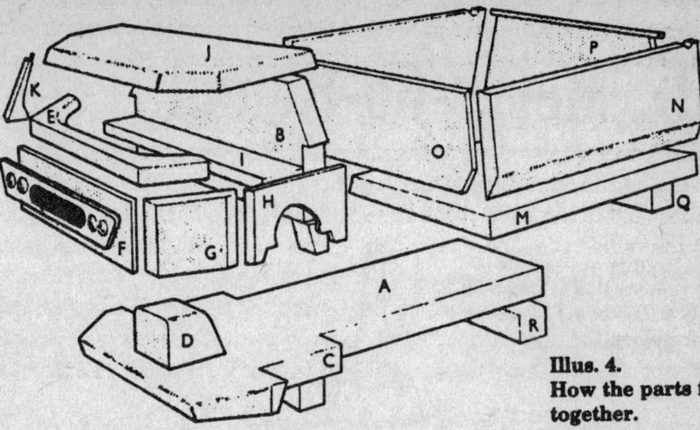

**Illus. 4.
How the parts fit together.**

of wood (Q) is hinged to the underside of the base and fastened to the chassis. This provides the tipping action. Two small turnbuttons are fitted to the sides to engage in slots cut into the back of the cab, thus securing the body when it is not being used for tipping.

Two strips of wood are fitted to the underside of the chassis, to which the wheels are fitted. All parts are glued and nailed or screwed as necessary.

Pieces F, H, L, O, and P are of thin plywood. The remainder of the sections are of softwood. The thickness varies according to the section being made.

26. Merry-Go-Round

Illus. 1.
In this design, the movement is imparted to the boats by bevel gearing.

THIS MECHANICAL TOY gives children endless fun. The movement of the merry-go-round is arranged by means of bevel gearing. These gears can be obtained in brass or plastic in various sizes. Model-making shops frequently stock them, and miscellaneous disposal shops often have them for sale. The exact size is not important, but it is advisable to obtain them first so that the sizes of the parts can be made to suit. The large gear wheel is fitted to the bottom end of the main spindle (A). To keep the spindle upright, a cross piece (F) is attached to the base (D) and a hole cut in it to receive the bottom gear wheel. To steady it at the top, a collar piece (P) is arranged in two parts to engage a groove turned in the spindle (A). In this way, the collar pieces can be added after the spindle is erected in position.

The small spindle (J) to which the handle is attached rotates in a

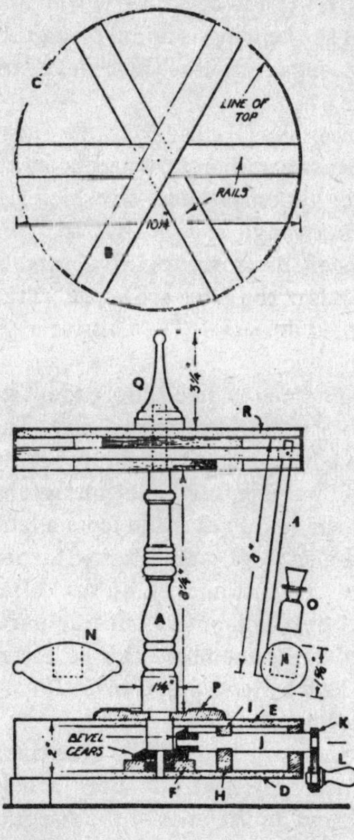

Illus. 2.
Plan of top and section.

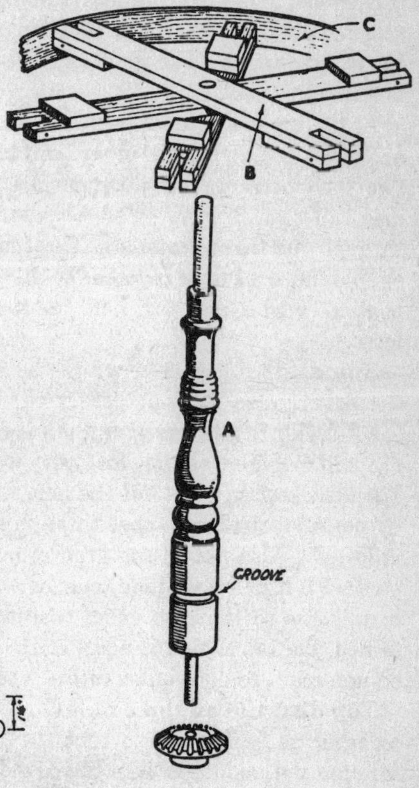

Illus. 3.
Top portion and main middle spindle.

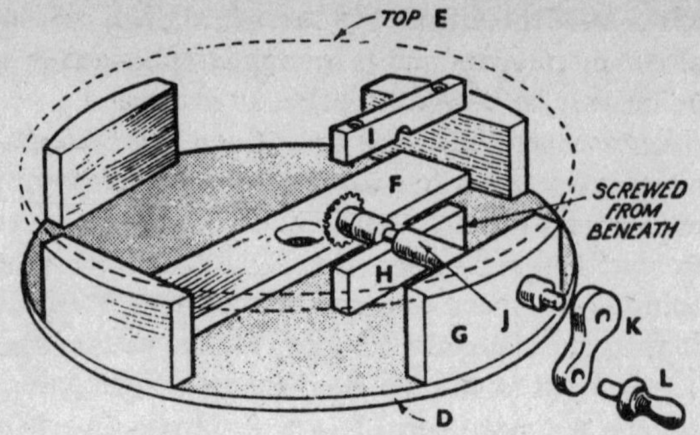

Illus. 4.
Lower portion, showing mechanism.

hole in the piece G, and at the inside fits in the bearing engaging in the turned slot. This bearing is in two parts: H and top-piece I, which is screwed on afterwards. The position of the bearing is found by adjusting it back and forth so that the correct engagement of the bevel gears is found.

At the top is a disc supported by three rails (B) (see Illus. 3). These are fitted one above the other, and blocks are therefore necessary on two of them to make a flush surface on the upper side, on which the disc can rest. The spindle (A) passes through a hole that is bored through the three crossbars. The ends of the crossbars are slotted to enable the arms to be pivoted. To the ends of the arms are attached the boats (N), which in turn hold the turned dolls (O). The dolls are left loose.

Spindle. As the size to which the spindle is turned is dependent on the bevel gears, it is necessary to obtain the bevel gears first. The exact design is not important, but it is a good plan to introduce plenty of small members as they look very well when painted in bright colors. Turn the bottom end to fit the hole in the bevel gear, and form a long ½" dowel at the top to pass through the rails (B) and into the turned finial (Q). Also put in the groove near the bottom to take the collar piece (P). It is a good idea to draw out a section of the working parts in full size so that the exact position of the members can be ascertained. The bevel gear is additionally held by long thin screws. It may be necessary to drill holes in the wheel to take them.

Top disc. Cut all three rails (B) to the same length, and glue them together as in Illus. 2 so that they are spaced at 60°. Bore a hole through the middle to take the dowel, and, to the ends of the top one, glue on pieces of the same thickness at the underside. To the bottom one, glue on similar pieces but on the top. These are to enable the arms

(M) to be pivoted from the same level. Cut ⅜″ slots at all six ends to take the arms, and drill through at the sides to allow little pieces of 1⁄16″ wire to be passed through, as in Illus. 2.

As the top disc (R) has to lie flat on the rails, it is necessary to put packing pieces on four of the ends (Illus. 3). Glue on the disc (R), driving a nail into the end of each rail. Level the ends of the rails with the disc and add the edging (C). This could be in thin ply or a good bending wood such as beech. Make the joint opposite one of the arms. Boring the hole through the disc completes this part of the work, except for the top finial (Q), which is added later.

Base mechanism. Cut out the top and bottom discs (E and D) to finish 10¼″. Plywood is suitable. To the bottom piece, glue and nail the four pieces (G as in Illus. 4), levelling the outer edges to the disc. One has a hole bored through it to take the small spindle (J). At right angles to the spindle, attach the cross piece (F), which has a hole in it

CUTTING LIST

	Long		Wide	Thick
	ft.	*in.*	*in.*	*in.*
(A) 1 spindle	1	2	1½ square	—
(B) 3 rails		10⅛	1¼	⅜
(C) 1 edging	3	—	1⅝	3⁄32
(D) 1 base		10½	10½	¼
(E) 1 top		10½	10½	¼
(F) 1 cross piece		10	2⅝	⅜
(G) 4 blocks		1	1⅝	⅞
(H) (I) } 1 bearing		3¼	1¾	½
(J) 1 spindle		5½	⅞ square	—
(K) 1 crank		2½	¾	¼
(L) 1 handle		2½	⅞	—
(M) 6 rods		8½	5⁄16	—
(N) 6 boats		5¼	2 square	—
(O) 6 dolls		3	1 square	—
(P) 1 retaining ring		5	5	⅜
(Q) 1 finial		4	2 square	—
(R) 1 top		10½	10½	¼

Items D, E, and R can be in plywood. Allowance has been made in lengths and widths. Thicknesses are net. Turned items allow for chucking and turning, but sizes can be adapted to suit method used. When a lathe is not available, construction should be adapted and sizes altered accordingly.

to take the bevel gear. The small spindle (J) is turned, as in Illus. 2 and 4, and once the correct position for the engagement of the bevel gears is found, the bottom bearing piece (H) can be fastened with screws from underneath. The addition of the top piece (I) prevents movement back and forth. In making these parts, the two should be screwed together and the hole bored through the joint. They are then separated.

The crank (K) is glued and nailed, and the handle (L) passes freely through its hole and is held by a cotter pin. When all is in order, place the vertical spindle (A) in position, and fasten the top with screws. The addition of the collar pieces (P) (fastened with screws) enables the action to be tried.

Thin plywood or veneer is used around the outer surface. Glue and nail it, arranging the joint opposite the handle spindle. Finally, make a neat finish by sticking ribbon or paper tape around the top edge. The base blocks are screwed on from underneath.

Boats. These are turned between centers and parted off. The large holes to take the dolls are also worked on the lathe. A special form of cradle is set up on the faceplate to hold the boat, and the hole is turned out with ordinary turning tools. A notch is filed across one side, and the arm (M) glued and screwed. At the top of the arm is a small hole to hold the pivoting wire. The dolls can be turned to various shapes.

Finishing. Flat oil paints can be used, if preferred, being followed by a coat of clear varnish. A rather more manageable method, however, is to use acrylic paints, which cover well. Various colors can be used, and the faces of the dolls can be painted in. After painting, use clear high-shining varnish.

27. Ping-Pong Table Top

THE PING-PONG TABLE top presented here is ideal for home use. The generally recognized size for a Ping-Pong table top for tournament play is 9′ × 5′, but, as a rule, this is too large for use in a small house. A top of 8′ × 4′ is the largest that can be used, and even this is usually made in two parts jointed together in the middle to enable it to be stored away when not in use.

The main tops in this design are in ½″-thick particleboard, which provides perfectly good play for home use. A rebated edging is mitred all around, which helps to stiffen the entire top and gives a neat finish.

The top in this design is 8′ × 4′ and made in two pieces, partly to enable it to be stored conveniently when not in use and partly to cut down the weight to be lifted. If you have the space, you could, of course, leave the board in a single piece. It is intended to rest upon an ordinary dining table, and if this opens out to the usual 5′ length, there is ample support. Particleboard is normally straight and flat, but it is of considerable weight. Consequently, when it is laid down flat, there is inevitably some slight sagging. This means that a stiffening edging or framework is needed. Apart from helping to keep the board flat, it protects its edges.

Particleboard panels. The board in Illus. 1 has an edging of 1½″ × ⅞″ material, which is rebated at the top. It is glued, and screws are driven upwards through it into the board. The corners are mitred

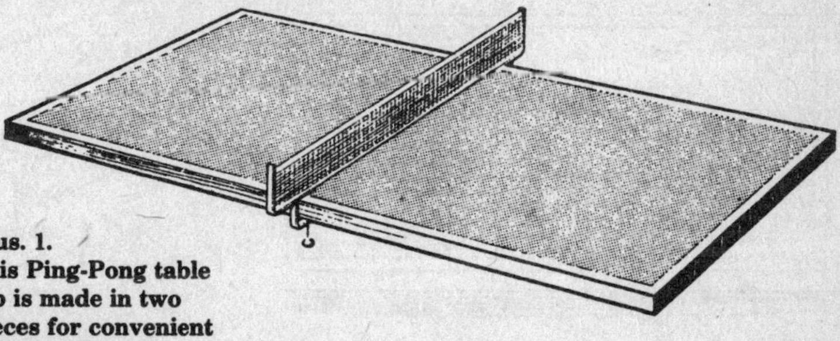

Illus. 1.
This Ping-Pong table top is made in two pieces for convenient storage. The size is 8′ × 4′.

and strengthened with angle brackets glued and screwed in. These stand away from the top by about ⅛″ so that they do not affect the resiliency. For the same reason, the intermediate cross rail fitted between the edging of each section is slightly curved in length so that it does not actually touch the underside of the top. If it were to do so, there might be a slightly different bounce to the ball locally.

Since the particleboard is 8′ × 4′ × ½″, it is necessary to cross-cut it at the middle to make two 4′-square panels. In case there is any slight tendency to curvature, it is advisable to arrange the two pieces so that they are in the same relative position when the table is in use. Put a pencil mark to make sure of it. The crosscut saw can be used for cutting, after which the sawn edge should be trimmed straight and square. You will find it a little hard on the edge of your plane, but there is not a lot of planing to be done. It is as well to go over the remaining three edges of each piece as a clean joint is needed for the edging.

Edging. A section through this is shown in Illus. 3. The material is 1½″ × ⅞″ and a ½″ rebate is worked at the top edge to take the particleboard. If you have access to a circular saw, you can work the

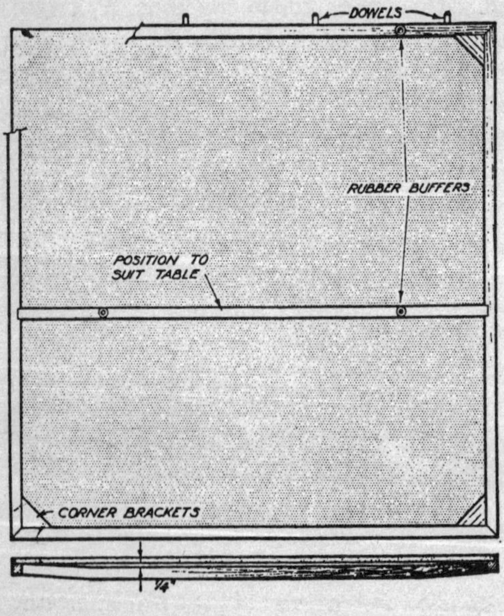

Illus. 2.
Underside showing cross rail.

Illus. 3.
Construction details.

rebate easily in two cuts: one with the wood on edge and the other on its side. You might also use a router.

The corners are mitred, and wood angle brackets are glued and screwed in to strengthen them. This, however, is best done after the edgings have been glued and screwed. The simplest plan is to plane the brackets to fit, glue them, and rub them in position. Screws are driven in after the glue has set. If this is not done, the mitre may be forced open by the pressure of the screws as the screws are tightened. The brackets are ¾″ thick and are fastened flush at the underside, thus leaving a slight gap beneath the particleboard.

The best way of dealing with the edgings is to cut the mitres of one piece, trim to an exact fit, and glue in position. Three thumbscrews will hold it in position. Screws are then driven in and the thumbscrews removed. (The screw holes must, of course, be bored and countersunk beforehand.) Now add the adjacent edging and attach it in the same way all around.

One detail to be noted is that the side edgings need small notches cut across them to take the cross rail. In some cases, the position of the cross rail can be central, but generally it is better to offset it towards the outer edge because this provides a definite tendency for the center to drop onto the table. Without this, the ends may sag downwards. It is better to cut the notches before the side edgings are attached.

Cross rail. Details of the cross rail are shown in Illus. 2. It is a 1¼″ × ⅞″ section, and the top edge is cut down ¼″ as shown. Gauge a line ¼″ from the top edge, and 9″ from each end draw a straight line to reach to the top corner. The waste can be either sawn or planed away. A corresponding sloping line is drawn at the underside. Glue in the notches and drive a skew nail into each joint.

To ensure that the two boards are level when put together, four dowels are let into the edge of one and corresponding holes bored in the other (see Illus. 2). To hold them together during play, a toggle clip is fitted at each side, as in Illus. 3. The addition of rubber buffers, such as are used for toilet seats, to the underside of the framework completes the job. They should be positioned to suit the table on which the top is to rest. One point to note is that many table extensions sag, and this may mean that some of the buffers may have to be packed up. The only way to go about this is to test the top on the actual table.

Painting. Many years ago it was possible to obtain a finish made especially for this purpose. However, it is practically impossible to find today, so the best thing to do is to use one coat of grey priming paint followed by one of dark-green undercoating. This dries flat without shine. A refinement is to paint a ¾″ white margin all around.

28. Doll Carriage

ALL CHILDREN WHO like to play with dolls would like a doll carriage.

Body. The construction of the body is shown in Illus. 4. There are two side frames put together with halved joints, joined by four cross rails. To be able to obtain the rail sizes and the shape of the sides, you need to draw in full size the side view of the body on a piece of paper. Sketch in the elliptical shape and mark in the positions of the rails.

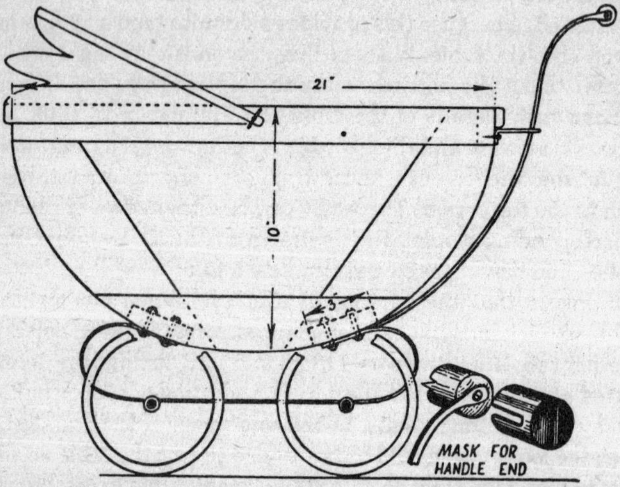

Illus. 1.
Side elevation with main sizes, and handle details.

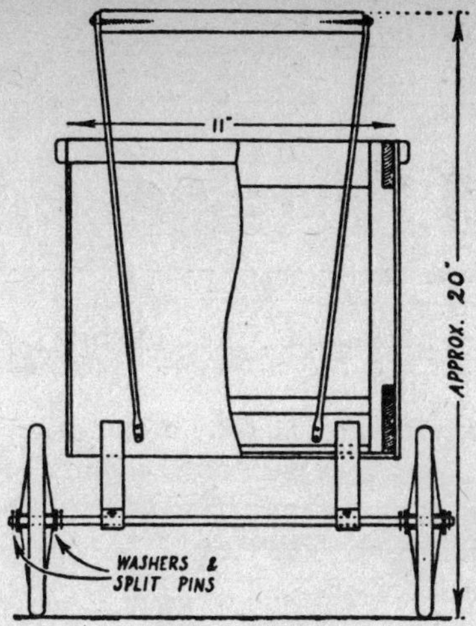

Illus. 2.
End elevation.

Top and bottom rails are obvious, and the sloping ones can be set at whatever angle best suits the shape. The chief point is to have enough overlap to provide good halving joints.

Cut out the wood, and, placing the parts on the drawing, mark in the shoulders by drawing a pencil line along where they cross each other. A lot of the waste can be cut away before marking in and cutting the halved joints, saving unnecessary sawing. Mark in the depth with the gauge, using the latter from the face side in every case. Glue the joints and put thumbscrews on them. When set, mark out and cut the shape, cleaning up with a spokeshave. Cut out the cross rails, and glue and nail them in position. Note that those at the bottom should stand proud of the shape so that they can be levelled afterwards.

Covering. The thinnest possible material should be used. Plywood 1.5 mm. thick is ideal and can often be obtained. It should be used with the grain running crosswise. Failing this, use thin aluminum sheet, which will have to be screwed on. Allow it to stand out about 1/16" so that it can be levelled afterwards.

Complete the curved portion first, and, if possible, have it in a single piece. If joints are unavoidable, arrange them in line with the bottom cross rails. When the glue has set, level the edges and add the side

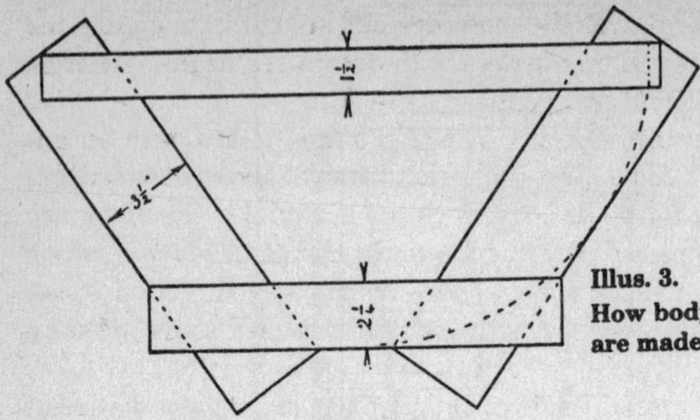

Illus. 3.
How body side frames are made.

Illus. 4.
Body parts assembled.

Illus. 5.
How springs are attached.

panels. Seats can be added as required. They are arranged to rest upon battens, but they are not actually fastened until after lining.

Chassis. Use ¾″ × 1⁄16″ strip iron for springs. To ensure both being the same shape, they should be bent around a piece of wood sawn to the inside shape. They are bolted to the bottom cross rails, as in Illus. 1. Axles are fastened to them by means of metal clips riveted or bolted on, as shown in Illus. 5. Axles are of mild steel rod of a diameter to suit the wheels, generally ⅜″. The wheels are held in position by cotter pins passed through holes drilled right through the axles with large washers at each side to provide easy movement. Alternatively, square axles with rounded ends can be obtained.

Handles are of ¼″ or 5⁄16″ mild steel rod bent to shape around a rounded object and hammered. Both ends are beaten flat for attachment, that at the top at right angles with the other as it has to fit the handle. It is easily beaten flat if first made red-hot. First, however, you need to make and slip on the brackets for fastening at the top. A 1″

dowel rod is used for the handle, and the ends are cut in to enable the metal rods to be flush. Either screws with decorative heads should be used for fastening or cover caps made as in Illus. 1.

Painting and lining. Apply a coat of priming, follow with an undercoat, and finally add a gloss coat. The lining is fastened to battens screwed around the top of the body. Tack the material to the underside of the battens, and pass it over the top to the inside. A layer of cotton wool or fire-resistant foam sponge gives a springy completion to the inside. Nylon ribbon fastened with brass dome-head nails makes a neat finish.

Hood. The main front hoop is of flat strip iron with holes drilled at the ends to enable it to be pivoted. The other one or two hoops can be in stout wire looped at the ends for the same purpose. Open the hood and tie string across to keep in the open position. Cut the material to suit the shape, allowing enough for the seams. Sew the parts together and fasten to the hoops with large stitches. The pivoting is on bolts passed through the body from inside. The bolts should have squares beneath the head to prevent turning, and they should preferably be fastened before lining. The hood stays pass over the bolts and are held by wing nuts. At the back, the hood is held by a couple of screws.

CUTTING LIST

	Long		Wide	Thick
	ft.	*in.*	*in.*	*in.*
2 side rails	1	9½	1¾	¾
2 side rails	1	2½	2½	¾
4 side rails	1	2½	3¾	¾
2 cross rails		10	1¾	¾
2 cross rails		10	3¼	¾
2 battens	1	10¼	1	⅜
2 battens		11½	1	⅜
1 handle		9	(dowel)	1
Metal parts				
2 springs	2	6	¾	1/16
2 axles	1	3	5/16 or ⅜ in. dia.	
2 handles	1	8	¼ or 5/16 in. dia.	
2 hoops	3	—	½	about 1/16 in. dia.
2 wires	3	—	⅛	in.dia.

Lengths and widths allow for trimming; thicknesses are net.

29. Small Birdhouse

CHILDREN ALWAYS SEEM to be delighted by birds and birdhouses. Using ½″ wood for this birdhouse, the gable ends (A) will be cut from pieces 8″ × 7″, the height to the eaves being 6″. The opening for the bird in the front can be 2½ or 3″ in diameter. The sides (B), 8″ × 6″, butt *within* the ends, while a floor (C), 8″ × 6″, fits within the four sides of the box. The parts are nailed together and screwed through the platform (D). Note that the roof overhangs ½″ at the back and about 3″ in front. The roof parts can be cut from ¼″ boards, 12½″ × 5½ or 6″. If you add a chimney, the stack can be cut from a piece 3½″ × 2″ × ⅞″, with a ½″ length of ¾″ dowel rod for the can. The stack should pass through the roof and be halved and screwed to the house side (B). The perch, or rail, consists of two or three ½″ posts 2″ high, with a ⅜″ rail nailed across.

Door and windows can be indicated by painting. It has been said that birds dislike red, but we have not checked this out. If the box structure is fitted over the floor loose and merely held with screws, it is easy at any time to get access to the interior for cleaning purposes.

Illus. 1.
Attractive birdhouse for wall attachment.

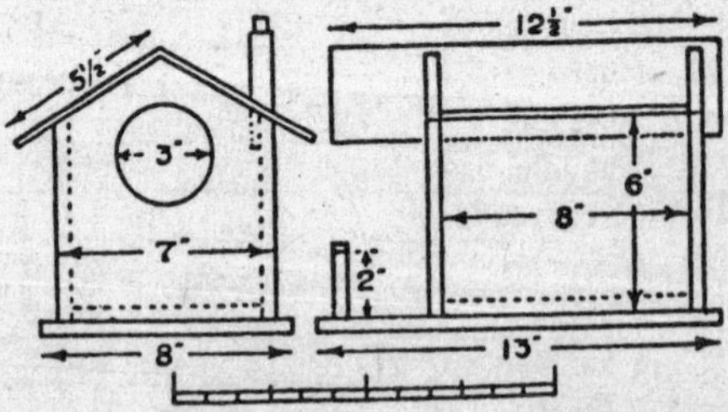

Illus. 2.
Elevations with sizes and scale.

30. Dollhouse

THIS REALISTIC DOLLHOUSE has four rooms and a garage. A size of 3′ 2″ × 1′ 6″ over the base is convenient in most cases, but if lack of space is a problem, the garage could be omitted and the base cut down to 2′ 6″ × 1′ 6″.

The left-hand front opens at a point level with the right-hand front so that the whole bay and a portion of the room opens with it. At the right-hand side, the front opens level with the inner wall of the balcony. Both these details are shown in Illus. 2. One of the roofs can be made to hinge, or a flap can be cut in it to allow batteries to be inserted if you want to light the rooms. If you decide to do this, it is best to arrange all the wiring during construction as it is much easier to insert it at that time.

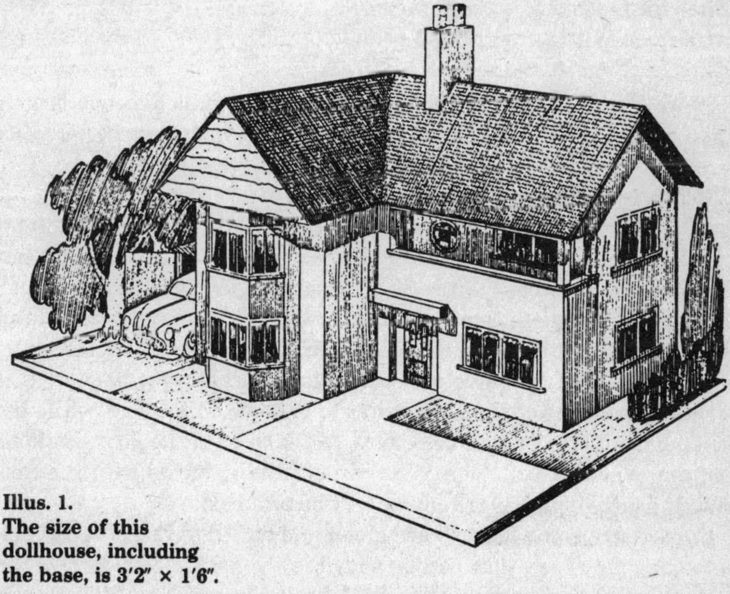

Illus. 1. The size of this dollhouse, including the base, is 3′2″ × 1′6″.

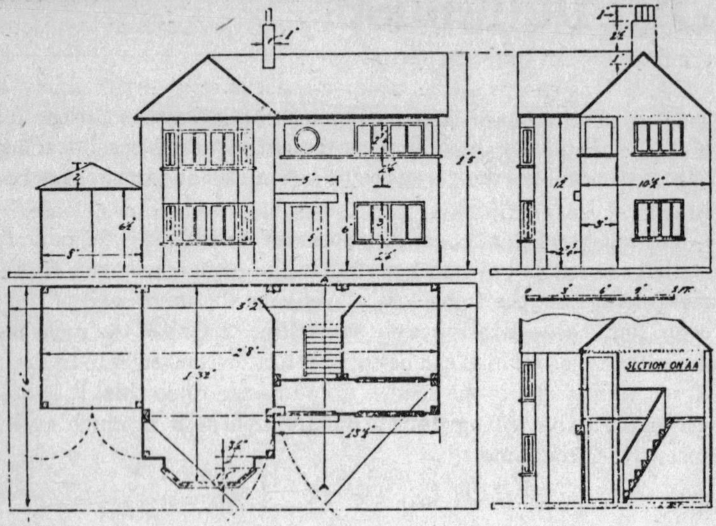

Illus. 2.
Front and side elevations, plan view, and part section.

Main walls. The construction of the main walls depends largely upon the material you have available. We favor using best-quality birch plywood as it is self-supporting.

Begin with the back, which can be in a single sheet, including the garage. Square upon it the positions of the walls, and, from it, mark the sizes of the fronts. The floors can also be marked in. Next, cut out the three front-to-back walls (the garage can follow afterwards). All three are the same depth because, although the right-hand wall reaches only to the back of the balcony, it has to fill in the space beneath the roof (see side view in Illus. 2). This right-hand wall is taller than the others because it has to extend to the ridge, while the others terminate beneath the eaves. Mark on each the floor positions and any windows and doors. You can cut the openings with the fret-saw. If neatly done, no trimming will be required.

Corner strips and battens are glued and nailed to these walls, and, once the glue is set, they can be added to the back. Always drive the nails through the board into the solid wood. The ceilings of the ground floor can be cut out, and it should be noted that in the hall it has to be cut away for the staircase. Again, fasten with glue and nails. At the top, it is advisable to fasten down a single ceiling over the whole piece. This will have to jut forward to fill in the space above the opening fronts, which include the balcony and the bay. The overhanging roofs can rest upon this ceiling, and there is thus no danger of their fouling the fronts when they are opened.

Base. This can be either a single sheet of stout plywood or a thin sheet of particleboard mounted on wide solid battens. In the latter case, the simplest way is to mitre the battens at the corners and glue and nail the board to them. Intermediate cross battens can be arranged wherever stiffening seems desirable—for instance, beneath the front-to-back walls. This will enable the strips at the bottom of the walls to be nailed down. When plywood is used, there is no difficulty; the strips can be nailed straight down.

Roof. To provide a suitable surface to which the roofs can be at-

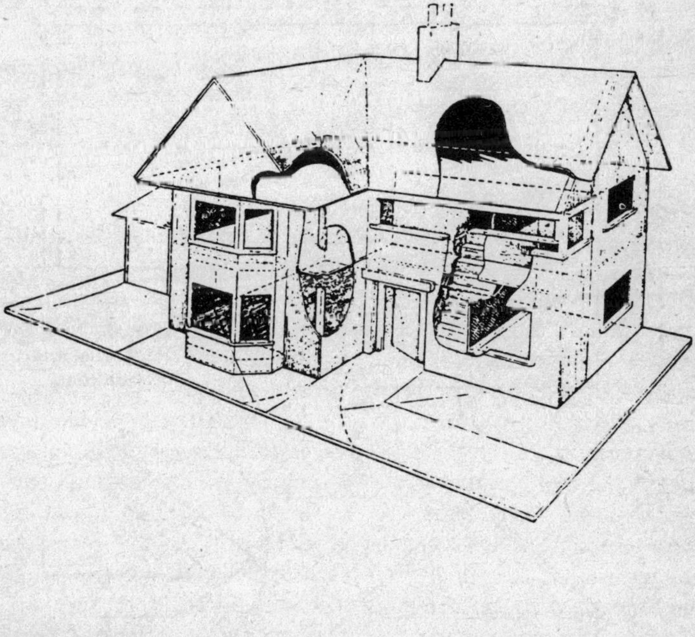

Illus. 3.
Perspective view,
showing construction.

tached, it is necessary to add triangular pieces, as in Illus. 5. That at the right-hand end already exists as a continuation of the wall, so all that is required is to add strips into which nails can be driven. The method of finding the shape of the roof panels appears in Illus. 4. Take the left-hand roof. The length at the ridge is known (10½″), also that at the eaves (16″), and the width can be taken from the elevation (7¾″). If these sizes are drawn in on the sheet of board, the angle at the hip follows automatically. The parts should be mitred where they meet, and it is a good plan to stick a piece of nylon ribbon along the joints. This provides a neat finish and creates the appearance of ridge tiles. A panel can be cut in, say, the large back roof to give access to the loft to enable batteries to be stored. It can also be hinged with a strip of nylon ribbon glued on.

Both the bay and the balcony front can be made up complete. Note from the dotted lines in Illus. 3 how a solid block is inserted in the bay at both top and bottom. This enables the wall and window pieces to be glued and nailed on. The window openings are cut to the size of the

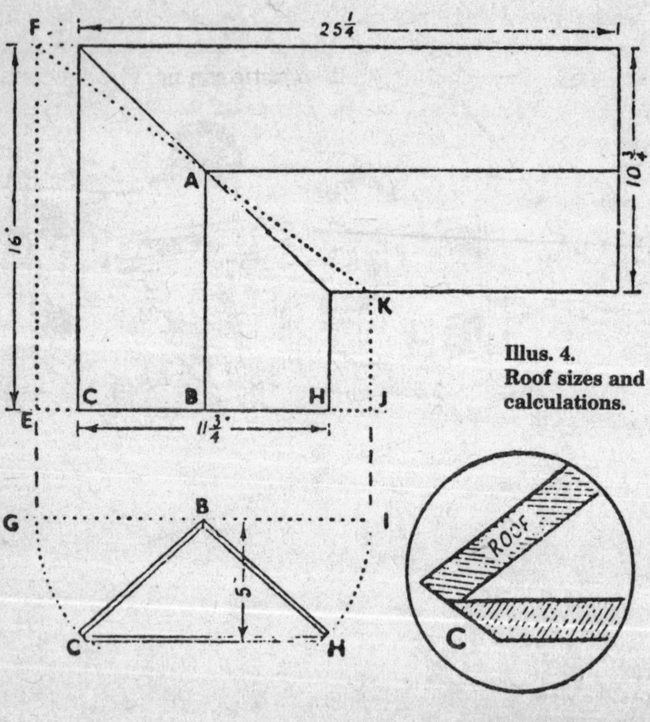

Illus. 4.
Roof sizes and calculations.

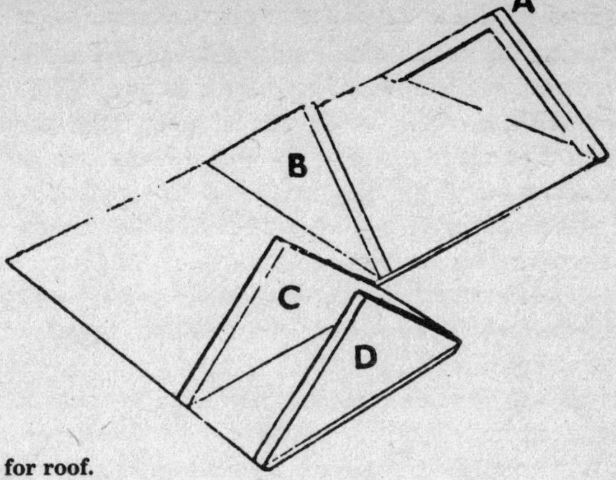

Illus. 5.
Supports for roof.

clear plastic sheet, and separate frames in thin wood or plastic board are nailed on at the front. The openings in these are made smaller so that a rebate is formed in which the plastic can fit. The windows are held either with small nails at the back or with little strips of glued wood or ribbon.

Details can be added as desired. Doors can be hinged with small brass butts or with ribbon glued on. The staircase consists of a flat board with triangular strips glued on and with a side glued on to form the panelled balustrade. The entire piece can be finished with paint, or dollhouse brick paper and tiling paper can be used.

About 25 sq. feet of plywood or similar material are required for the dollhouse. General standard sizes of panels are 6′, 8′, 10′, and 12′ × 4′. With careful planning, it should be possible to make the entire piece out of an 8′ × 4′ panel.